Acclaim for
A Map of the Harbor
Islands

"Young Petey and Danny are the 'bestest' of friends. And J. G. Hayes makes us fall in love with them from the opening pages of his first novel, *A Map of the Harbor Islands*. Hayes' engaging narrative style keeps us bound to the boys as they endure many challenges in their coming-of-age years, including the incident that strains their bond of friendship more than all others, when one of them discovers that he's gay. The effects of the revelation reverberate broadly and deeply in the lives of the adolescents, especially since it is the traditionally Irish-American Catholic neighborhood of South Boston that they call home. As life thrusts its terms upon these young men—whether in marriage, the military, alcohol abuse, recovery, or family secrets that surface—it is the power of friendship that Hayes poignantly beckons us to root for.

After Hayes' first two wonderful books of short stories (*This Thing Called Courage* and *Now Batting for Boston*), it is refreshing to finally read full-length fiction from this gifted writer. Here, Hayes displays his incredible storytelling talents with more confidence than ever, combining a rich Irish tale-spinning heritage with a modern American sensibility.

A Map of the Harbor Islands sets sail for the destinations of manhood, tacks passionately through the rough seas of young adulthood, and will find a safe harbor in the hearts of anyone who has experienced the aching discomfort of sexual awakening and the triumph of true friendship."

—James A. Lopata
Editor, *In Newsweekly*
New England's largest gay,
lesbian, bisexual, and transgender newspaper

"Stories of boyhood buddies growing up to be adult lovers are a gay-fiction staple—alas, almost a cliché. But few are as infused with as much poignancy and poetry, or brim with as much audacious originality, as this first novel from Hayes. His two earlier short story collections. *This Thing Called Courage* and *Now Batting for Boston*, explored t ____ en bewildered urgency of sexual blue-collar South Bost ____ n an uncommon, subtle artistry, craft-ing with muscula ____ s of lives that were sometimes sad and sometimes ecstat ____ [ayes as a writer in those short stories. This novel delivei ____ e. The story of Petey and Danny is lu-minous and luscic ____ with prose that glows with heartrend-ing l ____ ars again and again."

—Richard Labonte,
Book Marks, Q Syndicate

More Acclaim . . .

"With *A Map of the Harbor Islands* J. G. Hayes has stepped to the front ranks of young American authors. In this his first novel (he has two successful volumes of short stories, *This Thing Called Courage* and *Now Batting for Boston*) he demonstrates that all of the bright promises of a unique voice so evident in his stories about growing up gay in South Boston have been startlingly well fulfilled. This is a man whose mind is not only rich in stories and characters, but also is a gifted wordsmith who has a liquid language that effortlessly traces the lilt and flow of Irish-American expression as filtered through the air and streets of South Boston.

It would be unfair to limit classification of Hayes' output as gay literature, though he is certainly one of the most important writers of gay books in a field of fine compatriots. His newest writing in *A Map of the Harbor Islands* is on the same level as Michael Cunningham, Mark Doty, Edmund White, KM Schoelein, Jamie O'Neill, and the full range of both Irish and Irish-American authors in style and in ability to communicate meaningful stories, whether gay oriented or not. That he is writing so successfully about the tough times of gay youths in a homophobic neighborhood is a wonder and very much to his credit.

Once read, the ebb and flow of the magic of Hayes' writing lingers like a lovely Irish poem or tune. Hayes' descriptions of atmospheres are simply wondrous: '. . . the vermilion sunset, which lies along the shore like a throbbing smudge' or '. . . the beach is empty at this inbetweenish hour, drippy with day and night. A thin time, as Mrs. Harding would say. A time when anything is possible.' He places words and phrases in the mouths of the mothers of the two boys that sing with that special lilt only the Irish can evoke. This is a novel that when the final page is read leaves the reader with that sensation of sadness that the story is over, but also with the surprising realization that Hayes' writes so extremely well that every motive, every change, every happening is planted with seeds throughout the book and that in retrospect we the reader should have known all along just how things would resolve. Petey's altered world is a magnificent realm that bears re-entering time and time again. *A Map of the Harbor Islands* is one of those books to read again and again—and hopefully J. G. Hayes will send another along very soon. He is a gentle, articulate master of fiction. A helluva book, this!"

— Grady Harp
Author, *War Songs*

A Map of the Harbor Islands

HARRINGTON PARK PRESS
Southern Tier Editions
Gay Men's Fiction

A Map of the Harbor Islands

J. G. Hayes

Southern Tier Editions™
Harrington Park Press®
The Trade Division of The Haworth Press, Inc.
New York • London • Oxford

For more information on this book or to order, visit
http://www.haworthpress.com/store/product.asp?sku=5677

or call 1-800-HAWORTH (800-429-6784) in the United States and Canada
or (607) 722-5857 outside the United States and Canada

or contact orders@HaworthPress.com

Published by

Southern Tier Editions™, Harrington Park Press®, the trade division of The Haworth Press,
10 Alice Street, Binghamton, NY 13904-1580.

PUBLISHER'S NOTE
The development, preparation, and publication of this work has been undertaken with great care.
However, the Publisher, employees, editors, and agents of The Haworth Press are not responsible
for any errors contained herein or for consequences that may ensue from use of materials or information contained in this work. The Haworth Press is committed to the dissemination of ideas and
information according to the highest standards of intellectual freedom and the free exchange of
ideas. Statements made and opinions expressed in this publication do not necessarily reflect the
views of the Publisher, Directors, management, or staff of The Haworth Press, Inc., or an
endorsement by them.

This is a work of fiction. Names, characters, places, and incidents either are the products of the
author's imagination or are used fictitiously, and any resemblance to actual persons, living or
dead, business establishments, events, or locales is entirely coincidental.

Cover design by Marylouise E. Doyle.

Library of Congress Cataloging-in-Publication Data

Hayes, J. G. (Joseph George), 1965-
    A map of the harbor islands / J.G. Hayes.
        p. cm.
    ISBN-13: 978-1-56023-596-5 (soft : alk. paper)
    ISBN-10: 1-56023-596-9 (soft : alk. paper)
    1. Male friendship—Fiction. 2. Gay men—Fiction. 3. South Boston (Boston, Mass.)—Fic-
tion. I. Title.
PS3608.A93M36 2006
813'.6—dc22

2006006573

To Dermot, Perry, and Tom

Contents

Preface

On the bright morning of September 11, 2001, my mother called from Maine and instructed me to turn the television on, as a small plane had crashed onto the roof of one of the Twin Towers. I declined, as I bemoan the devolution of the news media into a carnival of mayhem and mishap. But my roommate overheard our conversation and tuned in; when he called me to the other room to say the accident was much more horrific than anyone imagined—indeed, could imagine, in those days—the three of us (my roommate, my dog, Biscuit, and I) sat involuntarily glued to the enveloping horror for the next five hours.

Finally Biscuit, displaying the animal sensitivity that science dismisses and pet owners routinely witness, started shaking—then he barked to get us out of the room. He had had enough of the emotional tsunami spilling into our home that day. As much for his sake as my own, we decamped to "Happy Land," our name for the 3,000-acre conservation area of hills, lakes, meadows, and cliffs 400 yards from where I live.

We were, of course, looking for escape. If I had known then the ramifications—direct and indirect—that would follow in the wake of that day, perhaps I wouldn't have come back—or not until, at least, the various Bogeymen who have appeared in the wake of 911 had been dispatched. I know some great caves up there.

There was something above and beyond that day's tragedy that was heartbreaking in its beauty. Every locale must have it halcyon days, and here in New England, our meteorological payback comes in a nebulous swatch of time and space and light that begins roughly in late August and extends—if we're lucky—into mid-October. How to describe the indescribable—softness to the air, a benign silence, a certain slant of light that contains cricket and cicada sound by night and flotillas of slow-moving cumulus clouds by day, punctuating a cerulean sky. Breezes carry a certain poignancy in the air, as if summer hated to be called last summer so soon.

A Map of the Harbor Islands
Published by The Haworth Press, Inc., 2006. All rights reserved.
doi:10.1300/5677_a

There are certain days that are meteorologically perfect—and yet we might plow through them without remark. But among these are some—two or three a year—that break one's heart with their beauty. Beyond the day's perfection, a je ne sais quoi, a spritz of harmony makes one feel, as the Zen describe it, as if one will live forever, even when one knows one won't. Everything conspires, and the soul soars. Maybe it's Jungian. Maybe it's me. Anyway, September 11, 2001, was such a day in New England, weatherwise if not otherwise; and Biscuit and I roamed the hills and fields of Happy Land—or *Tir na Shona* as we called it then (I was teaching him Irish so I would have someone to speak to in that lovely but listing language) until day smudged into night.

The greatest lesson the animals teach: everything is for the first time; everything is now. In Biscuit's case, he could go from despair to nirvana with just the taking down of his leash from its home over the pencil sharpener. And so we proceeded, up hill and down dale, seeking our escape: and while it was true that horror had come calling that day, the bees had found some secret stash of goldenrod, and were making merry in it; the clouds stalled over mirror water, and the light shifted, delighted and drunk; frogs plopped off logs to swim; we sought out Hawk Hill to see if any red-tailed raptors were riding the thermals, as the breezes were from the happy northwest; they were. We watched the skies, as Petey might say, with quiet eyes.

It occurred to me sometime that late afternoon that perhaps all this—the diphthong of the birds, the pine drench in the air, the dewdrops lingering in a golden gate of a spider web, spanning an upland meadow path—was reality, and what the world had witnessed that morning—and, alas, other mornings, and afternoons, and evenings: the hatred, the revenge, the rooms where people gather to plot murder, or invent terms like collateral damage—was the unreality, the nightmare we have dreamed up in our collective fear and greed and loneliness.

I had just begun this novel then. I put it away for a time, as it seemed I should be writing, or painting, about things other than the secret discovery two people make in their own version of Happy Land, the Boston Harbor Islands. But eventually I returned to it, of course, for it seemed Danny and Petey, the heroes of this work, would stomp on my stomach at night while I tried to sleep, demanding to be birthed.

In the same way it sometimes seems silly, in these times, to write about things like the dream-drift of clouds, or the numinous joy elicited by the secret discovery by two city boys of a tern's nest, or the bliss to be found in a friend's smile. But I am reminded of the story of a "high-powered" somebody or other who went into the hospital for dangerous surgery. A voracious reader by necessity, she didn't want the "important" works of the day, or the weighty journals of her profession, despite the pressure to keep current; she wanted *The Wind in the Willows*. "They're always making toast," was the only explanation she could offer.

The point is, it is in the worst of times that we must remember what is still beautiful in the world, and of lasting value—however esoteric and individual those things might be to each of us. And so I offer you, gentle reader, the story of Danny and Petey, and what they found of lasting value, in the never-never land of my own reality.

Acknowledgments

Although writing is an allegedly solitary pursuit, putting a book together is decidedly not; and the author wishes to thank all those responsible, beginning with those he will inevitably forget.

But those whose assistance I could never forget are, in no particular order, John Mitzel of Calamus Books; the wise and indomitable Peg Marr at the Haworth Press; Bill Palmer; the Fan Club: Grady Harp, Steve Susoyev, Tom O'Leary, H. F. Corbin, Chris Reidy, Rocque Dion, Clint Chamberlain, Jim Lopata, and all the many people who have written—your support and encouragement keeps me going.

To Fionn, and Biskey, who kept watch at my feet through the long years of writing—you are indeed Other Nations, and I am humbled by your unflagging devotion.

To my dearest friends Perry, Tom, Dermot, Roger, Robbie, Vonn, Clay, George and Bob, Bill, and Scotty—your care, love, and encouragement mean more than I can say.

To the big guy who makes it happen, Bill Cohen—many thanks for your continued faith in me.

And to my family—Margaret, Peg, Maureen and Wayne, Bob and Missey, Mike and Carol, Chris and Regina, Teddy and Mary, Rocky, and precious Will—you are my home.

And finally to the Great Creator, who brings joy to my youth, as well as valleys from which I can see joy.

A Map of the Harbor Islands
Published by The Haworth Press, Inc., 2006. All rights reserved.
doi:10.1300/5677_b

Nobody sees a flower really; it is so small. We haven't time, and to see takes time—like to have a friend takes time.

— Georgia O'Keefe

Dog Dinner Parties, Dog Funerals

The City of Boston was troubled by *ye great invasion of sundrie bears* in the year 1643. So say the historians—and so said Petey—

"Dad! *Dad!* There's a man up ahead with a boat! He says he knows you!"

My eight-year-old, Jamie, comes bombing back down the beach, arms airplane wide.

I squat down to receive him as he crashes into my shoulders. Tomato cheeks and the drench-smell of October on him, the blue eyes flippant but cavernous.

"There is, eh?"

"Mmm. And he knows all the names of the Harbor Islands." He drops his voice and says into my ear, "Not the regular names, Dad. The secret names."

"Really! Wow."

The imagination on him.

"He *does,* Dad," Jamie blurts, pushing away. His eyes enlarge until I look at them. He pauses dramatically before shouting, "He says this beach right here is the Pepperminty Coast."

Jesus.

"He's waiting up there. He wants to see you. C'mon, Dad, let's *run!*" And Jamie's off again, throwing himself into the vermilion sunset, which lies along the shore like a throbbing smudge.

But I stay squatting.

It couldn't be Petey. He's 5,000 miles and four years and too many unsaid words away from me. But it must be—who else?

Mussy hair from the sea wind's hands and I'm blue Home again, sea green Home again and soon to be with Petey.

Is it four years? Or five?

A Map of the Harbor Islands
Published by The Haworth Press, Inc., 2006. All rights reserved.
doi:10.1300/5677_01

Jesus.

His blacker hair ocean-damp will be slickety down his forehead. A stray piece of breezy seaweed, the same bright rubbery green as his eyes, might be dangly down his white swan neck and he'll fleck at it, then decide to leave it. That mouth of his, that's been out of town lately.

Petey. Petey Harding.

Me and Petey.

I say the words out loud, in my head, in, out. They soothe me. I smash the words together and they sound thundering and triumphant, a consecration from an ancient numinous religion *MeandPetey*. Twenty-eight years of my ten jillion moments connected, or not, four million years of Eve-olution resulting in this jabbery linguistic thing, and the end result is here I am at the shore soon to see Petey, maybe, and *MeandPetey MeandPetey MeandPetey* all I say and all I need to say.

To keep themselves from harm, Tibetan monks envision their bodies surrounded by blue light; but I've just always said *MeandPetey*. *MeandPetey* when I knew the puck was about to smack me in the eye during the All-Star game; *MeandPetey* when the car bomb went off in Lebanon, imploding half a city square, lifting Boomer's shoulders off him and splattering them against my legs; *MeandPetey* at the Shea kid's funeral.

MeandPetey. The noise of this seeps into me the way a lost dog perks to hear his name again. Listen, I know, there's stray dogs all over Southie. Me and Petey used to study their ways when we were kids.

"Jesus wept and where *do* these dogs all come from, that's what I'd like to know," Petey's mother, Mrs. Harding, used to wonder, shaking her sweating head while she pounded potatoes. "I think it must rain dogs, nights when the world's snoring. It must teem them."

She said they gave her the heebie-jeebies, but the alleys were draped with dogs, sniffing out baby-blue Rubbermaid trash cans, tipped over like syrupy dark continents ripe for the plundering. They'd look at you. Occasional squeals and whines of beseechment. Their liquidy eyes full-up with *buarthaí an t-saoil,* Mrs. Harding would say in her native Irish, *the worries of the world.* Something else too.

How they would vault into instant ecstasy if you'd take a second to chuck a ball to them, rumple your hand through the down-and-out fur and an odorous sheen on your fingers when you withdrew them. Quick adoring glances they'd throw you. They'd become wanton with tail wagging, remembering something they probably never had. A dog dream of something. Careful as the Cronin sisters, we always noticed, about where they went to the bathroom, like they didn't want to impose more than they already might be on a world that had finished with them. *I'll just go right over here where no one can see me.* There was an inquiring meekness about the most savage of them. You don't really find that with people. The meekest among us can be savage. Every Marine a rifleman.

The Cronin sisters—remember them? Their lace-curtain mother somehow found herself and her daughters still stranded in Southie after all these years—howsoever, that didn't mean they couldn't live in refined ways. *There are only three places a gentlewoman may use the facilities in Boston, ladies,* Mother Cronin commanded her five daughters. *Bonwit Teller; the Harvard Cooperative Society; and her home.* You'd see them on the City Point bus sometimes, sweating, squirming—or walking furiously up M Street and everyone knew just why. Recall if you will that accident poor Maureen had in fifth grade. She never got over it.

But the stray dogs now, they couldn't be bothered with etiquette gone wrong. Their etiquette was based on a poignant consideration.

"D-don't look n-n-now, Danny, but someone's doing their poopsters," Petey would sleeve-clutch whisper when we'd catch the strays doing their furtive duty, in the corners of seawalls, in the wet shade of alley corners. Behind a dumpster.

"D-Danny, what did I s-say? I said *don't* look, you'll embarrass them—"

It was after his accident that Petey began stuttering, stuttering and collecting these strays. His family's 18' × 12' backyard, wedged between his house and its saggy garage, became a kennel of sorts. The abandoned dogs he could lure home he would, use his paper route money to buy them—not dog food, never doggish food, but steaks, roasts and chops and Mrs. Harding never the heart to roust them out, though their barking plagued her something fierce, *a botheration and no mistake, in fact a malediction.*

One week the Now You're Living! part of the Sunday paper featured The Dinner Party Pullout Section and, inspired, Petey threw a supper for the strays. A Friday night it was, October. The dogs were temporarily sequestered in the Harding basement, oily muzzles pressed against cobwebbed windows, knowing something was up. Meanwhile Petey slit plastic garbage bags for tablecloths, arranged old fruit crates for tables. The *Company's Coming!* cookbook propped up on the stove. Name tags written in green Petey calligraphy on the backs of Mrs. Harding's file-card recipes, *Minnow, Fandango, Monstro, Wolf.* Gordian knots of Christmas lights got hauled down from the attic and polished. Glass jars became stuffed with dandelions for an atmosphere. Candles but two of them had to go. They proved aroma-therapeutic and the article had strongly cautioned against these—*They might obscure your guests' palates.* Mantovani squeaking through the tinny speakers mushed up against the kitchen screen window in an attempt to soothe the savage breast but no, chaos reigned when the cellar door was let fly, and the only thing that kept Mrs. McMurty next door from calling Animal Control was the butter-drippy homemade soda bread Mrs. Harding soothed her with. One defining mote of Southie, neighbors will usually advise you of their intentions before siccing the law at you. The law is frequently invoked in Southie but it can never be entirely trusted.

"What can I tell you, Margie, Petey took a notion," Petey's mother kept explaining over the fence, while curs roared and yelped for more. Petey in the midst of them, the wildest one of all, spinning in bliss at the excess of it. That Sheehan girl down the way got nosey, got bit.

Weep like rain Petey would when he'd find any of the strays dead, thumped by the side of the road after being three-in-the-morning thwacked on the Boulevard or Broadway, or curled up in the shroud of a dark alley corner somewhere, again not wanting to impose, even in death. A three-dimensional shadow of something that, once, was. Disintegration preying on the body but the sea breeze still lavishing caresses upon the fur.

One time Petey found a dead one all stretched out on the top stair of Gate of Heaven Church's locked front portico, as if the sad open eyes had been seeking the grace of a last Confession: a huge, tigerish lowrider with incisive yellow teeth. The unwashed fur the consistency of old newspapers, blowing off in feathery clumps. The long-loping, tireless gait of the stray made to desist at last.

"And Old Soul eyes, they were still open so I could r-read his spotless life," Petey sobbed to me. "A pussycat in the body of a jaguar. Danny! You should'a seen how l-light he was when I picked him up. F-four feet long not includin' the tail and light as a bag of rags. He must'a st-starved to death cuz he wasn't so old. In front of everybody, with everybody around here he starved to death and not a s-soul noticed."

Dog funerals would follow. Petey would load the deleted into a stray Flanagan's shopping cart and dredge them all-business over to the slowly imploding industrial West Side, where he'd bury them somewhere, I promised not to tell. We were twelve then I suppose. He'd slow-wail his pennywhistle while I'd help pick-dig through the dust and cigarette butts and heaved-out loser scratch tickets of the ages, but I'd always check just to make sure we weren't tossing away our fortunes. Debbie Morrison's grandmother found that thrown-away fifty dollar winner in the street that time after Mass, and it was the ruination of her. She couldn't leave a gutter alone after that.

A few suitable words Petey would intone over the new mound with a cross and whatever sidewalk-crack weeds he could find placed tenderly on top, dandelions mostly. Once a gorgeous pluck of Queen Anne's lace, but it proved too regal, airy. It immediately decamped, fluffering away in the sea breeze so never again. Petey would clear his throat the way Fr. McCarty did while sermonizing, for effect. *Emotional postmortems,* Petey called his little examinations that preceded burial.

"They c-cut up things when you d-die, Danny, people and things," he whispered before he began. "They w-want to see what m-made you die. They should find out instead what m-made you l-live. Your ways and means."

He always seemed to be wearing striped jerseys then, after his accident. Frayed at the collar, his eyes frayed too, open and foreboding as elevator shafts. But then a new joy would find him, and the result would be That Smile. We never had to wait too long for Petey Smile, the new feature of the universe he'd discover that must be shared and him the beaming transmitter. Flowers. Birds. The ocean. Stars. Rust and dust, secrets and mysteries. And then finally the Harbor Islands, paradise three miles from the Broadway Bridge and me shirtless in the midst of them.

But the dog funerals were solemn business. He'd look in the eyes of the departed, open them if they weren't already, then Petey would gasp, cry, and measure the stiffening ears and limbs with this broken half-yardstick he had found that had STUEBENS LUMBER stenciled across it in faded maroon letters.

"Stuebens Lumber, is it? No, I've never heard tell of them, and why do you ask?" Mrs. Harding said to Petey when he made inquiries. Her eyes tried not to show the absurdity of his question when she had seven fatherless children to raise and a factory job, nights. But she hacked into the hours to make time for Petey, her youngest, her pet. She was lavish with her time on Petey, on Petey especially and her plants. Joked that she managed to put food on the table by *discerning what my children abhor, then giving them plenty of it.*

"Acute Compassion in the eyes," Petey would report during his dog postmortems, writing it all down in his little neon-green notebook. Dog-eared it became. "With obvious c-c-complications of Loyalty. Hmmm, wh-what have we here . . . l-listening ears, lookit how big they are Danny, the b-better to hear you."

He'd dispatch a death notice into the *South Boston Tribune:* Daisy, about seven years old, suddenly last Tuesday, she actually would laugh when I took her swimming. But they wouldn't hear of it. He embellished, desperate for publication, desperate to incite a community-wide canine compassion: Spot, run down last Friday night on Broadway, saved the life of seventy-four seniors when the Nursing Home on Farragut Road caught fire last year, dragging them out by the hems of their housecoats. But no.

The point is, Petey's always been sensitive to others' feelings. Especially animals. And he loves words, even though he stutters and did lousy in school. Profligate in the heaps of Fs he accumulated after his accident, but much of that was probably due to his lack of interest, his attitude; his dress, which was a catastrophe—after his accident.

If it were a smaller dog or other diminutive creature, Petey would change *poopsters* to *poopsterinis*. A factory of words, he was. When we were twelve we snuck out one night and puff-shirted, stand-up leg-yanked our bikes four miles and a world away to Boston Common. Late May it was and the crabapples blooming for us, the midnight air liquid with their fragrance and us pedaling through it like a series of unseen pink water sprinklers. None to be seen at night, but always tons of ducks and geese intent on ribald fowl play here by day.

"C-c-careful, Danny," Petey shouted out in front of me. "Watch out for your b-b-ike tires, someone's done their poopsterinis all over the p-place up here."

They were like green Tootsie Rolls I remember, all sectioned up. Another time double bike riding to the beach he yelled in my fluttering ear, "Alexander Haig hastened to The Hague where he was m-met by a happy hag who thought he looked h-haggard, but she hesitated to h-harangue him as he was eating heinous haggis."

Then he'd finger-flick my ears, big ears, jug ears, Jughead they called me years later in the Marines when they weren't calling me Yank.

Petey'd say anything, turn American into a foreign tongue but sometimes I knew what he meant.

He has the memory of the world, too, Petey. Eight years later when I dragged him to the prom at the Casa de Fiori, disastrous double-dating with Noreen and Tricia, Petey asked the short, steely-haired waitress pushing petrifying antipasto at us if the poopsterinis were fresh. Thank God the girls didn't know what he was talking about. They'd already had it up to here with him that night. *'Course they are, my brother-in-law's makin' them in the kitchen. He's back there right now,* the waitress answered. Pointing.

"Is that this one here?" Noreen asked with no more than her usual suspicion, holding up an impermeable tomato slice on a Ritz with a runny clump of pimento on top.

But that was then and this is now. I've tangented, as Mrs. Harding would say.

MeandPetey. How many thousands of times I've initiated sentences with these words. Altered the course of a day, a destiny. Answered questions. Launched dreams. I say them again out loud and something perpetually skewed comes untangled. Me and Petey.

And now my son tells me he's just up ahead. Waiting.

I'm at the Place Where the Land Meets the Ocean—that's Petey's name for the shore. "You can in f-f-fact go home," he'd always say right before we spangled into the water. "Speaking from an e-e-evolutionary point of view of course."

The Place Where the Land Meets the Ocean and finally I get what he means: it's just a city beach, the heat-wavery-in-summer asphalt Day Boulevard shoved up alongside, the grit-floored public-pubic restrooms and hot dog stands and detritus of humanity scattered here and there: a slimy empty bottle of Hawaiian Tropic tanning oil with a black curly body hair stuck on the lips of its greasy open mouth; a crushed plastic Mountain Dew 20-ounce Big Gulp; one pink flip-flop half-buried in the dirty gray sand, thrust out like a tongue; a skanky rubber, 'tis true—

—But if you stand at the water's edge looking out: the horizon a building twilight, the rising moon throwing a dash of a shimmer on top of things. The sluice-sweep of the water, a poultice on my soul. The not-too-distant Harbor Islands, the same blue gray in the scattery sunset as mythical kingdoms. And a look and feel about this place that only beloved landscapes have, landscapes that have been caressed by thousands of eyes. We have taken the measure of this place with our footsteps. This place has taken the measure of us. A fervid, restless continent behind us, and now this. Projects and tenements, triple-deckers and barrooms, people living so close you can see the very crease of their slacks—and now this. The open window the Creator has perhaps chucked to us for all the doors that have shut in our lives. A gentle sweep of harbor and islands easing out into the mighty North Atlantic. On a night like this it seems nothing less than a gesture of divine benevolence.

It's the end of one world and the beginning of another. Like Petey always said. And that other world can be what you want it to be. How trite sounding . . . but how necessary to have such a dream-hatchery in this life. Our reality is fed by our unreality, our perceptions, slurping on, not career plans and major purchases, but cobwebs, smells, and oddments, the strange beliefs we pull to us in private. The barely realized, seldom articulated notions that dictate all other actions: not only the place we are led to, when we stash our extra rolls of paper towels *there* and nowhere else, but also our conception of what will come after, when the throb in our ears throbs no more. Thoreau said a man is rich in proportion to the amount of things he can let alone; but the opposite should be true for our beliefs, no? Our beliefs should be as vast, as gaseous wild-rumpled, as this life we inhabit. Our faith must be a biggy sky to wander in. How else—*go shopping and let the divil take the hindmost?* That was Mrs. Harding's oft-threatened cure for all ills, whether they be the unlooked-for sudden gushing of a pipe under the sink while unflagging children screamed, or bills tricked out in scarlet PAST DUE, sometimes the more thought-provoking SHUTOFF NOTICE. Or a visit from Mr. Bane her landlord, peeking through the porch windows to discuss Arrears, *the ditto of my existence,* she called him. She'd sneak out the back door and then *walk as if for a wager* in the opposite direction.

I stumble up ahead to where Petey waits. I stare out at the sky-water and the sky-water stares back. "Danny don't jump in 'til you feel it staring b-back at you," Petey would say whenever we'd go swimming. *Swumming,* Petey always called it after his accident.

A saffron wash blossoms up around the rising, cloud-louvered moon. The twilight becomes electric. A front is coming, almost here. It's mid-October. The day—forgettable for the most part until now—has been balmy, soft, gauzy blue. Puffing from the south, but now a bulldozer of a front's racing in from the sangfroid northwest and you just know it won't be warm again until April. High seventies all across New England all week but now Worcester is reporting forty-four and falling.

While we haven't felt anything here yet, the sky is starting to move, shoving out a few tulle-ish clouds of such a wispy color, you can't really tell where they end and the sky and ocean begin; soon white cumulus puffballs, bright white even at night, will roar in from the west. Leaves will be stripped from trees, will blow down Broadway in untold numbers, and hurl themselves lemming-like into the sea. Storm windows will be Windexed and lowered, doors will be shut, thermostats will be turned up and something in the heart will be pleased. Stews will be planned for the morrow—ask MaryEllen to pick up a coupl'a pounds of beef at the butcher's on the way home from school. A stalling of systems in the North Atlantic waters, in the North Atlantic skies for the past few days, but the season's first invincible autumnal front is having none of it and will march all the way to Ireland, bringing a bit of our breath with it.

Ah, here it is: the first puff of hard blue air from the northwest, a tang of Canadian woods wrapped up in it. An interior something spurts up in sympathy, rejoices. There is a pausing, then a larger blast behind it, running right through us, rippling the sea as it runs out across the waters of Pleasure Bay. Clouds scuttle. They cross the rising moon and you can see their innards like an X-ray. Terminal beauty. Traveling gulls rake the sky over us. Higher up, V-shaped flocks glide their invisible highways southward. The vapory air is swept out in an instant. Some kind of celestial focus turns, and the first stars leap into a hard fierce glitter.

The wind puffs up, breathes life into things—something at the hockey rink across the Boulevard behind us clatters and bangs. Darkness falls like a sledge, but there's a gleam to the night, except at the inky navy zenith. *Inky-dinky-parlez-vous.* Dad sang that song when the family with the French mother moved in next door but never again—Mom went on the warpath, denounced his upbringing and hid the *Sporting News* and his transistor radio on him.

Jamie comes running back to find me, our dog Buster in gallumping tow.

"Put this on, sweetheart," I tell him, pulling out his Irish knit sweater from my fanny pack.

"Whatever you say, *sweetheart.*" He complies without complaint, as much a testament to the plummeting temps as the racing clouds above us.

A shape takes form at the water's edge beyond us.

Petey. It's the wind in my mouth making me salivate, I tell myself.

I lower my head in the hope that he won't see me walking to him faster, faster.

Jolly Olly Petey

We used to half-watch after-school cartoons, the off-white noise of American children, in Petey's musty basement when we were kids. It was a large, cryptic room: bright along the walls, shadowed in the middle, impenetrable in the corners and suffused in the scent of slightly damp newspapers and fermenting dandelion wine, a yearly undertaking by Petey's mother. We would play Monopoly, occasionally Risk, or sometimes Petey would read aloud from *The Lord of the Rings.* Anyway this commercial would blare on a lot for these drinks—You made them from a powder. Probably just sugar and food coloring right, FDC #1975975333, triclyethelenesorbital added as a noncaking agent but kids don't give a care, they trust no one's out to poison them. But we loved those drinks, loved the names of the different flavors anyway, loved the commercial. *New, exciting flavors! Goofy Grape! Rootin' Tootin' Raspberry! Freckle Face Strawberry! And Jolly Olly Orange!*

It was two months after Petey's accident. We were twelve, and this was the odd first thing that had thrummed the strings of delight inside the strange new Petey.

"It's o-on!" Petey roared this one afternoon from the basement—the Rumpus Room his mother always called it with her brogue *Rrrrrruuuumpuss Ruuum.* I was taking a pee break up in his family's pink-tiled first floor bathroom, reading the T and A mags his dead father had kept hidden under a stained mattress pad in the bathroom closet. I came bombing down the stairs at his call—

Our mothers were upstairs in Mrs. Harding's kitchen, trying to find things to say to each other. *The dust was that thick under her kitchen table,* my mother reported later. As for Mrs. Harding, she thought my mother had airs.

A Map of the Harbor Islands
Published by The Haworth Press, Inc., 2006. All rights reserved.
doi:10.1300/5677_02

"The *grandeur* of that one," I overheard her say to Petey. Not with malice, only observation. "She's so high she's *haute*."

"Jolly Olly Orange! Jolly Olly Orange!" Petey was shrieking when I got back to the basement, not stuttering at all like he did most times. He was holding his stomach and rolling on the floor, laughing, wiggling his thrown-out arms and legs like a spider I watched once after inundating it with Raid.

"Jolly Olly Orange! *Jolly Olly Orange!*"

When the commercial was over, Petey calmed down a little and we went back to our Monopoly game, set up on the drunk-legged card table Mrs. Harding used for ironing—she was somewhat short.

There were whole years when we played Monopoly, both post- and pre-accident. We'd get so into it we'd have one game set up at my house and one at Petey's.

This particular afternoon I was murdering him, kicking his ass and taking his gas, as the local chestnut went. I'd just about taken over the whole world of Atlantic City with my lucky boot and Petey—Petey was always the doggie—was holed up down in scumbag Baltic Avenue, maybe one utility, awaiting a final fatal pass on my hotel-charmed chain o'greed. Like teeth those hotels, red bloody teeth ringing the board and mine all mine. My bills tucked away by the neat pastel denomination exactly halfway under the edges of the board, lifting up the board in fact in their swelling largesse.

Petey's love of Monops as he called it was one of the few things that hadn't changed after his accident.

I fustily rearranged my red hotels back in their precise lines—Petey's only delight when I was winning was to muss them up, accidentally on purpose. "They went awry and I can't s-say why," he'd explain, when I'd turn back/come back and find them askew. "Act of God, I s-suppose."

I handed him the dice, trying to look like I was trying not to gloat.

"Don't get a one, three, four, seven, eight, nine, eleven, or twelve, whatever you do," I said. He hated when I did that.

"Up y-y-your, up y-your a-a-a—"

"I catch your general drift, Petey," I said. His stuttering was always worse when the blood rose in him. "No need to wear yourself out."

He flung the dice, his black hair flung too, and they bounced within the box's cover, little tiny rattling pieces of fate. Like bones they sounded. They came up seven, considered most times a lucky number but before I could proclaim, "Oh what a shame, Pacific Avenue! It looks like you owe me one thousand, seven hundred, and fifty dollars!" Petey turned and grabbed this floor-mopping bucket he must've filled with water when I was upstairs peeing and snooping.

"TIDAL W-WAVE HITS ATLANTIC CITY!" he roared, dumping the water onto the board, sweeping all the pieces and money and cards and hotels onto the floor. I lost my breath, the table imploded in sympathy, amusement overcame outrage and I dove on top of him, laughing. We rolled around on the floor, wrestling and shrieking on the soggy money and the soddening board.

"Act of G-God, game c-cancelled due to act of G-God!" Petey cried as I knuckle-sandwiched him on the head. On the opposite side of course from where his indent was from the accident.

I like to remember Petey that way. I should say, it's one of my favorite cards in the infinite Rolodex in my head marked *Petey.*

It was after his accident, and Petey was no longer the sharpest tool in the shed in school, though he could've been if he wanted. But a pulling something in his eyes made you believe he knew everything important. You know that look—some dogs and cats have it, certain strangers on the bus. You wish you could ask them, *Ahhh, life, right? Like what's the story?* Petey didn't have that look before the Accident even though everyone called him the Golden Boy. No one called him that after the Accident.

The Accident.

Might as well talk about that now and get it over with. You tell me, was it my fault?

It was deep in the green tangle of June. Not that there were any more trees in South Boston then than there are now—it's the least vegetated part of the city. I read that just recently. So what there was of green stood out all the more. Shimmery. The neon tufts of grass beside the buckled continental plates of sidewalks, and you'd always have to look, like pubic hair on the very young and the very old, that much of an emerald surprise. The explosion of sumac and ailanthus from ends of alleys, from mere fissures in industrial parking lots. Squirming unstoppable some of them up from miasmic subway vents and where are their roots, you wonder. Springtimes, you'd almost swear the smokestacks and asphalt roofs, the soot-draped fill trucks that rattle-roared through the West Side at night, took on a softer color in sympathy with the reputed rebirth of the world, elsewhere. But we lived in community then.

One of those summer days in late June you dream about all winter, weird that It should happen then. Forever after referred to as the Accident, from the Broadway Bridge to Pleasure Bay and everyone knew exactly what you were talking about.

We were still locked up in school, tight as tiny drums the last week before vacation. _Must be hard on the kids, weather like this_, everyone said, but I never minded, dreaming out the lifted windows. Buildings had windows that opened then, so the mind could wander when the body couldn't. Windows should be a compound word, no? Open-, openable-, but instead nowadays it's a case of NO YOU DON'T, and toxic-breath industrial carpet to boot.

But it was Then, and summer smells and indolence waltzed right on into class: dropped lemon Popsicles, melting sticky in the streets and the dogs would lick them found treasure. French fries and dogs from Sullivan's when the wind was from the east. The yellow smell of ancient dandelions shoveling up puffs from the sidewalks. Always, the sea aroma—vital and variable as breath. Hot nights hanging out on the top slick stoop and you could almost lick the air so sticky with city summer smell, bricks and backs of necks sweating and Ma wouldn't call you in 'til eleven and the neighborhood crones concurred, _Good for your mother, too hot to sleep anyway kids_. Unless of course your window faced the ocean: _You kids behave yourselves, I'm putting yez all in Christopher's room tonight, there's not a breath anywhere else_, and when I slept over Petey's house, with all windows agape we could hear the neighbors in their living. We devised blackmail schemes to get rich quick at what we heard in the lights-outness; but these were all forgotten by the morning, left behind as we traversed the flashing Timbuktu of eleven-year-old-boy dreams.

Me and Petey both played Little League then. Senior Division that year, we were eleven almost twelve and on the edge of Something. Changes but not the Bowie kind. We'd no idea what we were going through. Petey played for the GasCo Cardinals. I should say he _was_ the GasCo Cardinals. They'd picked him, and Old Colony Glass picked me, and there wasn't a thing you could do about it. They had tryouts the second blue-blowy Saturday of March and then they'd call you that finger-biting week. A man's gruff voice, calling for you. A stranger to tell you your new team and that was that. You pictured a basement somewhere, men and smoke gathered. Rosters and charts and one lightbulb a-swinging like a detective movie and your name written down. You and your abilities being bandied about, extolled or repudiated.

Me and Petey got called for different teams. Petey got picked Saturday night right away—me they didn't call 'til Thursday.

Until Thursday.

"Don't worry, Danny," Petey said all that week. That smile. "Don't worry, Danny. They're fighting over you."

We were playing against each other that June night, me and Petey's teams. I was okay. Petey was the best in the league. Both teams 11-0 undefeated, one week before the playoffs started, believe me it was the talk of the town. *Ouf, that game of yours is a nine-day wonder,* Mrs. Harding said when she puffed in from the butcher's that afternoon. She went on to report that Mr. Green and the Kenealley girls had asked her all about it. She always called it *sporting. Are you sporting tonight then?* when she'd see Petey in his uniform.

"Who's gonna win tonight?" I remember Mr. McGillicuddy asking when we traipsed into his store after school that afternoon for lucky green ice pops. I felt integral, a necessary part of things. A part of the sun slanting sideways through the thick-as-mud dusty ketchup bottles on the third shelf, the winning scratch cards Scotch-taped to the cash register, jiggling and bobbing in the open-door sea breeze like the bottle-blonde night ladies down Park Square.

Me and Petey looked at each other and laughed. Petey was graciousness itself in those days, the best at everything. Of course he didn't stutter then. He turned back to Mr. McGillicuddy.

"May the best man win," Petey said.

"Here we go then, Danny," Petey said later that day, right before that night's game.

He'd showed me before but I could never see it enough. It was that weird. His pregame ritual. We were in his bedroom, the tiny one that looked out onto the alley. It glowed from above, that room. The light fell down between the buildings and then wobbled into his room. Gobs of light but once removed. So hot, his mother had wedged the old rattly fan into the window. An old white sock with a green stripe stuffed between the fan and the paint-peeling sill lessened the vibro-hum a little, not too much but that was fine, a summer sound and welcome back to you. The fan was an old GE model, gray. It looked like it belonged on a battleship, or in an office where battleships were planned. Funny how you remember. The fan's breath lazy, half lift-stirring the pictures of knights and Red Sox players, Gandalf and Aragorn Scotch-taped to the old roses wallpaper in Petey's bedroom. Any one of Petey's six wild older brothers would've received *a fanny-warming remembrancer* from Mrs. Harding for doing such a thing. Not Petey though, never Petey. He was her favorite. Even then, before the accident. All of them red-headed but for Petey, Petey's hair like wet coal, the fair-haired boy nonetheless. He could've Scotch-taped the world. Okay, probably oldest brother Donnie would get away with it too—just little things you notice, tone of voice, the lift and shift of eyes, smiles and sighs given or held in pursed-lip reserve. *If I have to come over those stairs,* Mrs. H's refrain those days—she'd shout it from the kitchen with everybody's bedroom upstairs, *if I have to come over those stairs*—and I pictured her like a wave rising up the stairs, coming like God in wrath with a rolling pin, but she never did except for once when Sean set Matty's bed on fire.

He was the world's favorite then, Petey. Like I say, referred to as the Golden Boy. A straight-A student and so polite you'd think it was parody. The nuns sweetened their ascetic faces with smiles when they saw him coming—*Let me get that door for you, Sister.* The girls had always loved him, but more now, our backs shoved up against the smelly abyss of puberty. An altar boy at Gate of Heaven Church, and a light around him after Communion. A bliss-glow coming out of him when he chanted *ad Deum qui laetificat juventutem meum,* to God who gives joy to my youth. If ever there were a poster boy for that prayer, it had to be Petey Harding. So clean and pressed and slicked, even after screaming recess. Smiles and yes please thank yous and a clean smell oozing out of him at all times. That good in baseball, all other boys worshipped him, while the men hereabouts held him up as an example to their less angelic issue. And the only parents who didn't like him had to be jealous—like my mother.

That went back ages. One of the big department stores downtown used to have a portrait studio on the basement floor, and every year they ran their Beautiful Baby of Boston contest. Petey won it three years in a row back in the day and my mother never forgot it.

"That family belongs in the Projects," she'd mutter over the sink. "Beautiful Baby, my ass."

She referred to Mrs. Harding as the Babymaker, though seven kids was hardly a freak in town those days. There was just the one of me, my older brother Brian having died before I was born. *The last shake of the stick, eh?* ancient Mr. Crosby next door used to call me, before they took him away.

In addition Ma couldn't figure out how Mrs. Harding did her vacuuming without leaving any lines on the carpets, and too proud to make inquiries. And then, the whole Donnie and Brian thing—which I didn't know about then. Ma would do anything for me, her only child, but there's a toughness about her you'd never guess, or, well, I don't know, maybe you would. *The tenderest parts of you are your fake fingernails,* Dad said to Ma once when he came home with a drop in. *And that puss on your face would scare Jesus.* Usually Dad so silent but that one night they were going at it, splotches of words hurled like paintball, Ma irrevocably committed to the final word. Not without a sense of humor though, Ma. When we were ten and *sap* was the saying at school, when something bad happened to you, as in you are one, it was constantly falling from my lips. When the can of cocktail sauce Ma was trying to open exploded thirty seconds before company came and she'd just had her hair done; when her lucky numbers never came out of a night; one time helping her with the shopping during a wild March deluge and her umbrella buckled, went airborne in the parking lot and her new leather coat became instantly corrupted, *Sap,* I'd intone at her, but drawn out in a pre-pubescent shrill, mocking, pointing at her, *Saaaaap.* She'd give chase but could never catch, my legs like sticks but endless in their energy. A few months later tired, not feeling good, Dr. McCarthy telling me, *You've got mono young man. You'll be in bed for a month.* A summer was just starting and on the crowded elevator ride down from the doctor's office Ma turned to me, waited 'til I looked at her, *saaaaaap,* she whispered as the doors opened to the lobby and the little bell went *ding.*

But Petey now, there was a shine about him. Some kids just have it. You wouldn't be surprised if they turned out to be president or at least very rich, rub-it-in postcards from Bermuda every Christmas like the Barrys who owned that fuel oil company.

But I used to wonder what people would say if they saw Petey's pregame ritual.

Petey's uniform laid out on his bed. The whole thing, like a flattened Fab-ed version of himself. The shirt by the head, the pants along the spread, the little puckery jockstrap with the frayed leg straps on top of the pants, even the sanitary socks and cleats. The shirt arms outstretched like an appeal. His glove threaded into one cuff sleeve, right at the edge of the bed. The smell of fresh bargain laundry detergent staining the hot room.

It was still about 90 degrees even though it was like seven. The big game, the battle of the undefeateds, started at eight, *Night game!* and the nuns wouldn't mind much if you were late the next morning. They'd ask you in front of the whole class and you'd try not to smile when everyone-turn-around and tell em how you won. *Well ahhh, see I was on third, right? Last inning two outs, right? Booger McPhee on deck? And then . . .*

I was already in uniform, slouched in the tipply green corner chair, watching Petey. I was a sloucher, a watcher, not smart at all. Nothing special. Intensely normal, forgettable *Danny? Danny O'Connor? Oh yeah,*

Danny. Yeah. Petey lived closer to the field than I did so I'd called for him. I was sitting in the green chair in the corner, watching Petey, my left hand sweating inside my Hank Aaron glove on my lap, the smell of it I still remember. Petey's room immaculate. Always. Petey had no clothes on at all. Our bodies were exactly the same, we'd measured them, except me with the red hair and freckles and him with the black and without blemish.

"Come to life now and we bless you and give you the honor," Petey said, waving his hands over his uniform. He was always getting these weird prayers and blessings from the knight books he read all the time, old history books from the library's tag sale every Memorial Day for a grubby quarter and they smelled like old people's breath when you flipped the pages, brittle and tired yes but whispering of mysteries and ways of living long gone by now. I couldn't be bothered—the writing too small, way too much to say and I pictured a withered hand up on a wrinkled brow covering the eyes as they murmured endlessly and you couldn't be bothered when you're young. Except for Petey. Petey wanted to know things.

The white naked length of Petey walked over to his bureau and took the tiny beveled-glass bottle of miraculous Lourdes water that the Mission monks sent Mrs. Harding once a month, along with their *Heartfelt Blessings*—she'd send them a little something when she was able. Petey unscrewed the black cap carefully with nimble antenna fingers, then sprinkled a bit of the holy water onto his white and red uniform. Number 7 he was. That was always a precondition.

He closed his eyes.

"We ask to win without bragging, and to lose without excuse," Petey continued. He had such a way of speaking then. All you could do was stare.

"We seek to bring honor to the game, to ourselves, and to our God," he continued. Then he raised his hands upward like an appeal, the back of him pink and white, bump-moundy with muscle and flesh and flank.

"Stand for this part, Danny," Petey tossed over his shoulder.

I slouched up silently.

Then Petey began intoning in a wild guttural language. It was the Irish again. He'd learned some of it from his mother and *this*, he told me when he finished, was a prayer 2,000 years old and yes, you could almost smell that it was.

Petey opened his eyes.

Then he began dressing, solemnly. Not a word out of him, the way we'd put on our cassocks and surplices when we did altar boy duty. Always in the same order. Petey sat down on the end of the bed, the cups of his hipbones pulling at muscle and flesh so white it was blue and me watching from the corner in fluttery fan shadow. I sat down again as he pulled on the right sanitary sock, then the left. Then his stirrups, cardinal red that year of course. The stirrups would have to be exactly as high as the sanitary socks. Petey was most particular about that. Then he stood, sighed solemnly, and wiggled into the little cotton jockstrap, putting those tiny white and pink things safely away where they belonged. Much was expected of them later, we didn't know that then. Our families, the Church, advertisers, everyone really, had plans for them. These expectations and boundaries. What were these expectations.

Then the shirt next, a baseball jersey underneath if it was chilly but not tonight, my ears red with the heat—nothing redder than a redhead's ears when he's flushed with June. Next came the pants, and the matte black belt always too long and wrapped halfway again around his tubular white waist. Now, Petey's cleats. Always the right one first. Finally the hat, like a coronation. Petey would turn to the mirror to do this, lower it slowly with both hands onto his black hair. Sometimes he'd ask me to put it on for him, not tonight though. He'd stare at himself for a bit, then turn to me—

"Who do you say that I am, Danny?" he asked. Like I say, he didn't stutter then. Never.

"Petey Harding," I answered, as usual when he did this, though I always felt funny. "My ahhh . . . best friend."

"Bestest," he said. "Always."

That smile. Something inside me rising up to meet it.

We march down to the Game on the clacky river of the sidewalk, which sighs out the day's heat. The air swings like a carnival. Our cleats clickity, we walk in unison. People shout out encouragement, luck as we stride you stride we all stride for baseball by their door stoops, everyone sitting out. Mrs. Lally now, relishing the view of upper O Street from her top stair smoking a Tareyton but she's a lover not a fighter, housecoat and scuff slippers and *Good luck to you, Brian,* she sings out to me. My name is Danny. Brian was my older brother I never met, my only sib like I say, he died the year before I was born. He was sixteen, drunk driver and that was that. This name fuck-up happens sometimes. I guess we look alike. Can't tell Ma. Can't ever talk about Brian with Ma. She bombs up the stairs to her room, slams the door and Dad fixes leftovers for silent supper. Other families round the way remember their dead, commemorate their dead, special

Masses, pictures on the mantle, the Lucky McGurl 5k Road Race but not us. We try our best to forget he ever existed.

"Take it easy on the hills, boys," an old timer cackles from across the street. He's *contraposta* in the open maw of a barroom, Pat's Place. You can see the smoke twirling lazy out into the honey twilight. There's no wind—it just sort of sifts out, that smoke. Wanting out.

"Look," Petey says as we click round the corner of East Broadway and Farragut Road. Beyond the tops of the triple-deckers there's a sharp glow to the south that is not the sunset, edging things in surreality.

We both come up short, stop.

"The lights are on at Columbia Park," Petey announces. I gulp. This means we're playing on the Big Field. The Big Field's only for playoffs and the 16-18 Senior League that lies in wait for us like all other good things.

For a second breathless and a jiggle bounces between us, but then *Why not the Big Field,* we're young and it's summer and we're playing ball *Night game!* and the world belongs to us. Miracles come every day, like the paper, like the first pubic hair and me waiting by the hour.

Depending on their sympathies, cars honk out derision or calls to *Kick ass* as they pass other shuffling knots of green-bubblegum players on their way to the Game. When they come to me and Petey, one from each side, the red and the blue, they get confused and a general tumult of noise ensues. It's Southie and that kind of night. I totally forget that other people driving by have other lives this night, totally unconnected to the Game. Then I remember that they do and pity poor them.

The ocean fifty yards across Day Boulevard shines pink and silver and flat, but way out at the horizon the shrouded light is green and yellow, with an ugly black oval like a bashed eye in the middle.

"Queer-looking sky." Petey points.

"Huh? Oh. Oh yeah."

"The ancients always said such signs . . . *portended doom!*" Petey waves his fingers in my face at these last words, blows a bubble and *snap* it goes. He laughs. Ironic now, looking back.

"Can you say it in English?"

"Here Danny," Petey says, thinking of something else. "I want you to have these."

He pulls a box of Good & Fruity from his back pants pocket with a flourish and a dimpling. Some kids are already warehousing cigarettes or airplane model glue for sniffing in those pockets, not Petey.

"Win or lose, I want you to have these, Danny."

Good & Plenty is like horseshit. It's everywhere, as my grandfather would say. Which isn't exactly true—there are in fact no horse poopsters in Southie any more, but that doesn't matter. Good & Fruity on the other hand is hard to find. Some of us at school that spring have chin-rub speculated about its disappearance from local stores' shelves. *They're not making it no more cuz one of the factory workers put LSD in it and some kid from Maine died,* Blubber Hogan, the school's rumormonger, announced solemnly one lunchtime. *My cousin Eddie O'Brien told me so.*

"I've ordered it," Mr. McGillicuddy would say when we'd make inquiries. He'd scratch behind his cauliflower ear. "I did order it."

"*AWE-SOME!* Where did you find them, Petey?"

"At this spa over in Dorchester. Cambodians run it. You should hear their music."

Petey was always off on his bike wandering. My mother kept a much tighter rein.

"If Petey Harding painted his ass purple, you'd do the same thing!" she said more than twice. The Halloween before, we'd done just that. I told Petey what Ma always said, so we got finger paints and painted each other's bums purple. When we went trick-or-treating an hour later, ski masks to protect our identity, everyone asked us what we were, dear.

"*The Purple-Butted East Side Boys!*" we screamed once we had the goods in our pillow-sacks, running down the tenement steps, then we'd moon them at the bottom. I chucked my white Fruit of the Looms into a trashy can in an alley before I went home that night—that would be something I'd never be able to explain to Ma, who did me and Dad's laundry with the eye of an archaeologist. I used to wonder what someone would think, if they found that underwear. Like I'd eaten a lot of purple plums and shit myself maybe. I mentioned this to Petey.

"Purple plum poopsterinis," he said. "That's called alliteration, when the words start with the same letter. They roll off the tongue like wiggly red Jell-O, no Danny? *Wa-wa-wa-wa-wa!*"

Half the town is clutched at the edges of the neon green ballfield when we get there, and they've summoned legions of lawn-chair-toting relations from Quincy and Milton, Dorchester, Hyde Park. Big Game. Day has shattered into night and you don't even notice. "Where goes the day when comes the night?" Petey asks but I ignore him. I'm nervous and not in the mood for Petey nonsense. Smaller children overflow the stands and spill airplane-arm screaming onto the adjacent playground. The excitement is croupy-contagious. Three competing ice cream trucks perfectly work the four sides of the Park, turning the square back into a circle and the geometry of it puzzles. Each one playing tinkly jingles that smear into a cacophonic symphony and a contented sigh from the ocean just across the rusty street. A jagged line of ruffling seagulls settles in on the telephone wires, peering, taut with Tonight like everybody else around here. Mothers muddled together, hobnobbing while checkbooks get balanced and diets get exchanged—*This is that one Marie Boyle lost ten pounds on and you know the appetite on her.* Young fathers are here, with three-year-old sons dressed in hats and baseball shirts too big for them, and as the squatted fathers point, trying to explain the holy intricacies of bats and balls and bases, their sons look skyward, their heads full up with baby blue thoughts.

"May the best team win," Petey says, extending his sweat-free hand to me as we decamp to our own sides of the field. He has to shout almost, it's that loud with the crowd and all. Petey's always saying stuff like that. We have this bearded long-hair of a janitor at Gate of Heaven School, one of the nuns' nephews I think, must be the last hippie in the world or at least in Southie. Yes, thanks, he's been to Vietnam and writes dirty-worded poetry on a filthy yellow pad he keeps in the back pocket of his greasy green chinos. He calls Petey "Peter Platitude." Petey's mother refers to him as *That poor miserable cray-chure.* His name is Larry but everyone calls him Scratch and Sniff, self-explanatory I trust. Went off to Vietnam shy and crew-cutted, big-eared, so tall yet baby-faced for eighteen. Came back wild-eyed long-haired, apt to declaim on the Broadway bus, *missing something God help him,* everybody says, but perhaps instead having been given something not entirely propitious. My mother says he resembles a vacant lot on the West Side gone to seed and what's he doing anyway working in a school *where he might do anything.* Everyone except Petey and the nuns laughs at him. Petey though calls him Lawrence and every day at school gives him an encouraging saying, *Good things come to those who wait, Lawrence,* next day *It's darkest right before dawn, Lawrence* or whatever. That's Petey. Larry always just grumbles back. But he cried when he heard about Petey's accident, *Cried like four babies,* Mrs. Harding reported glumly. Even came to see him at the hospital afterward but Someone called security and they made him leave looking like that, *the cut of him,* the old Irish matron at the registration desk kept saying to anyone who would listen. So many people visited Petey in the hospital. Even the mayor and the bishop and the pictures of it in the papers clipped out and sent back to the cousins in Ireland, along with fervid scribblings to Storm Heaven for Petey, prayers and novenas would you please to this saint and that.

Petey was the most popular kid in school, maybe in town. The Golden Boy. All that was about to change tonight.

Listen what happened.

It was in the third inning when that wind came.

One minute even oceanside here people fanning themselves with flattened empty popcorn boxes, the sports section from the *Herald*, anything, not a breath and the women's perfume spurting into the sweat-and-tobacco-ridden air like flowery unseen ejaculations. Then quick this invisible something whooshes in from the sea right across the Boulevard. If someone gets up from their lawn chair to pee in the sumacs behind left field or go talk to somebody about the upcoming primary—*Say Billy, could you and Trudy give Danno your vote next month? For my sake?*—the chair flips over. A few caps swirl off the players on the field like twirly maple seeds except up not down. An angry loop of sand raises itself like a fist between third and second and drives in toward the plate. About a hundred people go, *Oooooooooooo* and the ump raises both hands time out. A lady's hat becomes airborne and goes campaigning off into right field, tumbling over and over with urgent intention. Haystack Hogan's grandfather goes hobbling after in chivalrous but comedic pantomime pursuit.

Everyone looks up and around like they've forgotten we live in a natural world. These big inky clouds puffing in from the ocean, lowering as they advance the very weight of them, black purple water balloons swollen to the limit and they've chewed away the stars and moon and us not even hearing. The temperature dives about twenty degrees instantly, like in a cartoon when they show the thermometer plummeting, turning ice-crusted blue to Goofy's *a-DUH* chagrin. At first it feels good after the day's heat but then seconds later no, too cold. All of a sudden you can't see the Hennessey twins, can't see Little Pinky Quinn out in center field so good, it's like misty or whatever.

Then the wind gone. Poof. Like the snuffing of a candle. It's so quiet— what is up with that? But a heaviness stays in the air like a stranger in your dark bedroom. That hanging quiet before the thwack. Everyone stops for a minute. Sniffing around. A lady of a certain age breaks the ice. She's having none of it—she's buried two husbands—cackles *Oh cripes!* and reaches with salamander-spotted fingers and fuchsia pink fingernails for her More 120 cigarettes in the maroon leatherette case with the lighter tucked in its built-in pocket.

"Play ball!" one of the umps roars, and everyone back to normal, though if they've left a sweater in the car they dash for it. The Jurassic hip-saunter of

mothers after their children, but they don't have to go far. The chilly kids are seeking out Ma, the girls holding their skinny bare shoulders, the little boys with finger and thumb abstractedly grabbing their peepees through their shorts, looking around. The men remain motionless, pretending still to sweat.

Petey's oldest brother Donnie is sitting on the guardrail up there by the Boulevard, alone, married with two tots but essentially alone. He used to mind us times when we were younger, before he got married himself. Quiet. Solitary even in a crowd that one. Some people just are you know. *He's hung up his happiness for sure,* Mrs. Harding says with a shake of her head. Can't mention Donnie without eliciting that response. The way he stares at me all the time. What is up with that? Must remember to ask Petey about that sometime. *My brave soldier, my little man,* Mrs. H still calls Donnie in private, for the yeoman's shoulder he provided after Mr. Harding died and Donnie being the oldest. Maybe that explains the wet blanket Donnie could be with her—a prodigal spendthrift, she hired a pony for me and Petey's eighth birthday party (ten days apart we are) and for three hours one shining September afternoon, all the sky above the Harding backyard couldn't contain the unbridled joy there. I'd slept over the night before, and by the time we woke up there were red milk crates in the street in front of the house, reserving parking. *Oh Dolly would you be a love and keep that spot open, there's a surprise coming for the boyos. Oh, Mr. Hennessey, God's blessing on you this lovely day, how's the wife? If it wouldn't cause too much consternation, we need to save those—I say, we need to save those spots for the boys' birthday surprise.* And by noontime me and Petey, immovably clamped to the splintery front porch steps, could not eat, could not speak, could hardly breathe. *What have you done, Ma?* Donnie kept asking inside the house. I could hear them, and she shushing him with a *Hush now, look at them! There isn't a squeak out of them!* And when the riotously painted Mister Mysterio's Mobile Circus of Animals truck rolled down O Street, Petey commenced a laughingly earnest, frenetic Irish jig so he wouldn't burst, and I didn't remember to take the finger out of my nose, where it had been busy digging, until a laughing Mrs. Harding appeared with the camera to snap-shot our ecstasy for posterity.

You could've paid the water bill with that, Ma. Did you put something aside for the phone bill? I heard Donnie say to her on my twentieth pony-time around. *Oh hold your whist, love, and never mind the phone bill!* she snapped at him. *I'd lose the roof over this house before I'd swap it for the joy on them today!*

Tinker Kelley strikes out and whips his bat, the ump snarls a warning, then Petey steps up to the plate and expectant applause all round. Our best pitcher Billy Donovan's going for us tonight. Jimmy Whelan's our other pitcher and his turn tonight but he got benched for this Big Game. See Jimmy's okay for six innings but completely falls apart in the seventh (the last), gives up homer after homer which is why he's Way-Back Whelan. So it's Billy tonight instead of Jimmy. Petey in the first inning is the only one so far to get a hit off of Billy, a long screeching double it was, then Petey stole third and came home on a suicide squeeze bunt. It's one to nothing now, third inning. Two outs. Not a soul on base. The grass twice as green under the funky night light. Three seagulls pecking and preening out in right field, oblivious but still a part of it all.

I'm playing first like always. Leaning in. Bum shoved out in a disdaining crouch, *left right left right left*. I'm lightly grazing my glove against the dirt three times before each batter just for green luck. Luck's always green to me, it just is.

Billy and Petey stare at each other, then Billy vaults his whip frame into a windmill windup. He has dick bush but not me yet, he laughing showed us after a game when he was taking his cup off, *Wouldn't you little pukes like to have this now?* He throws a fastball. Petey's ready but swings a hair too soon. He cracks a screamer down the right field line, just one foot foul. It almost takes my head off. I feel the wind of it whiz by me. No one can hit Billy Donovan's fastball except for Petey. He creams it most every time. If there's a thing Petey can't do no one knows it yet. There's something about watching a boy do something to fluidy perfection, you wonder what ever will stop him when he's a man.

"Sorry, Danny," Petey calls out to me. It's the very lastest thing the old Petey Harding says. He whacks the dirt off his cleats with his bat, one at a time, spits, peers.

The next ball is a curve, low, in the dirt a wormkiller, and the next one same thing but too high a rainmaker. Coach calls time out and hustles out to talk to Billy on the mound the way they do. I think Coach wants Billy to walk Petey intentionally, because Billy keeps shaking his head, no no no. I go over to see what's up. Coach falls asleep in Mass, never during a game but nevertheless Mrs. Harding vouches for his *deep devotion to Our Lady.* He's a member of the local chapter of the League of Mary and she should know, isn't she the recording *sec-a-terry*. Big hairy paws I always notice, but something heartbreaking in how they fumble with a rosary when he jump-wakens right at the final blessing, never married as his fiancée married someone else while he was in the service, and his life now is all about Mary and Baseball. He was sent to Vietnam to kill people. Signed up for a stupor-second tour when the loved one repudiated him Par Avion. One time after a team meeting at his house he showed me and Petey his collection of cards, greeting cards birthday cards get well cards Mass cards, not the usual like you'd find around here there and everywhere in overly lit, hot fluorescent shops, *A Niece Is A Special Person, A Prayer For You, Father-in-Law, On Your Birthday,* but crinkly missives of wonder: rice paper ones from Southeast Asia, some hand-lettered in gold by Capuchin monks in Italy, another, layered tissues of paper thinner than butterfly wings, all unique but each a hallmark of wonder. I'm just telling you because TV would have us believe coaches are just coaches, half-dimensional recipients of indigestion right before the Big Game, shillers of athlete's foot and jock itch remedies and I want to set the record straight before coaches themselves start taking their cues from ads like everyone else.

"What are you doing?" Coach is saying to Billy, not rhetorically, when I join them at the mound. I'm not sure I'm supposed to be here but this is what the Big Leaguers do when there's a conference on the mound. The first baseman will trot over sometimes, an assistant-secretary-of-state-ish advisory capacity.

"I can get him out. I know I can!" Billy whines. He's six foot tall and has dick bush already but his voice hasn't changed yet which is strange, but I guess This Thing Coming to us all is like that telescope I got in the mail that year from Aunt JeanMarie for Christmas—the shafty-thing part came in December, the lensy thing not until February. But it was cracked and Ma wouldn't let me send it back because *that would be rude Danny, but I ask you isn't it just like that side of the family.*

Billy splays a cleated foot into the dusty pitcher's mound. The dust rises up, does not settle down and I watch it, wondering where does it go as it vanishes.

"One more pitch," Coach says, shoving his hands into his back pockets and rocking back and forth. "Throw strikes, hear me? If you don't, then you walk him. Hear me?"

"Play ball!" the home plate ump bellows. Coach slaps skinny Billy on his nonbum and trots back in. He's put on his Veterans of Foreign Wars Post #6536 blue nylon jacket.

Billy is a sore sport and hates to lose. He's mad now and going to throw the fastball, I know it. People who can't control their emotions you can predict what they're going to do ten out of ten times, no? I want to yell that out to Petey but I know he knows this too, fastball coming. I want my team to win but I always root for Petey too. Once Paul O'Rourke said to me—whispered it really on the way home from Altar Boy Guild, with Petey still back at church getting his picture taken for *The Pilot* for his Altar Boy of the Year Award—he whispered, Paulie did, "Okay Danny, listen—Petey, right? Sometimes, I want to see him . . . not fail, I don't mean like fail. Just maybe not be so perfect."

"Why?" I asked. Then, "Shut the fuck up, Paulie," before waiting for him to answer. The shove I gave him, you should've seen it. Fuckin' say that about my best friend.

Petey digs his cleats into the dusty home plate soil. From where I am, crouched beside first base, I can see Petey tighten up his grip on the bat. Fingerlings. He becomes absolutely still, a Hall of Fame statue in the making and me knowing the inevitability of this twenty years before the rest of the world and why me as his best friend when he could have anybody. An accident of kindergarten seating and not a day's gone by since that we haven't been the sight and light of each other. Billy Donovan's eyes are wimply and leaking nervousness, fierceness, but Petey's are hearing music. And Petey's uniform still gleaming in the gloaming, how he manages to keep it white the way he plays. There's some people and it just comes natural. All you can do is stare. For a second I picture Petey in his batting stance without any clothes at all. Just his cleats and helmet. I wonder what everyone would think if they saw Petey doing his ritual dressing. But I know it's something you don't talk about with anyone else. How do we know we shouldn't. I look down, spit nervously, try to reach the edge of the grass with the dollop but it plops far short.

"*Petey! C'mon, Petey! Petey, give it a ride now, Petey! All the way, Petey!*" But there's just as many calls out to Billy to blow it by him whip it by him, strike him out for Chrissake and a boozy laugh. Billy's mother in particular with the brassy red hair: a wicked whiny voice and her incessant call a rising crescendo like a stain above everyone and everything: *Ca'mooooooONNNNNNN, BILLY!* over and over again 'til you want someone to slap her please. For the sake of your own concentration. Billy's father, a cop and works nights watching from the edge of the road above the field in his uniform not too far from Donnie, spitting with a snake-jerk of his head. Staring down in a way that makes me glad he's not my father.

Billy winds up and The Wind comes back as if Billy's Merlin movements have summoned it. It cuts in like a rumbly driverless miscarriage of something from left field and roars right for the pitcher's mound. It knocks over somebody's camera-tripod thing. Patsy Flynn over on third does a little dance—he gets twirled around by the wind and looks a dust devil with all the sand. Billy Donovan closes his eyes as he hurls the ball. His gloved hand shoots up to his face to cover his eyes from the sand. I remember that. He half stumbles as he lets the ball go, dick bush and squeaky voice and inherited nasty spleen and everything else he's got thrown into that pitch, half the universe thrown into that pitch. I know the fastball will be wild. I know the fastball will be wild. Everything slow motions. The ball rotates as it approaches and its coming is cometlike, calamitous and heraldic.

"Petey!" I roar, to warn him, can't help it my best friend, everything oh Jesus—

Petey squints and his head shoots a look at me. We stare at each other for a second. The ball hits him then right over the eye, in between the helmet and his eyebrow. It came out of the sand while he was looking at me. The thwack of it. Crunch. It shatter-bounces his helmet off. The impossible has happened. Petey has erred, next the planets might go spinning out of their orbits—

Petey is still looking at me. His eyes rise big like moons.

"I'm numb! I'm numb!" he wails, dropping his bat and reaching for his head with both hands. Everyone hears this.

Then a silence as everyone watches. Silence is wonderful in a church, awful when there's so many around, no?

Petey's eyes shutter-shut, slow. How they louver—how it reminds me of blinds quick-yanked down inside a house where something horrible has just happened. His arms pause halfway to his head, then flop.

He heaps to the dust. Buckling and the slow pulling in of knees and elbows. Crumple. There is a second when nothing happens, then blood curdles from his ear onto the dusty dirt. The dust is too dry. It won't accept it. The blood makes a crooked spiral as it leaks from his ear. Something monstrous seems to travel underground out from home plate, out to me where it splits the ground between my legs.

It rained for three straight days after that.

3

WHY

He was in a coma for a month, exactly, as if the moon. Mrs. Harding never leaving his side. They squeaky-wheeled a cot in for her at City Hospital, and me thinking the only names worse could be Acme Hospital, Amalgamated Hospital, Hospital Inc. Mrs. Feeney and Mrs. Cleary, two ladies she worked with whom all my life I never met but heard about and they remained mythical figgers, ten feet tall in their plaid skirts, took over her night shift at the Necco Candy Factory *because that's what friends are for, Dottie.*

You had to be twelve to visit. I was eleven and three-quarters and rules were rules, but once finally they let me go see him with Ma.

Ma brought a crystal blue pair of rosary beads for Mrs. Harding that had been blessed at St. Anne de Beaupré or someone holy in Canada. I never knew there was anyone holy in Canada, all the saints seemed to come from Italy or Ireland. I pictured a woman, shining maple leaves in her brilliantine hair, but shivering as she prayed in the cold. The beads were in a black velveteen box that snapped shut with an invincible click and Ma finally on the ride over *Stop that Danny you're driving me to distraction,* and me struggling to keep my mouth shut at the obvious retort to avoid a U-turn.

A smelly confusion of elevators and endless yellow halls and *Don't stare Danny* when we'd pass people overflowing into the corridors in various forms of estrangement from what they used to be, mostly old people melting into caricature. But just beyond the walls, just beyond the glass glowed the brilliance of a late July day, and the hospital on a hill and the view shining off to everywhere, and I tried to hold onto that.

A Map of the Harbor Islands
Published by The Haworth Press, Inc., 2006. All rights reserved.
doi:10.1300/5677_03

"They've got him in the poor section. The *welfare* section," Ma murmurs decisively as we ease into Petey's room on timid steps, the way people do when visiting, our shoes announcing our tentativeness.

Mrs. Harding starts blubbering when we come in—some people are invincible until given one inch of sympathy and then imploding commences. Petey's oldest brother Donnie's here too, sitting quiet in the corner. He rises up, grim like in court. Not a word out of him, eyes so blue they're white and the red hair a relentless assault in so colorless a room, redder than mine. A last-night stale beer smell rises from him like he's slowly composting from the inside out, but he's here and Petey's other brothers aren't, has brought coffee and dognuts (as Petey called them) for The Mother and the nurses. A jolt whenever he stares at me—it can never be called just looking, the intensity of it, a puzzle because we haven't said a word for a year or two though he used to babysit us when we were younger.

But this mystery will have to wait for another time; for there's something with bandages on its head like a mummy and tubes everywhere in a bed beside us and a machine goes *bleeeep . . . bleeeep . . . bleeeep* as if it might stop at any minute if it cared to, if it was not placated and appeased, but you don't know its peccadilloes. I know the thing in the bed must be Petey—no I don't want that, but the eye unstoppable like a magnet and me not ready yet. Eyes have no fears, no? They'll look at anything.

"Tar isteach, tar isteach anois!" Mrs. Harding says, Come in, come in now, reverting to Irish in the slap-stupor of her grief. I've heard it enough at her front door to know. *Sghbrckgmcha* Ma will imitate cruelly later out in the car, spraying me with spittle. Intentionally? You never know with Ma.

"Dottie," Ma says, stopping on a dime and tilting her head like a gibbous moon.

"God bless you for coming! God bless the both of yez and leave you your healths!"

Mrs. H rises up from her chair and her knitting plunges to the floor. She steps on it not noticing. She and Ma brush-kiss on the cheek, like polite visiting spiritual potentates inwardly convinced of the other's charmingly heretical views. Ma wearing a dress the color of grass. An oval stain of violet remains on Mrs. Harding's inflated red cheek as Ma pulls back. Oddly I think of Judas.

I've brought a Classics Illustrated comic book, *Tales of the Knights of the Round Table,* picked it out special I did, and its glossy violent cover gleams slippery under the fluorescents. I hand it to Mrs. Harding and she doesn't even look, tossing it down at the foot of Petey's bed. It uncurls, slowly, hoping to be read. *Do me,* I think I hear it whisper.

"What a lovely shade of pink, Dottie," Ma says, looking down at the lump of knitting.

Mrs. Harding stares at Ma, sighs, then turns to me.

"Maybe if he hears your wee voice he'll come out of it so," she urges, snatching up the knitting and working it like bread dough. Then she tssks and hurls it over her shoulder back to the floor and puts her hands on me. The way she clutches my forearms—the stuffed hawks we'd seen on our field trip to the Museum of Science two months ago. On the pandemonium of a bus ride home Mark Riordan started at the back of the bus and crawled under the seats biting all the girls' calves, and there was mathematical perfection to the way the individual conversations came to a screeching halt in perfect domino succession, but that has nothing to do with this unless everything has everything to do with everything.

"Going out for a smoke," Donnie mumbles to the floor. Ma's tight smile follows after him. Pushes him out, you'd think. I turn to watch him leave and see him turn back and stare quick at me. He's old, twenty-eight, as old as my dead brother Brian would be and I always think that when I see him, how odd it would be to have a man for a brother, a big grown quiet man and me just a little puke still.

"Can I ring the buzzer?" I ask Mrs. Harding, pointing to the button on the wall.

"Ouf, please yourself child, but you'd be all day waiting for the response," Mrs. Harding says, but Ma says *Stay away from there Danny* before I can indulge this empty pleasure I've retreated to, ducking from the guillotine of horror here. See in my mind over the past month I've kept Petey at sea, floating out somewhere in the soft brine, a misty sun laving down Healing on him and me a rosary every night for him. The reality of This Instead pricks to the core. How can I keep from roaring?

"How is he today?" Ma asks. Mrs. Harding works her mouth, stares for a minute. Her eyes huge behind her glasses and they recall a nature show, denatured really, a vulgar buffalo hunt cable show and her eyes like the bow-and-arrowed buffalo's now, one panicked, the other stoic, remembering what no one else can.

"No change," she says quick, like it'll be easier that way. But last Tuesday afternoon Fr. Brennan down at Flanagan's said *Oh he's not well at all* to Mrs. Flaherty—he'd brought the Blessed Sacrament that morning and me almost fainting among the vermilion tomatoes hearing those words. That's Southie, we live in each other's shadows.

"I've made a novena," my mother says, smiling bigger and looking around. Even here she must examine, file. That look on her face. The room pants stuffiness, even with the perfume my mother has apparently swum a few laps in. I look here there everywhere but don't see no ice cream—they always said you got ice cream when you came to the hospital, a false promise just to get you here finally. A defeated-looking half-deflated purple balloon with a puckered GET WELL SOON in white letters rests like purgatory halfway between the ceiling and the floor on the other side of Petey's bed. I want to pop it, put it out of its misery.

"If ye'd been here a month ago, you'd've seen the flowers . . . piles of 'em!" Mrs. Harding says, shaking her head. No flowers now.

"Ohhhhhhhhh," my mother says.

"Mary Mother of God, a panoply of them," Mrs. Harding continues, jerking her head. "A fleet of flowers, you might say. The bishop sent birds of paradise."

"It's been so busy," my mother says, looking around still, but just last week she tossed down her thick paperback, crossed her nylon-stockinged legs, stretched yawned and complained of these *languid* summer days.

"Speak to him now," Mrs. Harding says, shoving me, ignoring my mother. "Discourse, if ye would. I've half a notion t'will do him a power of good."

I slouch over to the bed, slunkily. I've grown three inches so far this summer and don't know how to do it yet, Ma's constant *Stand up straight Danny, for heaven sakes* a momentary stopgap. Deep breath. I can see from the top of Petey's nose, down. His eyes half-bandaged, purple half-moons underneath them. They look like our bums that Halloween. A beautiful plum color everywhere in the universe except when calamitously spangled across soft human flesh. I burst crying, unexpectedly, a gawky retch-sob, just the one, but an explosion of hot tears and sizzling off my chin already. Ma looks at me funny. The way her almond eyes half close, the face moving in half an inch to appraise. Radar fully engaged, operational. What's she thinking always in that fragranced gated realm of hers?

"Be . . . be a little man now, Danny," she chides.

She pulls her plain black leather pocketbook closer into her green dress. Her fingers work its strap like she's blind and wants to see is the leather real, is it best quality.

"Be a little man now and don't be upsetting people."

"Whist now, whist!" Mrs. Harding hisses, whether at me or Ma I don't know. Her fists clench like she might start swinging. She shoves me closer to the bed again. "Speak to him now, Danny! Go on wi' ye now and say something to 'im! Don't keep your tongue under your belt!"

"Wh-what? Say what to him?"

There's a funny lump in my throat, too much cotton candy that won't go down yet. My arms dangling all the way to the floor. The emergent mother of all zits throbbing on my forehead, third eye blind.

"Anything, say anything. Tell him things. Regale him why don't you." Mrs. Harding smells of three-day-old Jean Naté dusting powder. But I love the smell, it recalls her even when she's right beside me.

I lean in a little closer and grip my hands on the iron railing they have around his bed. The room is hot but the metal railing sings cold. There's two tubes up Petey's nose. Also a breathing thing that looks like a vacuum cleaner hose except clear shoved into his mouth, as if Housekeeping has taken over medical duties for the poor in light of recent budget cuts: *Somedin' wicked in him and we gonna suck it on out!* a voodoo-professing for-eigner will come in and explain any minute, as they commence mopping. Petey's lips dry and cracky. His arms white sticks, with blue sting-smudges up and down like someone mean's been playing cribbage on him when no one's here at night.

Petey!

A vast something rises up inside me and wills him to get better, wills all this shit-that-happens away. I close my eyes to see it: the cold metal railing will be first to go. I picture it shoved out the window, smashing down seven stories where it will be continually run over by traffic and no one even look-ing stopping or caring like squirrel meat.

"We ahhh . . . we lost the game that night," I say. "You guys won."

I turn to look at Mrs. Harding. The edges of her eyes look like they've been permanently tattooed red like she's the *Star Trek* freak of the week, this time from the planet of Perpetual Grief. She's wearing a white dress with happy li'l rosebuds and for the first time in my life I am aware of irony though I don't know the word yet. Or maybe it's a talisman, her willful pen-etration of something hopeful into this chamber of dread. She wears no ny-lons and her drumstick legs very white with blue roadmaps of veins that don't really go anywhere in the end. Her long red hair puffy-out and wild. Just the very top of a lopsided barrette showing, lost in its midst, totally un-able to bring order into the chaos of tumbling red. She looks like a witch without her glasses when she's squinting but she's really nice, I've always loved her. From the west of Ireland and talks a lot, excessive with her vocabulary when things reel out of control. Another foreigner. We're all foreigners I guess except the Indians, and look at the freakin' shafting they got.

"That's it," Mrs. Harding murmurs. She's working her hands together like milking. "That's it love. Proceed wi' ye Danny. Go."

She pauses as I stare open-mouthed at her.

"Don't clam up now, wax loquacious for God's sake."

I turn back to Petey.

"They called the game after you ahhhh . . . when you got hurt there, and you guys beat us one-zero," I say. My mother behind me making me nervous, Seen But Not Heard. Watching.

I turn around and find her peeking at a get-well card on the radiator.

"It'd . . . it'd be easier like if yez weren't staring at me," I sore-throat mumble.

"Of course it would! Shall we away to the cafeterium for cups of tea," Mrs. Harding says, clutching my lip-set mother. Ma glares at me as the two of them stumble out of the room. Their heels clacking on the mirror-green linoleum like draught animals made to go faster. I can feel my mother's displeasure, like a hot radiator from across the room when you just walk in. For once she's been maneuvered. Out.

I stand here staring at Petey. The all of him. For a minute. I wait 'til I feel him staring back like the ocean for green luck, but I can't tell. For another minute. I reach out a finger and touch his left arm, quick at first like you're seeing if the WET PAINT really is. Then longer, the flesh of him. Very soft. Little tiny blond hairs on it. A thing has stolen my best friend and it occurs to me that I mean to get him back.

I raise my eyes to a round painting of the Blessed Mother on the wall over Petey's head. Her eyes of woe rue and anguish jutting right into mine—*You Did This, Didn't You? When You Called His Name? We Saw You. Oh! Ooooooooooooh!* It's not just a picture, it's a pothole into that other world. That Vast World. I move a little to the left but the eyes still looking into mine, one of those. No one's said nothing so far about me yelling out Petey's name right before he got hit. I'm not sure anyone knows. But at night when I try to fall asleep I hear the whole world. The pillow against both ears but still *Dan-NY, Dan-NY, Dan-NY!*

"I'm sorry, Petey," I mumble. "I just . . . "

This killer lump in my throat. A big Adam's apple since last month. Sore now. Something else to tell Petey when he wakes up. *Is yours bigger too then?*

"I wanted to warn you was all," I say. "I'm sorry, Petey, so Petey sorry."

I mean to repeat *so sorry Petey*—but it doesn't matter. He understands. Having said the words. Better now. I know he forgives me. Petey.

"Petey," I call. A deep breath, a good one. Sniff hard to clear the wet nose rubble. I take his hand in mine. At least it's warm anyways. Something leaps between us. I think of extension cords joined finally, lighting up something in the distance we haven't got to yet.

"Peeeet-eeeeey."

A little *mmmpphhh* out of him, like he's in pain, and very far away. I lean in closer and put my mouth up against where his ear must be, under the bandages. I smell the bandages, caustic, dampish.

"Someone's done their poopsterinis," I whisper.

Hoping he'll laugh but no. I reach over and carefully lift one of his eyelids. Open your eyes damn you. There are Monopoly games to be played and summer smells to be sniffed. Just yesterday the long-tall grasses growing between the abandoned railroad tracks and how they smell different here in roasting July—tarry, burny—than they did in spangly June when they smelled meaty, greeny. Life, its bizarre beauty, needs witnesses and I need Petey to witness my witnessing.

But when I pull back his eyelid his eyeball's way up high and it grosses me out. I *uhhhh!* and fall back a little.

A crack of my knuckles to regroup. Come in close again, a boxer sizing up his opponent. Scared shitless but must go on. Something I must do here, wish I knew what. Deep breath, here we go.

I unhitch the metal railing on this side and slide it down. Of course it doesn't cooperate but then finally after a clanging and screeching. *It's cussing for grease,* as my grandfather would say. I deposit what there is of me that's bum on the edge of his unmalleable bed. I take his hand again.

"It stinks. Without you around, Petey. You gotta wake up."

I rub his hand like they do to fainted ladies in movies. I pause. Out the window beside us you can see way far away the Mystic River Bridge. You can't see the cars and trucks themselves, but the sun's hitting their windshields and things are winkling, so you know they're there. Where's everyone going all the time in their cars, alone? Can't wait to find out myself, drive Somewhere. A ball game maybe. Me and Petey will drive to a game some summer's night, windows down to summer gush smell, radio on, seventeen and aftershaved and beautiful. So vivid is this picture I feel my foot lowering down to accelerate before I realize what I'm doing. Weirdness but I'm really there, bling-bling, Cadillac zoom in America.

Another *mmmmmmmph* from Petey.

"Hey Petey, lookit, I been ahhh . . . hanging a lot with Denny. Denny Foley I mean. You know. He said last week we were best friends now, but I told him I was still best friends with you. I told him that. I did. Right away, like."

Petey's mouth shifts a little. I don't tell him that Ma urges Denny all the time to stay for supper, entices him with the sizzling meats on her menu and she's never once with Petey. I can't say why.

"But ahhhh, I told him I'd be his best friend until you got better. Like them summer shows they have on TV? The replacement ones there. And then the real ones come back in September?"

I stop because I have to pick my nose for a minute, very dry in this room here. Hot too.

Somebody's looking for a certain doctor over the intercom thing and he won't answer them. They keep calling but no. I have nowhere to put Mr. Booger so I wipe it under the table next to Petey. It's also cold metal and ugly and no I don't like it. A kidney-shaped blue plastic thing on its top. No niceness to it, no kindness. How can you get better with a table like that beside you. Here, have a slimy booger why don't you on your underneath part. What about an airplane model kit on that table? What about a teddy bear but no too old for that now, but nothing else yet to take the place of toys. Nature abhors a vacuum and us winging through the air now, having left one trapeze but not at the next one yet, our hands eager to grasp but the next one still not in sight, but my observation of the older boys round the way seems to suggest this next stage involves girls cars liquor cigarettes deep harsh voices and me afraid one minute, ready to dive in the next.

"'Member that wicked cool dinosaur set Ma got me for my birthday last year? On the Fourth of July, I mean the day before, Denny got these firecrackers from his older brother and we blew the dinosaurs up in the backyard about forty feet. It was so cool 'til Ma came home. They're made outta wicked hard plastic and you can keep doing it without breaking them. They don't break. They turn black from the powder but they don't break."

I pause.

"One of them had this round hole near his bum and we stuck one in there. You should've seen it. It completely destroyed him. Split him right in two. Other than that there weren't any casualties. If you don't count the powder stains."

I think for a minute about anything else that's happened Since.

"Red Sox on a tear now, Petey. Ten in a row. Figures you'd miss it."

What else.

"Ahhh, Grandma Flynn's birthday party was okay, she asked me to blow out the candles cuz of her emphysema and I wished you'd get better. That was the wish I made. Even though it wasn't my birthday, I figgered I still had a wish comin' since I was doin' the blowin'. I know you're not supposed to tell it but I figger you can't hear me anyways so it doesn't count."

"*Mmmmmmph,*" Petey whimpers again.

I wonder if you dream in a coma. He must be having a dream. I turn around because someone's walking wicked fast past Petey's door and they startle the shit out of me. I stand up and walk over to the door and stick just my head out into Pine-Away sick-smell. There's a nurse reading some chart or something way at the end of a hall, about a mile away, getting longer as I look down it like a crazy horror movie when they do that Ex-Pand-O thing there. I can't see anyone else. Where did that walking person go?

I shut the door. I want to lock it but there's no lock on it, *Oh no you don't.* So I take the metal chair with the gray padding on it beside Petey's bed and wedge it under the doorknob like on TV. It keeps slipping but finally I get it with a whispered *Stay, stay.*

I stand beside Petey's bed. My heart starts going funny-faster a little, like right before you might steal second base. The gathering up of resources for Something. My mouth working. I do this thing with my mouth now since Petey's accident—you'd have to see it, *Stop that Danny* Ma says without looking up.

Now what.

I climb into Petey's bed up with him. One of the tubey things jiggles a little and I get nervous but then it stops. Drop drop drop going into him. A bag hanging over him like a collapsed lung. Turn away from it.

"This is like when we sleep out in your backyard when we make the tent outta that bedspread," I whisper into Petey's other ear. The one with no bandages. I want to be in the hospital and ride the wheelchairs and elevators and miss school and get cards and have people visit me and ring the buzzer 'til the cows come home and the nurses come bearing silvereens of ice cream, but I don't want to be sick. See things can happen. The youngest Mannion girl, what's-her-name, went in and never came out. *Sudden death!* Sister Ruth Anne told our class, *so stay in a state of grace at all times!* But *Infection!* said my mother, *so wash those hands when you come home mister.*

There isn't much room in the bed but I manage to stretch out beside Petey. I plop my arm next to his and regard the two of them. Mine's tanner now, a little bigger too. No man-hair on it though, not yet.

"My arm's bigger than yours now," I whisper. Then I feel bad and say, "But I bet you when you get outta here you'll catch up right away."

Push-ups, sometimes we'd do push-ups, how many in a row. Petey always winning of course.

It's wicked warm in his room.

Now what?

I just lay there for a minute looking at him. Strangely I picture what I must look like looking at him. I don't do anything for a while, then I lift up his sheet a little and look underneath. I don't know why. It's dark and secret but gray half-light seeps in like a musty cave. His legs are an open V and bare. They look long and smooth from this angle. He's wearing this white thing with blue dots on it. It goes down to his thighs but it's all mushed up on one side and I can see the edge of his white bum. Something hot jiggles inside the bottom of my belly, squirmy frog eggs. Why?

I reach my hand down, pull back, then reach it down again and shift the johnnie thing to the side until it uncovers Petey's Thing. I feel a certain inevitability, though I don't know that word yet either, the thrumming up of some scalding engine I didn't even know I was the manager of. It's rubbery and white and the head of it pointing up from the gathered wrinkles toward his belly button. It looks like a dead fish whose eyes have been put out, washed up on the shore of Petey's belly. Sad somehow, lonely like. I think mine is longer but Petey's looks fatter. I watch my hand go over to it. It gets rubbed between thumb and forefinger like someone else is doing it. It's warm and soft and meaty. A texture to it, how else to say it? It feels weird, to feel somebody else's. It feels important. A way to get to another part of him no one knows yet, not even him, maybe him a little in secret. A periscope to something. Or from something. The all I know of Petey, but now there's This Too, like waking up one morning and your Southie 8' × 8' backyard has been alchemized into forest.

Sweat on my forehead. Sweat on my fingers. Sweat inside me, I almost can't see. Rub. It's gotta be wrong but I rub. It shifts a bit, expands. Why? Jesus. Maybe if I wake up this part of him he'll wake up too.

"*Mmmmmmpphhhh,*" Petey says again. His head thrashes to the side and everything bounce-shudders.

I yank back my hand and at the same time I hear the doorknob all jiggly and what's-going-on-in-there.

"*Danny? Danny!*" Mrs. Harding's voice.

"Okay!" I cry, too loud. Petey's right leg kick-jumps and the sheet does a bugaboo.

I spring off the bed. I smooth the sheets down the way they were I think, lift up the metal railing, then scramble to the other side of the bed and put the chair back quiet as I can. Then I open the door.

"It was way too loud out in the hall," I blabber before they can start with the Questions.

My mother examines my face, which I know is reddening, but says nothing.

Mrs. Harding's eyes slide across mine and right to Petey.

"Blessed sweet Jesus!"

She yanks both her hands up to her mouth.

"Wh-what?" I stumble. I hear the sharp inrush of breath from my mother behind me.

"Holy Mother, what did you do?" Mrs. Harding cries. "Petey! *Petey!*" Not even looking at me. She starts laughing, or crying.

"N-nothing!" I stammer, sounding how Petey will soon sound for the rest of his life, a life-imitates-life dramatic foreshadowing, though I don't know those words yet either.

Mrs. H's eyes on Petey. I follow them to his face. His eyes are open and swirly. He's looking at me. Cruddy stuff around his lips. He moves his arms, tries to move them, one of them strapped to tubey things. The hose slips from his mouth. He lifts the other hand and points at me.

"D-D-Danny!" he moans.

"What did you do?" Ma asked calmly on the way home. Not right away, but halfway home, after she'd discussed the new neighbors, the deplorable state of the cafeteria food. Just when you least.

"Nothing," I said. "When?"

"Nothing?" she asked, after her white gloves had pushed down the blinker and she took a left.

"I just talked to him. It ahhh . . . it must be a miracle like Mrs. Harding said. All them prayers."

"All *those* prayers," Ma corrected. "Yes, that must've been it."

I couldn't figure out why I was sad when we got home. I mean I was happy with Petey, bounce-jig happy . . . but that was on the edge of myself, like Europe far away in sunlight, and me myself America in the dark of night yet. Why, and why did things, everything, look different? Slanty almost, but I decided that wasn't the right word.

4

Birdy Brain

Petey had one more operation because they said there was too much fluid on his brain. I pictured a dark interior ocean, a flood sea-swishing between his brain's continents, washing out its coastal cities. Half the town went to Mass special that morning at St. Brigid's. Coach was there too—not the Donovans though, they'd moved out over the summer and Billy Donovan having thrown that pitch.

Petey got out of the hospital two weeks later. A Frankenstein scar on his head but then the hair covered it by and by. Blacker now, his hair. Wilder, tuftier.

He was supposed to rest a lot, but I'd sneak him up to the roof of his house what a blue view from there so he could look at the sea five blocks away. One step at a time. Careful now. Pigeons on the other side of the jimmery roof door all a-fluffering when we'd push it open and they'd burst coo-coo-cooing into the air. That was what Petey wanted to do now all the time, look at the ocean look at the ocean look at the ocean five blocks away.

How to say it—he was a different person. Only way to say it, like those stories you hear about babies going home with the wrong families. Alien abductions. Petey stuttered now. Not that it bothered me, but it would frustrate him sometimes because he had so much more to say now. His hands going into fists like the unopened marigold buds on Mrs. Harding's front-porch-potted plants. I laughed the first time Petey stuttered, never again. The doctors said he might stop the stuttering any moment now, then again he might do it 'til the day he died. I guess that meant they didn't know but doctors can't say that.

The stuttering the least of it. I brought my Adidas shoebox full of baseball cards over one afternoon. I was going to let Petey take advantage of me in some trading. *Let's trade cards,* we used to sigh in bliss on certain still sum-

A Map of the Harbor Islands
Published by The Haworth Press, Inc., 2006. All rights reserved.
doi:10.1300/5677_04

mer days pre-Accident, when Monops got old, and the delight it gave the both of us as the August afternoons plopped by like fat honey drops. I left my Freddy Lynn rookie card at home though.

Petey couldn't be bothered. Sitting up in his bed and staring at me, the warming glass of water at his bedside getting still-bubbles inside it from neglect.

"Tell me about the o-o-ocean, Danny," he said, pushing the box away.

"I know it but I'll give you my Denny Mc—you should see how many new cards—"

"What I want now Danny is to h-hear about the ocean," he said. "The o-ocean, and anything that might lie beyond the ocean."

"Ahhh . . . how do you mean like?"

"Beyond," he said, waving his hand. "Beyond the b-beyond. H-Happy Land."

"Ahhh . . . huh?"

"Tell me what it's like t-t-today, Danny. The ocean. Tell. Go. Start n-now."

"Ahhh . . . blue," I answered. "Ahhh . . . wet, like."

One afternoon in his bedroom, three weeks before school started. Staring at me for an hour while I made tiny talk, then finally:

"S-something important. To tell you, Danny."

"Okay," I said. Relief, I was running out of things and him staring at me like that.

"Don't think the less of m-me."

Picking at the corner of his comforter.

"No. What do you mean? Never!"

Staring. The smile.

He slid from his downy bed, still wobbly, crossed the room closed the door. His smell was different now and it trailed after him, preceded him and never Before. A smell of the earth. And blood, drying crusty blood as things healed and re-formed within him. He was wearing a pair of pajama bottoms too small for him, lax at the ungathering ankles. The white tubeiness of him. Got back into bed. I helped him with the puffy hand-covers. Then I went and sat in the tipply green chair in the corner, my chair. His room was the same one he used to do his ritual dressing in, but it seemed different, the same but backwards-like, as if this place we were in now was a mirror room of his real room.

"What I'm about to t-tell you happened last w-week," Petey said. "My first d-d-day up. Note the s-s-significance of that."

"Ahhh . . . okay."

"About an hour before you came over. Sitting out on the fr-front stoop. Waiting for you. Watching things. I . . . Danny, I kinda g-got this feeling I'll be doing a l-lot of watching from n-now on."

"Nah, no you won't. You'll be back playing baseb—"

Petey did this thing with his hand since the accident. He would hold it up palm outward to silence me. He did it now.

"I w-want to," he said. "I . . . s-so much to see. So m-much to think about."

"Ahhh . . . so what happened?"

"The kids across the street were play-play-play—"

"Playing?" I suggested.

"Playing. Yes. The Barry kids and two of the M-Monahans. They waved l-little half-waves when they saw me come out. Whispered together, didn't c-come over. Danny—I got this other feeling people won't be c-coming over to me as much n-now—"

"'Course they will, it's just that—"

The hand again.

"So they were pl-playing. Running around the c-cars. And then one of them, the littlest, st-stopped. Moaned. Shrieked. The others c-c-came over. Found something. Between the cars. The bending of knees. Murmuring, spec-speculating. I watched them. Nancy Barry looked up, s-s-saw me. *Can you help us?* she said. I got up, got d-dizzy, walked over slow. A bird, Danny. Resting on its back. A little bird in the g-gutter, between the cars. Just there. Not moving. Clutchy little claws. The liquidy eyes. A blink now and then."

Petey gulped, looked at me, looked away. He was in danger of tearing the corner of the comforter so hard was his pulling and knotting. The August light sifting into his room. Still summer, but quiet, like summer was hearing fall's clomp-steps coming.

"The bird was alive but hurt. Still. Ly-lying on its back. The wings okay, not broken. I p-picked it up. The kids came in closer, their heads blocking out the light. Their sweat. The plopping and smell of it, summer kids' sw-sweat. The bird trying to turn its head to face me but it couldn't, you could see little muscles moving along its b-body but it couldn't. Broken neck Danny. The eyes oceanic and w-wondering why. Must've been in agony but n-not a sound out of him."

Petey stopped again. I was about to ask *Well?* then this noise from him, a wrench. A sob. Like mine at his hospital bedside, just the one of them. His lower lip shaking.

"What—what's the matter Petey?" I yanked up in alarm.

"Birdy!" he wailed. *"B-Birdy!"*

He pounded the pillow.

I wanted to go over to him but I didn't know how. I was afraid to.

Petey looked down into his hand. Opened it, closed it.

"One of the little kids asked me, *Can't you save it? Can't you fix it?* S-sure, I said. I told them that Danny, but I knew . . . I m-mean . . . broken neck."

"Nothing you can do about that," I said. But my mother's words, *He'll never be the same, they'll probably have to put him away someday* came back to me. Birdy? I lowered back to my seat and started bouncing my right knee. *There's such a thing as brain damage, you know,* my mother had added.

"What if there was?" Petey asked, and the question had more urgency in it than I could recall from him before. More urgency than his responses while altar boy-ing. Always smart before but easy, perfect. No urgency—

"I m-mean, that's what I thought but what if—what if there was something I could've d-done?"

He looked away and swallowed, seeing something I couldn't. There would be years now when Petey saw what I couldn't. I felt them open up between us like one of those South American chasms and the bridge between too shaky, made from palm leaves, sticks, and wishes.

"So like . . . ahhh . . . what happened?"

Petey looked back at me, so quick his black hair flung. He slid his top teeth over his bottom lip. I didn't know him, for the first time. It was August 11, a Friday afternoon half an hour before baseball practice and for the first time I didn't know him, didn't know his deal.

"I br-brought him back across the street, Birdy. I . . . I . . . "

He sat up in the bed, kneeled down, leaned forward, rocked back and forth. Years later in the Marines, I would be stopped dead in my tracks by a Lebanese woman keening for her baby and the gesture recalled Petey's then, now.

"Maybe we should just play Monop—"

"I n-need to tell you, Danny. You have to know this now. I . . . carried him up the driveway. Birdy. I knew what I . . . I brought him in. Shoebox, in the trash went my b-baseball cards."

"Jesus, Petey! You threw all your cards—"

The hand again.

"My bike, I w-went for it, Ma'am said *What's that clatter?* Told her I was going to the vet's, him down West Broadway. *Back in the bed with you. You're out of your mind your first day up,* she said. Told her, showed her Birdy. She went for me, took Birdy, c-c-could see I'd go myself otherwise. Called later, from the vet's office. Nothing they could do. Is it money? I asked. *No,* she said, *no, there's nothing they can do. Shall he put it out of its misery, Petey?* No, I said, bring it home, I'll do that."

Silence for a while. Petey and his brothers all called their mother Ma'am.

"I'm going undercovers for the rest of it," Petey said, getting under the blankets, pulling them over his head.

More silence.

"Tell m-me you're still here, Danny."

Muffle-voice.

"I'm . . . yeah, I'm still here, Petey."

"Tell me you won't l-leave."

"I'll never leave," I heard myself say. Something leaped up to say it, did battle with Ma's smears, won, kicked their ass.

Silence again. But a relaxing of him under the green and blue covers. I could see this. A passing seagull squawked as it flew by just outside.

"I'm glad of that. Ma'am brought it back from the vet's. Out b-back I brought it. My mother has this b-bucket out there, that metal b-bucket? Waters her plants w-with it. Full to the brim from rains. I walked over to it. Birdy in my r-right hand. I kissed him. The eyes still liquidy. Not moving, not shaking. Warm. Waiting. Watching me. Then a little chirp out of him, that . . . that . . . br-broke my heart to hear it. A tiny chirp, a little eggshell chirp. Just the one.

"I talked to him. T-told him what was about to happen. He was leaving this w-world. How this world wouldn't be the same without h-him.

"I . . . I started crying and plunged him under. Under the water. All the way to the b-bottom, n-nothing I could do, wanted to put him out of his m-misery. Oh *God!*"

Petey started fluttering under the blanket, fists pounding the mattress.

"Quiet at first Danny, then this b-burst of struggling. The life in him, Danny! How he wanted to *live!* Broken neck and a-all! The *throb* of him! The struggling, Danny! How he still wanted to l-live!"

Silence again, punctuated with sniffles and stutters. Later:

"Are you still here, D-Danny?"

"Still here."

Silence.

"Danny, how to t-tell you . . . everything passed through me then. When he was struggling in my hand. Like I'd put my hand on the . . . on the electrocuting Third Rail of Life. The w-wild fluttering heart of every thing that's ever sang to see a morning sun. *Everything.* Every . . . every thing that ever wanted to live, but died still, Danny . . . every heart that ever wanted to love, but . . . Danny, h-how can I make you understand what p-passed through me then? The leaking heart of this life? I still f-f-feel it!"

Too much heartbreak in his voice, too much pain. I found myself standing, sweating. Walking. To his bed. Lying down beside him. Shaking, the two of us. His arms flung themselves around me, through the blankets. A leaping up of our molecules, a jolt at the touch, even through sweaty sportscar sheets and his mother's homemade blue and green quilts and blankets.

My head and heart racing.

"What . . . what's it like, a coma?" I asked quick. What if we got caught now? What if someone came in? Something unknown inside me, soaring tall above me like a tsunami, run from it—

"Do you dream?" I persisted rapidly. "What's it like, a-a-a cave you can't get out of?"

Petey stopped shaking. His fingers appeared, on the edges of the blanket. Then his hands. The blanket lowered, his black hair, his black eyebrows, the hazel eyes. Wild.

"You . . . you really w-wanna know?"

"Yeah. Yeah."

A deep breath out of him.

"I was . . . I was w-w-wandering in the darkness," Petey said finally. "And . . . one b-by one, things were t-taken from me. They . . . bl-blew off me in this w-wind. Faculties. D-d-dispositions and inclinations."

"Ahhhhh . . . how do you mean like?"

Petey looked at me. His eyes bigger now. Endless, they went somewhere. I think it was at this moment he realized the amount of work it would take, to try and bring me to that place where he was. And before it had just been ball games and school, everything free and easy like breath.

"I was wandering in the d-d-darkness, Danny. Couldn't get out at all." He closed his eyes and half shook his head. His hands clenched up. Then he opened his eyes slowly and looked right through me.

"And then you called to m-me."

"I did?" I remembered that. Of course I remembered that. "You heard me?"

"I did. And then," Petey murmured, his voice dropping to a calm murmur, "you t-t-touched me."

The walls of his bedroom started fluttering in, like birds' wings but closer every time.

I sprang back, looked away, started picking a scab on my elbow. Inched my body away from his.

"You . . . touched me d-d-down there, Danny."

Petey pointed.

I opened my mouth then shut it.

"You must've been dreaming," I finally mumbled. "You . . . I think people must dream crazy stuff in a coma."

Petey stared and I looked away. After a long time he said, "It's okay, Danny."

"'Course it is," I said, deliberately misunderstanding. "You'll be better in' no time."

Another long silence, ticked off by a thud in my ears.

"I . . . I just wanted to tell you about Birdy, Danny. You . . . you know about the coma and now you know about Birdy. I'll never be the same. But it's not just the coma—it's Birdy too. I w-wanted you to know. I've touched the b-beautiful heart of this life, and now I'll never be the same."

I dared to turn and look at him. This close, I could see the golden flecks in his hazel eyes. He seemed ten years younger, but his eyes ancient.

"Ahhh . . . you wanted me to know what?"

"Life, Danny! *Life!* The m-miracle, Danny! I'm for life now. And it's not from tasting death, Danny . . . it's . . . from t-tasting *life!*"

Our faces close, the Red Sox on the walls, smiling down at us. A breeze-flutter from the window, cool on my hot cheeks reddening, aware quick just how shut the door was.

Our eyes going back and forth to each of the other's.

"I can . . . I c-can feel your breath," Petey whispered. His eyes shifted, then locked back onto mine. "I remember now! I felt it in the coma t-too, your breath. The breath of you. The Birdy of you."

He was whispering now. Nothing in the room now but four eyes and the rustle of something—

"Pee-tey! Pee-tey? Danny's mother's out front, beeping to wake the echoes! Is he that deaf?"

"Practice!" I yelled, so loud, leaping, the bed shaking. "I'll see you later, Petey. I'll call you tonight."

So long it was, the distance to the door. Another world outside waiting, my mother waiting, to take me to baseball, a world still solid, a world I still knew.

5 W ⊕ E
  N
  S

Miasma de Mustafa

When he could walk again, go off on his own again the days before school started, I'd meet Petey down at the ocean sometimes. Straddling the seawall, looking out. Pleasure Bay contained within the crook of his elbow. Beyond that, the causeway, keeping out the high seas, but unable to hold back Petey's eyes. His white skin flushing under the sun, the hazel eyes ripening under the black lashes and brows, the hanks of sea-tufted black hair curling at the ends and the sea-puffs having their way with it.

Laugh to see me, surprise, him a million miles out to see, to dream. Thick, Wisconsin-size art pad on his lap. He'd be making these maps. What? Yeah, crazy. Maps. The shoreline, the Harbor Islands, the bay, everything. Blue for water and green for land, the names ornate and glistening in black and gold metallic ink all calligraphied. I'd watch him for a while, get bored, get antsy. Petey's maps got more intricate and never any artistic leanings Before. But now sacrifices were made so that special pens and papers could be purchased at an art store downtown. He brought me there one after-school and the old goatee guy working there knew his name. Smiled to see him, hastened off the phone, called out, *Petey, Petey, come here, wait'll you see, the Arches order has come in,* a special new paper to show him and four hands reverently grazing its rag-bondy surface while I wandered the archaic aisles and by and by buried my nose in a *Painting the Nude* pamphlet.

Petey changed the names of things on his maps. Gave them his own. *Why keep dead men's names for the living things?* he asked. I had no answer for that and most of his other questions. Harbor Point over by UMass there became the Point of Lost Ribbons. Thompson's Island was now the Isle of Unopened Packages. The fogs that slurred into Pleasure Bay on August nights he dubbed the Mists of Misbehavior. The backside of Castle Island was now the Pepperminty Coast, the Atlantic became the Sea of Similes.

A Map of the Harbor Islands
Published by The Haworth Press, Inc., 2006. All rights reserved.
doi:10.1300/5677_05

"Not smiles, Danny, s-s-similes," he said, correcting my misreading of it.

"Oh, sorry."

Whatever that meant.

"That's a comparison using *like* or *as*. I was looking at it one whole Sunday m-morning, the ocean as light blue as what I couldn't s-say, as dazzly as what I c-couldn't say, as inviting, as endless, as hopeful, as b-beseeching . . . think about the j-joy of naming the Atlantic Ocean! Also the r-responsibility. It's a big thing. You know what I m-mean?"

"Uhm—"

"Finally I just jotted down Sea of Similes temp-temporarily 'til I thought of a g-good one, then decided I liked it, stuck with it."

"Oh. Okay."

Plain ol' immutable Day Boulevard was now the Street Very Close to the Place Where the Ocean Meets the Shore.

"Don't you think it would be c-c-cool to live on a street with a name like that, Danny? And get mail from a pen pal who lived w-way far away in the Midwest? And he'd think, *what a w-wonderful place to live,* and almost be able to smell the ocean? Just by your address? He lifts the envelope up to his corny n-nose and tries to sniff the ocean? Remember, D-Danny, think of Native American names. Always place names, full of the awe of Nature. They tell stories. They c-celebrate things, name their priorities. My Water Home; Place Where Three Hills C-Come Together. Not named after chiefs. Not named after aldermen on the make. Not n-named after people who were forced to kill a lot of people in a forgotten w-war. We shouldn't be bigger than the pl-places we inhabit."

"Ahhh—yeah I know it."

"Let's *run!*" Petey would suddenly announce, plopping his pad down on the other side of the seawall out of the wind and he'd be off, me chasing laughing, like the wind. You could never catch Petey and his laughs coming back at me in puffs and chops, wouldn't stop 'til we got out to the island, Castle Island, which isn't an island at all anymore since they built the causeway out to it a hundred years ago. Then flop down breathless on the ticklynose grass.

"What the fuck is this, *The Secret of NIMH?*" I asked him when he showed me one of his finished maps, like I say all calligraphied, all tarted up with windlasses and legends under his bed rolled up, the edges burned to make it look older. Stains on it. I thought he was going to show me dirty pictures, the way he'd whispered bringing me here. *S-s-something secret to show you upstairs under my b-b-bed, Danny.*

"I spilt t-tea on it to make it old-looking," was all he said, his eyes brushed shy, evasive.

"Ahhh . . . it's . . . it's really something. But ahhh . . . what does it mean, though?"

"What does it mean?" he echoed. He looked at me. He put his hands behind his back and rocked back and forth on the balls of his feet.

You know still looking at him you'd think he was the same but no.

"Half o'er, half o'er, to Labrador," he whispered, holding my eyes. So quiet in his room. Messier now.

"Ahhh . . . excuse me?"

"Wanderlust. Dreams. Dreams of a pl-place we could go to so that we could . . . could—there's tr-treasure out there," he whispered, still holding my eyes but waving his arm behind him with car salesman expansiveness. "It m-might be a treasure map somebody f-found. Or it m-might be an old Indian map. The way to get to Shangri-La. I don't know. M-magic? A way to bring w-w-wonder back to this franchised w-world? Disenfranchised. Name everything, make it ours, make it n-new. When you n-name something you claim it, no? It can be all ours out there, D-Danny."

Like I say, the way he stared at me now. Like he'd caught his brother Donnie's disease.

Always the warmest of welcomes at Petey's house since his recovery, not that there wasn't before. Mrs. Harding fighting the hours to get some sleep before her night job. *Someone'll be sorry if I'm not in that bed by the noon,* she'd say, then it would be *by one* then *by two* while Petey's three or four wild older brothers that still lived at home tore in, tore out, and crises erupting in their wakes. But always time to make me and Petey lunch, *Just a little something, out on the front porch with yez now,* and grilled cheese sandwiches and homemade pickles and teas would be set up on the wicker trays amid the jungle of her porch plants. The street would disappear by August, the screen-in porch a breaking wave of green between the house and the street. An explosion of vines running up the railings, spilling off the front porch roof, window boxes and pots stacked on steps and sills and floors and the light on the porch limey, filtery on the bright summer mornings, the long summer afternoons. The sea-breeze scent dyed lemon and rose and honeysuckle when it found a way to puff in through the greenery. Mrs. Harding stealing a moment one afternoon to watch us for a bit, make a peephole through the green to see the sky above and she murmured, *Horsetail sky, horsetail sky, never long wet, never long dry.* Funny what you remember.

"Not a word! Not one blessed word!" she would say after Mrs. Cleary and Mrs. Feeney would drop her off from work at 7:15 of a morning and a stampeding of boys to get to her first, clamoring of shoes and homeworks and milk monies gone missing overnight. She'd dispatch them all back upstairs 'til she had at least ten minutes with *my other darlings,* her flowers. But Petey never assailed her that way, never a thing he was missing or needed.

"Oh Danny! How you brighten our door! In you come!" whenever I'd ring their buzzer, but even more effusive now, after Petey's recovery. *The miracle your friendship worked,* she always said. Is that what it was? I used to wonder. Then stopped wondering, tried to forget what I'd done, what I'd been drawn to do.

"But why d-doesn't your mother like *me*?" Petey would ask the few times we'd find myself in my museum-quiet house, an illiterate scriptorium of spotlessness, of tablecloths and curtains so stiff-starched they could walk off on their own, of shades every one pulled exactly halfway down until the very moment of sunset when they would be yanked to their limit.

"She . . . does. 'Course she does," I'd say.

"No! No she d-doesn't! I c-can tell, Danny. But why would anyone n-not like me? What have I ever d-done?"

This really got to Petey.

"She just . . . she gets nervous," I'd lie. "Not used to the noise. C'mon, let's get outta here."

The shit hit the fan when Ma, waiting for me one afternoon at the kitchen table, tossing her henna hair back, exhaling on her cigarette said, *Someone's been stealing the upstairs bathroom towels.* She never said it was Petey but inferred this, dropped hints for the next three weeks until school started again, *Someone dirt poor and strange in the head and down the beach every day— who does it sound like to you?* or *Motive and means, Danny, motive and means!*

"Your mother's never been the same since Brian died," was all Dad would say when I mentioned her weirdness to him.

He's sleeping, she'd snarl at Petey when he called for me no matter the hour of the day, but Petey sneaking up the driveway, tossing gravel to the window. But now that you know, once every blue moon just the opposite with Ma. She'd pull Petey in, coddle him, pull the both of us together and *Pray for me, please pray for me,* she'd hiss while her tears fell down on our faces, and once a year or so gone, *She's gone for a little rest,* Dad would say, *Aunt Anne's,* Dad would say, though I never had met that one, never heard of her even. The next time it was *Aunt Ellen* and me pouncing on him for an explanation. *Oh, that's Anne's sister,* he said. After a shifting of eyes and something coming down behind his.

"Who d-do you say that I am?" Petey'd still ask sometimes, especially after he felt compelled to do something weird. Sarcastically? I couldn't tell, though I didn't know that word then either. This little smirk on his face. Looking at me from the corner of his eyes but they sliced me at that angle.

"Ahhh . . . my best friend, Petey Harding," I'd answer, like always.

"Bestest. Always."

But.

When we started school next month, seventh grade, Petey's differences were plainer to see. The contrast. He'd been everyone's favorite like I said, everyone's Golden Boy, and a light on the faces of all who talked to him.

Not anymore. See, he was different now—*peculiar,* Mrs. O'Rourke said carefully, and by virtue of her position as head cashier at Flanagan's she was kind of the town's Every Person, the Oracle, the depository and disseminator of public opinion. Petey's problem in a nutshell: different or peculiar wasn't really encouraged at Gate of Heaven School or Southie as a whole. *The nail that sticks up is the one to be pounded down* is an old Japanese saying, but it could have been the intonation the nuns were whispering in their Latin when we'd play Outs against the chapel wall and hear them at their Vespers, or the mantra the mothers mumbled when they gathered at PTAs and corners, oracle-ish ciggie smoke seeking out non-smokers for miles. Petey would watch us now from atop the parking lot wall during after-school games of Outs, scamper up the wall like a monkey but only to watch. Sometimes moving his hand, mimicking the flow of the ball back and forth.

"You did w-well," he'd say on the way home, nodding his head, falling in beside me like one of his strays.

"Thanks, Petey."

"But Danny, d-did you see the light coming through the dying sycamore? Redemptive, that light."

"Ahhh . . . yeah, I know it. Redemptive alright. Don't get ahead of me now, Petey."

"I w-won't," he answered, with a chuckle. "But if I do, sure I'll wait."

September, the scent of sharpened pencils and the newly waxed nun-quiet corridor floors, and Petey could walk and run again but he had taken to spending most of his free time down at the beach like I say. The Place Where the Land Meets the Ocean. Or out exploring on his bike, riding fast and frenetic to the point of *There he goes again. I think that bump on his head made him strange, God help us,* people started saying. This is when it started with the strays, the homeless dogs following him on the bike, yelping, or not. He'd hurl scraps of food behind him, pick through garbage cans or disdain eating his bagged lunch to provide for them.

"Birdy!" he'd sing out while doing this, and the eyes of all following after him, eyebrows lifted.

That's when the letters to the editor started too. Every town has one, the letter writer, carping about that awful situation in Swahililand, *If only people would skip one meal a week to feed the poor, if J. Paul Getty might be cracked open like an egg and the money sent to* blah blah blah land, and Petey continued making these maps of the harbor and its islands but the names all changed like I say, the Island of Broken Crockery, the Tropic of Afternoon Kindergarten, a dangerous rock reef out in the harbor, Fitzy's Woe. An island way out named Blessed Maureen Cronin Land. Maureen Cronin was this girl in town, one of the Cronin sisters and I've already mentioned them. Not a word out of her in seven years, since the morning she'd wet her pants in fifth grade during math and Pissafloor Cronin she'd been ever since, her story known to all and never a town-born child not shouting it out after her when you'd see her on the street. They said you could hear it dribbling that day onto the floor and then Linda Flint had pointed and laughed and the whole class falling into pandemonium.

"Maureen Cronin?" I asked Petey, smirking, pointing at his map. "Blessed Maureen Cronin Land? What's up with that?"

"Yes, that's r-right," Petey answered immediately. He snatched the map I was reading out of my hands. "Her m-m-march to the grave will be a silent one unless a miracle occurs. And so we pray for that m-miracle. One of the h-h-humiliated ones who will be quiet all her life. Things should be named after beautiful souls like hers. Not after m-murderers. Not after the grabbers of things."

As I watched, Petey grabbed a magic marker, crossed out Sea of Similes, wrote in Sea of Blessed Maureen Cronin's Miracle. Then crossed his arms and glared at me.

There were some kids you didn't associate with by virtue of one thing or another, shared inherent knowledge that everyone knew, like blue is the color of the sky, Maureen Cronin being her generation's example of that. Our generation being equally vicious, we had our own untouchables among our colleagues at Gate of Heaven School; but these were the very people Petey ran to now in the parking lot during recess, the ones he befriended and their walks down the corridor hitherto alone and horrific. Animal Head

Ed O'Brien, who had the rather unusual, exact profile of a bulldog; Marcia McKillop, who, it was said, with her pimply face and sticky-out bristly hair, was *as ugly as the back of your father's ball-bag;* Francis aka Francesca Murphy, a mama's boy who walked like a supermodel and always wore a cardigan sweater tossed over his shoulders; and the like. But Petey became their lord high protector now, eating with them like I say, walking the corridors with them, hanging with them during recess. Jackie Regal, our class bully, took fruit cocktail with whipped cream on it one day during lunch, and started applying it to the knocked-down Francis's face, saying *Francesca's forgot her makeup today so I'm puttin' it on for her.* Petey calmly lifted Jackie up and hooked him by the back belt loop of his pants onto the pointy part of the parking lot fence.

"Petey, what the fuck are you doin?" Jackie wondered. Petey was still a hero in most everyone's eyes.

"It's really f-funny when you dress people in a different g-gender's clothing," Petey said. "Watch this." He hopped a fence like it wasn't there and came back with a bra he must've purloined from a neighbor's clothesline. He affixed it around the now-blubbering Jackie—like most bullies Jackie was a coward—and left him hanging there for the rest of the afternoon.

"Hey Petey," I asked one afternoon when we were languid-hanging down at Castle Island, the sun not a sear now as it had been in August but a kiss, a buss. Petey was all business making a map, and I was trying to read homework. "What's this thing way out in the harbor?"

Petey looked where I was pointing.

"Miasma de Mustafa. There's fog banks out there sometimes, you've s-s-seen them." He jerked his head. "Out in the bay here. They sit there. Then they shift. This is what I've named them."

"Oh. Okay."

"Do you know what it m-means, Danny?"

"Ahhh . . . yeah. I think so."

Petey big-eyed me as he gave me the lie. This little smirk.

"M-miasma is like this poison gas or something, a d-dangerous mist," Petey said. "It's like our own little B-Bermuda Triangle out there. Mystery. What's known and unknown. Pitfalls and e-epiphanies."

"Oh. Ahhh . . . what's mustafa?"

"Mustafa is a person. I forget his last n-name. I read it last w-w-week when I was delivering my papers. He got blown up last Wednesday morning in the Middle East and no one will ever r-remember him, but n-now forever here he is. You see I f-felt for him."

Way at the edge of this particular map a gilded arrow, pointing out beyond the map, to the open seas, the horizon's mist-softened edge. To Happy Land, the arrow read. I never asked.

"What's the matter?" I'd ask Petey sometimes, when we'd be waiting in line at the cafeteria or walking home from school and he would just stupor-stop, looking at something. Or nothing.

"I'm seeing the w-w-world so differently now," he'd say. Almost impatiently. "You don't see that?"

"Ahhh . . . what? See what?"

"The l-light. The way the light's f-falling through that windowless building there."

Or it might be a spider's web entangling a bus stop sign on Broadway *out to c-catch this morning's beauty.* A cloud that looked like Arkansas with a dog head on top and *Lookit Danny, the state dog of A-Arkansas! Let's race it down to Castle Island!* A flower bud about to pry open. An old bent woman trudging up Broadway with her shopping, stopping to rest. *A Jungian archetype,* Petey called her, whatever that was. It could be anything. Weird. Weirdness. Anything. Everything must be studied and pondered and these maps had to be drawn while everyone else moved past him, while the flushing junior-high glory that had been his was snatched by others.

And then of course he started reading everything in sight.

Sometimes a silence for days, the tremble of him, *What is it, Petey?* and the only answer *Danny, I'm so afraid!* Then the next minute silly, gushy, racing and handstands on the school-way home. *It's one of those days where you know you'll live forever!* he'd cry, the eyes leaping green from his sockets. One time stopping by his house, I found him leaned over the kitchen sink, motionless, his mouth right above the drain.

"Jeez, Petey, what's a'matter, you puking?" I asked.

"Oh God n-no," he whispered. He lifted his face up to me and it was radiant.

"There's magic in the kitchen sink, Danny."

"There is?"

"Oh yes. The drains and how d-do they work. Secret tunnels leading out to the sea and the creatures that lie in s-secretive wait along the way. Ultimately c-connecting to the sewers of Paris and crystal caves where the *Flying Dutchman* and *Nautilus* are m-moored. Can you keep a s-secret?"

His eyes were dancing.

"Yeah."

"There's magic everywhere," he whispered, clutching me by the forearm.

"Do you wanna play catch?" I'd ask sometimes. "It'll be spring before you know it again and—"

"Oh God no," he'd answer, his smooth, wet-looking black eyebrows lowering. "I have no interest in that *at all*."

"I understand," I'd say. "No can blame you, Petey. But something like that only happens once in a li—"

"Oh no it's n-n-not that," he'd answer. The hand again.

"But don't you want to be . . . I mean . . . don't you . . . "

I didn't quite have the heart to say what I wanted.

"Don't I w-w-want to be Petey again?" Petey asked. "But I am. I am, Danny. New and improved. Birdy."

First Cs then Ds then Fs started appearing on his papers and tests and never before. Driven to scholastic perfection before but now it appeared he couldn't care less, crumble them into balls and finger-flick them off his desk, fold them into paper airplanes and launch them out the window. Go back to the book he'd be reading, even in class now. Weird books. Couldn't begin to tell you.

Once Sr. Teresé in geography was quizzing us on principal products of the nation, and that week we were doing the South. You know, like what grows down there and what people make in those sweaty factories. The only thing I knew about the South was once Dad let me stay up late to watch the convention and a big fat man in a big white suit stood up and said *the great State of Tennessee casts fifteen votes for . . .* I forget now. Someone with three names. But now we were learning other things.

Sr. Teresé called on Petey, who'd been daydreaming out the October-hot raised window, staring at the wavery ocean a few blocks away. Like I say, buildings weren't hermetically sealed then. You could open windows and strands of things would waft in, lifelining you to the World. The sound of a Red Sox afternoon game squeaking from somebody's tinny transistor and *crack* you were there; lug nuts being *wha-wha-wha*-ed off tire rims from Andrew Autobody right across the parking lot; the smell of the sea: happy when the wind was gushy and blowsy from the south, ill-humored and raw when it chopped in from the northeast—

If the sounds and smells of Life coming in did that to me, I can only guess what they did to Petey. This new incessant Petey.

Sr. Teresé must have been keeping an eye on him that day.

"Maybe Mr. Harding can tell us."

Petey slid up to answer, like we always had to. We had to stand when called on whether we knew the answer or not. Blinking, he looked truly confounded, yanked back into the tiny contractions of Gate of Heaven School from that Universe he wandered in now. A calamity now in his dress, a shirttail that wouldn't stay tucked with rivets, pens that rushed to leak in his white shirt pocket, zippers gaping open, shirt cuffs for a hankie, the hair longer now and bordering on wildness and sea-curling at the ends.

Petey's eyebrows jumped up and his eyes enlarged. His words always lagged behind his facial expressions now, like twins born a week apart. His hair like I say longer too. Maybe to hide the indent that didn't go away? On the side of his head between his left ear and eye?

"Well?" Sr. Teresé asked. "What do they make down South, Mr. Harding? What do they grow? Manufacture? You weren't paying attention so I assume you know all this already and we're boring you."

"You're half r-right, Sister," Petey answered. "No I don't know, but yes you are b-boring me."

You could hear the gasp throughout the room, Petey Harding talking to a nun like that, but quick I whispered beside him, *"Cotton,"* covering my mouth with my sweaty pencil-nubbed fingers. *"Soybeans. Textiles."* Though what a textile was I wasn't sure. A kind of small schoolbook, I believed.

There had been about a week when Petey's return had been celebrated, then a week where he had been left alone, then another month where he was granted favors and breaks. The next month was one of silence; now he was like the rest of us, liable to nun interrogation.

"I'll see you after school for that, Mr. Harding. But surely you must know *something* about the South, smart young man like you. Smart with your mouth anyway. Come on, give a guess. Name one thing that comes from the South."

Petey's eyebrows puckered back down and his lips came together and jutted out.

"Well, Mr. Harding?"

"Ahhh . . . Di-Dixie C-Cups?"

Sr. Teresé's smug shrug signaled the class it was okay to laugh, and they did. You wouldn't credit how ready everyone was to laugh at the once golden Petey Harding. I glared around and behind to silence it. Petey always told me *No Danny don't b-bother,* but I'd have to set an example later, out in the parking lot after school. *Hey Hogan, HOGAN, where you going? Get the FUCK over here, you got something to say about Petey?* I wouldn't have Petey laughed at. I wouldn't have my best friend laughed at no.

"If that's all you know about the South, Mr. Harding, you don't know much," Sr. Teresé commented. "I suggest you pay closer attention. Or . . . I'm sorry are you still . . . "

"I'm *F-FINE!*" Petey blurted.

He reddened up, like the wine-stained faces of the drinking men you'd see at night, roaring home with eyes like darts. Even then. Seventh grade but even then—or still—Petey had his pride. I didn't see this until later. Why didn't I?

"Well if you're fine you should pay closer attention so you'll learn something."

He snapped up to his full height. He was growing apace since coma's end. Caught up to me and quick. Maybe taller and his voice jeep deep.

"W-well, I know that there are s-seals out in the h-h-harbor now."

Sr. Teresé had half-turned to the blackboard by this time. She wisp-of-habit floated back around to see Petey still standing, his chin out, his hands balled into fists. I can't say enough how much I had to look twice at such scenes, a nun confronting Petey. It was like catching your grandmother doing crack.

"Excuse me. What did you say?"

"S-seals. Out in the h-harbor. They're b-back now. They've been g-gone for almost a hunnert p-polluted years. But they're b-b-back. H-harbor seals." He paused dramatically. "You m-might ride a seal from here to Ireland."

The class went stone quiet. Sr. Teresé made a tssking groan of annoyance.

"That's all very interesting, but we're talking about the South, Mr. Harding."

"I know it. B-but they're back. The seals. They are."

Petey turned around and told everyone.

"They are," he said. "You know what that m-means? Where there's seals there's fish. Where there's f-f-fish the water's getting cleaner. The sea's not bad anymore, our sea. We can s-swim in it again. We c-c-can walk in it again, stand in it. We can breathe it. Pee in it. We don't have to think of ourselves as l-l-l-living by a dead thing. A dead thing that we've killed on our d-d-doorstep. It's healed itself. This place is blessed again. Birdy."

"Birdy?" Sister asked. "Who in God's name is Birdy?"

"That's right, Birdy," Petey said. "B-Birdy is l-life. Birdy is the thing inside us that wants to live. Birdy is a s-seed opening up. Birdy is Jesus up there on the cr-cross. We've all b-been given the gift of Birdy but can we s-see it, I wonder?"

"That's enough, Mr. Harding. Please sit down now."

"I know it, but Birdy."

"That's enough, I said. Never mind Birdy. Sit down, please."

Petey sat down. As all of his ilk are eventually sat down. He turned to me, got busy biting his nails. I looked at him, wondering who he was now. Expecting still for that first second that he'd be the way he used to be—that smile, the straight As. Baseball, polite, congratulations on a lovely class this morning, Sister. The halo of him, but no and never again.

Fascinating, but scary because anything could happen to you, to the other half of you.

"It'll all be okay," I told myself at night, last thing before I slept and dreamed that me and Petey were running, running.

The Song of Sealamon

Later that night on his roof, three worn-lino flights up and a view of the sea in case you're wondering—

"Danny? Hey D-Danny!"

We were lying on our backs kinda side by side. Petey with his hands behind his head, watching the night sky do night things. His ankles crossed, his eyes as swirly as the dodge-em clouds and a general air of bliss leaking out of him. Me I had my Walkman on, listening to the Red Sox. If that cloud catches that other cloud then we'll score a run here. Toes crossed inside my Adidases/Adidasii for green luck. The calendar said mid-October, but this night still chattering summer-ese, fluent in summer-ese.

"Tenderer tonight, because it's gotta s-say goodbye soon," Petey murmured. How did he read my thoughts like that?

The wind lavish from the south, from the south tonight all across the universe, doing things—rustling the roof door, snapping at Mrs. H's clothesline that stretched from the bulkhead to the chimney. I wanted to stretch lines of clotheslines from here to every chimney in the world, to try and contain my happiness, Petey here and well again. Well, somewhat well. Jury still out.

"DANNY!"

"Okay! What?"

"Turn that absurdity off and l-lend me your ears."

"Absurdity? It's . . . the Sox!"

"I r-repeat."

"Okay, what?"

"Today in cl-class. What I said? About the seals? It's true. They're b-back."

"Huh. Really?"

A Map of the Harbor Islands
Published by The Haworth Press, Inc., 2006. All rights reserved.
doi:10.1300/5677_06

"I've seen them, you know. An article in the p-paper about it last week too. The most important thing in the paper pr-probably all year, and they buried it. Half-sacred to the Irish, seals. Did you know that? *Roan.* That means seal but for once I prefer the English word, *seal*. Thing of the sea, just add an l. Like adding a l to *you* and where you live and calling you Earthl. Ma'am says broken Irish is better than smooth English, but h-here's an exception. So yeah, sacred to the Irish. You're Irish. Are seals s-sacred to you, Danny?"

"Ahhhh . . . I never really thought ab—"

"That's what Ma'am tells me anyways, they're sacred. Bad cess to them that hurts a seal. Calamitous and why w-would anyone want to anyways? The eyes like that, their f-faces. Everybody's faces really when you think about it. Birdy."

"Ahh . . . I know it, yeah."

A pause and the sky spinning above us.

I was just thinking it was safe to return to the game. A tinny rally was sounding from the earphones round my neck—

"I have a story that p-perfectly illustrates this point."

"Ahhh . . . you do?"

"I d-do. And you're anxious to h-hear it. You *l-long* to hear it, don't you D-Danny?"

Not really, but then I thought of him in the coma, the way he crumpled at the game, and I sat bolt up.

"I really do, Petey," I said. My voice catching—I coughed—

"Fr-frog in your throat?"

"Yeah, I guess."

"Well don't croak, whatever you d-do."

He was teasing, and that smile.

"Okay." He sat up and rubbed his palms deliciously. "Well, this is in Ireland n-now. Long time back. A f-farm by the coast. Look. Lookit."

Petey jerked his head and we both turned to face the ocean, or not, night now so you had to guess where it was, no moon to slither its surface.

"Right there," Petey said, pointing. He knew of course. "Between the chimneys right there. Keep looking. K-keep going with the eye. Not them baby blues D-Danny, the ones inside. Go all the w-way across the sea. To a farm on the north coast of Ireland. Fields, stone walls running up the hills, flecked white with sh-sheep. Soft those hills, like a woman's back. A stone farmhouse tucked in the l-lee."

"Tommy Lee?" I asked. He was this goofy kid in our class.

Petey eyed me.

"A m-man and a woman in that farmhouse. More than two hundred years ago. No children. One night a storm, wild, w-w-wildness. The sea a bubbling froth—"

Petey stood up and started waving his arms—

"—The w-wind a-scream and a m-mo-mo—"

"Moan?" I suggested. This was something I could do to help him out. I liked doing it.

"Yes, a moan of course. A ferocious moan. The mother of all m-moans. The boom of the surf, like c-cannons, a mighty frozen rain falling sideways, boom, boom, b-boom—"

Petey started spinning, ducking under the clotheslines, thrusting out his arms—

"Boom boom boom let's go back to my room," I teased. That was a song then.

Petey stopped.

"How about you tell the story, Danny, and I keep inter-interrupting?"

"Okay, sorry. Go ahead. Boom, you were booming."

Petey was glaring. Touchy, this new Petey.

"Try to remember, Danny—when I'm t-telling a story, the only acceptable interruption is applause."

"Ha ha. Okay, sorry."

"Boom boom boom let's have no more of your cardoon. So the surf booming like c-cannon. The man and woman inside the farmhouse, in b-bed, safe, that feeling when it's wild outside, you warm, the howl outside, their eyes quiet and b-big like animals'. You know that feeling? Don't answer, it's rh-rhetorical. But that w-wind now—so powerful, it's even making the candles dance. Through stone walls that wind must pass, and st-still it's making the peat fire, the candles, flicker-flucker."

I opened my mouth to comment but Petey eyed me, held up a finger.

"Sounds, all these sounds . . . the boom like I say, the mo-moan of the wind, a hiss, hissing of fr-frozen rain lashing on the windows, on the roof, on the stones outside. But this other sound too—like a flap, a t-tap . . . at the door—

"*Listen,* says the wife. *Whsst, Eamon, and hark to that, would you? What is it?*

"*The wind, woman, the wind! What do you think?*

"Now Danny—might I di-divert? What I've just given you is a Jungian archetype of s-sorts. It's okay if you d-don't know what that means, but I'll explain through c-context. Not the people themselves, you understand, but the s-situation, that's the archetype. The c-couple in bed, the wife hears a noise, tells the disbelieving husband—you've heard this before. You know what's coming, yet you don't know. You know what's c-coming but you wanna hear more. And you do, too."

"Alright, I do," I admitted. I shut off the Walkman—I'd read about the game tomorrow. Petey always left a paper at my house in the mornings anyway. Like a part of him, I'd see it and smile out the window. "So what happened?"

"Here's where the archetype goes awry—the woman gets out of bed and goes for her ax.

"*Maire,* the man says, for that was his wife's name, *come back now and don't be daft.* Maire puts down the ax but pauses, listening, straining to hear. *It's coming from the other side of the door!* she says, so she makes for it. Undoes the latch, pushes open the door, but the wind pummeling against it and she can hardly open it. She heaves hard but then the wind catches the door and hurls it open. Maire screams and a mighty wind pours into the h-house, floods into the house like a wave, and it snuffs out the candles, snuffs out the fire on the hearth, plunging them into darkness. *Eamon!* the woman cries, struggling to get the door shut again, and Eamon leaps from the b-bed but can't find his way at first, the wind roaring around the house, smashing things, tipping things over like a thousand scalded cats run amok and the howl of it. He m-makes the door at last and between the two of them they grab it, all their mights c-combined and finally, finally they pull it fast, and the both of them in the prime of life. They slam it shut, they fall against it. Eamon resets the l-latch. They stay like that for a minute, snatching at their breaths, in deepest darkness now, leaning against the door, hearing the scream of the night outside, the pounding of their hearts against the wood.

"But then Eamon feels his wife beside him tighten—a gasp spurts from her—she reaches for her husband, snatches at his hand—

"*I don't know what it is, Eamon,* Maire says, her voice hardly a whisper, but frantic, like spitting, *but I don't dare move for my very life!*

"*What is it, then?* Eamon whispers back, and at the same time a shiver runs through him, the hair on his arms jumps up, a tingle all over him—

"*For God's sake, Eamon!* Maire hisses. *Don't move!*

"*What, what?* Eamon asks.

"*By God and Mary, we're not alone in this house! Listen!*

"They almost stop breathing the both of them, and there—wait, there again—a sound. Someone—something—breathing. Right before them on the floor. But even if they didn't hear the breathing, they could both *feel* it now, this . . . *pr-presence*. But beyond that there was this smell now, this odor, as if the sea itself had come into the house, the sea itself roaming all the rooms.

"*Who's there?* Eamon shouts, but he's shaking. *Who's there!* But there was never an answer.

"*T'isn't human at all!* Maire whispers. *Tis the Sídh, Eamon! The Sídh have come!* The Sídh are the spirit people, Danny.

"*Sídh or not, we've got to make a stand in here!* Eamon says, his voice hardly a breath in Maire's ear. *There's hell's own fury pounding at the door, t'will do us no good to flee, and a stone couldn't live out this storm. Where'd you leave that ax, and wasn't I the fool to tell you to drop it.*

"*Against the pantry door, but have a mind, Eamon, for God's sake have a care!*

"*Stand fast, Maire,* Eamon says, *don't move at all! Think of our Lord now, who stilled the savage sea!*

"By inches, Eamon m-makes his way from the door, across the room the long way, keeping his fingers on the walls behind him, but his fingers rattling like leaves.

"There isn't much in the room, just a wheel for spinning in one corner, a few stools before the h-hearth, and one by one Eamon comes to these landmarks, making his way slowly.

"Whatever is in the room with them hasn't moved an inch, an *orlach*, but still the *breathing* of it, the *feeling* of it—and though it's darker than a blind man's midnight in that room, the both of them could p-point to the exact spot where the thing is—"

I swallowed my gum with a gulp—

Petey sat down cross-legged right in front of me, leaned his face close to mine. His eyes bug-huge, looking into mine and yet they weren't. It was like he wasn't just telling the story but reporting it, eye-witnessing it—

"For a long while nothing happens. Maire against the door thinks she must scream or go mad, r-roar, go shrieking out into the storm, and the storm growing wilder by the minute. A booming around the house now, a clattering on the roof, and she pulls herself closer onto the door, feeling the thing right at her feet.

"At length she hears a soft clatter, and her ears leap up to hear it for she knows Eamon's got the ax now. She holds her breath—in his last desperation Eamon lets out a roar and makes a lunge for it, screams as he lifts up the ax, but at that moment a flash of lightning through the windows and *No, Eamon, no!* Maire screams, and herself almost getting the ax as she rushes against her husband to stay his arm. She makes for the hearth, grabs the scuttle, rakes up the fire and feels for a peat chunk, tosses it onto the smoldering ashes.

"They both turn—and there on the floor is a seal, a seal pup. Half-dead, by all appearances.

"*It's still a coílin, a whelp,* Maire whispers, and it's true. It hasn't even f-finished its molting yet. She stoops and lifts it up. It doesn't weigh any more than a b-baby, and all Maire's heart rushing out to it somehow.

"*There's life in it yet, Eamon,* she says. *Fetch my shawl—the poor miserable creature's cold as a miser's Christmas, but there's life in it yet. Hurry, man!*

"They wrap the baby seal in the shawl, stoke up the fire, and Maire pulls a stool close to the hearth and sits, rocking the seal back and forth in her arms, putting it inside her shirt for the warmth, for the feel of her heartbeat.

"*It wants milk, and us without a drop,* Eamon says. *I've got to go to the shed.*

"Maire looks up, says, *How will you do it, and the wind like a riptide out there?*

"*I know how,* he says. *T'was a storm like this when we were young, and my father having to get out to the animals. I'll do it like he did it.* Eamon fetches a rope, takes off his shirt, and tying one end round his waist, the other to the bedpost, he goes n-naked out into the storm. *If I'm not back in a bit, pull like Christ himself was at the other end,* he tells Maire.

"He comes back looking like a drowned thing, gasping for air, half frozen and red from the tips of his toes to the crown of his head. *I wouldn't have another tussle like that for the Five Kingdoms,* he says when he catches his breath, handing Maire the bucket of milk. *A power of rain's got in it, but t'was a good rich stream she gave, pure cream by the looks of it.* At first they can't get the seal to take note. It still hasn't opened its eyes. *He wants to sleep but he'll not live this night without something to nourish him,* Maire says, getting frantic. Finally Eamon takes her hand, dips his wife's fingers into the bucket, guides them into the seal's mouth. It stirs, tries to move away—then sucks, as if for life. A gurgling noise out of him. Maire and Eamon look to each other with eyes that are shining. There's a thing, Danny, inside us, that can take a kind of perverse pleasure in destruction—but there's another thing that rejoices in Creation, in healing, and I think that one's a lot stronger than the first, and more a-akin to what we were meant to be.

"Well, they saved it that night. All n-night before the fire Maire held it. Singing to it, rocking it, watching it sleep, then feeding it again the two of them whenever they had the chance. The storm blew itself out, moved on, and the dawn saw the sea still seething, but the sun shone strong into the cottage.

"Like a pet it became to them, more than a pet, like a child, and when it grew so big that it couldn't share the bed with them, it was fond of climbing .into the oven overnight. Eamon would put out the fire and Maire would leave the door of it open. A kind of latch Eamon contrived, with a rope that ran down to the floor, and couldn't the seal let itself out of the house when it wanted, though it must bark and flap against the door when it wanted in again, as it h-had that first night. *Poor motherless creature,* Maire called it, but eventually just *Roan* became its name, Seal. Smart it was, too smart, making them laugh at its antics, filling their lives with a wonder and power of life, sometimes following Eamon around the farm at his work, sometimes staying with Maire as she baked and washed and mended the fishing nets, for they would fish in their small curragh when the notion t-took them. Most days the seal would spend some time in the sea, but always it would return by nightfall, and they'd wait for it if it was late.

"Now, at about this time, a cattle sickness struck that part of Ireland, and many of the beasts fell ill and died. There's always a thousand reasons in the people's mind for s-such a thing, but somehow the word went round that there was an unclean beast living with Eamon and Maire, and the British, who were still a power in the land then, c-came round to make inquiries, for they had a great fear their own gr-grand horses would catch the disease. Maire always thought it was the old woman had started the rumor, the old woman that some thought was a witch, whose son had hoped to marry Maire and get her land and home, when instead Maire had chosen Eamon.

"The seal was in the bay the morning the British came, four of them on horseback, and Maire and Eamon told them nothing, pretending they had no English; but j-just as they were riding away, didn't the seal come bounding up the field, barking in delight at the sight of visitors—for it had not a thing to f-fear from people. It had learned n-nothing but love from Eamon and Maire.

"*Take this man's boat and bring that beast out past the islands,* the colonel in charge said to one of his men. Maire and Eamon's hearts went hot with hate, for the islands were thirty miles down the coast with a power of currents and tides between them. But there wasn't a thing you could do. Irish were hung in those days for less."

"Why?" I asked.

"Why?" Petey answered. "Why not? They were being c-civilized, if you'll excuse the e-expression, by an occupying power, and that's usually deadlier than a pl-plague. You don't know your h-history? What a pity but never mind n-now, Danny. Anyways, the seal went willingly enough, but when one of the soldiers slipped a noose round its neck and bundled it in rope, it began barking and yelping in a way so pathetic that Maire must run to it, British or not. But the soldiers grabbed her and threw her to the ground, laughing that Brigit wanted her baby back and no wonder, wasn't it the spitting image of its father. Eamon went red with rage, and had half a thought to get his pike, for all the good that would do against four barbarous soldiers and them with their guns. But Maire stood up, watched the British leave and the seal bundled into their own boat with two men, and she cried after them, cursing, *Go ndeine diabhal dréimire de cnámh do dhroma ad piocadh úill I na ghairdín Ifrinn!* which is, May the devil make a ladder of your backbone, and pluck apples in the garden of hell with it.

"It was a black day in the house without the seal, and the sting of their rage, and they comforted each other as best they could. But the next morning, and a comfortless night before, they were awoken at dawn by a sound at the door, and hadn't the s-seal returned—braving the many ocean miles and currents. Exhausted it was, and they took it in quick, and what a joyous reunion that was!

"*We must keep it hidden, Eamon!* Maire said, but how was there a way to hide such a thing as a seal, even on their large fields, and with the sea at their door? For there's no p-power on earth, Danny, will keep a seal from the sea. Eamon went about with a cloud of resolve over him, but also a burning, to be free in his own fields, and the sea stretching all round he thought only mocking him now, and his powerlessness.

"Some t-time went past, but ever in fear of discovery did they live, and the cow blight getting worse by the week. But the seal the whole while coming and going as he always did, the only joyful thing they saw from one end of the day to the other. Until one day, the inevitable day the British came back. But this time they had the old woman with them, the witch. They had been right. It was she had played informer all along.

"*There's the source of our ruin!* she said, pointing to the seal. *Take it away again, my lord,* she whispered to the colonel, *far off to the islands, but this time put its eyes out, and it won't see its way back.* Well, it was done, and Maire set up her keening as if she had lost her only child. They blinded the poor creature and tossed it into the s-sea.

"But wasn't it that very night the blight worsened, Danny, and took the horses and many of the people too? Including the old woman. But not a blade of grass was struck at Eamon and Maire's, not a lamb or calf was touched. But their hearts were broken for all of that, and Maire went strange in the head, and took to sitting outside her door, staring at the sea. But wasn't it t-two months later, there on their doorstep one morning—the seal, eyeless and all. Dead he was, of starvation, for he couldn't see to hunt. But even starvation had not stopped him from returning home. And they say that Eamon and Maire were never seen again after that—and all the people said, that evening there was a trail leading down to the sea—across the fields and sand, and into the ocean. Two sets of footprints, one a man's, one a woman's, and the sliding scuddling tracks of a large seal. Going into the sea.

"And that is my st-story, Danny."

I lay back against the tar paper shingles, let out a deep breath.

"Wow."

"Did I do o-okay, Danny?"

Shy all again now Petey, and a moment before wild and rousing.

"Petey, that was amazing! Are you kiddin' me? That was better than the stories the nuns tell!"

"Thanks, D-Danny." He lay down beside me again. "Better than the R-Red Sox even?"

"Ah . . . yeah."

I had forgotten about the Red Sox.

"The moral being, of c-course," Petey said, lying down and putting his hands behind his head again, "B-Birdy."

Have You Seen the Button Man?

Petey knew things.

The new Petey showed me how to wave my fingers through the fat yellow candles on the altar when we were altar boys during Mass without burning them. He said it was magic. *Don't try this at home, Danny, with candles that aren't holy.* I believed.

He taught me too the next spring how if you planted a dried-up shrively seed in dirt—even the choke-dusty trash-ridden dirt of that empty lot down by the old railroad yards on the West Side, cheek by jowl to where Petey had his dog cemetery—it would turn into a beautiful plant with fragrant flowers by summer. I didn't see how this could be, and I said so.

Later that summer on a sticky Fudgsicle night we rode double on his bike over to the West Side, and Petey showed me the secret garden he'd made over there. *Waiting 't-til it got big to show you, Danny.* Waves of color and smell pushing up through the rusted beer cans and rat shit. I couldn't believe it. Seven big drums of shattered glass, metal cans, and other trash that Petey had raked up as the earth vomited back what people had thrown down there.

You had to part the tall grasses to get into the garden, to see it. How had he done this? On the sunny summer mornings we'd peddle over there, Monopoly tucked under our arms, or balanced on our heads like the pictures of the African missions women. *Can You Spare Them Your Milk Money One Day This Week?* We'd spend the day flopped on our shirtless bellies playing Monops in the middle of his garden, the flowers a fluttering wall all around and the blue sky bluer above us 'til you thought you weren't in Southie anymore, and you were just as good as any Brady kid out in their suburbs in their architect father's sprawling backyard.

A Map of the Harbor Islands
Published by The Haworth Press, Inc., 2006. All rights reserved.
doi:10.1300/5677_07

Petey said wasn't it amazing, how the poopsters and poopsterinis of his strays, buried into the ground here with leaves, grass clippings, and anything else that grew, turned even this concrete-colored quasi dirt into fragrant, rich loam that grew flowers of such a size and hue there was nothing to compare them to in any of the florists along Broadway. He was right, too.

"It's like a twelve-step p-program for the earth," Petey said, whenever we'd bury the stuff in his garden.

"Lookit, D-Danny!" Petey hissed one day, a finger describing the jagged parabolic flight of a butterfly bouncing above his flowers. Petey held his breath—he snatched my arm—and then it landed on one of the sunflowers he'd planted. I heard the sharp inrush of Petey breath. He couldn't have been more wonder-whacked if the Pope had come to visit. We watched as the butterfly's body pumped in evident ecstasy as it took in nectar.

"It must've crossed the Expressway s-somewhere to get here," Petey whispered, his eyes working. "It had to have. Miles of industrial w-wasteland and then this. H-how did it know? They know. How did it know?"

Battle stations, battle stations! Petey's talking G.I. Joe would bark out from time to time. Its pull-string was stuck and this was the only thing it said now and you never knew when. Petey had removed Joe's uniform and painted one peace sign on his chest, another on his moundy plastic bum.

"The Mugloids are attacking! It's the M-Mugloids!" Petey would cry, and we'd grab our mop handles and shoot down the invisible but pervasive enemy that wanted to destroy Petey's garden, or the recently returned harbor seals, anything beautiful it found in Southie. Mugloids, he'd say. That was Petey's name for the shadowy forces that set fire to dumpsters in parking lots, left smashed beer bottles on the beach that tender toes would find at night, dumped oil barrels or missing people out in the harbor. Beat people. Made people beat other people 'til they stopped moving sometimes. Dealt drugs to kids, some of them our age. Southie was changing now and the old folks who lived near the projects wouldn't go out at night so much anymore. *Your life's not worth a plugged nickel to some of these people!* Rita Hennessey told my mother when we saw her down at Flanagan's one time.

But Petey's garden: this silky grassy patch in the middle of a 20' × 20' secret plot. On the north side, a six-foot-high wall of flowers Petey had planted. To the south, the same, to the east and west, the same. In the middle of these flower walls, a sun-warmed swath of grass, which Petey cropped by hand every other morning with one of those hand-trimmer things that go *gee-CHAW gee-CHAW gee-CHAW*. The grassy swath was just big enough for two sprawled and Monopoly, the grass leaving little pink itchy dots on our bellies but we never minded when our shirts were off and one afternoon we counted each other's belly dots laughing. Funny what you remember. I had 242. Above, the sky, like the cobalt bowl my mother only used for company to put her Irish step-dancing medals in tipped over above us. We could've been anywhere—most times we were.

"I suppose you'll be finding other friends now?" Ma said casually one afternoon when I came home from school. "He's that *strange* now though, isn't he? And those towels still haven't shown up."

She was reading a magazine in the parlor and didn't take her eyes off the page.

"No," I said, when I came back downstairs from changing. "No, I won't."

Would you get a new leg, for Chrissake? Get a new head?

"No you won't what?" Ma asked, idly flicking a page and taking a sip from her iced tea.

In spite of myself, Petey made me see there might be more to life than Southie, school, TV, Saturday chores and grocery shopping Thursday nights and Ma—*C'mon, Danny, get down here, help your father in with the bundles, where are you, did he go out on a Thursday night when he knows it's grocery night?*—while at the same time I began to be yanked in other directions, in the directions of others. A secret he became, nothing you'd talk about with the other guys pickled in normalcy who were starting to keep their distance now from Petey. A place to be one of me he became—Petey was that weird, I could be myself. One of myselves. Couldn't care less what I wore, what I'd watched the night before, what teams I rooted for or what my batting average was that season. Whether my face was clear or zit-ridden. Just me he wanted. Just to be with me. Not something to be taken lightly, even then. *Is é an duine an t-éadach,* he consoled me one time, Petey-arm on my shoulder. I was upset Ma would only get me two pairs of the Adidas sweats everyone was wearing that year, not the five pair I wanted. "The man h-himself is the clothes, D-Danny. Old p-proverb and nothing new under the sun, eh?"

Stories, he began telling me more stories, writing them down too sometimes. No stranger to drama when he told his yarns. I can still see him atop the seawall by the beach, the arms and hands wildly outstretched, encompassing the Atlantic in their skinny white ken, or pulled in and miserly, getting down to nitty-gritty details of human character. Gesticulating while eggs of stories gestated inside and bubbled to the wide-mouth surface.

Listening to Petey's tales, all of which he claimed sprouted from his time in the coma, via the Button Man (I'll explain), I saw heroes and giants in the

dirty seaweed, Spanish diamonds floating on the surface of the harbor, sparkling in the sun. This latter illusion, Petey said, was enchanted treasure that
sank away as you approached it, pirates' treasure the sea had storm-stolen
400 years ago.

.   . "That's j-just what that is," Petey explained one day, pointing out to the
dazzled ocean. The smile of him whenever we'd be down there together and
the world Maying again, Juneing.

"I thought it was just the sun on the water there, Petey."

"Oh no. God no." He paused, lowered his head and eyed me with the
green eyes. "That's just what they want you to think. No, it's t-treasure."
Then he jumped up onto the seawall as if he were addressing a throng and
hissed, "But there's a mighty c-c-curse upon it! It's d-d-diamonds on the
water but they s-sink when you get near. Captain Kidd was bringing it
ashore when the storm struck, r-r-right out there. Right out in what's Pleasure B-Bay now."

"Really?" You had to be careful—lots of the stuff Petey said was true.

"R-really. That would be the Great B-Blow of 1633. Sit ye down and I'll
sp-spin you a yarn about it. All about it."

That was just one story out of a million.

"Listen to this," Petey said another day down at the beach, reading from
one of his library books. I'd met him here after my baseball practice. I was
late, and him waiting for me. He came running at me with the book open,
his black hair curling in the sea wind. "Listen, Danny, you w-won't believe
this!"

"What? Don't you want to hear about practice? Eddie McDaid—"

"*Bother Eddie McDaid,* no, listen."

We flopped down on the sand Indian style facing each other and Petey
read from his green-covered book. *"The C-City of B-Boston was troubled by ye
great invasion of sundrie b-bears in the year 1643. They came up from Braintree,
roaring into the city from the south. They even swam out to some of the Harbor Islands
when the tide was low, and s-several were dispatched by m-men in boats."*

"Okay, wait a minute, what's sundrie? What's dispatched?"

"Sundrie is an old word for several, or a certain undetermined n-number.
Dispatched is a c-c-cover-up word for killing. They smited them."

Petey put the book down, cleared his throat, and improvised from there.

"See D-Danny, God speaks to the animals directly. We've fallen asleep
to h-his voice, so we only hear it in dreams, or visions. That's what Jung says
anyways."

"Who's Yung?"

"A very sm-smart man. He had a dream one time that God was doing his poopsters onto the top of a church. No faces, Danny, listen. But the animals, well, they hear God plain. No attitude or the smugness brought on by a s-sexy figger. What h-happened was, the King of the Bears around here at that time—his name was Skovo—was visited with v-visions of a future world. He told all the b-bears what he saw in these v-visions. Dead rivers. Mugloided seas empty of fish. Oceans bl-black and full up with sludge and nervous diarrhea and *fresh scent* chemical t-toilet paper and changed motor oil. Woods paved over with strip m-malls and McMansions, streets choked with cars and tr-trucks where once berries and nuts and honey trees grew.

"*These cars, now,* the other bears asked Skovo. *We wonder now who's in 'em?*

"Skovo answered, *Full up with p-people on the way to strip mall stores in search of plastic potato chip bag clips made with human m-misery in China, and the other necessities of l-life.*

"See, Danny, Skovo, with his k-keen insight, foresaw that the ultimate p-postmodern gesture would be shopping. Skovo explained all this to the other b-bears, and in a r-rage b-born of desperation they invaded. What else was there to do Danny, when they knew these p-p-people, infected with g-greed, would m-m-multiply like bacteria, breaking down the world? As it were? You listening, D-Danny?"

"'Course I am, infected with greed. Ahhhh, you sure you don't wanna play catch? Eddie McDaid forgot his glove so I have a spare—"

"No! I w-wanna tell you another story."

So many stories, some spoken, some he'd write down.

"This is f-f-for you, Danny," he'd say, walking to school some morning. A five-, fifteen-, twenty-five-page story. *Just a little di-version I whipped up last night,* while me, I marveled, I recalled my own profligate sweating over a two-page book report, each single word a triumph but wondering when would the next one come. My writing big and swirly so as to get more bang for the buck.

"Is this another Button Man story?" I'd ask Petey.

"Another B-Button Man story of course, Danny, they're all Button Man stories."

The Button Man.

"Listen, Danny," Petey said to me the morning he gave me his first story. "There was this old man down at Castle Island. Sat out on one of the b-benches behind the Castle. He was always there, you could always see him there, any day of the year. Always looking out at the sea. Again, another one of those archetypes there. Almost like a necessary part of the sea—there's the sea, and then there are the old men who sit and watch it. Remembering. *Half o'er, half o'er, to La-bra-dor . . . "*

"Huh?"

"That's a line from a poem. You've questioned m-me on it twice now and only once is acceptable. Signifying, at l-least to me . . . outishness. The beyond. The wanderlust of the ocean and the sh-shining light just over the horizon. The sea. Anyways, I finally asked Ma'am, my mother, she knows everyone, I said, who's that old man always sitting out at Castle Island? *That one? I think he's called Casey,* she said. *I can tell you no more. He was here when I first come over when I was a girl o' twenty, and that was some thirty years ago. He's here yet, God bless him. He was old then.* But why? I asked her. Why's he always looking out at the sea? Why's he always there? *Ach, you'd no more ask that than ask the stones why they're in the ground,* my mother said. *As much of a fixture as they are.*

"The thing is, Danny, he was always looking out, always. Scanning the harbor. Not with the slack eyes of the s-senile, the sad lumpishness of them that's been ab-bandoned. There was p-purpose in his looking. Steel. Steeliness. The posture of him. Like a m-mizzenmast for heaven's sake. I needed to know—what was he doing? Was he remembering? Or was he waiting? Do you remember ever seeing him when we'd bike ride out there?"

"I don't know, maybe."

I always seemed to miss the things Petey saw. Petey saw everything.

"I asked him. I finally got to talk to him a few weeks b-before my accident. The timing, Danny. The t-timing of it."

Petey grew big-eyed and silent.

"Go on," I said. That was what I'd say when I wasn't sure what Petey was talking about. I'd seen it in an old movie—Ma really went for old movies on the long afternoons, the drama-dialogue puffing upstairs all the way to my room and sometimes I'd sneak onto the top stair step to listen when it got good—

I'm crazy about you, Monica.

I'm . . . fond of you, Frank.

No more?

Why should there be more? You're still a stranger to me. You never speak of your past.

That's because I prefer to think of the future—our future together.

Ha! Not so fast, Frank—I like you but I don't want this to mushroom. . . .

"Earth to Danny!"

"Okay, sorry."

"Okay, the first day I got to t-talk to him. The Button Man. This one day. Two weeks before my accident. I br-brought my bike right up to him. I stared. Something m-made me. Finally he tore his eyes away from the sea and regarded me. It was early June. I was c-c-coming home from my paper route. Why did I g-go out there that afternoon, Danny? I had n-no time for idleness then, do you remember how I was? The Golden Boy? Homework and ironing my own c-clothes? But I rode out there after my paper route that day. Something called to me. I saw him. I pedaled right up to him. I stopped and stared. Rude I know and I was never rude then."

Petey got vacant eyed for a minute, like he himself couldn't believe the great distance between what he'd been and what he was becoming now.

"He stared right back at me, Danny. *Well?* he finally asked.

"What are you waiting for? I asked him. Or are you remembering?

"He looked at me hard, a-appraising. Eyes going into sea-slits, sea lanes. The eye lines creaking up like a t-topographical map. You know them? Like the Rockies all in shade, you know?"

"I guess."

"I expected him to be kind somehow but he wasn't par-particularly kind. Not c-cruel, Danny, you understand, but not especially k-kind.

"*You've got the Life in you though, haven't you?* he said to me. He patted the empty bench space beside him. I sat down next to him. *You're the Golden Boy. I know who you are. Petey Harding.*

"How do you know? I asked him.

"He shrugged. *People talk,* he said, looking down at his hands. *I listen. Sit down, boy.*

"You know the view from there, Danny: the harbor, the Harbor Islands, the ships going out, the ships c-c-coming in. The stream of river-water wiggling out, the salt water wiggling in. It was the beginning of s-s-summer.

"*Boy, there is a remembering that's stronger than the present, stronger than the future,* he finally said to me.

"His hands, D-Danny. Like lobsters, b-big and red. Like mitts, big red mitts. He consulted them often, looked down at them. Scars and spots and c-c-calluses and lines. Maps of lines. Stories in themselves, those h-hands."

Petey looked at his own hands, midsize and white. Then he shoved them in my face and laughed.

"The old man was fingering a button between two of his reddy f-fingers. About the size of a ha-ha-ha—"

"Half dollar."

"Yes. That big, this b-button. He was fingering this button. Beige-ish. Thick. Not plastic—something else. Old it was. Carefully made. It had a j-job to do that was taken seriously.

"Without taking his watery eyes off the sea—he had watery eyes, Danny, you look at something long enough and it comes into your eyes—without taking his w-watery eyes off the sea, he saw what I was looking at, he saw I was staring at his button.

"He squeezed it tight like he w-was wringing one more memory from it, then handed it to me, but like he was reluctant to.

"*My uncle's,* he said. *From my uncle's sea coat.* He couldn't have handed it over more reverently if it had come from the hem of the dress of Our Lady, Danny."

"Uh-huh."

"*I'll tell you about him, my uncle,* the old man said. And he did."

Petey shook his head. He squatted down on his haunches, leaned forward, clasped his hands together, peered up at me.

"Danny, the world faded—I mean, the world I thought I was in at that m-moment: the mothers lumbering by sh-shoving prams, the oil tankers steaming past—two squalling little kids fighting over a baseball glove right in front of us. He told me the story. The st-story of his uncle. His uncle the seaman. He said seaman not sailor."

"What was the uncle's story?" I asked.

"No real story, Danny. Just about him, about his life. The best k-kind of story."

"Like?"

"Like . . . the way his uncle would c-come home from sea every two years, when the old m-man himself was only ten. How red-lusty his uncle's face he said, how alive the man, how thick and bl-black his hair, how pert and blue his eyes, how he'd bellow swinging him up to the thick sm-smoky rafters first thing he come through the door. Hams and herbs hanging from those rafters. The tattoos he'd show him, the leg scars from h-h-harpoons, the tales of chase and privation, headhunters and the bare-bosomed queens that ruled S-South Sea islands."

"Really?"

"Yeah, but right then and there, Danny, the w-world smeared into the past. Like, all you had to do was look into a different corner of your eye and it was all there before you again. Still happening. The pa-past but still happening. He told the story and I could see it all before me."

"What happened to his uncle?"

"Th-they that go down to the sea in ships, Danny, that's what happened. Lost. Never again. The sea swallowed his life. But bigger. Bigger and sadder and more beautiful and un-unutterable, like life. And every st-story encrusted with the sea. I'll tell you someday. I'll write that story down someday when I get to be a *seanchaí* myself. I want to be a *seanchaí* myself s-someday, Danny."

"A what?"

"Shan-a-kee. *Seanchaí*. An old storyteller. It's an Irish word."

"I thought . . . didn't you want to be a baseball player?"

Petey made a repelling gesture with his hand.

"Oh God n-no."

"Sorry, but that's what you used to—"

Petey got up to come closer. He looked out at the sea, then looked back to me. Something fierce in his eyes. We were down by the seawall at City Point beach.

"Danny l-listen to me. There's only one story, and we're all in it—it's one big story and we're all in it and it g-goes on and on like it's never been told before, that powerful. Almighty. Are you listening, Danny?"

"'Course I am."

"Danny, this is important. The st-story of my accident is the same story as his uncle going under the waves forever and Cain and Abel fighting and Madame Curie discovering—whatever she discovered, I forget n-now— and then the date she had later that night. It's the same story, D-Danny. You're in it too, we're all in it. What part d-do you want to play in it? You can write it as you go along, m-make up your own story and have it come true. That seagull over there's in it. Jesus raising Lazarus. And Birdy running through it all."

"Ahh . . . I know it. So what happened to this old man?"

"The Button Man. It was the time r-r-right before my accident like I s-say. I went to see him every day after my p-paper route, after that first day. The last two weeks before my accident."

There was a silence, like there was every time Petey mentioned the A word.

"You never said so," I finally mumbled. "What was his name?"

"He n-n-never said. I guess I never asked. My mother said Casey but I don't know. But every day I went to see him. It was like my l-life was turning. It was right before the accident, and it was like the w-w-wave of what was coming into me was raising itself up and curling and billowing up, right before it smashed into me, broke over me. It was gathering up and I think I sensed it. I went to s-s-see him every day and that wasn't like m-me. I had everything ordered in m-my life then."

"You did?"

"I did. He told me his stories, Danny. A different story every day. Ten days of stories b-before my accident. I didn't go on the weekends.

"This is how h-he'd do it: he pulled something out of his p-pocket that first day. It was a jar, a b-button jar. A jar full of buttons. An old thick glass jar. *My mother put up quinces for me in this jar, gave it to me the day I myself went to sea—almost eighty years ago,* he told me. *The particular day of all days came when it was my turn to go to sea, and my mother gave me quinces in this jar. Some days are bigger than others, boy. So much has broken in my life, but this jar still holds, and it's brittle glass. What do you make of that?"*

"Wait a minute, Petey, what's a quince? Old money?"

"No, Danny. S-something you eat. A kind of fr-fruit. They used to grow wild all around here. Skovo and the bears would f-feast on them then fall asleep in the sea-brine smell of sunny September hay marshes. No more, we've dispatched them all. Sea-sun r-ripened once and light orange, an edible g-garden this whole place was once, before pantyhose yanked up nervously l-late for work again and copy machines and d-deadlines and traffic jams and acres of asphalt sm-smothered upon the p-pink raw flesh of Mama Earth and us feeling powerless all over the place."

"Ahhh—pantyhose?"

"Never mind. But the old man—his j-jar had buttons in it. Buttons."

"Button button, who's got the button?"

"Jolly Olly Orange," Petey said. "But every afternoon the Button Man'd tell me a st-story. He took out his Button Jar from his coat, unscrewed the rusting cap, picked a button out. Would tell me the st-story of who it belonged to. Every button a story.

"The d-day of my accident I saw him. I saw him that a-afternoon before my accident. Before the game that night."

Petey paused, and me inwardly cringing.

"But you never told me," I said lowly. "You . . . never told me you did this every day after your paper route."

I couldn't believe it. A little hurt? Yeah, of course.

"I admit it, Danny. I was holding back from y-you." Petey folded his hands and looked down at them. "N-not . . . you p-p-personally. I was holding b-back from everyone. Not . . . not on purpose really. There comes a time you discover things, step out into Life, Danny. You know? Step away and b-become yourself? You can't bring anyone else to those m-moments.

Then after a while, you spend a big part of the r-r-rest of your life trying to find someone to discover what you've become. Where you've gone now. Someone to help you understand all you've b-become and vice versa."

"Ahh. . . ."

"That last day, the day of my . . . accident. He told me I could pick out which button that day. He'd tell me the story of who that button belonged to, what happened to them. He handed me the jar. His hand was like a lobster's like I say but it wasn't shaking. I expected it to b-be shaking but no. He unscrewed the cap. I knew the one I wanted. Halfway d-d-down it was, I'd seen it. Beautiful, Danny. Triangle-shaped. Purple it was, very plummy in the sun, dark purple in the shade. Like a melted m-m-mandolin it looked. Shaped that way. Do you know a m-mandolin?"

"A . . . something Chinese, ain't it?"

"Ahh . . . great guess. I think you're thinking of Mandarin, Danny. A mandolin's an instrument. A kind of string instrument."

"Oh."

"It's okay."

Petey put his hand on my shoulder and patted.

"When I picked out that button, the old man smiled. *Carved from moose bone, that button is,* he said.

"He told me the story. He never looked at m-me when he told his stories. Just staring out at the ocean, like he could s-see them all out there again. He sat back and sighed and told me the story of the Indian Princess. The purple mandolin button belonged to this Penacook princess and he told m-m-me her story. He told me the part of the Big Story that c-c-concerned her."

"What was it? Who was she?"

Petey shook his head.

"When I'm a *seanchaí,*" he said. "Like the other stories, it's big and powerful and too big for me now, too sad and too h-happy. The same story, Danny. The one big story. Later, when I'm a *seanchaí.* The Button Man had heard it at sea when he was a young man from a fellow crew member of his ship, a Native American from M-Maine. But later that night I got hit. Coma time. My first day out of bed two months later I went d-d-down to find the old man. But he was gone. Gone. For the first time in a million years, gone. No more on the bench, no more l-looking at the sea. Part of the sea now, in the story still but somewhere else, not here."

"You mean he died, like?"

"In a w-way. In the way that we all do."

"You haven't seen him there since?"

"No one h-has. I've asked. But listen, Danny—lookit. This came to my doorstep while I was in my coma. It had my name on it, on a slip of paper wrapped around it with an elastic. Wavery writing. My mother saved it for me. Didn't know what it could be but she s-saved it for me. Lots of things came to the house then—flowers, pans of lasagna, holy medals h-holy water but this h-had my name on it."

Petey reached into his pocket and brought out a jar, full of buttons. The glass was tinted barely green. Very thick the glass, like it had been made out of seawater, as if the lightest green seawater had hardened into glass. I'd never seen a jar like it, never seen the type of buttons that were inside it. He handed it to me.

I shook the jar.

"Wow," I said. What else to say?

Petey took it back and returned it to his jacket pocket.

"See, Danny, you n-need to know this about me. When I was in my c-c-coma, the Button Man came to me. He came to me in the wandering darkness and told me his stories. Told me the Big Story, as much of it as he knew. Kept me company sometimes when I was w-wandering in the darkness. Always s-sitting at a bench he was, with his hand covering his brow as he spoke, half shielding his eyes. A big lobster hand.

"And then when I c-came home from the hospital, there it was w-waiting for me, the Button Jar. He s-s-sent it to me, Danny. My mother had put it on my bureau and I smiled when I saw it, knew. Knew everything would be fine."

Petey nodded, but looked out at the sea, like he was agreeing to something.

"So I'm to b-be a *seanchaí*. I want to anyway but now I h-have to be. Do you know what the l-last thing was he said to me? The Button Man?"

"Ahhh . . . no."

Jesus Christ, what had happened to my best friend?

"I was p-pulling away on my bike the night of my accident, that afternoon. *Times were tough in 1957,* he said. He was sm-smiling as he said it."

"Ahhh . . . I see."

Petey was quiet for a bit. He crossed his arms then said slowly, "I think he m-meant . . . I think he meant, b-bad times don't last. Wait. Wait them out. It was like he knew what was coming to me. Like he could see into my future. And why not, Danny? The future and the past are just two sides of the same door, when you think about it."

Petey was saying this more to himself than me. He turned and refocused on me.

"See, Danny, it wasn't just a c-c-coma. It was a cocoon too. Three things, Danny, things come in threes and so do I now: the coma; Birdy; and the Button Man. Now you know. And h-here I am."

Petey was staring at me, hard. He always stared at me now but this particular day his staring had a ferocity to it—

"Who do you s-say that I am now, Danny?" he blurted, half smirking, our old thing but us different now, him different—

"Ahhh . . . Petey Harding. My best friend."

"Bestest," Petey said. "Always." But that night I dreamed that Mrs. Harding was searching her house. *Hasn't anyone seen my button jar?* she kept asking, but Petey was old and hunched and sitting at the kitchen table, mumbling stories to no one.

The Woods Are Full of Bittersweet

It was a day of blue radiance that summer—that was really our summer. Do you have one, an *our summer?* Who was it with? Where are they now? What did you do?

This is what ours was like.

Petey dragged me down to the beach the second day of vacation, lugging an old gray two-by-four. Actually three of them stuck together.

"You look like the ragpicker's son, draggin' that shit around town," I yelled behind him.

"Only to enlighten you to that old ch-chestnut, one man's trash is another man's treasure. Your r-ride, sir," Petey said. He lobbed the plank into the water. "Hop on and start k-kicking."

He pulled off his shirt, kicked off his smelly sneakers, waited, then dove into the water and leaned his arms onto the floating wood. His hair slicked down and I saw the indent on his head.

"Huh?"

"C'mon, h-hop on, D-Danny. Get b-beside me. Start kicking now. I mean it."

I de-sneakered and de-shirted and complied. We used it as a floater. Its simpleness made it magic and I laughed as one does at sudden, simple elation. A thrown-out piece of wood with a rusty sticky-out screw on the bottom could take you away, take you out to sea. There was more magic, tucked into the bright pockets of the sea air, sparkling in the water's flash. The feeling of it hit me when I tinkled my toes down and felt nothing for once, no bottom, just the sea swirling, doing things. You couldn't see Southie for once all around now, now nothing but the sea and the waves before you and the gulls and the white puffball clouds in the bluest blue above. A wave-lap up your nose but it doesn't matter because of all this new now

A Map of the Harbor Islands
Published by The Haworth Press, Inc., 2006. All rights reserved.
doi:10.1300/5677_08

and we looked at each other and shrieked. Every sense and thought woken up. Arms slickety with salty wave-wash. The cool water up your legs and butt, the place between your legs a cave and the cold water seeping in there. Your mind unlocked and floating out like the sky-water. Something inside singing as I looked at the shimmered horizon, bouncing away in the distance up and down up and down up and down with the waves and all our stroking.

"Pretend we're one p-person," Petey ordered. We scrunched together, put one arm around the slippery other and flapped with the free hand. We went faster somehow.

"Do you s-see those dark shapes way under? Down there?" Petey asked, head-jerk to the depths.

"No. I don't think so. Not really."

"L-look harder. They're like navy bluish amidst the green."

"Maybe. Oh okay, yeah."

"Those are the b-b-bodies of the bears, Skovo's disciples, the ones that were k-killed by men during the bear invasion. God won't let them rot, he wants a m-m-monument there for their b-bravery. They fought for their country. By which I mean of c-course, Mama Earth. God's beautiful creation."

Later, slicky paddling and the sun bouncing off the sea smell, we saw a rusting car in twenty feet of water below us, wavery. A drunk someone had probably driven it off the causeway, or sometimes stolen cars were stored in the bay here, for vengeance, like miser's gold never to see light of day again, but all-powerful in the thought of it, in the constant remembering.

"That's the bears' g-getaway car," Petey said. "Three h-hunnert years before Ford. It r-ran on seaweed."

That first day we dog-paddled just around Pleasure Bay, the small contained body of water in between the beach and the causeway that keeps out the sea when she turns ill-humored.

"Pleasure B-Bay, Pl-Pleasure Bay," Petey kept warbling, water in and out of his mouth, in love with the sound. He leaned forward and sucked more green ocean into his mouth, then said it again, gurgling. Then he spit seawater at me and a quick, indecisive water fight ensued. Seagulls squawked at our joy.

"Why do p-people murder each other and go to jobs they h-h-hate when there's this to do?" Petey asked as we drifted contented. "See now, D-Danny, here's Pleasure Bay, a circle of light and water all around us. And off to the l-l-left there is Castle Island, where the ghosts of Skovo and his bears still dance on the parapet on the silver-watery nights of the full m-moon. Way to the right over there is L-Long Island, and then beyond that Spectacle Island, Georges Island, Gallops Island, Graves. And in between them way out you can see the high seas—the blue-white shimmer on the h-horizon, the sun like diamonds on the water. Let's keep going, Danny, and n-n-never come back."

The floats got bigger. Petey loved ritual—*Joseph Campbell says what's missing from modern life is ritual, and mystery, Danny.* Who's Joseph Campbell, someone from the West Side? *No, h-he's a writer*—and as soon as we would be able to jiggle our legs and toes through the water without touching slithery sand bottom, Petey'd make this little tour guide speech, the same one every time we went out—sometimes just saying it but most times sing-chanting. Weird, but he never stuttered when he sang:

> Danny and me, Danny and me, Danny and me and the sea,
> Bobbing out of Pleasure Bay, the islands on our lee:
> Spectacle, Georges, Gallops, the sun-wash on the brine—
> Castle Island where Skovo danced a bear-dance in bear-time.
> The Golden Boy has chosen, I know what I will be—
> Danny and me, *seanchaí,* Danny and me and the sea.

You might think it weird—I never got tired of hearing Petey say those words, and he'd say them every single time we went out. When he forgot, I reminded him to stave off nautical disasters. It got to be like a thing I'd repeat when I was sick, or when I twisted my ankle sliding into home a month later and the pain sucked so bad I wanted to scream, staring at the suddenly vicious two-in-the-morning race cars on my bedroom wallpaper the first two nights after it happened. Or if I'd be nervous right before a test. Or a fight. I'd hear Petey's words again, see it all a-shining before me. Comfort and joy.

At night Petey would work on his maps if he wasn't being wanton with moon watching. It took him a while to show them to me again after my previous unkind comments. The Pepperminty Coast, Zanzibar, Svengali, the Mountain of Seven Sorrows and One Joy.

"But what's it all mean, Petey?"

Petey smiled and the sea lighting up his green eyes.

"The s-sounds, Danny. The music of l-language. Dreams. The wonder. No m-more wonder in this franchised world so we g-gotta make up our own. We have to explore for wonder, d-drill for wonder like the oil companies do. Maybe we'll apply for government s-s-subsidies, call your congressman. Tell 'im you're hot for w-wonder. I think there's a big load of it waiting out in the harbor for us. I suggest exploratory afternoon junkets by the dozens, you and me."

"You know, Petey," I said, as we were side by side on our float drifting in, "I don't . . . like always understand what you're talking about." The tentativeness of my tone told him if there was any reproach in my words, it was directed at myself.

His smile then was so warm something jiggled at the back of my throat.

"It doesn't matter at all, D-Danny."

There were other maps sticking out from under his bed. He didn't show me them. Turned red, got shy, *Maybe l-later, Danny.* I saw a corner of one of them before he toe-nudged it further out of peerage, and Boston Harbor on it had become the Sea of Love.

A month later after a storm, Petey found a little wooden boat with punch holes in its bottom upside down on the side of the causeway's rocks, as if the sea had disdained it. Risk and Monopoly got dusty and wondered maybe where we were as we fixed the dory. Petey said it was a *d-dory* but his mother called it a curragh, the c's of the word hard and like she was hacking up a bit of choked lunch. Like Dad's roses blooming over the arch in the backyard under which they took my confirmation picture right as the yellow jacket stung Ma on her sleeveless shoulder. It was time for the sea and these trips now.

"It's called the *Argo-eeni*," Petey said. We were lapping in the water of City Point Beach up to our knees, ready to launch it for the first time. "By which I m-mean of course *Little Argo*."

"I don't get it."

"It's from G-Greekish mythologicalia. It was his boat, the n-n-name of his boat."

We were wearing cutoffs, half sliding down from our belly concavity, the only thing keeping them up the hard small mounds of our almost-thirteen-year-old bums.

"Whose boat?"

"J-Jason."

"Jason who?"

"Ahhh . . . I don't believe they had last n-names then, there weren't s-so m-many people like now. Jason went looking for the Golden Fleece. He had adventures. We'll have b-better ones."

I believed Petey, though why someone would want to sail around the world looking for fleas was beyond me, even if they were golden.

Petey's green eyes were squinting slits among the salty black lashes. Mrs. Harding always said Petey had his father's eyes. A career navy man, he'd died three months before Petey was born, had come home the year before from Vietnam missing a leg. After praising God for his mercy in not taking the both of them, Mrs. H would always add, *Well, at any rate, it did inhibit his campaigning somewhat.*

We hopped into the boat. So far so good. It was creaking but not leaking.

"It's creaking not leaking," I said, pleased with my phrase. Petey stuttered but he loved words, the music they could make.

"Jolly Olly Orange," he answered, addressing my meaning, plashing me.

Delight came in on the tender lapping waves and off we went.

"Are we gonna do it?" I asked, delirious whereas this morning I'd been bored, depressed at my still lack of man-hair. We'd be taking the *Argo-eeni* out of Pleasure Bay and into the Outer Harbor. Today was the day. We'd talked about nothing else the whole time we'd been fixing it. The high seas, the Harbor Islands, Cadiz and Ireland across the water, everything.

"And d-don't let's forget Los Mavroules de Sancta Concepcion," Petey said, reading my thoughts again.

"Who?"

"It's an island off the Spanish M-Main," Petey said. He laughed and said the words again. "Admittedly I m-made that one up. But it sounds r-real, no? Better than real if you ask me. P-ports o' call, real and imagined and them all slip-sliding into each other. Fragrant with s-sea smell of course, these names, but something else too, something fr-fruity, exotic. No?"

Petey wet his finger and held it up to the warm gushy baby breeze.

"Set a c-course for starboard!" he laughed.

"What's starboard?"

"I dunno left or right but it s-sounds good. Go that a-way. Out. Out-ish."

Petey waved vaguely at the horizon. Then he said the words again:

> Danny and me, Danny and me, Danny and me and the sea,
> Bobbing out of Pleasure Bay, the islands on our lee:
> Spectacle, Georges, Gallops, the sun-wash on the brine—
> Castle Island where Skovo danced a bear-dance in bear-time.
> The Golden Boy has chosen, I know what I will be—
> Danny and me, *seanchaí,* Danny and me and the sea.

Our bare feet slapped together and we started kicking and laughing in the tiny boat facing each other. Petey, having languished pale during the school year, was getting strong again, pubescent and full of possibilities again, drinking in the elixir of this new world of his.

We had two rusty shovels for paddles. We'd found them over by Petey's secret garden, down by the old train yards. They worked beyond expectations until the first one broke after five minutes of sea work. The boat started leaking not long after.

"She's going down!" I yelled, one hand to the side of my mouth, laughing and sunburned nose. "Abandon ship!"

Petey said nothing but I saw that look pinch his face. The open eyes then peering, the tight-jammed mouth, his chin hard and jabbery. Relentless white hands, he started scooping water out.

"B-bail with a will!" he cried. I didn't know what that meant but just did what he did. The waves got rougher, laugh-slapping in, adding to water woes. The boat started sinking. We were about a hundred yards out from the beach, fifty yards from the causeway dead ahead.

"She's creakin' *and* leakin'!" I laughed. "Flip 'er over and we'll float 'er in."

Petey was not amused.

"N-NO!"

A few leaks needing caulking was all. I slid out into the water, holding onto the sinking boat for leverage. My cutoffs sliding down a little and the feeling of seawater sluice-gating down my bum crack.

"NO!" Petey screamed again. It was the world to him right then.

I laughed.

"N-NO! N-not funny and N-NO!"

He folded his arms across his heaving bare chest, the penny red nipples, and sat back down in the boat with relish. I watched as they both went under. I don't think there ever could've been anyone in history who looked as resolute as Petey did then, arms folded as he went under, no efforts made to swim. Resolute, there was a poster of pilgrims in our history class on one of the walls, a picture of them dour-walking back from church in the snow and one pilgrim was looking at the other beside him, and Sr. Janice Mary had written underneath in swirly nun letters *See how resolute they were.* Someone else though one time crossed that out and wrote *Did you just kick me in the hindquarters forsooth?* and the whole class got detention.

But resolute or not, Petey was more so as he went under. His black hair lifted up and wavery like a mermaid's through the green water and I could see it which was interesting. I took a deep breath and went down to go get him.

"Why would you die over something like that?" I asked him ten minutes later, hauling his ass onto the Causeway Beach. I'd had to swim for both of us the whole way. Petey hadn't lifted a cheek.

"I w-w-wouldn't!" he panted. "That's j-just it, I w-w-wouldn't!"

He was sputtering and foaming, never so mad!

"The f-f-f-f-f-f-fuckin' q-question is, why would Life si-sink our b-b-boat, then drown me just c-c-cuz I stayed w-w-with it? This was our d-d-day! It was s-s-supposed to be our perfect d-d-day!"

"You said fuck," I reported, blowing sea mucus out my nostrils. "You never said that before. All your life."

"Fuckfuckfuckfuckfuckfuckfuckfuck."

Petey rolled over onto his belly and started pounding the sand at the base of the causeway with his fists, his white feet. A few mothers passing by on the causeway above stared as they marched past. It would not be the last time.

"Tomorrow," I said. "We'll fix the leaks tomorrow is all."

"Tomorrow? FUCK TOMORROW, I wanted it T-TODAY!"

"Shhh!" I whispered. "People are looking!"

He slapped the sand with his feet. "Let 'em look! Why w-w-would Life do that?" he panted.

"The boat just leaked is all. We didn't fix it as good as we could."

"Yes we did. We're only k-kids. Life should've known that."

I should've remembered, later, how stubborn Petey was, how the injustice of Life was nothing to him. If he didn't think it was right, there was nothing else to be considered. Say what I would, the walk home from the beach was funereal and Petey kicking stones along the way.

That night though Petey chucked Good & Fruity, which had reappeared in stores, at my window, so I shinnied down the drainpipe. He couldn't talk, so bug-eye excited was he.

"The b-b-b . . . "

Pointing toward the ocean.

He pulled-pushed me down to L Street Beach and our boat had low-tided up on shore, an old black rubber boot sitting upright in it, as if someone had borrowed it and this their payment. The moon was out and riding the waves. Teenagers were drinking, hooting and hollering but further down and away from us.

"It came ba-back," Petey said quietly, reverently. He folded his hands across his midsection. "Danny, L-Life reconsidered our c-case." Suddenly he started jumping up and down in his exuberance and I was glad it was pitch.

"Something else, Danny. I've been a-pondering as to what was a-missing. Spent the rest o' the day a-researching n-nautical tomes, sea chants and lore. You might have seen my c-corporeal being at the library, but really I was out to sea. But the answer is o-obvious! I know where we w-went wrong."

He pulled something out of his raggedy jacket with a flourish.

"A f-f-figurehead!" he announced, thrusting a topless Barbie doll in my face.

I started laughing.

"Danny, listen. I was d-disremembering the rituals, the ways and m-means of the sea. No wonder she s-sank, no figurehead. Go figure."

"Where'd you find the Barbie?"

"She's not a Barbie at all, she's a cheap knockoff. Down at Everything-a-Buck. I was their last c-customer of the day. I flew down there on my bike once I realized the mistake we'd made. The Button Man would've known of course. She was made in China. I think there was a t-translation issue cuz her n-name is Linda, City Girl. There was another one beside her except black hair called Attractive, Pamela but I only had enough dough-ray-me for one. Besides, all we n-need is one anyways."

It took us three days to recaulk the boat. We tried to test it out in a kiddie pool we found in someone's backyard on East Fourth Street. Petey had seen it one day flying by on his bike when he was out *a-roaming and a-racin', and all them stray dogs flyin' behind him God help us,* as Mrs. Harding phrased it. We rang the kiddie-pool house's doorbell one afternoon just to make sure no one home, then lugged the *Argo-eeni* up the weedy cracked driveway to the small backyard. The boat was tiny but heavy and always leaving red bumps on the red bumps of our shoulders.

"Get away from there you kids!" a neighbor lady with orange-juice-can hair rollers called from an adjacent window.

"What l-light from yonder w-window doesn't break," Petey said.

"Huh? Don't get fresh with me, you! Get away from there I said!"

"Why n-not?" Petey asked. I was already halfway down the driveway.

"A little boy drowned in that pool last week. A little four-year-old boy. You didn't hear? What are you doing with that boat?"

Petey's eyes got huge. He looked down in the four inches of shimmery baby blue water, as if the kid might still be there.

"What was his n-name?"

The woman scrunched her face up.

"That Foley boy. Andy. Little Andy Foley, God help us. Requiem High Mass this weekend, you didn't know?"

"We've been at s-sea," Petey answered. He turned and stared at me, then looked beyond. I turned to see a boat-big Buick behind us at the end of the driveway, rusting, half hove-to up on cinder blocks. All its tires missing, like they were rolling along the U.S. highways far from here waiting for the car to catch up. Cobwebs were settled like ghost turds in the corners of its smashed-out windows.

"It's a ghost car, and the k-k-kid's in it!" Petey hissed.

Terror then, and us running all the way to the beach, lurching the boat between us on our bone-bumped shoulders. We dropped it twice. Before we launched it the second time, Petey whispered to the boat that it was hereby being rechristened the *Little Andy Foley.*

Right before we launched it Petey took out Linda, City Girl and super-glued her to the front, which Petey called *the bow as in wow, Danny.* Linda, City Girl seemed to be enjoying all this as the smile never left her face even though she was topless and Petey hadn't been able to pry her bright pink high heels from her feet.

We launched it, hopped in.

Petey said his magic tour guide words again, then whispered, "Little Andy Foley, if you're l-l-listening: we say that all the time when we g-go out. Please keep this boat from leaking if you're in h-heaven now, watching us on God's Big Console TV."

A miracle, we made it all the way out to Long Island that afternoon in the recaulked *Andy,* Petey and the sky brightening with every inch from shore. Little slappy waves destroyed Linda, City Girl's hair but still she smiled, *And why wouldn't she,* Petey wondered, *out of the c-city at last and f-finally free of the confines of lookism and sexism.* The colors of the water changed as we progressed, navies and greens and when the sun went in everything transformed again to the point of confounding me just when I had a system. But delight was the common denominator. We looked at each other when the boat made a sliding scud noise coming ashore onto Long Island: delight was in the sound, in Petey's face, in something white and green and blue throbbing inside me.

"We made it, we made it, we made it, we made it!" we chanted, doing an Indian dance in a circle around the boat and never thinking we really would. *Jungian,* Petey said it was all Jungian.

"Oh my God," Petey whispered, once we secured the boat ashore and turned and faced the island. Every instant of our lives had been lived in the shadows of projects and barrooms, triple-deckers and car exhaust, squabbles and boom boxes and bus exhaust and now this: a wave-lap silence; beach and dunes and, beyond, more trees than we had ever dreamed there were in the world.

"Paradise three m-miles from the Broadway Bridge," Petey whispered.

We never thought to run at first—it would have been like racing in church. We wandered the island barefoot like we were the first and it 10,000 miles away—in most ways it was. Wild grapevines brambling everywhere and wave-licked forests, a shut-up lighthouse on one rock-piled hilly edge of the island with a fairy-tale mist around it, a closed-down children's tuberculosis hospital on the island's other end POSTED: KEEP OUT. When Petey drew a map later he named it Constant Coughing Island, which he said was an *allusion* to my mother's Constant Comment Tea, which only came out from behind the old cookbooks on the top shelf for company and her side of the family. *Guineas don't know tea, they know wine,* she'd whisper to me out in the kitchen when Dad's relatives came, serving them the generic cheap stuff. Dad was half-Italian, his mother an Italian woman, squat and suspicious-eyed and built like a quarter and what a row there was when Ma caught her snooping, reading our phone bill out in the kitchen. Dad's father, Irish, had died young which was a shame as Ma liked him, *Whereas that other one will live to be a thousand I suppose,* Ma would mutter.

Petey made us stop there in front of the boarded-up kids' hospital and listen and he made me believe we could hear the voices of the dead children laughing just around the corner, up in the glimmery interstices of those trees right over there and cured at last of coughing.

"Can you h-hear it at all, Danny, the coughing?" Petey asked, his eyes endless.

"Ahhh . . . no."

"See," he said.

A very thick muss of trees and bushes lay around a corner, a conspiring tangle, as if anything might happen within it. We'd never really seen woods before.

"Look," Petey whispered. His body tightened. He turned to me and his eyes were electric. "Woods!"

"Wh... do you do with them?" I asked.

"You go in them," he said. But Petey made me stop again and wait while he explored it ahead of me.

"No s-sense both of us dying if there's trouble in there," he said. "Methinks Morgan le F-Fay might be ensconced in there, ready to a-waylay."

I sat down on an old log and picked at a scab on my knee the shape of Nebraska but sideways. Still no man-hairs on my knee yet, or anywhere else. My smooth flesh seemed eternally impervious to it. But today that didn't matter.

Five minutes later Petey came back. I heard the rubbery half-snap of fallen sumac branches as he came. I looked up. Hard to say what was brighter, the sea-washed sky or Petey's eyes.

"The w-woods are full of bittersweet," he announced. A viny wreath of orange berries circled his black hair and tangled down onto his bare shoulders. I lost my breath because he looked like he'd walked out of a storybook, like this was the real Petey and him having to hide it all these years, the king's son or princeling of the gypsies or something.

"I am the voice of Skovo, King of the Bears," Petey said. "Kneel d-d-down, I say, and pay me homage, and I'll showest thou the t-tern's nest I found in yon tangle."

I followed him through the catastrophe of brambles and sumacs and it reminded me of the Mideast, everyone fighting relentlessly for the same sandy land. So tight we were forced to single file and Petey reached out his hand behind him for me to grab so he could lead me through the leafy jumble. A big puff cloud paused above us and shaded out the world. We stopped. A finger raised to Petey's lips, a pointing, a quiet itchy waiting and the urge to pee and then at last, a carefully raised white and black cap head like a periscope going up.

"The m-mother," Petey whispered. He took my hand in his again. "Lookit, D-Danny."

We ate our bucket lunch that day on a tumbled down seawall facing east and out, the green-and-blue checkered high seas spread before us like our pic-a-nic blanket. Meatball sub for me, cheese sandwich for Petey, both from McGillicuddy's, Petey eschewing meat since his accident and Mrs. Harding in a fit about *the state of his blood, for as anyone will tell you it takes blood to make blood.* My sub cold now but nothing ever better even though its consistency recalled sawdust. The sun it seemed would be in a totally different place every time you looked at it, over here, then way over there on the other side two minutes later. Anything was possible out here. I asked Petey.

"Oh, s-simple: Jolly Olly Orange," he said.

A minute later he spread some of his mother's homemade piccalilli onto his lunch and said, "Danny, lookit, I'm eating with relish." For once I got one of his jokes and I laughed so hard I almost choked.

"This is for you, Andy," Petey said, tossing half his sandwich into the lapping waves a minute later. He never finished a meal. It floated on the surface for a few seconds, like a laugh, then vanished. A burping contest followed. Petey's hands would clutch when he let loose.

"My m-mother says life is a dream," he said. "But what if it's a burp?" And he burped again. The high spirits of him.

The tumbly stone block wall we sat on was splotched with lichens and sun-warm against our bums. Some of the growths were yellow and some white and some a grayish green, and in places they overlapped as some had gone aggrandizing like Napoleon with conquest in mind. There were thousands of them but none of them seemed to look like states I knew. Instead they looked like ancient crusty countries lost to the memory of people. Petey said his mother claimed the lichens gave prophetic dreams back in Ireland when used in a tea, and maybe we'd see our future that night for sitting on them. He didn't pluralize *future*. A buoy dinged like a hypnotist on TV right offshore ten yards away. We could smell the sun sizzling our shoulders, but benignly. Nothing could be bad this day. In between Petey's toes was very white. The rest of him was sea-flesh pink. Petey's eyes turned greener, his hair blacker, as his skin reddened. He never tanned but got golden instead and became once more the Golden Boy but only I could see. My idea of where I lived zoomed out exponentially. Southie no longer ended at the boulevard but continued on to Spain and Ireland, like Petey said Cadiz, to the lurking, shining places right before one would get to Ireland and Spain.

"I still see the diamonds," I said, pointing out to the dazzling water.

"As I say, that's p-part of the curse," Petey explained, immediately and briskly. "Once you've s-s-seen them, you always see them. Give thanks to God if they don't inspire the tr-treasure lust in you. By which of course I mean gr-greed and snatchericity."

The next week we told our mothers the old we-were-sleeping-over-the-other-one's-house and camped out on Long Island one August moon night so that on the next day we could expand farther out with such a head start. Fortunately Ma was on a mood upswing that day and grudgingly fell for it. We arrived at Long Island just at sunset and the world behind us a melting masterpiece of purple and silver and gold. We ate Pop-Tarts and made a fire over which we shook hell out of Jiffy Pop. I fell asleep to the Further Adventures of Skovo, a story Petey would pick up every now and again, like his mother her knitting. I awoke at three to a wildness of silver, the moon on the water, in my eyes and dreams. In what was one of my last boyish instincts, I wanted to go home. Petey said we couldn't anyway. The poisonous Portugese jellyfish came out at night and would get us on the way back. Get us good, he said, especially in the nuts should the boat capsize. That was enough—I stayed.

"I'm cold though," I mumbled, curling up fetal, the sea air heavy with damp licking into our bedspread tent held up by sumac sticks.

Petey's eyes became liquidy.

"I'll keep you w-warm, Danny," he said, and he pulled me into him never warmer and I woke up once and he was stroking my red crew cut in his sleep and something hard pressed against my never-warmer flank. A sad, cleaving history of the world written in gestures like these, but us not knowing it yet and I slept the sleep of the deeply loved with the outside of me never knowing.

We made it to Spectacle Island after a dawn of sea roving. We had to keep looking back at Boston because the sunrise was turning the city into liquidy golden sun and it liked that picture so much it made another one like it dripping in the water shine around us. Petey said he couldn't decide if the gargantuan fair-weather clouds were galleons or castles, and he finally decided they were galleons hauling castles.

"There's people like ants scurrying to work n-now in that city and they can't see it," Petey said.

"They're part of it b-but they can't see it. Isn't that f-funny. They can't see the p-p-people for the ants."

The only weird part was I had to do number two outside when we first woke up on Long Island, and use leaves to wipe up matters. Petey said the world would be a better place if everyone did it like that often. It would keep people humble no matter what they did and drove.

"Don't look n-now but someone's done their poopsters," Petey said when I came back from the woods. "Don't turn red, Danny—I did m-mine too while you were gone, and now we're no b-better than the stray dogs. But that's okay because there's nothing nobler."

Spectacle Island was our next port o' call and it proved even more deserted and we found a beach on the ocean side and went swumming. Someone official or maybe just officious passed by on a boat with a bullhorn, and a dog on the bow, and said something rendered unintelligible as the dog began yelping hysterically. But the message was clear. We weren't supposed to be there. Petey gave him the finger and then we ran into the woods and hid. Petey explained he had given the finger to the *idea* of the man and authority, not the man himself and certainly not the dog. He said when we emerged from the trees later we shouldn't wear our bathing suits when we went swimming again, so we didn't; felt like I was swimming for the first time, the water seeking out the mysteries of me, my thing rubbery and waving back and forth underwater with the whim of the current and it looked, and felt, as if it was laughing. I kicked my legs out further to give egress and thought it might be an occasion of sin but I kept doing it, feigning ignorance. I was ignorant.

Afterwards we laid on the sand and compared our bodies like we'd done all our lives. I put my two hands around Petey's thighs with my fingers a-spread like I was measuring a tree trunk to see if his were wider than mine. They were the same again still. So were our arms again. And our feet, we slapped them up against each other. Petey said he wanted to see my bum and I stood up, turned around, and showed him. He rubbed it for a little while to get the sand off and I started laughing and dove back into the water, which was not just one color but all colors, and the smooth pebbles and golden sand grains beneath magnified through the waveryness like kind old people's eyes when they're wearing glasses.

"We're the same p-person," Petey said when he came up for air. He'd dived in right after me. We'd talked about this before the accident but never since and it felt good to hear it again but I wasn't sure.

"Did you w-wait until the water was l-looking back at you before you dove in, as I s-suggested?"

Petey always asked me that.

"Oh jeez, I forgot this time."

We got back in the boat by and by and hit the high seas again, as Petey said there were epiphanies awaiting. The fair weather puffballs above us laid anchor, drifted, exploded slowly, brilliant whites and brilliant grays sieving the slant sun rays, all without a peep. A few cottony-wool ones slung away to the east, to the high seas, that might have been only mist.

"Miasma," Petey said, seeing where my eyes were. "But g-good miasma."

"Miasma de Miami," I said, pleased I'd remembered something from one of Petey's maps.

"It's Mustafa," Petey said, but still I got that smile.

Petey said, "Lookit, Danny—wait—lookit that l-li'l island over there. It's g-got . . . it's got like a little indent or inlet or something. Whatever you c-call it. A canal."

We made for it. We got closer and went up it in our boat, this tongue of .shining seawater cutting into the island. Petey announced that he had it. It was a *penetralia*. Maybe it was a river. It got narrower as we went up it, by and by stabilized at about ten yards wide. The current slowed to a suggestion. Drifting commenced. The trees closed in on the banks either side like they wanted to jump in to go swumming. Over our heads, the trees met, they almost met, they met, they almost met, and result of this was that the sun came down all dapply on our bodies, on the boat, on the brine. Like we were traveling by vessels and arteries to the heart of something wondrous and chartreuse and private. The trees thickened above, commingled and confabbed, and the light stretched syrupy. The sun filtering through the trees and, Columbus-like, we discovered the colors of things were lime and yellow, edged with a wobbling dark where the shaded reflected water was. Petey's face flushed up with a silent sunburnt bliss. The whites of his eyes shone through the limelight, like the stray dogs at night a-raiding the ashcans when the car lights sweep up the driveway and morph peepers into prisms. For once not thinking the world belonged to grown-ups and us just borrowing it 'til we became them ourselves. For once this was ours all ours. It was enough. It was much more than enough.

We lay flat in the boat, face up, Petey's feet lean-to against the edges of my head. The sun off the water where it leaked through the trees shimmery all around us, and it reflected onto the trees above and beside us. Wavery, gobby. You could tell we were floating in water just by looking up at the trees above is what I mean to say, whereas the land doesn't know how to do such things with light. The *Little Andy Foley* slowly drifted along this canaly thing of its own tender volition.

"T-tunnel of love," Petey murmured. "Cozy Cove, I dub you. I'll s-say it again, Danny Boy, people wouldn't want to murder if they c-could do this instead. No more wars if they were m-made to do this. Peace conferences should be held here. But one thing I always w-wondered, why don't they hold peace conferences b-before a war instead of after?"

He leaned a moth-white finger outside the boat and lazily traced circles in the water. He was always doing that. They spread out and then became one with the flow of water and light. The sun hit his sea-slicked hair and lit up for an instant his indent. Heart-shaped it looked, almost.

We got closer to the other side of the island. This thing was like a canal cut right through its heart. A tunnel of lime-yellow light, you could look through it and then see its end through the arch of trees, see the bright shining sea water and an endless sky beyond.

"Our future," Petey announced, waving his whole hand, like the lady-models who displayed prizes of toasters, jars of popcorn, new cars, on game shows.

We hushed with beauty, clammed up as the clouds and all of us drifting. The current sifted us finally back into the Sea, on the other side of the island. There seemed to be a sweet music in the air that we just barely couldn't hear.

We paddle-drifted home that twilight, not in silence, not in talk, but in occasional licks of laughter. We had seen a great and beautiful thing.

A gasp of Petey breath a little later and I thought it was the sunset flaring behind the Boston skyline as we came in, but when I looked back at him his head looking behind, and behind that the moon, full, just there like it always had been but not there a minute before. Pink and whole, dripping its color into the darkening mystery of a sea behind us. A few puffball clouds lit up around it like an entourage.

"Stop rowing, Danny," Petey whispered, but I had already, with wonder.

The silence of it. A flock of something raced across the face of the moon, and their squawk was like to break my heart with beauty. One just one moment, I was given Petey eyes.

"I think I'm r-ready now, Danny," Petey said after a bit. "Ready to tell you another Button Man story. I'll tell you the Indian Princess story."

And he did too, while the veil of night lifted, and the ho-hum sky became star-streaked universe.

We came upon another island, way out, one day some day another day. Some day, a day in that stream of days, the days we went to the islands. A Tuesday afternoon, a Wednesday afternoon, a blue-bright Thursday morning. The whole world *filleting souls with its weary r-roars and entanglements,* Petey said, but out here only sea, sky, sand. A little breeze gushing off the water, the islands beckoning like unopened presents. A gull cry every now and again, and a soft lapping of things.

As we approached the deserted island it could have been 10,000 BC.

"A m-million years ago," Petey said, reading my thoughts again, or perhaps the same thoughts shining down. We rowed for the island automatically. It was understood, understood genetically, anyone would.

"I don't think anyone's ever been here," Petey said. There were no build-ings, no driftwood even, no mark of people's messes. As the *Little Andy Foley* skidded ashore, there was no reason to refute him. A eureka was around Petey. He couldn't contain it. He had to jump from the boat and run, run laughing. He came back to me again and again, only to take off, except once he lingered long enough to close his eyes, spread his arms and declaim, *I claim all these lands for Queen Birdy!*

"Oh w-wait," he said, laughing and shrugging. "Birdy already owns all this." Then he vanished again.

When I finally finished dragging the boat ashore, I gave chase, following his sand-prints. He'd vanished over a small dune, a fold on the island's silky skin. I came upon him and he was pacing now, deliberately, across the sand; stopping now and again, his head cocked. Then a smile and nod, a beckon-ing wave to me, and then he resumed his funny walk.

"What are you doin'?" I asked. The happiest I'd ever seen him?

"L-listening."

He tilted his head down again, the black hair shadowing his sunburn.

"I'm listening, Danny. I f-feel the earth has something to say, and I'm lis-tening as best I can. You have to be barefoot. The earth w-will talk to us in barefeet, si-singing through our bodies. Try it."

"Jesus, Petey, I'd rather eat. Starving now, aren't you?"

"Pl-please?"

"Okay."

What the heck, I was barefoot anyway.

"The Universe," Petey said, whispering now, "the World, is song, and only wants us to sing back. That's all, just s-sing back."

We stood still side by side, the gush playing with the threads of our cut-off dungarees.

"Close your eyes and ears and l-listen," Petey said.

Petey, he could really almost get you to start believing all this wacky stuff. I could almost feel a million years of tides oozing up my legs, through my sea-slicked calves and into my thighs, my guts. Moons and half-moons and new moons. Lavishings of storms. Landing parties of jillion starfish un-der stars so bright they turned midnight to midnight blue. A shipwreck once but not what you'd think, one of cavemen's canoes.

"Aha!" Petey murmured, his eyes still closed. "Skovo's been here."

Then suddenly "Run, Danny!" and he took off, me chasing.

"Danny this is S-Sanctuary Island," Petey panted when I finally caught up to him. He was sprawled on his stomach where a dune hill sloped down to a grassy patch toward the other end of the island. He was staring intently at a little white flower.

"Or maybe we'll call it Begin Again Island," he mumbled. "Danny this is trailing arbutus. A very endangered plant. B-but it knows it can begin again here. Don't you?"

Petey rolled over onto his back and I flopped down on the sand beside him, the twirl of the white puffies above us in the blue endlessness overhead.

"Ah—"

"Do you know w-why, Danny?"

Petey propped up on one elbow and looked at me.

"Why what?"

"Why this is Sanctuary Island?"

"No."

This close I could always see the golden flecks in his hazel-green eyes.

"This is important, D-Danny. You know, almost every c-culture speaks of a Fl-Flood, a Great Disaster that wiped out almost everyone. It might c-come as a plague, or a weather ph-phenomenon, or a terrible scourge of war where even children are shown no m-mercy.

"Usually God gets the blame for all this. But Danny, listen, we bring it on ourselves. We do it to ourselves. We forget that we belong to each other. That we belong to the world, rather than the other way around. And so we kill, and pollute, and hate, and h-hoard while others starve."

His eyes looked beyond my sun-burning shoulder.

"Something's coming again, Danny. Something awful."

"Do you think?" I asked.

"Duh! Every day you see the signs in the p-papers. A thousand octopus dead on this beach, thirty whales dead on that beach on the other side of the world. Diseases jumping between animals and p-people, whole species of trees being wiped out by a new blight. American chestnut, American elm, flowering dogwood, Canadian hemlock, white birch, mountain ash—they're all gone, Danny, or going. And every one of these in-incidents is treated as if it were a freak, an unrelated occurrence. *Gee, scientists are puzzled, we don't really know why all those whales washed up on shore. Gee, the polar ice cap is melting, and we don't really know why.* But the world is roiling, Danny. It's thrashing as we p-pinch and twist the howling nipples of Mama Earth, m-milking her for all she's worth."

"I know it, Petey, but—"

"And then you have wars and h-hatred. A Mugloid stepping out of a limo, reading updated war reports with satisfaction. He skims over the reports of c-collateral damage, and meanwhile an eight-month-old fetus inside a running mother gets vaporized. Danny, that kind of thing can't happen without an equal and opposite effect. It's just Natural Law. The world is turning again, Danny. It's like right before my accident. Something's coming. When it happens, if we're sp-spared, we'll come out here, me and you."

"Jesus, Petey, do you really—"

"We'll start the human r-race all over again, Danny. But in our world, trailing arbutus will be riding in the limos."

"Ah . . . wait a minute there, Petey. I think you know as well as I do it takes a boy and a girl to keep the race going."

He met my eyes again and smiled.

"Don't worry, Danny." A chuckle floated out of him and I was glad his dark mood was over. "With Skovo, all things are possible."

"We'll come b-back every day," Petey vowed as we rowed away from the island four hours later, a green and vermilion sunset spangling around us. But somehow we never did, not once, and by the end of the week school had started.

I remembered Petey's words when, some years later, his paper route bag slung over his shoulder was heavier with tales of a new war. I saw him on his bike out delivering. He was leaned to the right with the weight of them, his teeth gritted.

"The Liberation of Kuwait has b-begun," he sighed when he saw me. He stopped and pointed to the headline. He looked in the gutter for something to kick but couldn't see anything.

"Just when some trash would be h-handy," he said. "But you know what that means, Danny, right?"

"What?" I asked. "Freedom?"

That's what everyone was saying. Already American flags were popping up everywhere, like mushrooms.

Petey made a face.

"Not exactly. What it really means is a whole shitload of p-people are in for it."

Moonlight and Man-Hair

Oh it's a marvelous night for a moon-dance,
with the moon all aglow in your eyes,
a fantastical smooshing of Skovo,
and the Mugloids all cut down midsize—

Mid-September, still warm in the evenings, the curtains in the dining room where I'd do my homework all fluffery, billowy in the breeze and the warm, yeasty smell of the sea like ghosts murmuring in the corners of rooms.

Of course it could only be Petey, outside, calling for me. He didn't stutter when he sang which was weird and my mother quick-treading from wherever she'd been to launch an investigation. It was just thinking about getting dark outside. Balm of balminess.

"What's that singing when you're doing your homework?" she asked, her nose uplifted like an animal's sensing danger.

"Singing . . . I didn't hear no singing."

"You didn't hear *any* singing."

"You're right, I didn't."

When I die, bury me,
hang my balls from a cherry tree,
Walk right by, take a bite,
Don't be surprised if you die that night.

Petey was growing bolder in the face of my mother's antipathy.

"*I knew it!* It's *him!* How *crude!*" Ma intoned, though there was a joke she told once a year when her girlfriends came over for their Christmas party in

A Map of the Harbor Islands
Published by The Haworth Press, Inc., 2006. All rights reserved.
doi:10.1300/5677_09

November, about a woman and a horse and a guy with a harelip, and the punchline was *twat twat twat,* which I didn't get 'til later but I always heard her say before she told it, *I hope Danny isn't listening.*

"Ho, no, you're not going out on a school night, mister," Ma announced as I sneaker-sprang through the Dad-and-TV-ridden parlor and out the front door.

"I'm just gonna talk to him," I called back, but rare thing, fate intervened in a positive way. The phone rang with theatrical timing and it was Ma's shut-in cousin Mary Donnelly from Buffalo and that was always good for at least an hour and usually two. *Cripes my teeth hurt from talking,* Ma'd say upon hanging up.

"No t-time," Petey said when I came down the front steps. "C'mon, Danny, no time!"

"What is it? What?" I asked.

"The moon! The m-moon!"

"What's with the oatmeal?"

"My drum," Petey said, a big round empty box of Quaker Oats tucked under one arm.

"What about the moon?" I asked on the way to the beach. Screen doors and windows open, inside and outside blending on the sidewalks car radios and living-room game shows and the clatter of kitchen cleanup.

"I told you in school today. You d-don't remember?"

"Oh. Oh yeah. You said it was . . . full tonight?"

Petey nodded his head quickly. At least he wasn't wearing stripes and plaids mixed tonight, which was always a good thing when I'd be seen with him. See there was a certain way of dressing now—

"All day I've been f-feeling it," Petey said. "Seeing it. C'mon, run!"

I didn't care what it was. I was sprung free.

Sun-sinking had occurred behind the skyline back of us by the time we reached the beach. We vaulted the seawall and after going down a ways we plopped on the still-warm sand, our backs resting against the toasty seawall and us facing the ocean. An occasional jogger or couple plodded by behind us. Otherwise we had this lovely part of the universe to ourselves. Before our eyes the sky turned silver, then purple, then a velvety navy blue.

"It won't be long now," Petey said, rubbing his palms together.

"What's occasional furniture?" I asked Petey. I had waited out in the car that afternoon after school listening to the radio while Ma went into a big store down in Quincy with a sign out front that said OCCASIONAL FURNITURE.

"You f-fornicate on it," Petey said, laughing. *"For-an-occasion."*

"Really?" I asked, somewhat appalled.

"Oh Danny," Petey said to me. Sympathetically? He put a hand on my hair and tousled it, his eyes getting serious like his strays.

Then he looked away quick and consulted his watch. The late summer evening gush-wind did things with his black hair, mimicking what he'd done to mine. The color of the sea was a silver green, and it was flatter than glass. A quietness, amazing how something as big as the sea can be so quiet, times.

"Fifteen more m-minutes 'til showtime," Petey said. "Danny, listen to me—all day long I've been feeling it."

"Yeah, me too," I said, grabbing my bits and pieces through my sweat-pants. Petey stared, turned red, turned away.

"Okay, just kiddin', go ahead."

Petey jumped up in his excitement.

"It's coming—the moon is coming. Can't you feel it coming?

"I guess," I said, pulling my knees up to my chest. It was grand to be out, liberated from homework and the confining web of my parents' nightlife, Dad in the parlor with the TV way up, then with a silent burst out to check on his darlings, his peonies and roses, during commercials; Mom here there and everywhere, busy when there was really nothing to do and me the whole time trying to figure out fractions at the dining room table while a part of me must keep track of every parental coming and going, especially when they kissed which they did whenever they passed each other.

"We get m-myopic," Petey said. "It's gonna rise from that spot r-right there in . . . twelve minutes now, that spot right between Long Island and Spectacle Island. But it's not just full here, Danny. Full all over the place, all over the w-world. What it sees. What it's shining on. Those are the th-things that make this a Global Community. Not Globalization. Not gr-greedy business."

"Ahhh . . . yeah, I know it."

Petey stood up, put his hands on his hips, stared out, stared back at me.

"There should be a law, that every f-full moon everyone comes out of their houses and goes to some communal place, even if it's just a parking lot—to watch, to s-sing and rejoice. Maybe no more war then."

"Maybe," I said, gulping back a yawn.

"I m-mean, right now . . . oh my God, Danny."

Petey had to sit down again with the weight of his thought. He looked seven in this light, or seventy.

"Think about this, Danny. Right now it's shining high in the sky on . . . a funny mosque onion t-tower in Istanbul. The Bosporus all murky-choppy-silvery."

"And the Bosporus would be . . . ?"

"A body of w-water separating East from West. Site of many the ancient empire. Cr-crossroads of the world! Oh, I can use that in a m-map."

Petey took out his little notebook from his back pocket and started scribbling.

He turned to me when he was done, his face flushed, the eyes electric.

"All day I could f-feel it coming, Danny. This m-morning during English, I *knew* it was rising just then over the Russian steppes. I could f-feel it, Danny, I could see it. I could see during English a Russian p-peasant couple standing in their d-doorway of their blue door, watching it. It was c-coming up over harvested fields. At lunchtime I thought, the Sahara, the Sahara, rising over the desert d-dunes now. A cheer g-goes up from a Bedouin camp, the d-dancing and drumming begin. Elsewhere in the desert there's no one to see it, but it floods the desert with l-light just the same and God s-sees that it's good. Every grain of sand turns into glass, the way it's done for a billion years. Ants launch out of holes and get b-busy doing ant things. The night animals in the savannas south of the Sahara sift out of their grassy lairs to do n-night stuff. The moon is in their eyes, D-Danny, reflecting in their m-mirror-green eyes, and something inside them is both aroused and pl-placated at the same time."

"Ahh . . . you think so?"

I wondered who was pitching for the Red Sox tonight.

"I *know* so. And then, and then all afternoon, the p-pull on me got stronger, Danny. When we got out of school I *knew, just knew,* swelling huge mustard c-colored over the lavender fields of Pro-Pro-Provence. The bees, drunk on purple smell, stay out later, moon-drunk-dancing in the lavender fields. French bees—rude to American bees? *Mais oui!*"

"May we what? Where's Provence?"

"Fr-France, Danny. Southern France."

"I see London, I see France, I see someone's underwear in Provence."

"They're purple but not from p-purple plum poopsterinis," Petey said. "Purple from lavender smell. And then when I was d-doing my paper route, D-Danny—"

Petey lowered his voice, put his hands on his knees, leaned in closer to me like he was telling me the most important thing in the world, "This image came into my head of the moon, the r-rising moon shining electric blue and green on icebergs in the North Atlantic . . . what a sight! Danny, listen, you have to know I'm not making any of this up. That's the most important part. The *mostest* important part."

Just that afternoon Petey had been made to stay after for refusing to change *mostest* back to *most* in a composition he had written, insisting that everyone knew it was more emphatic that way, and this fact precluded any other considerations of *a-alleged right or wrong. Language like the S-Sabbath was made to serve m-man, not the other way around* but Sr. Marie would have none of it. *You'll thank me the longest day you live for correcting you now.*

No I won'test, Petey kept repeating.

"What I m-mean, Danny," Petey continued, getting more excited, "is that I call on the moon. I do. A person-to-person call. And the moon calls back. Loving-God-created-thing to loving-God-created-th-thing. I make a m-mental connection to it, and it shows me what's it's d-doing, where it's rising, what it's shining on. Anyone could do that. I just empty my m-mind and it sends me these images. Because I've asked it to."

"Huh."

"Danny, listen, it's almost time. Right over there is where she's going to c-c-come up. Watch it. Soon, five m-minutes I think. It's just come up right to the east of us, off Cape Cod. Portuguese fishermen are coming home n-n-now across Provincetown Harbor. The sky is p-purple, Danny, and they're looking at the moon with quiet eyes. I know this."

Petey started tom-tomming on his Quaker Oats drum, making these funny noises. I turned around to see if anyone was watching.

"Danny l-listen, we live in a world where there's more and more d-d-disconnect. Funny huh? When we got phones and satellites, but everyone feels more and more i-i-isolated. We don't know the people next door. We don't know the n-name of the tree growing in front of our house. The birds that s-sing in it. So when there's no more birds singing because of global community pollution and loss of habitat we d-don't even notice, because that's not as important as the Midnight Madness sale down at Wal-Mart. Birdy, we've forgotten all about Birdy. We're l-lonelier than ever. More isolated. What do you th-think the answer to that is?"

"Ahhh . . . I don't know."

"Well what d-do you think?"

"I ahhh . . . never really thought about it to tell you the truth."

"The antidote to that is b-being connected, Danny. To life. To each other. Living in the now. Noticing things. Like . . . l-like how blue your eyes are in this light. That streak of red in the sky behind you that's the same color as your hair when the sun shines on it out in the harbor. The warm breeze now that's going up my shorts to . . . g-going all the way up my shorts. Those s-seagulls over there, intent on s-seagull business. Can't that be as important as the current scandal running in the papers every day? Depressing us all? *Seagulls doing seagull things last night on City Point Beach!* The headline should read. Why c-can't that be as significant as this other crap that no one will remember a year from now?"

"I know it."

"Danny, l-listen, every single thing we notice in the now is a strand that connects us, Danny. Don't laugh, Danny. Please don't laugh at m-me. Everyone else in the w-world can but not you."

"It's . . . I'm not, Petey! It's . . . it was a nervous laugh. Not even a laugh, somethin' halfway between a laugh and a cough. I got a little cough is all."

I coughed again.

The way he was lurking his eyes at me—

"I'm . . . I'm sorry, Petey."

I put my arm out and pulled him into me, beside me. I wanted to hug him to me sometimes the way you'd hug a dog. Then other times I wanted to push him away. Petey giggled, then thought better of it and hushed up. The funny thing was, he still looked sometimes like the Golden Boy, the straight-A star athlete, and sometimes I almost thought this was all a dream or an act. Almost.

Then the moon came up right then in front of us, purple and veiny and swollen, like the Wizard of Oz's head.

"Jesus Christ," Petey whispered. He was trembling.

It really was amazingly beautiful. For at least five minutes we sat there and watched it slide up the sky in unseeable increments.

"Do you think, Danny," Petey whispered, "do you think right now in a cornfield out in Iowa there's two best fr-friends, waiting on the moonrise, and one of them is saying to the other, who doesn't really believe it, *Right now it's r-rising over the beaches of South Boston, and two best friends are holding each other, watching it?*"

"Ah, get outta here!" I laughed, pushing him away a little.

Petey said an hour later down the beach still but sitting out on the rocks getting *moonrays* as he called them—we were wearing just our cutoffs cuz we'd gone in for a *moon-swum*—"Danny, d-do you have any man-hair yet?" and I didn't, but redheads are late the doctor told me. I'd asked him finally at my last *cough* physical. But Petey did—I'd seen it at the beginning of the summer when we wore shorts for the first time, when we went skinny-dipping that time, a line of it running up his legs and on his forearms between his wrist and his elbow, black and dangerous-looking and beyond me. I was hoping mine when and if would be black too but I had the horrible belief they it be red because Petey's oldest brother, Donnie, a redhead like me, had red man-hair on his arms and legs, whorls of it, like the twirly cyclone stuff on top of barbed wire fencing around industrial buildings on the West Side.

"Ahhh . . . not yet," I answered.

"Don't worry, Danny," Petey said. "Don't worry."

I shrugged.

"No moon, no man," Petey said.

"Huh?"

"I was r-reading this book about the moon last week, or m-maybe a few years ago, and it said how some ancient culture—I forget which now—thought a baby boy b-born during the dark of the moon would never m-make it to manhood—*No moon, no man,* they believed."

"What's the dark of the moon?" I asked, suddenly nervous.

"Strictly sp-speaking, it's when we can't see the m-moon, right before it becomes a new moon, which is when it's all slivery and getting smaller every night. In the br-broader definition, it's the time between the full moon and the new moon."

"Oh."

Clear as mud, as Mrs. Harding would say. Jesus, where did he come up with all this stuff?

"Do you like Noreen?" I asked Petey after a minute. All talk and thought of man-hair and things like that eventually led to a perusal on my part these days of the charms of this particular girl in our class.

"Noreen *B-Butler?*"

"Ah, yeah. Her."

Petey stared at me for a bit but I didn't meet his eyes.

"She's a bully though. She was one of the ones who used to make f-fun of some of the other kids. She's like head of that little tough girl g-gang with their white l-lipstick and everything."

"I know it but I think . . . ahhh . . . I think she's changing. I think she's a nice person deep down, like."

Finally I snatched a look at Petey and his eyes were big, unreadable, fixed right on me. His mouth was open like he'd just been thwacked in the back of the head.

"It must be v-very deep," Petey mumbled. He crossed his arms across his bare chest.

"Well I think . . . see, don't tell anyone, Petey, but her father beats her and her mother sometimes, I think. I betcha that's why she like . . . acts so tough."

"How d-do you know that?"

I shrugged.

"How?" Petey repeated in a mumble. His voice sounded soggy all of a sudden.

"Well one time I was . . . after school I heard them all fighting, and heard Noreen crying and . . . stuff crashing around like."

"You did? Where were you when you heard all this?"

"Ahhh . . . out in her driveway."

"What were you doing out in her d-driveway?"

Petey shifted and the moon on the water behind him all silvery and I couldn't see his face anymore.

"I just . . . I . . . I followed her home from school one time."

"You did?"

"Ahh . . . yeah."

"H-how come? Why?"

I found that I was picking at a piece of lichen on the rock we were sitting on.

"I dunno. I just did."

Petey opened his mouth, then shut it.

"But the next day in school," I added, "she was wearing a turtleneck and had a lot of makeup around her neck and when Sister Janice told her to take it off and change into her uniform in the girls' room, she wouldn't. And then she went home but I think she was crying when she left. I think there was a big bruise there, that's why she wore the turtleneck."

We sat in wave-lappy silence for a bit. I didn't know why but I could feel like this . . . wall of tension between me and Petey now, almost like you wanted to hold your breath. I wanted to tell Petey that when I saw Noreen outside through the school window running home when it looked like she was crying, this . . . like big thing rose up in my throat and I wanted to . . . hold her, like. Make it all better. Beat the shit out of her father.

But . . . I don't know—it was weird. It was like I couldn't tell him that. For some unknown reason, and odd as it seemed, I could tell Petey didn't want to hear that.

"So . . . you don't like . . . really like her then," I said after a minute.

Petey didn't answer at first. I saw him look at me again, then look away.

"You're a g-good . . . it's really nice of you to . . . feel b-bad for her and everything," he finally answered. He hung his head a little. "But . . . no, I guess I don't . . . really l-like her all that much."

It was very quiet again for a bit, except for the little wave-laps. Way from the other end of the beach a police siren shrieked. Then it bled into the night far away. Petey kicked one foot through the water. It made me jump a little. Then he stood up and took two steps toward me. He ran a hand through his hair to get it out of his forehead, then let out a deep breath and said, "Danny, I have m-more hair here."

He slowly stretched down the front of his cutoffs. His fingers were shaking again a little, which was weird because the moon was way up high in the sky now. He shifted into the moonlight to show me a few black curly ones around his pecker, which all of a sudden was bigger and darker than mine—they'd always been about the same size, small and white like edelweiss, clean and bright, thin and floppy and harmless. It was right in front of me, like.

For once I felt Petey had gotten ahead of me since his accident (he was always ahead of me Before) but I said nothing. One more thing however to consider at night with the lights out and there was so much already.

It seemed very strange though to see his thing, to be reminded that everyone had one (well, everyone had *something*) which you would forget by day riding the bus and in school and so forth.

"You'll g-get them too, everybody d-does, Danny," he whispered. He didn't pull his cutoffs back up right away. His thing shifted a bit in the moon-air, or maybe of its own volition. I was reminded oddly of the creatures in *Aliens* right before they attacked, noiselessly swirling, full of calamitous intent.

"Your thing'll get b-bigger too," he murmured. "Look at the texture of my m-man-hair. It's like . . . m-mossy now that it's damp."

"Do girls get hair down there too?" I asked.

Petey let go his hand and his shorts flopped back against his body with a wet slap.

"How should I kn-know?" he said, looking away, but by October's end I had my first man-hair and I didn't feel like showing my body to Petey anymore because I think his thing always got hard when I did and eventually he stopped asking.

My man-hair was as orange as carrots on the boil.

Birdy with a Boner

That school year we turned bumpy-voiced thirteen. I got a razor and shaving cream among my Christmas booty, but more important limbs and hairs and organs were erupting in jerks. When I screamed now during hockey games my voice had authority and never before. I loved to hear its rasp.

Petey told me that May he knew how to talk to the sea.

I believed him but asked him prove it. I wanted to go right down to the beach after school that afternoon. I was becoming more obvious and certain about things, but he told me it wasn't that simple. You had to wait for the right time. He said things like this were wrapped in *mystery, subtlety, and whim, and s-something else too* and must be approached with a proper spirit. Nighttimes were best, he said. It was also good during storms, or when the moon was just rising especially if it was full, or on your birthday or feast day.

"I m-mean, you d-don't feel like t-talking all the t-time, right? The sea d-doesn't either."

It wasn't until a month later that he showed me. I had the feeling he was getting desperate in his attempts to show me things, his claims getting more outlandish as he sensed me drifting toward a normal boy's Southie adolescence. He needn't have worried. Despite the other friends I had now, see we are loyal to the death here and sometimes—well, once or twice anyway—I pictured me and Petey old, elderly, done with the botheration of wives and kids and both of us doing the things we always had done.

But for now we had finally bumped up against the ass-end of eighth grade. It was the night of our graduation, preceded with a Solemn High Mass, from Gate of Heaven K-8 Grammar School. On the way home from Maureen Murray's graduation party (where there was a couple of bottles of Seagram's and all kinds of making out going on in the damp backyard there behind her garage in the sea-smell shadows, and I found out girls like it as much as boys, but most times they require reassurances before anything happens) Petey brought me down to the beach, his favorite spot down at the beach.

It was the first night I'd fooled around with Noreen, back at the party, Noreen Butler. I'd kissed girls before but Noreen had also let me feel her tits this night o' nights. I got hard the second I did, no transitory period, like a light going on/off. Waiting for so long now to do this kind of thing with anyone really and she the first to step inside My Space, My Erotic Space, a new place inside me where it was peppery hot. A fire blew up inside me that I thought must show on my face. My cheeks hot to the touch. Later peeing in the bathroom, I felt them with one hand as I rubbed tentatively with the other. I finally knew what it meant to be an adult, finally understood ads, related to them. *Yes I'm like the rest of you now, where's my truck, where's my beer, where's my woman?*

"I can't be-believe you k-kissed her," Petey mumbled to me and his shoes on the two-block walk down to the beach after the party. Petey had come out to the garage at one party-point for lemonade and seen us in the act.

"Why not? She's hot, no? I felt her tits too."

A sudden inrush of Petey breath? Or did I just imagine it or was it the approaching sea?

"She's . . . you did? Well, she's . . . she's kinda d-dumb. If you ask m-me. And a bully like I s-said before."

"Well who's asking? You don't think she's hot? Everybody else does."

"But h-how c-can you talk to her? She's st-stupid. She's s-so . . . she's other."

"Other? What's that mean?"

"She's dumb. A dummy. Linda, City Girl on our b-boat is smarter than her."

"No she's not. Besides, I'm not lookin' for no . . . bridge partner. I just want her to put out a little."

I paused to hear those words emerging from my mouth. Yes. Oh Yes finally, here I am.

"She let me feel her tits," I repeated. How dare he rain on my pubescent parade.

"B-but if you d-don't like her as a person, why would you?"

Petey was *upsetting himself* as his mother would say. The fingers balling into fists, the scrunching up of him.

"Why not?" I asked. Getting mad for some reason. "I . . . I do kinda like her. I do."

Petey turned and looked at me.

"What you take into your h-hands, you t-take into your heart," he said.

"Whatever. I do like her though, Petey. She's very nice and friendly."

Saying it like a slap to him.

"She's . . . she's a phony. A f-fake. She's just nice to you b-because she . . . she likes you."

Petey had gotten man-hair and a bigger pecker before I had, but he was still behind me when it came to this girl thing. He'd catch up of course. It was like we were jumping peak-to-peak along two parallel mountain ranges. He'd go on, then me go on ahead until him again.

"Awright, show me. This sea-talking thing."

I wanted to talk about the straps and hooks of Noreen's things, the scorching intricacy of her separate odors and equipage, but I knew it was useless with Petey. I'd have to talk to some of the other guys about it and I would, too.

We hopped the cement seawall lining the Boulevard and walked across the beach, which tonight was a catastrophe of wind-carved lumps. Something different in my walk now tonight and I accentuated it, a manly walk, feeling my nuts swinging through my spread-apart legs.

"What are you walking like an ostrich for?" Petey accused. Little wise-ass.

The sand proved unobliging or maybe it was the burning Seagram's I'd gulped. Sometimes the sand took you right in, welcomed you. Other times it was resistant like tonight. I kept sand-thudding.

"First d-day with your new feet?" Petey wondered.

"Ha ha."

Khakis and a navy blue short-sleeve shirt I was wearing, Petey some ragged street-person jeans and a T-shirt about a rain forest or something. *Petey why you always dressin' like a freakin' slob?* I'd asked him earlier on the way to the party, but he didn't say anything, just kicked at an empty beer can in the gutter. Like I say there was a certain way of dressing now, everyone cool did.

Now the half-moon half-dodging in and out of these gray and navy clouds after the party and Petey had been waiting outside Maureen's house for us to walk to the beach together. For an hour he'd been waiting, sitting on his bum on the edge of the sidewalk like a 'tard. Here at the beach now to see this sea-talking thing and me only half-interested, semihard still from small firm yet jiggly eighth-grade tits. He'd said *I'll show you after the party*. I even saw it on his calendar in his bedroom, *Friday the 17th, show Danny how I talk to the sea*. I didn't need no calendar. I had a calendar in my head and it said *Party Friday Night!*

Moonlight raced across the water, got smudged out, then came back again farther out to sea as if it couldn't find a place to rest finally. May had swollen into June and even the nights were warm now, open, even with the breeze that always licks the ocean's edge like some kind of reminder.

Petey looked up at the sky and took a deep breath, like he was finally getting air. Very high that night, the sky somehow.

"The stars are flying, the w-wind is sighing."

"It's wicked nice out," I agreed.

"Sh-shoes off, Danny. We need bare feet now. Sacred sp-pace."

We never wear socks in Southie much so that part was easy, off flopped my Top-Siders. We'd gotten a little dressy for the graduation and party—everyone but Petey that is, like I say, and that had proved a line of demarcation of almost papal significance. He was shunned at the party, except for Maureen's wigged-out grandmother before she went to bed, who kept telling Petey about the stamp collection she had when she was his age. *Did you know there was a country named French Guinea?* I heard her say to him at one point. And when she cackled after she said that, smoke came out of her mouth. She'd been left to babysit when Maureen's blue-mascara-ed single-parent mother left on a date. *Keep an eye on the kids Ma, Ma, you hear me? You listenin'? Maureen's havin' a few friends over, keep an eye on them*, but within the first five minutes inroads and advancements had been made, and chaos reigned once the liquor cabinet above the refrigerator had been breached. All the girls Omigod-squealing for peppermint schnapps, the boys gulping everything in sight. An entire big-ass bottle of clug-clug-clugging vodka added to the tropical fruit punch Sr. Jeannette had sent over with her CONGRATULATIONS, CLASS OF '86! written on the side of the bowl in something glittery that instantly began falling away in tiny spangling pieces onto the tablecloth after all her nun-effort.

"The sand's st-still warm," Petey said.

"I know it," I said. I wiggled my toes.

"That's b-because the sand holds onto the sun's warmth, like a m-memory. It h-holds onto it and re-remembers in the winter. You can c-c-come down here some winter nights and if the s-sand is thinking about the s-summer, it'll be w-warm. God gave all things memory, Danny, so we could have Christmas in July, roses in winter."

There was a desperation almost in Petey's voice.

"Yeah. I know it."

We walked down to the water's edge, rolling up our pant cuffs. Our legs were long and skinny and even hairier now. Mine orange of course but I was getting used to the idea. My dick was getting bigger by the month so that was a nice consolation. A tape measure under my bed and Ma one time after vacuuming—*What's this doing here when I've been looking all over for it for those drapes I want?*

Tonight it seemed like we were different people than the ones the summer before. We hadn't been out on the boat since then together. I was kinda busy with Junior League Hockey, Pop Warner football practice, the boys, the thrill and alternate nonthrill of thrice-daily beating off and Petey was off on his own weird missions, stray dogs, map making, secret gardening, though sometimes he'd come and watch my baseball games, way off to the side like a stray pencil mark on ruled paper, away from parents and girlfriends and the fat boisterous grandparents wedged into their web chairs and everyone mumbling *Oh what a shame* when they took the trouble to stare after Petey way off quiet like that beside right field on his own, picking his nose or his ass or a flower and the divil take the hindmost as to being watched or not.

"B-breathe," Petey said.

"Yeah, I was forgettin' to do that."

"D-don't be a w-wiseass. D-deep I mean."

"Deep."

I did. Petey's voice was deeper than mine, deep jeep. I thought how Petey would like that phrase but I stayed silent, rearranging my allegiances. Fuckin' not congratulate me like this over getting some tonight.

The moon gonzo again and the ocean with it, and we were on the edge of half the world. You could feel it though, the ocean, its breath raking through our hair, stuffing our mouths with its taste and smell, swirling all around us, that sound.

"In, out, in, out," Petey said as he breathed. "Just like the ocean. Like a-any l-l-living thing. See? Nature repeats her s-successful patterns. In and out."

"Like people fuckin'," I said. I laughed. Petey didn't. His rain forest T-shirt had a small tear near the shoulder, I now noticed, the flesh beneath it the color of the white-pink peonies Dad grew out back and woe to those who threw a football into them.

The moon flashed on again, but way out. You couldn't see it but you could see its beams shining way out, way out at sea, like an airport searchlight but upside down. The dark spaces over the water became vast and expansive and somewhat threatening. It was like watching an uncertain dream of the future.

"Someday the s-sea will take me away to my h-home," Petey said.

Whatever.

"W-way out," Petey said, extending his arm. "Happy Land. S-someday. And you'll be with me, Danny."

And a pig's ass I will, I thought. Like he was talking to himself, reassuring himself. Whatever.

"I am Skovo, King of the Bears, and I wait there. I live there way b-beyond the islands that we don't go to anymore in the place I c-call Happy Land."

Then a sudden spurt of sympathy for him. Little bastard, how he could wrangle my feelings.

"We'll go back," I said, though I was unconvinced of this at this time. "We will."

"T-tomorrow?"

"Ahhh . . . probably not tomorrow there, Petey. I told ahhh . . . I told Noreen I'd bring her to the beach tomorrow."

Petey silence followed this remark.

"See some of the other kids are goin' too, we made plans. Like a after-graduation beach party?"

"Sounds gross and c-c-conformist. With d-dates?"

"Yeah. What's conformist?"

"The life they got laid o-out for you. The life you're l-livin' now. Doing what you're told."

I said nothing because nothing could dissuade me from eighth-grade tits and Future Possibilities of that ilk. Petey kicked his foot through the water.

"Why don't you come, Petey, and ask Jen Shea? You seen the way she was lookin' at you tonight. Earlier tonight there in the kitchen."

Petey was sodden, sullen.

"Why don't you? She went out with a junior in high school last year. She's a babe." She always liked the weird ones, did Jen, and that was Petey all over nowadays.

"I got b-better things to do with my t-time."

"Suit yourself. I'd go out with her in a heartbeat though. Denny Murphy said one night she put on a strip-show for him down in her basement with this funky disco light and him watching through the basement window."

"Sounds like a b-bad Fellini movie."

"Whatever that is."

"It's a b-bad Fellini movie, like I said. Speak'a the English?"

"Alright, so you're fuckin' smarter than me and I'm ignorant."

A noise out of Petey then and he turned away from me quick—a sob, .pulled back quick?

After a while I said, "You alright?"

"Just . . . I don't w-wanna do this!"

"What, hear the sea talk? Fine by me, this was all your idea—"

"No, ar-ar-argue!"

He held up his palm.

"Leave me alone for a m-minute, Danny. Just leave me alone, for a m-m-minute."

"Whatever."

He started walking away, then stopped after only a few feet. This big-ass sigh out of him, I could see his shoulders go up, down, with the power of it. He ran his hands through his hair, which was too long, longer than any of us were wearing it now.

"I . . . I didn't mean anything, Petey. I only thought you should take Jen Shea to the beach tomorrow and hang with us, you'd probably have a—"

"I'M NOT GONNA TAKE J-J-JEN SHEA OR ANYONE ELSE TO THE FUCKING BEACH TOMORROW!" he roared, vaulting around.

Both of us staring at each other now. Him panting, me with my mouth open. His eyes wet?

I looked away first.

"Alright fine, don't bring Jen Shea to the beach tomorrow. Fine. Forget about it. So you gonna talk to the sea or what? I gotta pee."

Petey turned to me and glaring commenced again. The moon slurred off and all I could see was his outline, a suggestion of him, like the instant before he'd been created. He'd gotten taller, I suddenly noticed. In the dark he could've been anybody, like when you're young and your mother brings you into the bathroom to pee at midnight, and when she puts the light out on the way back to your bedroom and you're blind for a second, a throbbingly illuminated monstrous blackness takes her place.

Another deep breath out of him like he was trying to calm down.

"You . . . alright. Alright. You c-can't rush this, D-Danny. I d-don't know if y-you have the r-right frame of mind for this t-tonight. Drunk and all and—"

"Drunk! Who's drunk, I'm not drunk. Just had a few sips is all. I just had a little."

"Whatever," Petey mumbled. "It's oddvious you're not into this."

Petey always said *oddvious* when he meant *obvious*. He did it on purpose.

"I am I am, I just gotta pee is all."

"Well g-go ahead and pee then. N-no wonder you sound *pee-vish*."

"Ha ha. I'll be right back."

I lurched back up toward the street and peed against the seawall, trying to write my initials with it, then Noreen's. It recalled a joke Dad had told about somebody's pee in somebody else's handwriting and finally I got it now. My thing felt rubbery and alive, as if it were plotting things for now. Couldn't wait to get home and beat off, both me and It couldn't wait, something real finally to think about, my hot spurty white stuff all over Noreen's firm creamy tits and then making her walk down the street like that, point out to everybody she met, Fr. O'Shea, Mrs. McGuiness who owns the bakery, *Look what Danny did to me!* and her rubbing the stuff in, smearing it all over—

Relieved, I wove back down to the water's edge. I saw a shadow and made for it, Petey.

"F-feelin' better?"

"Much. You?"

"There was n-nothing wrong with me."

Petey said the words like he was pissed, like we had another argument while I was gone.

"I know it. I'm just kiddin'. Calm down, alright?"

"I'm c-calm."

"I'm glad to hear you say so. Okay then. I'm ready. Are we ready?"

"It's not that s-simple, D-Danny. One must . . . pr-prepare oneself. Okay. We have to s-scoop up some water now."

Petey bent down to the water and filled his two pressed-together hands with a bit of ocean, then poured it over his head.

"All water is the s-same, Danny. The trickly streams run into b-brooks and the b-brooks run into r-rivers and the rivers run to the s-sea. The sea e-evaporates and m-makes the clouds. The clouds rain down their w-water, and fill the trickly streams . . . and the whole g-gorgeous poignant cycle starts again."

"I see."

"C'mon, do it. Scoop up some w-water and pour it over your head."

I hesitated because Ma would notice if my shirt was wet and then there would be Questions.

"Okay," I said. I took off my shirt and threw it behind me, where it landed muffed up. The wind started playing with it, puffing it. When I turned back around Petey was staring at my right nipple. Something heavy and unseen fell down between us. He kept staring. He reached his hand out, stopped halfway, then kept going. Two rubbery fingers fell against my nipple and pinched.

I didn't say anything but I stepped back. I felt something rise in me, like a thermometer when you're sick, and you can picture it bursting up inside its brittle glassness. I turned away from it in my head.

"Ahhh . . . what about the water? You were saying," I asked after a minute, but my voice was jiggly. I couldn't read Petey's eyes.

"Ahhh . . . also," Petey continued, like he was waking up from something, "all w-w-water t-touches all other w-w-water. It m-moves. Swirling commences. C-c-currents move water all over the w-world. Mingling occurs. The w-water that f-falls into the sea in autumn from Lake Su-Su-Su—"

"Superior," I said, yawning—

"—Is breaking on the coast of Sp-Spain the next spring. And this w-water right here, s-some of it anyway, came from a melting glacier in Siberia, last s-summer or it could be the one before that."

"Irkutsk," I said, mentioning one of the countries they had in Risk up by Siberia. Petey had explained years before, when we used to play Risk taking a break from Monopoly, that this was a place where bear-large Russian women served as wardens when they shoved you gibberish-speaking into a gulag, whatever that was. A stew, I think they ate you.

Petey didn't smile at my allusion but his eyes grew wistful.

"Who . . . who knows where this w-w-water has been," he said.

I stared down at the dark water. Mysterious suddenly. Plotting. Suspicious and foreign. I wondered if foreigners had peed in it, thick orange pee, people with strange headgear and open flaps on their long dirty robes, or when it was steamy, diaperlike short-shorts that would be *none the worse for a washing,* as Mrs. H would say.

"So there's never any new w-water, Danny. It's all the same water, just going r-round and round like. So this w-water here that we t-touch, it's the same water that watered the Gardens of Babylon. It's the s-same water that M-Moses parted. It's the same water that John the Baptist baptized Jesus w-w-with, the same w-water that Jesus turned into w-wine. Sacred. Or slated to be sacred at some later t-t-time. It's the same water that rinsed the parched l-lips of dying heroes at Th-Thermopylae."

That would be Petey. He could always get you to look at a thing different-like, even when you weren't in the mood and your mind fingered the idea of fingers on tits instead.

"So it's old," Petey said. "It's oooooooooold, and it knows things. But always being reborn too. It's like our mother, our f-father. Does it c-care for us? Yes of course. If you know this, you c-can talk to it. Ask it q-questions. Get it?"

"Hey, am I gonna end up gettin' somewheres with Noreen?" I laughyelled into the swirling darkness.

"It's no j-j-joke!" Petey cried, and his getting-bigger hands balled up into fists. He splashed me with his foot and I jumped out of the way.

I'd seen Petey lose his temper plenty of times but not much with me. He got my pants wet and I didn't relish the idea.

"Hey, chill, okay? What the fuck's the matter with you tonight, Petey?"

"Nothing! Wh-what the fuck's the matter with you?"

"You're just . . . I dunno. You seem so . . . you get pissed off all the time now, over nuthin'-like."

"THERE'S NOTHING WRONG WITH M-M-ME!"

"Alright, fine, there's nuthin' wrong with you. What are . . . don't scream at me! That's the second fuckin' time tonight you screamed at me!"

I kicked my foot back at him, splashing him good. He didn't move, except for a pitiful shudder when the cold water hit him. Damn him, one minute he was invincibly pain-in-the-assish—the next defenseless, helpless.

We stood there in clammy darkness, staring from a great distance. Not a flat empty distance but one bump-and-fissure-ridden. All you could hear was the sea, and the panting of our angry breaths.

When I heard Petey's breath slow a little I said, "Okay, c'mon. Show me. I wanna see. I'm sorry I splashed you. I do wanna see. I do believe you, Petey. About talkin' to the sea, I mean. I'm sorry. C'mon."

Petey let out a deep big breath. He looked down at his bare white feet—ridiculous, so white they looked—and shook his head. Then he turned and looked out at the sea. He shoved his hands, still balled, into his nerd-pants pocket.

"Alright," he said finally. But soggy, like his voice had gotten wet too. He turned back to me. "This is wh-what I do. W-wait here."

Petey vanished into the darkness and left me alone. I felt very alone because I couldn't see him and the black swirl of the dark water's edge swallowed him up. I turned back to face the sea. It did feel like a living thing—you could almost feel it pulling you. I fought it. I didn't want to think of this stuff—I wanted to think about Noreen. Besides I was tired and a little groggy from the Seagram's. I wanted to go home and beat off thinking about Noreen and the feel of her tits. The smooth jigginess of them—how they could be solid and loose at the same time—like Petey's thing had been in the hospital when—

—But that was then, kids' stuff and this was now. Growing up now.

A resolution formed in my head. I could feel this. I crossed my arms, then undid them to put my shirt back on.

Petey came back in a few minutes. He was carrying an empty Diet Pepsi plastic bottle that seemed joyful in its squished abnormal shape. He pulled the pen and the little memo notebook thing he always carried with him out of his rear pants pocket, to jot down ideas he had, to write out words when his stuttering froze him and calamity threatened.

"This is w-what I do," Petey said.

He wrote something down on a slip of paper, tore it off, rolled it up, shoved it into the Pepsi bottle. Then he screwed the cap back on and tossed it out onto a wave.

"*Breascheigh go nas gnoc marinach!*" he cried, some gibberish.

"What's all that?"

"Irish w-words Ma'am taught me. You can only d-do this when the t-tide's going out, Danny."

"What did you write?"

"I asked the s-sea a question."

"I thought you . . . I thought like you really talked to the sea like."

"I do, but it doesn't t-talk like people. It talks to m-me in my h-head. In my heart."

Petey was being so serious, I didn't joke him about it. Sensitive tonight. I couldn't believe but really I was wasting my time on this.

"Does the bottle ever come back to you?"

Humoring him now.

"Not y-yet, none of them have. But I get the answer in my h-head like, or in a s-sign."

"Oh."

"I'm hoping s-s-someday there'll be a r-reply. Like a class of children on the coast of Ireland or Spain or Portugal or England will f-f-find it, and then we begin a c-c-cor a cor . . . a dialogue."

"Oh."

I pictured boring letters from overseas nerds. *My sister's name is Muriel. I am ten years old. I have a pet cat named Hector. The autobus takes me to school every day* or whatever. I couldn't be sure what an autobus was but every foreigner seemed to speak of one when you learned their language. It implied a double bus maybe like in London but maybe that was just me.

"I got you a bottle t-too, Danny. Do you w-wanna ask a question? Go ahead, ask a q-question."

Petey handed me another empty bottle and the notebook and pen. His hands were trembling. The pen was skinny and blue with white writing on it, but you couldn't quite read the writing as if it wanted the night off from advertising.

I thought for a minute then wrote something down. I rolled up the paper, put it in the bottle, then heaved it out onto the dark nothing.

"GERONIMO!"

"It's very p-powerful to invoke the names of powerful Native American sages," Petey observed. Sarcastically, but it didn't matter. I didn't get it. That was just something they said in WWII movies before they charged. The moon sliced out again and I could see my bottle, riding up a wave, then riotously down. Then it got black again and everything vanished.

Petey turned to me. The wind lifted up his black hair, then thought better of it and let it go again.

"What d-did you ask, D-Danny?"

"If I was gonna be rich when I grew up. How's about you?"

"Ahhh . . . secret. It's s-secretive."

I opened my mouth to complain, then shut it. The thing was, I really didn't give a shit right then.

"Okay then," I said.

Petey snapped his head to look at me. He waited a while until he said, "Yeah. Yeah I guess we're done."

"Alright then, I'll . . . I'll see you later I guess."

"Yeah. See you l-later, Danny."

I learned something on my walk home that night, alone—Petey said he wanted to stay down by the ocean for a while. I think Petey had learned this thing a few months earlier, and that's why he'd been pissed lately: we weren't the same person anymore.

It wasn't like I exactly wanted it that way—

It was just the way things were working out. Or not.

As I ran across Farragut and Broadway, my jigging sprang a boner. Naw, it wasn't just my jigging, the flopping around of it in my pants—it was Life. Not just Noreen's tits, but Life, a world full of tits and parties and beers and fast cars. Waiting just up ahead for me, it was like I could've run up to the end of Broadway and it would all be waiting there for me like a carnival come to town—

I stopped running. Turned my head. In front of a triple-decker. All the lights out already. All the shades pulled down exactly halfway, eighteen fuckin' shades and all pulled down exactly halfway. Old people. Losers. Outta my way.

I felt the thud running through me, my blood pumping, Life pumping. I listened, and my thud was the same throb that was the not-very-distant roar of Boston, at midnight, on a summer's Friday night. Waiting for me, and me stronger and taller every day.

"Birdy!" I laughed, running again to get home, strip down, beat off, strain every muscle I had just to feel them popping. I laughed because I finally understood something Petey had said: Birdy. The throb of Life running through.

But my Birdy was different—

Birdy with a boner. Ready to take on the whole fuckin' world.

Are the Stars Out Tonight?

Yup, things were changing with me and Petey, with me and life, me and school, me and everything. My grades, never stellar, flopped a bit. Ma didn't complain though. *Well he's all boy, what do you expect?* she'd say to Dad, braggingly, and certain ones of us, who had always known each other, sniffed out each other's coolness and attractiveness and formed a bit of a gang. Petey wasn't in this gang and Ma relished that. Hockey baseball football Ma selling raffles and making new friends of the mothers of said gangees, and the days and nights swept by with outrageousness, pimples, and partying. And me and Noreen, whose abusive father had dropped dead at Park Street Station, were going steady. But then a week later, a month later, there'd be a night I couldn't sleep, some kind of worry, wanting, on my mind.

"Petey," I would whisper to the ceiling, the way you recall a long-dead pet that gave you a comfort that seemed to have died with the first man-hair.

And half the time if I whispered his name hard enough, there would be a shoveling of thrown-up gravel against my window within the hour, and Petey outside at driveway's end, the light in his eyes a match to my soul.

I was tossing and turning one of these nights when Petey-gravel swooshed against my window. The smile tugged at the edges of my face as I sprang from bed.

The moon was slanting into my room, wobbly on the hardwood floors Ma had just resanded and varnished two weeks earlier. The awesome part of this was, I could slide in my socks from the bathroom down the hall to half-way across my room, from where I could leap into bed. *There was on-going debate in the household as to the wisdom of me continuing this habit.* That's a euphemism. We were doing euphemisms that week in English class and

A Map of the Harbor Islands
Published by The Haworth Press, Inc., 2006. All rights reserved.
doi:10.1300/5677_11

these are the words I used to describe the particular warpath Ma went on whenever I'd do this. *Christ on a crutch, Danny! You're giving me nervous diarrhea every time you do that! I think the house is falling down!* But see I couldn't stop. Every time I came out of the bathroom and saw them shinin' floors I was mentally transported to the Olympics—me, Danny O'Connor, competing for the USA against a bevy of bearded Bolsheviks on steroids in the ever-popular Floor-Sliding Event. My particular bed-launching dive, which always landed me the gold, I called the N-D Move, in honor of Ma. Think she'd be pleased but no.

I chucked back the covers and headed over to the window.

"Hey! What's up?" I whispered, opening my window to sea breeze and Petey, which is not to be confused with "Sixpence and Lucy," Grandma Flynn's favorite song. She was Ma's mother. "What are you doing?"

"I fo-followed the moon to your house," Petey said. "The moon was westering, and my feet wanted to follow it. I was tired and didn't want to, but then my arms w-wanted to follow too. Soooooooo . . . here I am. F-follow?"

"I think so," I said, yawning. Why didn't I ever tell Petey I'd been hoping he'd come by?

"You have b-bed head," Petey said, pointing.

"That's cuz it's after eleven."

"I know it but tonight I'm on Finland time. C'mon."

"Where?"

"S-something to show you. I think tonight's the night."

Petey started laughing.

"What's so funny?"

"I'll tell you when I come down. I m-mean, when you come down."

"What?"

"I said I'll tell you when you come down."

I chucked on some clothes and snuck down the stairs, ever mindful of the sixth step, which was the creaky one that squeaked out to Ma notice of my after-hours Petey forays.

"So what was so funny?" I asked Petey.

"I'll tell you on the way, c'mon."

For once we didn't head in the direction of the beach. I wondered where Petey's feet and arms were taking us.

"Okay. My m-mother knows this guy who works the night shift with her at the Necco Plant. His n-name's Ted. He's kind of a f-fusty old bachelor—you know the type, always keeps his top shirt button buttoned. He's got this g-girlfriend named Esther, and everybody thinks she's after his money. They go out to d-dinner one night a week. He's kinda the nervous type. Anyways he has one of those b-bags on his side, they took out some intestines or something and he has to wear one of those bags, and he has to sc-scour it out every few days. He doesn't like doing that at all and who can blame him, and he's e-especially quiet on those nights—he walks around telling everybody, *I'm not myself this evening because tonight's the night.* But my mother always thought when he said that, *tonight's the night,* he was talking about having a date with Esther, so she'd give him a big smile and s-say, *Oh Ted, that's grand! Have a great time!"*

"That is funny, Petey. What would he say to that?"

"He'd just look at her. My mother said she could never figure it out."

"So anyways. Where we going tonight?"

I loved being out this late with Petey—Southie all closed down on a Sunday night, the red lights flashing to nothing, the world all ours for the taking.

Petey turned to me, his lips set, and seized me by the shoulders.

"Danny, I've d-discovered a place. It's a p-peephole into heaven."

"What is it?"

"I'll show you. But we have to stop at my house first."

When we got to Petey's house we climbed upstairs to the second floor. Petey, the youngest of seven, was the only one still living at home, and his mother of course worked nights. Petey stopped me in front of his bedroom door, which was always closed. One of the first things he'd done after his accident was to strip the door of eighty-seven years of white paint and expose its raw oak essence. It took him a whole week. *Oh, I suppose he took a notion,* Mrs. H dismissively telling the brothers when they wanted to know what Petey was up to. But now, really looking at it for the first time, I could see it lent some kind of . . . deeper presence in the house, and not just because of the sign on his door that read *Embrace Hope, All Ye Who Enter Here.*

I was trying to figure out exactly how, when Petey said, "Danny, we're going to go on a pilgrimage tonight. Danny listen, for as far back as time tells, people went on p-pilgrimages. Journeys from where they lived to s-some special place that had meaning to them."

"Ahhh . . . what do you mean? Like the Crusades or something?"

Petey's face jerked up.

"Well, I wasn't thinking of anything that fr-fraught with violent, imperialist m-machismo. I mean a journey that's as spiritual as it is physical. Like a trip to a saint's town, or to some place where a m-miracle is supposed to have happened. A mountain dr-drenched in spiritual energy. Some place with a special kind of feel. And you always h-had to walk."

"Ah . . . . okay."

"We're going to a place like that t-tonight."

"We are? In Southie?"

"In Southie, yes. R-Ripley's Believe It or Not."

"We going to church or something?"

"In a way," Petey said. "But n-not exactly. Though there are some times—especially at night, when just one candle is burning, and you can really feel God's presence, and feel the energy of all the people who have ever prayed there, rejoiced there—times like that, a church really feels like a church. But this is something a little d-different."

"What should I wear, like?"

Petey looked me up and down. He paused. I noticed this close how long and black his eyelashes were.

"You're fine like that," he whispered. "Only, take your sneakers off."

"Ahhh . . . they probably smell a little."

"That's alright. If I can st-stand it the Spirits probably can too."

I followed Petey's example and wedged off my sneakers.

"Okay, r-ready?" he asked, his hand on the bedroom doorknob.

"We're going on a pilgrimage to your bedroom?" I asked.

Petey laughed.

"No."

"What's so funny?"

"Nothing. No, the pilgrimage isn't to my b-bedroom, but first we have to prepare. People always prepared themselves when they w-went on pilgrimage. Ritual and mystery. Symbols, b-but they stand for an inner shift. Sometimes they can act as the pr-precipitator of the inner shift."

"Ahh. . . ."

"Like what you do before a b-ball game. When you put your s-socks on inside-out and say three Hail Marys. When you lean forward and shake your b-bum three times before every batter gets up."

"You noticed that?" I asked, scandalized. Who else knew?

"Yes. Those rituals put you in a state of mind to play b-ball on a higher level."

"You remember that?"

"I d-do. Of course I do, Danny."

I felt a glitch in my stomach, like I always did when me and Petey talked about baseball. Kinda brought the night of his accident back—

"Forget about it, Danny," Petey said, reading my thoughts again. "It wasn't your f-fault."

I nodded but avoided his eyes.

Petey slowly turned his glass bedroom doorknob. We stepped inside. He closed the door behind us. Old doors always have this great click to them, no? His room was dark, no lights.

"The n-night," Petey said, but there was a light in his green eyes, "is sacred. We used to be nocturnal, Danny, and not just diurnal. We'd go on pilgrimages at night, hunt by night, f-fish by the light of the full moon. Have ceremonies. But we've banished the night from our lives, really. Drenched it in brown sodium vapor light and n-neon blasts of advertising, and could there be anything that casts uglier light? And something died in us when we turned our backs on the night. Some part of us that is mystery and d-delight. We're going to try and get in touch with that part of us t-tonight."

Our eyes adjusted a bit, and I could see now that Petey had moved his nightstand from its normal spot beside his bed to the center of the room, up against the wall, underneath one of the two large windows in his room. The bird's nest, jar of acorns, stack of books, candles, and other Petey paraphernalia that usually sat on the table were gone now. In their place was a large clear glass bowl. The table had been polished. The smell of lemon oil lingered in the room and to tell you the truth that's a smell I've always liked. The bowl was full-up to the rim with water. Something was floating on the surface of the water, I couldn't tell what. The moonlight cracked through the alley and fell with a slant onto the bowl, lighting it like a non–sodium vapor spotlight.

Petey gasped, stiffened.

"What?" I asked.

"I knew the m-moonlight would eventually fall on the bowl," he whispered. "But I didn't know exactly when. And now we walk in, and b-boom, there it is. Talk about s-synchronicity."

"What's that?" I whispered back.

"That's when you take a step in the direction of the universe and the universe responds by taking tw-twenty steps in your direction. The timing of it. Recalls Jung's words, *I don't believe, I know.* C'mon."

We walked, slowly, across the room to the table. Petey reached into his pocket and pulled out a book of matches. He struck one up and I could see that the thing floating on the water was a candle, and he lit it. Petey put one finger in the water, then gently stirred it. The candle began moving around the bowl, casting the room into changing, liquidy flickers. You could hear the faintest of lappings. A room I'd been in a thousand times, yet here it was, transformed. And trying to transform us. I could feel something whispering to me, beckoning—tried to fight it—

"Come to the b-bowl, Danny," Petey whispered. What a smile he had on his face. I guess he could tell I was moved by this.

Something I couldn't name, some warmth beyond me that at the same time found a home within, started spreading inside. Following Petey, I took a step closer to the bowl. We took up positions on either side of it, facing each other.

"Since ancient times," Petey said, "water has always been a p-powerful tool in ritual and spirituality. It's cleansing. It's r-restorative. It's contemplative. Every religion in the world uses it in ceremonies and rituals. Our bodies are three-fourths water. For thousands of years, we were nomadic, searching for water. Water is l-life."

Petey dipped his finger in the water, and made the sign of the cross. He closed his eyes.

"Lord/Lady Skovo, the maker and lover of all life, one of your prophets said whenever two or m-more of us are gathered in your name, you would be in the midst of us. That's not just a call to come to you, Lord, but a call to connect with others, a reminder of how much we need each other. We come here tonight to engage your mystery and beauty, and we ask you to come to our m-midst."

It was still so strange to hear words like these from Petey, the once Golden Boy, the home-run-hitting, straight-A, perfect normal boy-next-door. Every town has one—but how many towns, I wondered, had the type of boy Petey was now?

Something like gratitude nipped at me while a feeling of . . . safety filtered into the room, like heat in winter.

Petey's hands fell into my own. Oddly this felt right, like we were standing in the presence of something . . . something. *Ohmigod Danny, what are you doing?* I heard for just a second, Noreen's voice as if she were watching and all of Southie behind her—but this other thing was too strong, too good.

"This is my b-best friend," Petey said, opening his eyes and smiling at me, his face radiant. "And we ask that you open our eyes tonight and always, to let us see the b-beauty that surrounds us."

Then Petey raised our locked hands to the ceiling.

"Feel yourself opening up to the l-light, Danny," Petey whispered. "Only when our b-bodies and minds open can we take in the light."

I don't know how long we stood there like that. Time stretched and melted. I must have felt deeply connected before in my life to someone—my parents as a child—but I couldn't remember that. In feeling so bonded to Petey now, I felt bonded to everything.

"Can you feel it?" Petey whispered. "Can you feel it, Danny, the Birdyness of life?"

"Jesus Petey, I think I can," I whispered back.

We stood there again for a bit, our hands still locked over the bowl. After a while Petey began humming something, and swaying a little, taking me with him.

"I think we're ready now, Danny," Petey said finally. "Ready to go on our p-pilgrimage. Though there's a peace here that makes me want to stay."

I nodded my head. An enormous and sudden appreciation for Petey soared up in me. One time I dreamed Ma had been in a terrible car accident. When I woke up, I ran downstairs and tumbled into her arms, and I told her I loved her until she wept.

"You're my best friend," I blurted. "I ahhh . . . feel so lucky to have you, like."

Petey stared at me, his face jerking back a scootch.

"I . . . I do," I stammered.

His face squirmed a little.

"Be right b-back," he said.

He bolted from the room, so jumpishly I started. He left the door open—wicked unlike him. I heard him scurrying down the hall into the white-tiled bathroom with the transom over the door.

The bathroom door was shut. From the open transom I could hear water running—and a muffled sound of sniffling.

I booshed open the door to find Petey seated on the edge of the bathtub, his green eyes ablaze with tears. He leaped up when I came in, turned away from me.

"Petey," I said. "Petey, shut the stupid water off, will ya?"

"S-sorry Danny," he mumbled, and a little laugh out of him. He sniffled deeply then turned around. He laughed again and turned off the faucet.

"I get embashful," he said, avoiding my eyes for the most part, but little darts of them when he did look at me. "You're . . . my best friend too, D-Danny. It's just . . . you haven't come out with it like that since . . . since—"

I didn't want to, but my arms wanted to. I tried to resist, but then my hands wanted to also. I spread my arms wide. Petey hesitated, a startled, unsure look on his face. Then we fell into each other, hugging hard. I started laughing at the release of it.

"Your face is r-red, Danny," Petey said when we finally pulled away.

"It can't be as red as yours."

"Okay, so where we going?" I asked, walking down N Street ten minutes later.

"You'll see," Petey said. He looked up. "The night's clear as a virgin's conscience, as Ma'am would s-say. Look at those stars."

Petey had his binoculars slung around his neck. They caught the light of the night and spangled it around a bit.

We cut across M Street Playground and then turned down Broadway. A few more rights and lefts, then Petey stopped at a chain-link fence between two triple-deckers. A police car raced by us and both cops turned and looked as they flew past.

"Okay," Petey said, rubbing his hands together and falling into whispers again. "Here we are. Hop over."

We hopped the fence and found ourselves in a narrow passage running between the two three-story buildings. Out of the streetlights' blobbing, intrusive reach, it was about as dark as it ever gets in Southie. I wondered what we were doing in an alley.

It wasn't too cold but it was October, and a leaf-rattling clearing front had come through earlier today. Everyone noticed it coming out of school that afternoon and I had given Noreen my sweatshirt to keep her warm. I had jerked off with its soft perfumery over my face right before Petey had come over tonight, but that still hadn't helped me fall asleep, *the best little sleepin' pill in the world!* Bunso Burns had called it, making That Gesture.

Petey was almost quivering with excitement. "C'mon," he said, "and be quiet."

We skulked down the alley. One of the windows from the house beside us shone blue with rapid-flicker TV light. At the end of the alley we came to a half-tumbled stockade fence panel, a slowly decomposing blowery of trash gathered at its feet. On the other side of the fence a trio of alley junk trees fought for dominance, reaching beyond the roofs of the buildings beside us.

"Okay," Petey said, cracking his knuckles and deep breathing. He looked all around, then turned to me.

"Danny," he whispered, working his mouth and grabbing me by the forearm. "I've stolen an alley!"

My scrunched eyebrows told him I needed more of an explanation. Again.

"See, Danny, it's too bright in the city to see stars. I m-mean, you might see a dozen on an especially m-moonless, clear night—but it's usually too hazy, too bright and gl-glary. Stars, Danny. Infinity. Imagine if you could climb up to your attic and s-s-see all the way to Paris—could see the Taj Mahal in India at night from your kitchen window while you did dishes. Could see the Grand Canyon—you'd think it was quite a m-miracle, no?"

"Yeah, I guess."

"Well, when you look at the stars, you see things b-billions of times farther. And if you ever get out to the c-country—I mean the real country—you can hardly see the dark for the stars. No wonder all the peoples who came before us had such rich myth and spirituality—you can't help but believe, Danny, in something so much bigger than ourselves, and yet a part of ourselves, when you see the stars the way they were meant to be seen. That's been taken away from so m-many of us now, Danny. We have pizza signs and b-bank skyscrapers instead. So those are the false prophets we w-worship."

Petey wet his lips and looked around again, looked up into the waving enclosure of the sumacs and ailanthus over us.

"Tonight, we're gonna take it all back, Danny."

"How?"

"I told you, I've st-stolen an alley. I was riding my bike one day last summer down Broadway, and out of nowhere this big bird soared about a hundred feet over my head. A hawk it was, Danny, a r-red-tailed hawk. In Southie! Using the ocean as a flyway I suppose. I'd never seen one before in real life. I followed it here. It roosted for a bit right in these trees here. And then I did a little exploring while I was here.

"On the other side of this fence, Danny, three alleys come t-together. The ailanthus and sumacs have taken over one end, and this silver maple that must be two hundred years old is at the other end. It's the biggest tree in Southie—I know, I've checked. I'm not sure anyone r-really knows it's here. The houses all have their backs to it and that's been the saving of it, the land's undevelopable and l-landlocked.

"Anyways I've been coming back since then. Cleaning up the alley a little, watching it. Making sure no one comes h-here. They don't. Opening up the view from the middle a bit. But Danny! Come on! Let's g-go!"

We climbed the fence to a sweeping-down of leaves, a rustling. It was so dark on the other end—when I let go to jump, I was vaulting into darkness. Funny feeling, but with Petey beside me I trusted him.

"Wow," I said when I plopped onto a ground I could only feel, not see at all. It was cushioned with a pile of woodsy-smelling leaves.

"I put them in the corner here to soften landing bl-blows," Petey said, whispering still. "Don't look up, Danny, 'til I tell you."

We stood up and brushed off our knees. I'd never been in such darkness, and the tree-muffled silence felt like a big fatty pillow. I didn't know Petey had taken my hand until I felt him pulling me on, farther into the darkness. A part of me hoped that just because we had held hands for a while in his bedroom, he wouldn't think we were going to do it all the time now.

"This space here is rectangular, about a hundred and fifty by ninety feet," Petey murmured. You couldn't talk loud at all in a place like this. "The old plot maps show a glass fa-factory here in the old days. Everything got divvied up eventually and this was the one c-corner of Southie left over it seems. Hidden. Forgotten. A hundred and fifty by ninety doesn't s-sound big I know but it goes down to the center of the earth in one direction, and up to the stars in another.

"I want to show you s-something else before we see the main attraction," Petey said. He pulled me over to the right. It was hard to believe it could get any darker, but it was like ink beneath the trees. He pulled out a penlight from his shirt pocket and turned it on.

Under the trees were old chairs of all shapes and sizes, some of them with their seats rotting out. Petey shined his light and we could see that on every chair was an old teddy bear or doll, a little bit the worse for wear. I jumped—Petey felt this and squeezed my hand—for a second I thought they were small, misshapen people, creepy in their motionlessness. There must have been about thirty or forty of them, and the chairs made a rough circle as if this was some kind of eerie gathering.

"What is it, Petey?" I whispered. "What . . . what does it mean?" One of the teddy bears had floppy red-felt lettering proclaiming I LOVE YOU.

Petey gulped and wiped his nose drip.

"I was afraid to ask around, cuz I didn't want anyone knowing I'd discovered this place. But finally I asked one of the neighbors when I saw them out one d-day. I said I'd lost my ball back here, an acceptable excuse for a young male, when *searching for meaning and wonder* is always looked at with askancity, no? She told me there was an old Lithuanian woman who used to live around here years ago. She kept to herself and had a little garden back here, and this was her work. She said they heard she'd been in a concentration camp in Eastern Europe years ago, and whenever she f-found a thrown-out doll or teddy bear she brought it back here and added it to her collection. Okay, let's move on, Danny."

After a minute he started slowing down a bit, sticking out his other hand like he was feeling for something.

A lonesome cricket sounded very slowly from the right; then another one answered from somewhere in front of us and the sound wasn't as lonesome. A smell was in the air, of crispness, woods—something I hadn't smelled since our trip to the Harbor Islands last summer.

"Land buoys," Petey said, hearing the crickets too. "Sounding out the channels and n-narrows of the earth. Taking the p-pulse of the night."

We stopped when I heard Petey's fingers rapping on metal.

"Here it is," he mumbled. My eyes had adjusted just enough to reach out my hand and feel the object in front of us. It felt like heavy solid metal.

"A car?" I whispered.

"A car," Petey said. "At first I objected to its pr-presence here, but then I realized it was perfect for a viewing platform. It may have been another of the bears' getaway cars when Skovo was king. C'mon, lookit what I d-did."

Petey led me over to the side of the door. He flapped his hand around until he found the door. He swung it open.

"It used to creak something awful b-but I oiled it," he whispered. Petey slid in first, then me. I didn't mean to slam the door but it was so heavy I couldn't help it.

"*Shhhhhh!*" Petey hissed. We both stopped for a moment but didn't hear anything. Any kind of sound seemed a violation here, except for the crickets, which were now sounding all around, a bunch of them if you could believe it in Southie.

"Okay," Petey said. "Sit back and look up."

The seats were marshmallow-cushy, and engulfed me as I leaned back into their musty smell. I looked up. Petey pulled a blanket from the roof to reveal a sunroof with jagged edges.

"I cut it out myself," he said. "Took me about a m-month I suppose."

I looked straight up. The trees all leaned into the open middle of the small clearing here, stretching trunky necks for the light. But right in the leaf-fringed center was a large semicircular opening of black sky. And there were the stars, shining all the brighter for the darkness. You could actually see the things they have in science books, constellations, how some of the stars were grouped together into funny shapes.

"Jesus," I said.

"Now take a look through these," Petey said, handing me his binoculars. "Just focus anywhere and tell me what you see. Turn that thing in the middle 'til it's c-crystal-clear."

I turned the focus until one star jumped into jagged clarity. Like frozen fire, blue-white. But behind it, beyond it—one two three four—wait a minute—a big fuzzy lump of something—seven eight nine—

"Jesus Petey, there's more and more of them!"

"B-billions and billions and billions, as the man said. And Danny, some of them aren't even there anymore. We're looking down a t-tunnel of time."

"How do you mean like?"

"They're l-light-years away," Petey said, scooting closer. "Which means the light coming from them takes years and years to get here. Sometimes millions of years. So if some of these stars b-burned out ten thousand years ago, the light from that hasn't reached us yet. We're actually looking at a smattering of the very distant past and present, all smeared into one."

I struggled hard to swallow this, really grasp it. I couldn't understand how no one had told me this before. It seemed the craziest thing I'd ever heard.

"Wait a minute, you mean . . . you mean like some of them aren't there anymore, and we can still see them?"

"That's q-quite right," Petey sighed, leaning back in the cushy seat.

"Jesus Petey," I moaned low. "It's like . . . lookin' into heaven and seeing the dead. I think . . . I think it's the bestest thing I've ever seen."

"I hoped you'd like it," Petey sighed.

As I shifted the binoculars around there was more and more to see. I handed them to Petey for his turn.

"That group up there to the r-right is Cassiopeia," Petey said. "See? Looks like an upside-down W. She was a proud queen. I'll tell you the story."

And he did, too.

"You're very quiet," Petey said on the way home an hour or two later.

"I just . . . I feel like I've been somewhere far away."

I turned my head up and looked at the sky again. With the streetlights all around I couldn't see any stars at all.

"They're still there, Danny," Petey said. "And we'll see them again."

I did, that night in my dreams. I was in a forest with Petey, and we were approaching some kind of pillar in a clearing in the forest. The crickets were very loud. As we got closer to the pillar we could see a clear glass bowl of water, sitting on its top. Petey smiled at me and we approached it. We looked down into it, and saw millions of stars, and soon we were flying through them, laughing, realizing we were as bright as they were. Everyone was back down on the ground, Noreen, Ma, Dad (even though he was watching TV) calling to me to be careful, come back down right now . . . but I didn't want to, even though there were tall buildings straight ahead that I knew me and Petey were bound to crash into.

12

The Man Behind the (Nixon) Mask

John O'Callahan sat in front of me in homeroom for four straight years in high school, due to a quirk of alphabetization, him O'Callahan me O'Connor. Homeroom started at 7:35 in the morning, a speculative time of day when the better part of you is still wrapped in the cocoon of blankets and sheets. If there were any butterflies among us you'd have to come back later in the day to view them.

As such John O'Callahan was a subject of involuntary study for me: for four long years the first person I'd see every morning for any length of time. I mention him only in contrast to Petey. Maybe by saying what Petey was not, negative space, I might convey a better idea of what he was. He was not John O'Callahan.

John O'Callahan was a mouth breather to begin with, which, right or wrong, has never communicated to most the presence of a keen and hungry intelligence. Sr. Patricia, sophomore year, in an uncommon display of frustration, once called John an *evolutionary cul-de-sac.*

He was a large person, John, always had been, solid as a telephone pole and about as nimble. During football in the parking lot at recess he'd be one of the first picked, to block. *Okay John, you just stand there, got it? Don't let no one near me, use them ham elbows to advantage for Chrissake.* His presence in school strictly ornamental—his father, his father before that, worked for the Edison and John aspired to follow in their footsteps, up ladders propped against utility poles and all the way down manholes, to ensure the continued delivery of power to the residents and businesses throughout the City of Boston. First grade, *I'm gonna work for the Edison,* and he'd draw yellow trucks during art, big men smiling in yellow gear. Tenth grade, *I'm going to work for the Edison* and he set up tables showing how much his pension would be after retirement.

A Map of the Harbor Islands
Published by The Haworth Press, Inc., 2006. All rights reserved.
doi:10.1300/5677_12

I envied his decisiveness. John could not be moved. I was often tempted to stick him with a pin. A stockyard sound when he laughed, but maybe people like that know more than we do, with our ropes and pulleys of plans, that grim upward mobility. Before enlightenment, work for Edison; after enlightenment, work for Edison.

Petey unlike John O'Callahan was a sensitive-tuned instrument. Especially after the accident. Everything around him, everything that was seen and said and done, a particular cloud formation in the sky, an offhand comment overheard, what someone was wearing, the smells of things, affected him for better or worse like grit in a delicate watch's mechanism.

No, forget it. This is no good—because in saying this, a number of times when Petey acted in just the opposite way come to mind, when he was not to be moved.

There was the whole Rexall Drug thing. As property values went up in Southie, and the news circulated among the suburban house-hunting set that the natives *probably* wouldn't eat you (though some of the younger ones might steal your hubcaps), Petey's older siblings one by one were chaffed out of town by the buffy wind of gentrification, unable to afford the sky-rocketing rents and mortgages *and where in the world will it all end, I wonder,* Mrs. Harding mused. We were sixteen that year, and Mrs. Harding was, she said, concerned about the lack of masculine role models in Petey's life. She'd read an article in *Parade Magazine* on Father's Day that extolled the virtues of same. That is to say, Petey, like the rest of us, had finally started drinking, and Mrs. Harding wanted some guy to keep an eye on her wee Petey. A good influence. Her older sons weren't around to do it anymore except for Donnie who still lived in town but was *married now and troubles of his own,* so Mrs. H asked her brother *Don't call him Bill* Liam, a confirmed bachelor from Dorchester one interstate-divided neighborhood over, if he might take Petey under his ample, God-fearing wing. Plans were laid and a Saturday morning was selected for Petey and Liam's first official get-together.

The first thing Uncle Liam did was haul Petey out Castle Island way for a double-time quick-march and man-to-man chat, Petey later reported. Uncle Liam had to run home though halfway through for a minute because he couldn't remember, had he left the kettle on? Or not? *Probably not,* he kept saying, *probably not, but better safe than sorry.* As fate would have it he got into a little fender-bender on the way back, at the Old Colony Rotary there, and the occupants of the other car as it turned out had green card issues, were summarily arrested and then sent back to Wherever. It made the back pages of the papers, all because Uncle Liam couldn't remember if he had left the kettle on. Which he hadn't. *And isn't that the strange w-way of this world?* Petey kept saying to me.

As it happened Petey was in a communicative humor that day. Since the accident you never knew, red-silent when spoken to and bounce awkwardly one foot to the other, an hour later telling you *as many stories in an hour as you'd want in a month* in his mother's words.

Uncle Liam—a serious bureaucrat for the City of Boston's Revenue Division, and a volunteer sexton at St. Margaret's Church—with *beautiful priest's hands, look at them now, and how 'bout that shine on his shoes!* Mrs. Harding would always say—attempted to educate Petey about the facts of life in general, the hydra-headed perils of Sin, and the ill effects of too much booze and masturbation in particular. Petey only half listened and interruptingly pointed out to Uncle Liam instead the whims of tidal surge, the natural history of the baby-blue drumlin Harbor Islands, *Oh l-lookit,* the many and intricate ways the seagulls, Petey's favorite birds, swam the gush-fickle ocean winds.

"They're fl-floating to music only they can h-hear," Petey said, pointing up and beyond. "There. There. Lookit. There are some people say the whole u-u-universe is music and it directs us all."

"We've a grand choir at St. Margaret's, come and hear it some time," Uncle Liam answered.

When they stopped for hot dogs at Sullivan's, Petey tried to convey his own feelings of faith and God in general, and masturbation as an occasion of sin in particular. Petey produced a folded-up page from *National Geographic Magazine* out of the little notebook he kept in his back pants pocket. He opened it up and showed Uncle Liam this glossy pull-out picture of one small sliver of Our Milky Way, depicting billions untold of stars. Petey explained how this was just one dinky corner of our galaxy, in a universe filled with billions more galaxies, each with trillions of stars.

"I d-don't think of God as buzzing around his big-ass universe in a sp-spaceship, shining his flashlight under my covers to see what I'm d-doing," Petey said. "He g-g-gave us our bodies to experience some pl-pleasure with the pain, no? God knows, we get enough p-pain, without feeling bad about the pleasure."

Uncle Liam was quiet for a bit.

"It's a question of ownership, Petey. Will you determine your own life, or will your desires? Will you be a slave I wonder, or the master of your own house?"

"It's a g-good point, Uncle Liam, c-c-cuz I've come to believe I'm in-clined to addiction, l-l-like my father before me," Petey said after thinking for a minute. "But—"

"That's right, Petey. Take drinking, now. A man takes a drink, but soon the drink takes the man. 'Tis a slippery slope and no mistake. Is there a re-cord of a motor car accident where drink wasn't taken?"

"But sometimes, Uncle Liam, we've g-got to get to the b-bottom of our own swamps, n-no?"

"I don't follow."

"And you're not m-m-married, Uncle Liam, don't tell me you don't whack it once in a while, then r-r-run to confession. Give yourself a b-break. T-take it from one who's been crushed, overwhelmed, by g-guilt, h-hit and left for dead. It's the m-most useless of emotions, a real m-monkey on your back. God doesn't want that. God is l-l-love and vice versa, or should be anyways, no?"

(I asked Petey later what he had to feel guilty about, but he just looked at me, looked away, spat.)

Petey went on to tell reddening-faced Uncle that the God they'd been handed was a toxic God, an Old Testament X-Man scouring the universe with a flyswatter to squash bugs that displeased him.

"Now, a b-b-baby I can accept as God," Petey said. "A helpless l-l-little baby, the son of indigent shepherd people, an unwed mother, we got n-n-nothing to fear from. He's . . . *accessible,* as they like to say in the art world when they don't understand the rest of s-somebody's w-work. Or Buddha, now. Big fat smiling happy Buddha. All the same, Uncle Liam. Birdy."

Uncle Liam scratched his big red ears. Petey hurried to add that he had changed the name of God to cleanse himself of this patriarchal toxicity. Sometimes he called him/her Birdy and sometimes he called him/her Skovo, Skovo King/Queen of the Universe, the Great Creator/Creatoress Birdy. Then he recited the Apostles' Creed to Uncle Liam, substituting *Skovo* or *Birdy* every time the word *God* came up:

> We believe in one Skovo, the Lord/Lady and the Giver of Life, who proceeds from the trees and the bees. . . .

"The trees and the bees!" Uncle Liam sputtered.

"Yes, that's right. I c-c-can't look in the face of an animal or b-bird or in-sect without seeing the face of Skovo st-staring back at me," Petey ex-plained. "By which of c-course I mean Birdy too." By then Uncle Liam was almost blocking his ears. But Petey was just warming up. He had his own ideas about God etc., and the questions he posed about these matters, *Sure they'd puzzle a bishop,* in the proud words of his mother.

Lastly, Petey went on to correct the small errors Uncle Liam had conveyed in explaining the facts of life. *It's called ovulation, from the Latin for e-e-egg.*

Uncle Liam concluded that Petey had too much time on his hands and needed a job. Besides he was a young man of sixteen now and there was no good reason why he couldn't contribute to the household. *Your mother's worked so hard, hasn't she now, nights, all these years Petey.*

Petey concurred (*We conversed, I concurred, and then we had con carne,* Petey told me later, even though that wasn't true—they had hot dogs) but told Uncle Liam he'd traipsed up and down Broadway the day of his sixteenth birthday 'til he was blue in the face and sore in the ass looking for work, but no one would hire him.

"My st-stuttering makes people unc-c-comfortable," Petey said. "To say nothing about the n-notions that fly through my head. And I have to say them! S-s-sometimes I think I'm the only one with thoughts!"

Uncle Liam said he knew lots of people and could get Petey a job quick as a wink, and never mind with the thoughts.

"I know it but r-right now, for example, r-r-right at this moment, all I can think of Uncle is the night before my accident. I keep going back to that night. How I sh-shone then. How different I was then—a different p-person. And yet still me. I think all of us could be different, there's like a million different p-p-personalities squiggling inside us like so many spermy things, wiggling and squiggling and rushing to the fore for dominance, and when I got h-hit, a different personality swam into my ego. F-follow? I had everything laid out for the next day at school, the r-rest of my life really when you think about it. My homework was d-done. It was hot in my room, twilight t-time. I was waiting for Danny to come by. I was n-naked. We had a game that night. My room so clean and h-hot. My uniform laid out on the bed. A pigeon fluttered outside my window and I thought it might be the Holy Ghost and then she was gone in a festoon of fl-flappery. Outside d-down the way girls were jumping rope and echoy-singing the Miss Lucy song."

"I'm afraid I don't know that one," Uncle Liam confessed. Uncle Liam, circumspect as he was, reserved Saturday nights to go drinking and singing in the Irish pubs along Dorchester Avenue, stumbling distance one from the other, and he was always on the lookout for a catchy new jig.

"Oh God it's an old one, American I think. I'll s-sing it you," Petey said. He didn't stutter when he sang like I say.

> Miss Lucy had a steamship, the steamship had a bell,
> Miss Lucy went to Heaven, the steamship went to
> Hello Operator, give me Number Nine,
> And if you disconnect me, I'll kick your fat
> Behind the 'frigerator, there was a piece of glass,
> Miss Lucy sat upon it, and cut her big fat
> Ask me no more questions, I'll tell you no more lies,
> The boys are in the basement, zipping down their
> Flies are in the meadow—

"That's enough of the nonsense," Uncle Liam interrupted. "You need a job. Never mind Miss Lucy."

"I know it but speaking of f-festoons," Petey said, "look at them clouds, Uncle Liam. Festoonery. High festoonery, no? So high it's haute."

And so it was that Petey got hired by Leggett's Rexall Pharmacy, a drugstore/lunch counter over in Fields Corner. The Kelley girl used to work there. Before she ran off with that ska band. She could play "The Rose" on the school piano with only three mistakes and all the girls would cry.

You couldn't turn around in there they had so much junk in the aisles. *Like friggin' Gimbels,* Ma used to say. Uncle Liam knew the owner and the owner owed Uncle Liam a favor, and so the deal was done. But Fields Corner was a neighborhood *changing by the hour,* Mrs. Harding said carefully. The result of this was that arrangements were made. *No no,* Mrs. H wouldn't have *my wee Petey* taking his bike back and forth there every day, *with n'ary a good Catholic within earshot.* She didn't drive herself so insisted Liam drop Petey off the three days a week he worked there, pick him up too when he was through. Saturdays was different now, he could take his bike as long as he left for home before sundown. Though we were sixteen and a half now Petey eschewed getting his license, an unheard-of anomaly and something to do with global warming and *the world looks better by foot or bike D-Danny, no?*

Uncle Liam, whose work schedule for the City of Boston was *ahhh . . . flex, don'chaknow* in Mrs. H's words, reluctantly agreed to chauffeur—he was afraid of his sister's tongue, Petey said. *The only tool I know that grows sharper with constant use,* Uncle Liam had muttered but Petey had mudder ears and heard him.

"He has a b-box of Kleenex too in the back windshield like a ninety-year-old," Petey said after the first day. "A mystery of the universe, D-Danny: how these people could ever reach that box when they needed it in traffic, w-way back there like that when they have to sneeze quick in a hurry. Like they got octopus arms or s-s-something. Or maybe they hire someone to ride in the back and hand them one when they need one."

"I know it. So how was the job?"

"Okay I g-guess. B-But they got a f-f-filthy lunch counter too and the s-smell of the cold cuts g-gets you after a while. By the end of the d-day I smell like a large Italian with everything on it. And I don't mean that in the good sense. See? Go ahead, sniff me, Danny. See? But it's a j-job. Hey D-Danny, you ever read the ingredients of what's in those c-cold cuts? No? You should."

It *was* a job, for three weeks anyways, until Petey cultivated the habit of telling the paying customers what they were really eating.

"Here's your p-p-processed, sodium-sorbitoled, m-m-mayonnaise-laden, bread-crumbed *hint-o-tuna* sandwich," he'd say, handing over the goods to a mailman on his noon break.

"Try the hot dogs t-t-today," Petey suggested another time, to a hungry taxi driver. "There's not as much s-sawdust and p-pig intestines in them as per usual."

The whiter the bread, the sooner you're d-dead! he sang-song to someone one day. The only bread they had there was thin white floppy stuff that came in bulk in unmarked brown wrappers, *Like porn, p-porn for the body,* Petey said. Petey called it either faux bread or tastes-like-bread, depending on his mood, when he would tell customers the kind of bread they had today. He said he'd suggested to Mr. Leggett that they get some healthier stuff in there. Lots of people wanted to eat healthier now, but Mr. Leggett was seventy-seven, he said, and that stuff hadn't done him any harm, even though he'd had many's the heart operation and was fat and took twenty pills a day for this and that.

(Since he'd come out of his coma Petey had refused to eat meat, wondering how he ever had beforehand. He said it was da Vinci, wasn't it, who called the body of a meat eater a rotting graveyard of dead animals. 'Course Petey said this right before I was about to chow down on a Triple Deluxe Big Beef Bacon Burger from the fast-food joint up the way and him taking all the juicy joy out of it. But Petey's veggieism was a queer notion indeed in that time and place and like I say caused fits for Mrs. Harding. But Petey seemed to thrive nonetheless.)

He said he only wanted to share his wealth of information with helpless consumers who had *the right to know*. Plus he said he was bored out of his mind at the store, and found that nothing livened up any situation like a frank discussion of Truth.

The end result of this was catastrophe as one might expect. See the customers didn't share Petey's thirst for knowledge. At last one of them loudly complained to the hard-of-hearing Mr. Leggett, who was at the other end of the pharmacy, filling prescriptions with a shaking hand.

"What? What?"

"I say, I axed him for a roas' beef sa'mich, and he gimme this dead cow buttock thing instead!" the outraged woman roared, pointing back at Petey. "He's a *racist!*"

Such a calamitous charge, even if unfounded as was the case, is never good for business and Petey was summarily dismissed that instant, Uncle Liam or no Uncle Liam. I suppose anybody else would have just walked home. But not Petey. Petey had his pride.

He didn't tell a soul he'd been shit canned. About a month later I went over there one night to see if he could get me a very good deal on some rubbers. By that time me and Noreen were ready for the Big Cahuna. *Yes! This weekend!* she had written to me on a note during Spanish. I'd been after her for at least a year now. The dot above the i in *this* was a heart instead of a dot. My thing had become large and fat and was always wanting attention and a comforting confirming touch. But before I even got inside the drugstore where Petey worked, I was approached by something standing outside, wearing a cardboard Halloween Nixon mask.

"It's m-me," a muffled voice said, when I was about to give this weirdo a shove for getting too close.

"Huh?"

"It's m-me, Danny. It's Petey."

"Petey! Wh-what the f—what are you doing?"

"Waiting for my r-ride. Waiting for the uncle."

"Well . . . what do you mean? Why aren't you workin' inside?"

"Ahhh . . . okay. I . . . got f-f-fired. Don't tell anyone."

"You got fired?"

"Yeah. Don't tell anyone."

"When? For what?"

"I dunno. About a m-month ago I guess."

It was hard to talk to him with Nixon smiling back at me.

"A month ago? But—Jesus, Petey, your uncle still picks you up from school every day to bring you over here!"

"I know it. I d-don't want him to know. I don't w-w-want anyone to know. Don't tell anyone."

"So . . . Petey, what do you do, have him drop you off here every day and then you put on that stupid mask and stand out front here 'til he comes for you at night?"

"Ah . . . y-yeah. I don't w-want anyone to know is all."

Nothing I could say would convince Petey to tell his uncle he'd been fired. But I couldn't have him standing out in Fields Corner wearing a Nixon mask every day. Sooner or later someone would've beaten the shit out of him or something. I don't think white people in general and Nixon in particular were too popular in that neighborhood.

I called Uncle Liam myself that night when I got home.

"Your nephew's been fired," I said in a deep disguised voice and a paper towel between me and the mouthpiece thing. "Go pick him up now, right now. He's wearing a Nixon mask and standing in front of the drugstore. Now."

"Who is this?" Uncle Liam asked.

"A friend. And don't yell at him, or we'll come and beat the shit outta you," I added as an afterthought.

Then I hung up.

Petey wouldn't speak to me for a week after that. I denied it but he knew it must've been me. But eventually he got over it. I mean, we were still best friends, I mean more or less. What are you gonna do, not talk to your friend for the rest of your life? Stand in front of a drugstore wearing a stupid Nixon mask?

I guess what I'm saying is, John O'Callahan never would've done that. He would've gone home the minute he got fired, made himself a cold cut sandwich, drifted off to hammy sleep in front of the TV in the wall-to-wall carpeted, paneled den, dreaming of working for the Edison.

But not Petey. Just when you thought you knew the limits of his weirdness. . . .

And then the Tree Personals the next spring, Petey sent Tree Personals to the *South Boston Tribune.*

"Sex sells," was the first thing Petey said to me one day. I was driving home from school, just dropped Noreen off and I'd picked him up. He was stopped at a dying sidewalk tree, examining it, when I saw him. "Jesus, D-Danny, we've got to get people more interested in the trees around town, and I think I know how to do it. Sex s-s-sells."

"Huh?"

"It does, sex s-sells. Ask N-Noreen."

Petey's plan was to get people to adopt a tree, volunteer to take care of one city tree half-languishing along the buckling sidewalks, many of them dying for the lack of TLC, Petey said, and once they started, malingering ruffians would snap the younger trees in two if they were able. "Nothing de-succeeds like de-success," Petey explained. "Lookit how people trash a trash-filled street, but don't drop trash where it's nice and cl-clean."

The *Tribune* had started running photos with their women-seeking-men and men-seeking-women personals. Petey took out a few ads, took pictures of his various favorite trees around town, especially the ones that needed looking after, and submitted them to the *Tribune* personals section. Somehow they made it in.

Betty, one of them said under a picture of this particular listing-to-starboard, dehydrated fir on L Street, sharp-needled but gentle on the inside, looking for someone to take care of me. Prefer younger, less than 100, but no saplings need apply.

Like to Drink? Me too! So Let Me Quaff Deeply of Your Waters, another one was headlined. **I'm Nancy and I've a Terrible Thirst.** The picture accompanying this one showed a languishing young locust way down on West Broadway not too far from Amrheins, dying a slow death from a lack of water.

When these got no response, except for the Heavy Breather (as Petey called him) who kept calling asking for Betty, Nancy, and what were they doing now, what were they wearing now, Petey got a little more daring with his copy.

June, hot female ginkgo, just coming into maturity, looking for good times, no reasonable request refused. Cum on guys, I got it going on! But the *Tribune* pulled the ad after it shut down their automated phone messaging system due to issues of overloading, and Miss Mary Shea, the late founder's eighty-year-old niece, got reassigned from Proofreading to Circulation. They never did print the ad that was headlined, **Listen Up Ladies, They Call Me Mr. Oak Tree.** But Petey didn't get discouraged, especially after he enlisted the help of Sr. Mary Alice's third grade class, and some of the old retired Raisinet men down at L Street Beach. He gave them the ball and they ran with it: bunches of flowers began sprouting up around the city trees around town. Little fency things were installed so dogs wouldn't nose-waffle affairs in the immediate area of struggling young trunks. One began seeing green plastic hoses, shimmery in the August heat, coily laid out for the afternoon soaking duty that was undertaken by the older folks with all the immutability and solemnity of their bimonthly trips to the bank on the first and fifteenth. *The early bird special at the Farragut House? Oh Helen I'd love to, but see I gotta wa-tah lay-dah, I'm takin' care of the tree out front now.*

"Lookit," Petey would say when we'd be driving around town once in awhile—most of the times it was Noreen or some of the other guys in my car but once in a while when they weren't around Petey—"Lookit, Danny, that one. And that one. And that one too." He'd be pointing out trees that had been rescued by his efforts, were thriving now due to the people he had enlisted.

But still, I'd have to say there was a change come over Petey—I can see it more clearly now the further I get away from those years. Something musty and cynical crawled into him. I suppose that comes in due course to anyone as different as Petey was. Still, knowing he was so different from everyone else, he nonetheless had always labored lightly under the illusion that there was a place for him in this world—up until the time we were like seventeen-eighteen. The sense of irrepressible wonder that he saw in all things flowed back to Petey like his theory of all water being one, and replenished him even as it flowed out from him.

But then there seemed to be a stop in the flow. Something dammed up somewhere. A backup of things. Clogging happened.

13

For Spacious Skies

Cynicism breached Petey eventually, like an infestation of Nixon-faced worms, like pollution from Gary, Indiana, settling down as acid rain on the sinless forests of Nova Scotia. Those are similes and metaphors and personification, we had them all senior year English, and I realized I'd seen them all before, via Petey.

I attributed Petey's downward slide—when I thought of it at all, which wasn't much in those wilding days—to his increased beer drinking, the pot smoking as we crawled into our late Southie teens. But the more I think of it, the more I see those things as symptoms, not causes. I really think it was the whole Young Entrepreneurs of America thing that proved the coup de grace to Petey's previously invincible Petey-ness.

Because, September at the beginning of senior year at Gate of Heaven High found Petey as green-eyed lustily hopeful as always—though he still hadn't had a girlfriend yet. Nor of course did he play sports anymore, at least within the bellowing cat's cradle of a team or league. Still though at recess, when the notion took him and you never knew when, he'd burst into an impromptu game of keep-away, stickball, sometimes touch football, and there was none could make headway against him. Even the kids on the track team left in his dust. You couldn't catch him, even if he was right in front of you. He'd stop to dare you. One lunged of course, he'd fake left, dodge right, then he'd be off, leaving you grasping arm-swipes of air where only a second before he was. The coaches of the various teams would pursue him for a week or two after these incidents—*Jeez Petey, with moves like that you'd be one of the best this school ever saw!* But Petey would always decline vehemently, though before walking away he'd try to convince said coaches that they needed to adopt a stray dog, and he had the perfect one for them.

A Map of the Harbor Islands
Published by The Haworth Press, Inc., 2006. All rights reserved.
doi:10.1300/5677_13

That was September, October. Another summer of bike-ride moons and sailing suns and God knows what else had left him darker of hair and greener of eye, flusher of face. A little taller, fuller in the shoulders and deeper in voice. Quieter? A speck more thoughtful? Like the secrets were festering up inside him, the hours spent alone leaving their marks? The way he'd look at me now. He'd stared at me since the accident, but a wisdom and a sorrow mixed now in his look, and always as if from a distance. I hardly noticed. The thing on my mind now alas was coke and fucking Noreen and how to get more, more, hockey and the half-remembered parties down at the beach on Friday and Saturday nights.

Girls had given up on Petey as a matter of practice, but in theory a different story. They quiet-watched him walk into class; they quiet-watched him walk out. Not speculating anymore, not laying plans, but envisioning things still. Mental scenarios and impromptu We're-All-Alones to brighten up algebraic conundrums.

But by June and graduation, cynicism covered Petey like a blanket of snow in the morning when the skies were spotless, quiet right before you went to bed the night before and the weathermen all *If you liked today you'll love tomorrow*.

I'll tell you about the Young Entrepreneurs of America fair, which was held in January every year, and you tell me, was this the thing that instigated Petey's downward slide?

Young Entrepreneurs of America (YEA!) had been the brainchild of William *don't call him Liam* Brennan, this guy. He owned an insurance business on West Broadway back in the sepia days right after World War II. His son Billy Junior ran the agency these days, and they had branched out like cracking ice onto the South Shore where they all lived now, lace-curtain SUV drivers, a boat someone said, *Coast Coverage, get it, oh please*. But every January, Junior as he was still called round town, though he really didn't deserve it, would come back to Gate of Heaven High, his and his father's alma mater, to run the YEA! Program. Any member of the senior class could enter the contest.

The idea was simple but somehow beyond me. Which I suppose doesn't say much about me those days. Any student who wanted could put together an idea for a small business. You would draw up a marketing and business plan, and present it, with any charts or props you could put together (the more confounding and colorful the better), in the auditorium during a day-long program. The YEA! Program was always held the third Saturday in January, when things were frozen and my dick most times tiny huddled shrivelly within the cotton field-folds of my BVDs when I was outside hanging on the corner, while insatiable business marched on fully tumescent in all weathers.

Three winners of the YEA! Program would be selected every year, and each would be given a $3,000 scholarship to the college of their choice. They used to give out cash, but a few years back Bunso Burns, who'd invented a home grocery delivery service long before lazy yuppies did, used his money to finance his own budding pot distribution ring, which in turn financed various forms of questionable bamboozle. When Bunso finally got to the court appointment he had so long worked for, the Proddy judge asked him who had spotted the dough to get him started in the first place. Bunso answered immediately, truthfully, *Oh, Gate of Heaven High, Yer Honor,* and there was no end to the talk. Consternation ensued and even Sr. Maureen John on her weekly call-in local cable show *Let's All Pray the Rosary* had to air explanatory protestations between the Second and Third Sorrowful Mysteries. So now it was college scholarships instead of Handy Mister Green.

The notices went out in early October to give students ample time to get their marketing and busines plans in order. The notices were run off on the mimeo machine and thus emitted that great fresh purple ink smell, which somehow I always imagined was what octopuses smelled like. In the upper left corner was an old-fashioned graphic of a man in a business suit and fedora yelling into a bullhorn thing, *Announcing the 34th Annual YEA! Program!* We got it in economics class, one of two classes me and Petey shared senior year. There weren't any really hot girls in that class, or Noreen, or any of my other friends, so I sat next to Petey, who always sat in the last row, last seat, from where he would occasionally declaim when he took the time to put down one of his own books and address the class.

"I like sitting here because I can s-s-see whatever's coming," he explained. But really that wasn't so. He spent most of the time dreaming out the window. That was Sr. Jeannette's room and it was on the top (third) floor, and faced the ocean. You could see the Harbor Islands all the way out to the Graves, the last spit of rock twenty-five miles out in the harbor before you hit the high seas. What was he thinking all the time looking out back then? Sorry, you can't always believe me. I know now, knew then too, could have guessed anyway but didn't care to then. Was afraid to.

I usually took Petey's mimeo notices too. He wasn't interested in any of the handouts. See, I loved to inhale all the inky smell out of them. A little buzz or maybe you'd just imagine it. But after a few minutes of staring out the window this particular day Petey turned to me and asked for the notice the day the YEA! Program's handouts went round, so fresh they smeared purple. ·

"What d'you got a business idea?" I asked dubiously, giving his back.

"I d-do indeed," he said. Petey read the notice, then went back to staring out the window. After a bit he turned back to me.

"Let me ask you s-s-something, Danny," he murmured. "Without looking, now—what's the sky doing today?"

Petey curled a black hair lock in his fingers while he stared. There almost always seemed to be a smirk at the back of his eyes when he talked to me now—and behind that, something else again.

"Ah, how do you mean?"

"I mean what I say. What's the sky d-d-doing right now? What's it look like? Don't l-look!"

"I dunno. Sunny, I guess."

Petey held my eyes. He nodded.

"Ex-exactly," he whispered.

I looked beyond him to see a sky gray as a saucepan, blackening in the east.

Petey's new obsession for the next few months was that same question. Notebook in hand, he began boulevardering up/down Broadway after school and on weekends, ambushing people if they didn't walk away fast enough when they saw him coming.

"Without l-l-looking up," he'd ask, "what's the sky doing right now?"

At first he reported he was doing a project for school, but then one of the nuns at bingo one night told someone she didn't know the first thing about it, so everyone became further convinced of Petey's increasing weirdness. *God bless him and the poor creature's never been the same really since the accident has he.* But they humored him of course, in memory of the Golden Boy he once had been, and *for the sake of his poor mother.* And of course he was One of Our Own, a Townie, a perpetual indulgence being granted as a result. He had his paper route still, which was the only job he could find or go back to after the fiasco at the drugstore, and the money he didn't give his mother or the stray dogs he bought a camera with and set up a little darkroom in his attic.

Petey wouldn't tell even me what his idea was, but when I did see him that fall and early winter outside of school—which wasn't too often; I was usually tied up with Noreen or hockey or partying or whatever—he'd usually be on his back, or perched on the corner of somebody's roof three stories up or something, taking pictures of the sky. In fact it was this kind of thing that got Petey in a bit of trouble with the law that winter.

On one of these mysterious missions, he climbed halfway up the impossible-as-heaven tower of St. Peter and Paul's, and shinnied through a window into the pigeon-poop belfry, from where he started ringing the shit out of the tower bell. This was only done on Sundays, though they say they used to ring it during World War II when someone thought they saw German U-boats out in the harbor.

Everyone came running of course—*Fire! Foe! Flood!*—and when several score were gathered seventy feet below around the church—including displeased representatives from the fire and police departments, who always seem to arrive in ill humor like you interrupted a card game and them wining for once—Petey stuck his head out the belfry window, pointed up and cried, "The sunset! Look at that friggin' s-sunset everybody! The west wind! The east w-wind too! SHAKESPEARE!"

They eventually dropped charges because the judge in the case happened to have a sister who was at the ball game when Petey got his whack five years before and she'd told Hizzoner all about it. No damage done, except Helen McQueeny did sprain her knee refugeeing down into her basement. *Cripes*, she told anyone, *I thought the goddamn Red Chinese were attackin'*.

Petey asked me a week before would I come with him to the YEA! Program the next Saturday morning, would I come, *Please Danny won't you come*. He said he needed help carrying things, and also that he wanted me there, wanted me to be present when he unveiled some of his philosophies publicly for the first time.

Whatever that meant. I had hockey later that afternoon but said yes, though really I wasn't terribly interested, and was somewhat hungover when the day at last dawned. Petey had a duffel bag slung over his shoulder and a big box of stuff in his arms, and he handed me another big box when I came down my front steps after him calling for me. *He's sleeping,* Ma had said, her unvarying response no matter the time of day when Petey called, and Petey, just as invariably, had thrown gravel up my bedroom window.

"Don't l-look in the box," he instructed as he thumped it to me. It was freezing that morning, overcast murky and the wind like gray darts off the water.

I expected a lot of people to be in Monsignor O'Flaherty Auditorium when we got there; but no, only a scattered pepper-shot handful, sitting in isolated clumps like they'd been plopped from the ceiling any which way.

About twenty kids had signed up for YEA!, but most of them had dropped out before the big day now. Petey signed in and he made the third entry, so that was good. They gave out three scholarships so he'd get one automatically. When he had to put down the name of his business, I looked over his shoulder and watched him write *For Spacious Skies* in his almost indecipherable mental pigeon scratch. I went out for a smoke, then came back in and sat in the seventh row. Seven was lucky just like green was.

There were about twenty people in the audience, mostly family and stuff of those involved, a few teachers too, especially the boring ones and, Get-a-Life Department, it was easy to picture them not having anything better to do on a weekend than hang at the place where they worked all week. The panel of judges was sitting at a perfunctory table off to the side. There was a bit of yellowish paper tablecloth still Scotch-tape-stuck to one corner of the table—there must have been a time here the night before. You could sign up free for the hall when the nuns weren't using it, Grandma Flynn's eightieth, the big time when the cousins from Cork came over, Jackie Carr's election party but no one showed cuz he lost, except for the Mulligans—they could smell a free meal a parish away but there were twelve of them so who could blame them. Nominally free of charge the hall was but a little something always smilingly accepted.

The judges included Mr. Brennan from Brennan Insurance of course and a few teachers assisting him. Mr. Brennan, a portly gentleman as most middle-aged businessmen are, or were before corporate lookism took hold, was just sitting there red-faced with his hand slurred over his mouth. You could tell he was pissed at the low turnout. Across the back of the stage, on which the three entrants were setting up their displays, there was a big-ass banner that said YOUNG ENTREPRENEURS OF AMERICA, SPONSORED BY BRENNAN INSURANCE, CALL TODAY FOR A FREE QU because the banner had slipped down a little and you couldn't read the end of it. Everyone could see this but it seemed Mr. Brennan was too discouraged at the miserable turnout to ask someone to straighten out the banner and he couldn't be bothered. Still it didn't leave me, a future insurance purchaser of America, with a very good impression and I began to resent him for curdling cynicism within my seventeen-year-old breast. Plus the fact that I was hungover.

MaryEllen Collins and Kevin Kilfoyle (the other two entrants) were already seated behind little nervous desks on the stage, their hands folded efficiently on top of the small tables and visible knees bouncing to beat some band. Poor MaryEllen looked like she was having sweating issues. They were both dressed very smartly. In fact I didn't even recognize Kevin until his big fat mother called his name from the second row. She was filming video. I remembered that Petey was wearing jeans and a T-shirt. And sandals, even though it was the middle of winter.

"What's up with the Jesus sneakers?" I'd asked him on the way over.

"My b-boots are all wet. I tried to w-w-walk on the water last night."

Petey however was not visible to the audience now; he had hung up a bunch of sheets as curtains (that was what was in his duffel bag) and you could see them occasionally puffing out as he got busy behind them. See Petey never liked to be discovered in the act of something, but preferred to spring out fully armed and clothed into any situation, like that Athena lady we read about in Greek mythology, who came out of somebody big-boobed with a helmet on and a sword, ready to *Cleave injustice,* Sr. Anne said rapturously with both hands upon the lowest part of her throat. Two of the sheets were blue and then there was a white one and a light yellow one. Funny what you remember. The yellow one had a big cum stain on it though, like a gray puddle of a country that had miscarried and unfortunately that was the sheet Petey had hung front and center. Talk about your dirty linen in public but I guess he hadn't noticed. Or maybe he had—you never knew with Petey.

There was still ten minutes to go when Petey reappeared on the stage. He squinted out into the audience, saw me, then came rushing down, tripping on the last stage step which wasn't like him, he was usually so birdy agile-like.

"The others got all d-d-dressed up," Petey said, looking back.

"I know it. It's too late now though so don't worry about it. What's that in your hands?"

"Who says I'm w-w-worried? Questionnaires. Can you collect them in five m-m-minutes, Danny?"

"What are they?"

"Questionnaires I said. I'm going to hand them out n-n-now to every-body. Can you c-c-collect them in a few minutes?"

I paused.

"Awright."

"What's the m-m-matter, you don't w-w-want to?"

"No, I will. I said I would."

Petey still held them clutched in his hand like he was uncertain. There was a question in his eyes that went beyond this particular time and place. I looked away, back up at the stage. I wasn't giving him attitude I just didn't feel that good, hungover and so forth and would be exhausted now at hockey later because I didn't get to sleep in.

"Never mind then, I'll c-collect them myself. B-but please fill one out, if it's not too taxing on your booze-pickled br-brain," Petey said. He flung me one, along with one of those little dinky pencils you keep score with at miniature golf, though we never played it of course. That was geeky and for suburbans.

"I'll collect them for you in five minutes," I said. "I said I would."

Write down what the sky looked like this morning on your way here, Petey's questionnaire read.

I rolled my eyes and let it slip to the floor as Petey went off, handing them out. Most people stared down at them with scrunched brows like they were waiting for more writing to appear. Mrs. McGuinness (she was connected to the Kilfoyles) complained that she'd forgotten her reading glasses and *Could someone please read it to me please.*

"The sky!" someone called out from the second side row. *The sky!*

"What about the sty?"

Mrs. McGuinness was very hard of hearing. She owned that bakeshop on Dorchester Street there and when her sister-in-law or the Cummins girl wasn't around to wait on you, you had to either point or tell her forty times what you were after. She preferred to talk about the Red Sox, soaring real estate prices, the state of her corns. She yelled. You could hear her coming, except in reverse I mean, she never left the store hardly.

"He wants you to write down what the sky looked like this morning," the woman yelled back.

I didn't want to, but after three minutes I got up and collected Petey's questionnaires. Most people had written down *blue* and nothing else. Which was wrong. I think. Some didn't even write anything. Someone else left their name and an address, wanting information about the YEA! Program sent to their nieces back home in Ireland, *If you would please. They would find this very interesting I think!* I pictured three tall homely girls, sitting out in a green field somewhere taking turns on the harp, watching sheep. Anything would be interesting under those circumstances. I trotted up the stage steps, pulled back the curtains and handed the filled-in questionnaires to Petey. He didn't say thank you, just snatched them from me.

"You're welcome," I said, heading back to my seat.

Ten o'clock came and after some whisperings between them, the panel of judges sent a delegation consisting of the retired but still fearsome Sr. Marie Celine up to the stage to see if Petey was ready. The sheets came down with yanks and there was Petey, and then he seated himself behind his desk. There were two partition things behind him, with posters attached showing many big blown-up pictures of the sky. Another poster was titled A GUIDE TO THE SKY and it showed pictures of about forty million different types of clouds and what their names were.

They started first with MaryEllen Collins, quite sweaty-moist by this time and the bright lights not helping matters. Our principal, Sr. Margaret, spoke first and thanked everyone for coming, then thanked and introduced Mr. Brennan, who got up and mumbled a few words. You could tell he was bummed out, so few people here.

"I remember years ago when this place would be packed," he said to no one in particular, looking out into the near-empty auditorium. *Shut the fuck up,* I said in my head to him. He annoyed me though I couldn't say why. Then he sat down and beloved Sr. Agnes got up. She was the head of the Business Department and she spoke a little about the YEA! Program and all the scholarships it had given out over the years. She said our next speaker was Ms. Marie Curtain, a former YEA! scholarship recipient who now owned her own business, but then Sr. Claire John pulled on Sr. Agnes's sleeve and said, "Oh please excuse me, Sister. I just remembered, someone called this morning and said she wouldn't be able to make it today. Something about picking someone up at the airport. That must have been her." She said the words in a hush but they came over the microphone nonetheless, the b's and p's popping as they will to the microphone-uninitiated. There didn't seem to be any reaction one way or the other from the lamby audience, but Mr. Brennan put his hand up to his forehead and shook his head. And then one of Petey's posters fell off his partition thing behind him. He got up and stuck it back on. Everybody watched.

"What did she say?" Mrs. McGuinness stage-whispered.

"All . . . alright then, let's start this morning's program with a prayer then," Sr. Agnes said. The other three nuns on the panel and Brother DeFillippo the science teacher (I'm not sure what he was doing there) stood up and then everyone in the audience stood up. Usually just a Hail Mary or Our Father would suffice on generic occasions like this, but Sr. Agnes had taken a year off to work with the poor and shat upon in Central America, and since she'd gotten back she was all about the Poor and Exploitation and the Evils of Technology and the Sin of Greed Regarding Third World Debt, which was a bit out of the everyday for the head of the Business Department. She was the only teacher that still really adored Petey, still thought him the Golden Boy.

"In the name of the Father and the Son and the Holy Spirit," she began, bowing her head, and everybody made the sign of the cross.

"Great loving Creator, we ask you to bless all here, and to infuse us all with a love of justice, to create in our hearts a power of love rather than the love of power, for business that seeks to share all of your bounty and beauty with all the people of this world, amen."

It didn't look like Mr. Brennan liked this any more than he had the missing Ms. Curtain.

"I wonder why she won't speak up?" Mrs. McGuinness wondered out loud.

Then Sr. Agnes introduced the first entrant, MaryEllen Collins, who stood up so fast when her name was called it looked like she'd sat on a hornet. She read rapidly with her head hanging down from a clutched handful of sweaty file cards and said her business idea was called Teddy-O Pop. She talked too fast and wouldn't speak up either and even I couldn't hear a lot of what she said, plus I was also checking out her ample Texas titties while straining to hear.

But it seemed like her idea was to make healthy drinks marketed to kids. She said people were interested in living healthier lifestyles nowadays and there were lots of healthy drinks on the market geared for adults, but none for kids. She said her drinks would come in a bottle shaped like a teddy bear and have no sugar in them. She said the drinks would be sweetened with fruit juices instead, and would have added healthy things like echinacea and ginkgo biloba.

"What'd she say, *bingo all over?*" Mrs. McGuinness chorused from the second row. "Where?"

MaryEllen had a chart behind her that showed how largessey the market was for some of these adultish drink companies like SoBe and Nantucket Nectars and a few others and they were all in the many many spondulicks. I recalled a mountain bicycle race I'd seen on boring TV last snowy weekend at Petey's house, a competition, TEAM SOBE, TEAM BALANCE, TEAM ADIDAS, humans turned into *pedaling billboards* Petey said and he added that one wanted to blow cigarette smoke in their faces, take away their gear and make them talk for once about something relevant.

But I digress.

All the letters in MaryEllen's chart slanted up from the left to the right. Then she said that she had already perfected a few drinks, and if anyone cared to come up and sample them they might. She said she had a few doughnuts and cookies too. Mrs. McGuinness heard this all right and led the charge that ensued to the stage. Having a hangover is dry work as anyone knows so I scampered up too. MaryEllen had little paper cups filled with her samples, four different flavors, those dinky dentist-office sanitary cups, with the rolled edges and the lines on the sides that always remind me of tiny worms somehow. Petey had walked over to her by this time and was suggesting she should call one of the flavors Jolly Olly Orange but it might be copyrighted already. *Yeah whatever,* she told him. She was more or less ignoring him like most people did those days except the girls who had crushes on Petey, who never knew what to say to him.

MaryEllen's flavors were VeryBearyBerry; Minty the Bear; Coconut Koala Cola (gross!), and Luscious Lemon Dee-Lite, which tasted okay if you could get past it looking like the first phase of a drug test in the little white cups she had on the table there, which was a poor aesthetic choice I couldn't help thinking but MaryEllen was always cheap. The first one was the best and I clugged about a dozen of them before she clutched my hand and muttered, "Save some for the fish, O'Connor." Her soft white hand was all fleshy and sweaty and I asked her as I wiped my hand on my pants if she served towels with her handshakes and then she told me under her breath to drop dead.

"If I had one more of them cola ones I probably would," I shot back.

Mr. Brennan had trooped up to the stage with everyone else and he kept going on and on about what a wonderful idea it was but I noticed he, too, kept eyeing MaryEllen's breasts. Sr. Agnes seemed to observe this too and finally she put her hand on Mr. Brennan's elbow and asked somewhat icily wasn't it time now to move on to the next one now.

Kevin Kilfoyle's idea was something about combining video and audio and stereo and God knows what else. It was way over my head so I'm not even going to try and explain. But he was all excited about it and was of course spittling a little in his zest as geeks will. Mr. Brennan fingered the change in his pockets, asked a few polite questions as did Sr. Agnes, but Kevin answered them all with his snickery little laugh in a kind of sarcastic way as if any idiot would know the answers, and that didn't go over too well with anyone. He was always such a dinkweed, and if his older brother wasn't Krazy Kilfoyle, whose MO when fighting was to get people down and then commence removing their ears with his teeth, Kevin would have been roundly beaten every day of his life until he smartened up. And good for him too.

Then it was Petey's turn.

The bright white spotlight swung onto him and he shielded his eyes and asked Blubber Hogan up in the control box to get the light off of him, he couldn't see.

"I mean it Bl-Blubber, t-t-turn it down," Petey said after a minute of silence and no response from Blubber. Everyone looked up and behind and there was Blubber, doughnut powder delineating his mouth and more being shoved in with the back of his palm. I thought of a movie we'd just seen in geography class on Canada, giant cut-down logs being rammed into a sawmill. The light turned orange then purple then turquoise and finally dimmed a little and then Petey jumped off his seat and rubbed his hands, like he'd been waiting all his life for this chance, though he still turned scarlet with embarrassment.

"My b-b-business is called For Spacious Skies," Petey announced, "and it seeks to gen-gen-generate an appreciation of the miracle of the s-sky."

"Is he on drugs or something?" Mr. Brennan mumbled to Sr. Agnes, referring I suppose to Petey's stuttering—but again unfortunately the microphone was on and everyone heard. Sr. Agnes's celestial smile—she always had that look on her heart-shaped face when Petey spoke—soured instantly into Medusa Nun-Glare, the full battery of which she turned and directed at Mr. Brennan. Then she whispered something emphatic into his ear, making sure she covered the table microphone with her hand first. Her head jerked in her passion, causing her little nun veil to bounce up and down, vicarious exclamation points at the beginning of her sentences like in Spanish as it were.

Petey's eyes sought out the floor and he seemed to shrink into himself, like he'd sprung a leak.

"*SHUT UP, BRENNAN!*" I heard myself yell from the seventh row, before I could even think about it. Everyone's head snapped back around to see who said this and, old Southie trick, I did the same and stared at the one person sitting behind me, Kevin Kilfoyle's great-grandfather, who was like ninety in the shade.

Uh uh uh uh, was all Great-Grandpa could get out under these discomfiting circumstances, with these little spasmodic jerks of his limbs.

"Now now," Sr. Agnes remonstrated over the microphone, "let's have no rudeness this morning."

But she couldn't have said the words more gently, approvingly, if she'd called him *Darling.*

Mr. Brennan turned redder and Petey cleared his throat theatrically and began again.

"Unlike s-s-some companies that think only of m-m-making profit through insurance schemes or other d-dubious chicanery, For Spacious Skies seeks only to make people appreciate the sky. No one really does you know, as my intensive s-s-surveys have indicated. On twenty-ni-nine different oc-oc-casions, I asked passersby on B-Broadway without looking up to t-t-tell me wh-what the sky was d-d-doing, and n-n-not one person c-c-could to my satisfaction. Yet on most of these occasions the sky was nothing short of s-s-sublime, and once at sunset it was mi-miraculous. Again this morning, I asked e-e-each of you to write down what the s-sky looked like on your ways here, and only one person could, Sr. Agnes. Which is interesting, because there's a nun t-tunnel that connects the convent to the auditorium here, and Sr. Agnes wasn't even outside probably."

Petey little-kid waved his hand in her direction. She beamed back, leaned into the microphone, and said, *"I lift up mine eyes to the mountains, from whence cometh my help."*

"Exactly," Petey said. "Right on, Sister. Now listen everybody, I'd like to begin with a little story if I m-may. A B-Button Man story. None of you know what that means except for Danny O'Connor but that's okay, I just have to give credit where credit is d-due. Ready? Okay. So, there was this psychiatrist, right? A big deal, Harvard, whatever, his clients all these messed-up rich people, the horror of it all, achieving the American Dream, no? And anyways one d-day, this psychiatrist was driving ba-back to Boston from this conference on the North Shore, where he was the keynote sp-speaker, and there was almighty traffic, I think there'd been an accident. So he gets off the highway and thinks he'll try and find a backroad somewhere, even though he d-didn't really know the area. So he's driving along, driving past strip malls and new developments and the usual eye-as-saulting excrescence of sub-sub-sub—"

"Suburbia," I called from the seventh row.

"Thank you, suburbia, and by and by the road starts rising, the strip malls thin out then vanish, and he finds himself on this amazing country road. Twisting and turning past farms and abandoned farms, fields and the half-veiled s-suggestion of fields. On and on he drives, and the road still rising, and him still wondering where the f—ahhh, where he m-might be.

"Then, this s-sudden noise! And not the twittering of happy little birds, as I bet you were all thinking. N-no, this sound henced from beneath the hood of the doctor's late-model imported luxury sedan. Arctic Gray its color. Now, if I may d-digress: this color—our good doctor had been careful in the selection of it. Black was the strongest contender of course because that was the thing, b-but he suspected his patients might find it a speck too f-funereal. White might work but he didn't want patients thinking of him as their savior, though m-many of them did and really, to tell you the truth he really didn't m-mind all that much. The Arctic Gray seemed a happy m-medium, if you'll excuse the expression, our doctor not caring tuppence for the occult and Reiki and meditation and s-such like.

"So, this noise now, out from under the hood—what a freakin' clatter! A v-veritable Oedipal rebellion, by the sound of it. And then red warning signs of an im-imminent panic attack flashing across the usually cool, Swedish brow of the heretofore sangfroid of the d-dashboard; an anxiety attack, a grand mal of anxiety attacks, signaling in the sudden beeps and whistles, as if he'd left four hundred doors open, lights on, keys ignited, scores of seat belts unhitched. In short, his car was h-having a complete breakdown.

"It stalled. He glided it to the s-side of the road. The steering locked up. An intelligent car, marketed as the intelligent clone's choice of c-cars, but like a smart person's breakdown there's more can go wrong when the st-stuff hits the fan. The doctor tried restarting it but a puff of vapor, with a density that recalled to him films he had seen in grammar school about the industrial revolution, discouraged him.

"The poor doctor! You can imagine! What to do, what to do, he d-didn't know what to do. The sign on the visor above him, extolling the ease of calling the toll-free number for roadside assistance anywhere in N-North America, seemed to be mocking him. Intermittent cars hurtling past him were eager to stare, to slow down and gawk, but were of course loathe to offer help. He thought he might get out and fl-flag someone down, but this seemed beyond him.

"He became aware of a growing hostility, of almost clinical d-depth, flaring up inside him at these same gaping, sneering passersby."

"What's your business, son?" Mr. Brennan interrupted. Everyone seemed to wake up, with a jolt.

"We're g-getting to that," Petey said. "But I thank you for the interruption, normally c-considered rude, as I'm dry. I shall qu-quaff, while the members of our audience are free to momentarily mull over the sweet rewards that m-might result from our modern American businesspeople being hauled off to ch-charm school."

Petey leaned behind him and drank from his bottle of water.

"Ahhh!" he gasped. "Wonderful! If a mite t-tepid. As Thoreau wisely noted, water really is the only drink for the w-wise. No o-offence," he added to MaryEllen beside him.

"At length—after a long frustrating hour—our good doctor abandoned his car. Usually a stone face of stoicism, he could be seen to slam the Arctic Gray door; but such was the air-tightness of his vehicle, such was its, one might almost say, *anally* engineered solidity, that the door wouldn't slam, but only puff-close, if you f-follow. Alas! I regret to report that a passerby, if there h-had been one at that moment, might have seen the doctor, usually a laving hand (albeit chemo-therapeutically) on the hot brow of temper, kick the side of his car. While this same model had been demonstrated, in legions of commercials, to withstand oncoming vehicular br-broadsides of almost asteroid-like strength and accuracy, our doctor's Italian dress shoes proved in this case the gnat that stung the elephant into submission—a foot-size indent on the once flawless side panel was the result of this kick. Nor did it do the doctor's toes any good either. As there are children of all ages pr-present here this morning, I shall refrain from reporting the doctor's ensuing commentary. I will say though that after hopping about on one foot for an undetermined amount of t-time, the doctor abandoned his vehicle and limped off—to seek his fortune, as the old a-adage goes.

"It was a m-miserably hot and humid afternoon, as these car breakdown days almost always are. The road, sad to say, was still rising, and the doctor's suit, while boasting m-magnificent lines for a man of his size, as his salesman had pointed out more than once on the afternoon of its purchase, seemed incapable of shedding the sweat that now ran freely about the d-doctor's person. Nay, in f-fact quite the contrary, the suit seemed to be manufacturing as much water as the doctor's body, as if in sympathy. Italian of course, that suit, and a v-veritable Venice now of flooding, if you catch my d-double drift. The road became steeper still, almost to the point of disbelief. A colleague would have looked twice, hardly knowing the doctor for his dishabille, or the state of his complexion, which recalled the flag of any of our c-communist countries, see usually he was so p-pallid. A car— of approximately tw-twice the value of the doctor's, who was loathe to be ostentatious, though of course he could have afforded something similar— swept round the corner just then, hard-dr-driven by a sun-glassed, ash blonde woman who, by the looks of her accoutered backseat, was returning from a shopping orgy. After all, by now this was the exurbs; *horsy country*, as the realtors like to say, and what else to do, other than hunter-gatherer shopping trips and extramarital affairs, as no d-doubt our host this morning could attest."

The two or three people in the audience still listening to Petey snapped their heads in the direction of Mr. Brennan. However, it seemed Mr. B had perfected the trick of some dogs, and certain high school students, of appearing to be awake when in fact they are not.

Petey waited a polite moment for a retort, his head cocked in the direction of the panel. When none was forthcoming he resumed.

"The doctor could actually feel the c-c-cosmic wind of this woman's c-car as she raced round the corner. Another coat of paint, as the local saying goes, and the doctor might have become roadkill. But before the doctor could even give vent to the v-v-vituperative words that were beginning to form, like stellar clouds, in the chaotic universe inside him, this woman actually *b-beeped* at our doctor! And not the friendly semi-toot of *Please Be Careful Watch Out I'm Coming,* but the long, violent, aggressive, intrusive, demeaning blast of the eminently entitled being forced to momentarily share the very edge of road with the less fortunate. An *F U* blast, if I m-may, a *Get the F Out of the Road!* blast. Alas, there were no sidewalks—picture a pleasant Sunday stroll along Route 128, if you will, if you're wondering why; you see, roads aren't made for people, certainly not for pedestrians, they're made for the car and oil industries. This realization occurring to the doctor, he thought it might behoove him to d-decamp from the road, notwithstanding the four-foot-high barbed wire cow fence separating him from the field on the road's other side. I won't detail the doctor's attempted climbs over this ancient, rusting, wobbly but somehow insolvable barrier, only to say: first, that the doctor would never wear this particular suit again; and second, to briefly allude to a vast, unfortunate coincidence, that being, the owner of this field having decided to use *this very spot* to warehouse his extraneous cow and pig m-manure. The poor doctor! It wasn't pr-pretty.

"Thus it was a changed doctor who stumbled through a fallow field of waist-high grass, to escape, first, the heat of the road, and second, the frustrated r-rage of shoppers hoping to have their souls filled with purchases major and minor, but alas, returning home emptier than when they l-l-left.

"And now here he is. In a field. The temperature in the mid-nineties, the h-humidity insufferable. Now of course such a field on a summer's day is a glory of God's myriad Creation, but it seems the doctor cannot at this time share this slap-happy sentiment at the discovery of the mosquitoes, bees, hornets, yellow jackets, midges, gnats, blackflies, white flies, no-see-ums, and other testaments to Our Lord Skovo's diversity. He thinks instead how his degrees, his pedigree, Dr. Sally MacGee, his wife, the who's-who-ness of his clients, the boo-hoo-ness of his self-pity, the icy-clean rationality of most of his thoughts, words, and deeds, even the profundity of the address he had delivered to some of his colleagues earlier this very day, avail his legs not a whit as he tries to negotiate his Italian-shod way through this rumbly f-field. To wit, he runs out of gas, to continue along the road of the auto-ish metaphor of my tale, and he collapses! From exhaustion. In this middle-of-nowhere f-field. For some time, the only move he can make, like a turtle on its back, is to squiggle his head a bit to the left to withdraw into the n-niggardly shade of an adjacent but parched swamp maple, or *Acer rubrum*, as the botanists call it."

Petey held up a *wait a sec* forefinger and then turned and reached again for his water.

A sort of stupefaction-by-overwhelmification seemed to be pressing down on the audience, myself included. But Petey had lots more to say. You wouldn't think a stutterer would be so good at public *seanchaí*-ing.

"The prostrate doctor recalled—I'm referring now to his position, rather than his Position, if you follow—he recalled I say with the only relief he had felt all day, that he would now m-miss his luncheon appointment with his professing wife. He realized suddenly—profoundly—how invincibly she bored him. There had been a puff story on her in the local paper some months before—he wondered how she'd swung it right before salary negotiations at her university—which rhapsodized how she was *on the very edge of academic critical thought.* He himself could vouch for this, from the very few but acidic words they exchanged at the breakfast table. Too, her smell rankled, almost beyond the doctor's endurance—what was it? What was it? Something inherently her own, soury-sweet smelling, immitigably welded, as with iron clamps, to her herbal bath powder—both odors singularly offensive to the doctor, but the whole being so much more than the sum of the p-parts. It quite p-piqued him that all the relationship workshops, all the discussions and conversations, to say nothing of medication, could not seem to save this relationship—dammit, it all came down to *smell.* He didn't like to ruminate over this because it bothered the doctor no end that a man of his intellect and rationality could be so moved by the b-baser instincts. A National Authority on Psychiatry, and yet it all c-came down to odor. He might as well be a dog.

"The one part of the d-doctor that wasn't sweating and gasping wondered who bored him more, his wife or his mistress. He recalled with just a s-s-soupçon of discomfiture that he couldn't at this precise moment recollect his mistress's name. *Oh, of course, Nancy, that's it.*

"Or was that, he wondered, the new secretary's name in his Cambridge office? At any rate I do believe the doctor slept for a time, out of sheer exhaustion.

"Now, when he awoke, it was as if to a d-different world; though this did not immediately occur to the doctor. Instead he recalled the dream he had just had, in which his m-m-mistress was nibbling his limbs in this kinda painful but pleasy-teasy way. He raised his head and observed a host of mos- .quitoes—it might have been a convocation—quivering about his face and neck with that hovery yet unerring flight of theirs. Some had even, he discovered after further c-consciousness, managed to ascend the cuffs and collars of his c-couture, and were making hay where the sun didn't shine, as it w-were. He leaped to his feet, giving homage to St. Vitus, shedding the pests as best he could, then forgot all else at the scene that lay before him, beyond him, above him.

"Without knowing it, the doctor, almost in sp-spite of himself, had achieved the cr-crown of this particular hill in Essex County. The view alone would have given anyone a bon—ah, would have st-stunned anyone—a sun-dappled valley, in a thousand shades of fl-flickering green, gathered within the ample blue bosom of hills, and more hills, and more hills behind, fading from green to blue to gray to something that wasn't even a color, but a gleam, a promising shine. But above all this—really, right before the doctor's eyes, because of his altitude—the sky was up to s-sublimity. You see everybody, S-H-I-T Happens, as we are reminded when perusing certain no-brow bumper stickers, and so does sublimity. The turgid, b-bitchy horror of the heat wave that had r-rotted over New England for the p-past week was now being swept away by water-cool Canadian air. Sweet, that air, but how to d-describe the smell of its non-fragrance to folks of your limited v-vernacular, the good Sr. Agnes b-being the exception that demonstrates this rule?

"The sky was of the softest, gentian blue, and the light that bounced around this sky was electric, t-tender, shimmering. It might have been the first instant of Creation, or maybe God's dream of Creation, right before He/She Did It. Clouds of castles, castles of clouds, sailed through the skies, leaking fractured yet whole shafts of white and gray light. Moses Horns, I believed people called them in the olden days. Swirling, b-bursting with light, lazy-lolling, majestic. The soundlessness of it all. The diphthong of birds through the azure, the growing glow the color of ripe guavas on the horizon, the benign kiss of the sun, which only an hour ago had been a malicious sear—suffice to say, Nature was having a moment—and for once, so was the doctor. He thought for the fractionest of a m-moment that he might have expired, and this was some Afterworld. But then he remembered he didn't b-believe in such things. While I can't v-vouch for the size of our doctor's id, I will say, 'tis a mighty ego that can swipe out Eternity, no?

"B-but if there are few atheists in foxholes, there might be fewer still when the wheels within wheels shift, and Rapture comes a-calling. The doctor fell back onto the breast of Mama Earth, as if he'd been whacked; as indeed he had, with the Wonder Stick. He watched the sky swirl s-silently above him. He thought his h-heart might break. He thought he might not survive this; he didn't care. He wept. He got up and paced. He knelt. He fell upon his b-back again.

"The in-intense rapture did not last—r-really you know it can't, we wouldn't survive it. A calm bliss t-took its place, and the shifting of the sky, the interplay between the place where there was light, and the place where there was less light, seemed the most informative thing he ever had witnessed. His mind opened, his heart opened. For the first time since c-college, he began to think there might still be things he didn't know in this world—vast things, systems of things, ranks and files of things. Universes of things. The most r-rudimentary of things. He looked at a half-squashed daisy at his feet and it seemed beyond him.

"This realization—that he had much still to learn, that life was a box o' delights—was the biggest leap of all for a man like our doctor; but he took it without a s-second thought. The moment after that was perhaps the most joyous of all for the doctor that late afternoon. This was followed, almost immediately, by a c-compassion, a big-butted one, to share what he was learning. In f-fact in a eureka moment it occurred to him that, could he only get his patients to go and do likewise—lie on their backs and stare at the skies—he might affect more h-happiness within them than he had before, ever, despite the p-prodigious chemotherapy, despite the weary hashing and rehashing of past rights and wrongs, the one-hour-a-week-at-three-hundred-dollars-an-hour picking over of old bones of wounds and resentments.

"A sudden determination to share all this with his patients was born within him.

"And so the following Monday morning, when his regular round of patients began a-gathering in his minimalist professional suite, somewhere in the bowels of the Goat Cheese Belt in C-Cambridge, the doctor announced to each in turn, and continued to do so during the week, that—well, the d-doctor was no fool. There was hardly, he knew, an uncynical breast among the l-lot of his patients, and a Pollyanna-like reporting that the hills and skies were alive with, if not the sound of m-music, then h-healing, would have been met with canceled checks and an exponential re-reduction in his elevated stature among his colleagues. To say nothing of arched p-patrician eyebrows, and you know how dr-dreadful those can be. You see, these folks longed to hear of *complexes.* They wanted to hear about deep-set, fatal mistreatment at the hands of toxic parents and s-sadistic spouses that had left canyonlike scars which could n-never be wholly cured, only br-bravely endured, with the help of course of a little chemistry. So the d-doctor, knowing all this, craftily announced the development of a new, cutting-edge prescription that the folks in the white coats had only just developed. It promised to r-revolutionize the profession, this medication, and he, the doctor, humbly enough let it be known that he was the sole d-dispenser of this medication, and his patients therefore the sole recipients, should they have the courage to serve in this exciting new v-vanguard. A simple *I can't naturally name names, but the most prominent of my clients have all agreed, but of course if you'd rather not* ensured that everyone signed up for it. And they did, too. A further caution from the doctor—*I must rely of course on your utmost discretion*—guaranteed that this new good news would spread like wildfire. The final directive—*This medication is most efficacious with exposure to the outdoors, and I must therefore demand that after taking it, you lie on the ground and look up at the sky for at least an hour*—seemed a bit queer at first, but the doctor wrapped this qualifying condition in such a haze of confounding nomenclature as to slaughter any ob-objections. And as everyone knows, if you say anything in the right way, people will do it. Just look at all the boys who m-march off to wars at the drop of an ethnic stereotyping.

"And so his patients went forth, doctors and professors, deans and editors, pompous old lions and fierce-eyed d-dowagers, formidable every one, with a month's supply of tiny blue pills that had, alas! been the placebos in a more l-legitimate drug trial some years before. They were each given a journal to record whatever changes of m-mood they might experience. The terrible sobriety of the American Psychiatric Association logo emblazoned on each of these journals' covers sealed up, as if in a Lazarinian tomb, the last of any dubiousness among his patients. And so they went off.

"Within the week results started dribbling in. The first was not promising: *No change whatsoever, none, none, no, but now I see my sense of hopelessness and despair as less a personal symptom, and more a courageous, realistic response to this world,* from an associate dean and author of some twenty sociology texts, was not a good harbinger. It seemed that, like vinegar, this man's exposure to sunlight had made him only the more sour; but like the Tr-Trojan War, where the first to fall came from the eventual w-winning side, as you Greek scholars in the crowd will recall, this old sourpuss was the exception. Intermittent happiness broke out throughout the Boston-Cambridge-Brookline belt. The journals, which were turned in each week for the doctor's examination, became sprinkled with reports of cautious yet obvious changes: *I'm sure it can't last, but I feel a certain buoyancy, a lightness of being. . . .* Sketches, snatches of song and poetry, began appearing on the margins of these journals. Five of his patients reconciled with their estranged spouses. One patient, whose father made B. F. Skinner look like Captain Kangaroo, sent his dad daisies on his birthday that he himself had plucked from a sy-sylvan hillside. Another patient, a heretofore humorless and greatly feared academic department head, suddenly became proficient in a rather underappreciated form of the dance made popular in the hills of western Pennsylvania, and even postponed what was to be her seminal though non-Oprah work, *Deconstructing the Postmodern Czech Suicide Poets,* to pen the sunnier-named but less academically welcomed *Clogging Your Way to Sublimity.* Yes, the sky had done its magic!

"But alas . . . about a year later, on a c-certain plane ride, in the first-class section of course, one of the doctor's now-rosy patients happened to sit next to a prominent, somewhat d-dour New York psychiatrist, and one thing led to another as they say—though not of course in the pr-prurient sense, both men were hopeless br-breeders—and the patient c-confided to his planemate this new, exciting medication that had completely changed his life. The psychiatrist grew increasingly suspicious as the patient waxed lyrical, like the moon rising as the sun sets, until finally he demanded that the patient turn over a sample of this Wonder Drug, saying there was no such thing, that surely if there were, he would have h-heard of it himself. He promised to send it to his laboratory for analysis, and twenty-four hours later a fax machine in the patient's home spat out the shocking news that the pretty blue pill was just that—a nothing, a placebo, a specious r-rendering of sugar and gelatin and water.

"My, how the sh-sh stuff hit the fan! The papers, always eager to detail a gentleman in distress, ran with the story. The colleges the doctor was associated with severed all connection with him. He was debarred from practicing. A hearing, in which the doctor sought the testimony of his patients, produced only three still-believers among the hundreds he had helped, and these were shouted down by the learned men and women in attendance.

"But there was one woman who heard the doctor's call for help too late—she would have been there otherwise—for she was leading the clogging troop in the Homer Days Parade somewhere in West Virginia, I believe, that weekend. Some were not so blind as not to see.

"So, I say to you all—believe that beauty is out there! Believe that happiness is not a whim, an illusion, but the birthright of all! But beware! It might change your life! Beauty might snatch you! Change you! Look what it's done to *m-me!* In other words, would you accept belief in God, in Joy, in Happiness, handed freely to you, if it meant you had to change your ways?"

"Right on, Petey!" Sr. Agnes laughed from the panel table. She started clapping while Petey bowed, and a few others joined in politely, thinking Petey's ramble was now over. But we had still to hear about his business, and so Petey turned to the charts behind him.

"Now, about my b-business. I won't b-b-bore all of you with scientific explanations of the w-w-wonderful atmosphere we h-have on this pl-planet, even though it's a miracle, because if people really c-cared about that then they wouldn't l-live the polluting lifestyle that we do. Especially business types. I mean let's face it, you c-c-could really substitute the word *entrepreneur* for *polluting exploiter,* and you wouldn't be f-f-far from the truth."

It was Southie, and the applause seemed to have awakened Mr. Brennan, so, with the delightful prospect of a row in the middle of what must have been otherwise a dreadful bore, everybody looked at Mr. Brennan, who started squirming in his chair, and getting even redder if you can believe it. *Might like you better if your head was redder,* I thought to myself, trying not to laugh, paraphrasing a popular alternative song.

"But I will ask y-y-you," Petey went on, "to think of the s-sky as an ocean, a river, a sea of air that is always sw-sw-swirling around and above us. C-compared to the earth's size, the layer of sky in which clouds form is like the cover on a b-b-baseball—but miracles occur here. It's the only pl-place where one of the basic elements of earth—in this case that most wondrous of substances, w-w-water—comes in all three forms: liquid, s-s-solid, and gaseous."

At Petey's mention of the word *gaseous,* one of MaryEllen's two ten-year-old terror twin brothers, who'd been dragged here, put his fleshy forearm up to his mouth and let loose with an extremely elongated fart sound. Mrs. McGuinness started bounce-laughing as did the twins, both of whom were instantly dragged out by the ears by the humiliated Mrs. Collins. She always punished the both of them for whatever a one of them did, claiming it saved time.

"The sky is a joy," Petey resumed after this interruption, "showing us s-s-something new every minute, if we would but look up. Now, my investigations led to watching p-p-people generally as they walk, and the cl-cl-closer you get to downtown and the f-financial district, the more people l-look down when they're walking. Psy-psy-psy—"

"Psychiatrists," I hollered from my row.

"Psychiatrists will t-tell us that the eye and brain function differently when they look down as opposed to up. To p-p-put it simply, happier chemicals are released in the brain when we l-l-look up."

"What he say?" Mrs. McGuiness wondered aloud again.

"I said LOOK UP!" Petey cried, throwing his arms skyward. "Look up I say, and see the b-b-beautiful sky all round us! It's always ch-changing. It's a vision of heaven. It protects the planet, but more important, its beauty has been g-given to all of us. It will be h-here after us, it's been here before us, and it's up to us to m-m-make the most of these things that have been g-g-given to us. You c-c-can look up at any time of day or night, and see a miracle for free. And not feel so boxed in, even if your life s-su . . . ahhh . . . stinks. Stinks out loud."

Jesus! He's right, I thought, remembering the night of the stars in the alley, how that had made me feel—

"And how will this venture generate *profit?*" Mr. Brennan asked, intoning the word the way I mumbled *wet pussy* to myself over and over when I jerked off at night. Everyone's head went toward Mr. Brennan, then back to Petey, like they were watching Ping-Pong.

"Profit?" Petey asked, tilting his head to the side the way a dog will when you tell him a word he's never heard before. "Who said jack about p-p-profit?"

Mr. Brennan smiled and half shut his eyes. "The first priority of any business is to show profit, son. Otherwise," he said slowly, looking toward the audience, "it won't be a business for long!"

He folded his ham hands on the table and started chuckling at what he thought was a joke. Mrs. McGuinness belly-laughed, even though she couldn't no way have heard him. God love her, she was a jolly old soul. Petey though up on the stage was frozen solid. Except for his face, which was squirming and his mouth was opening and closing. I knew from experience this presaged an outburst.

"That's the p-p-problem with businesses t-t-today, they only care about profit, which is why we have a dying planet and people g-g-going hungry and no medical b-b-benefits. It should be profit and concern, profit and concern, this should be the systole and diastole of the heartbeat of business."

"Well, let me tell you about business in the real world," Mr. Brennan began, but Petey interrupted him.

"J-Jesus said *I must be about my father's business.* What kind of profit did that g-g-generate?"

Everyone's head snapped back to Mr. Brennan again but this time his mouth was a big red O. He wanted to say something but when his eyes shifted to the left, then to the right, you could tell he knew better than to mess with Scripture with nuns fore and aft and a brother to boot.

"Right on, Petey!" Sr. Agnes said again.

"Ahhh . . . thank you son," Mr. Brennan said into the microphone, a tactical retreat, but he got too close this time and it came out all poppy and deep, like a horror movie.

"No I'm n-not done," Petey said, not even looking in Mr. Brennan's direction. He half turned and pointed toward one of his charts. "Now. Did you ever i-imagine there were so many different types of clouds? I know I d-didn't. There's cirrocumulus, and cirrus floccus, and cirrus uncinus, cirrus spissatus, cirrus f-f-fibratus, cirrostratus—"

"Excuse me, Petey," Sr. Agnes asked, raising her hand halfway and inserting a sense of urgency into her voice. "What exactly is cirrus fibratus?"

"Thank you, Sister, we'll be g-g-going over each type of cloud in some d-detail in a moment."

Petey then went on to list about 20,000 more cloud types, and the promise that each one of these would be explained in turn at some stuttering length was enough to make me slip out of the auditorium. But I guess I wasn't the only one who felt that way. Mr. Brennan lasted about ten more minutes, then said he had to go and the panel of judges had to confer first about who the winners would be. You would think that was a moot point as every year there were three winners and there were only three entrants this year.

But I guess what happened was, Mr. Brennan decided Petey wasn't going to get any scholarship money no way no matter what. Even if he was the only entrant. Either he didn't like Petey's idea or maybe he didn't like Petey. Probably both, especially after the cracks Petey had made. I heard there were some heated words between Mr. Brennan and Sr. Agnes, and finally Sr. Julia, our assistant principal, had to intervene. Someone had to wake her up first though—she'd fallen asleep in the front row. She'd been doing that for years. Everyone always thought she was praying. *She looks so peaceful,* everybody always said.

Eventually Mr. Brennan announced that the winners this year for the YEA! Program were Kevin Kilfoyle and MaryEllen Collins. They say Petey just sat there in his chair in front of all his pictures of the Skies Over South Boston, stunned and open-mouthed. Then he gathered up his stuff and left. Sr. Agnes tried to go over to him but when Petey wanted to vanish he was too fast for anyone, let alone a sixty-year-old nun.

Noreen picked me up for my hockey game about an hour later at my house where I'd gone back to bed. I woke up with messy bed hair and boner issues. A headache to beat the band but a coke snort set me to racing ease. Noreen had her own car by then, an ancient white Buick with 2,000 miles on it that had been her eighty-seven-year-old Great-Aunt Teresa's before she went into Marion Manor for Our Aged. Her car still had the daisy thing on top of the antenna and Petey's Universal Mystery Kleenex box way in the back windshield. We used them to wipe up my prodigal loads when me and Noreen had car sex down the beach, and I remember thinking right before I'd commence clean-up detail what a surprise them Kleenexes was in for—forty years of old lady icy nose dribble—and now this. There had been a plastic glow-in-the-dark Mary on the dashboard but Noreen had removed it, and in its place was a petrified ring of glue residue that had dirty gradations of elevation to it, as well as the look of something having been deposed but nothing to take its place.

Noreen's four golden bracelets jangled as she turned the wheel, and I liked the sounds they made, tinkling on about a future life we would have, of our money, and things that were specifically, intrinsically ours, a big-screen TV from Best Buy, a new fridge chock full o' steaks and cold ones. We turned the corner onto O Street and then another, different image, Petey big as life, trudging up the way. It had started freezing raining by then, and the wind was whipping off the sloppy ocean, lavishing the streets with an intolerable half-frozen mush. The different cloud pictures pasted to Petey's posters were flying off in the wind, as if coming to life at Petey's touch and retreating back to their sky, and he was putting down all his boxes to give absurd chase. Noreen *uugghed* in disapproval when she saw him like he was a tard or something.

"Sandals in the middle of winter," she whined. "Why am I not surprised?"

"Pull over," I said.

"You'll be late for your game," Noreen said.

"I said pull over."

"I couldn't stop for cigarettes but you have time for this?"

"Just fuckin' pull over, will ya?"

Noreen groaned and complied, though it was a five-minute walk to the curb. She wasn't exactly Mario Andretti when it came to driving and the art of parking especially evaded her. I got out.

"How did it go?" I asked Petey. "I ahhh . . . I had to leave early."

Petey said nothing.

"Well?"

A car pulled up behind Noreen and beeped.

"Pull over a little," I said to Noreen, turning around. She held up her hands like there was nowhere to go.

"Did you get the scholarship? You won, right?"

I knew he must have—there was just the three of them in the contest.

The other car beeped again. Then Noreen beeped. I turned around.

C'mon Danny! she mouthed through the glass.

I shoved my hands in my pockets and hunched up my shoulders in the slash of wind and ice.

"What happened?" I repeated. The wind tore another cloud picture off Petey's poster and this time he just watched it go, flip-tumbling over and over down O Street. His eyes slurred back to me. I couldn't tell if he was crying or was it the frozen rain in the squinty green eyes. His exposed toes redder than Mr. Brennan's face. Sorrowful somehow, those toes.

"You l-left me," he said. "You w-w-walked right out in the middle." He paused. "That was l-like my World Series. And you l-left."

"I did no— . . . I'm sorry, Petey, I had to . . . I had to go get ready for hockey. But what happened? C'mon, tell me!"

"Forget about it, D-Danny. Go on to your h-h-hockey. The n-never-ending hockey game that's your life now. I'm a f-freak, and freaks don't g-get anything in this world but shit on."

"What are you talkin' about?"

The driver behind Noreen beeped longer now and so did Noreen.

"I gotta go," I said.

Petey waved me off, though his eyes stayed stuck onto mine.

I shrugged and got back in the car.

I didn't score any goals that afternoon at hockey but I did manage to get in three fights. We were playing these fast prissy kids from a private school in the suburbs with $400 skates who would slash you when the refs weren't looking, then fly away from the corners. But I finally managed to nail a few of them. I was in a really lousy mood for some reason. Finally Coach benched me.

"You're a fuckin' animal today, O'Connor," he said. "What did I tell you? Don't hit anyone until I tell you to!"

He turned back to the others on the bench.

"Boys, if any of you ever lose your mind and become a hockey coach later in life, don't ever, EVER, have redheads on your team! They're animals! They have tempers! They can't control themselves! They'll give you ulcers! They'll make you old before your time! They'll . . . "

It struck me how Coach said *animal*. Petey always said the world would be a better place if we were like the animals, and he said when an animal acted savagely we should say, *That animal is a real human,* rather than the other way around. I guess I was a real human that day.

Noreen had gone out between periods and using her fake ID went down to Roxbury to get a case of beer (*We all look the same to them,* she explained). Jackie Regal was in the back for a ride to Old Colony and I had already sucked down two brews on the way home when we saw Petey again. He hadn't moved an inch from where we'd left him three hours earlier. He was just sitting in the corner of this closed-down building's entrance, half-sheltered under a little overhanging roof thing that reminded me of a smile pulled back at the last minute. His posters and whatnot were scattered about him, flopping in the wet and icy wind. There were no pictures on his posters anymore.

"Should I stop?" Noreen asked.

"Ahhhh—"

"He's seen us I think." Noreen giggled.

"He's a fuckin' weirdo," Jackie slurred from the backseat.

"Shut the *fuck* up, Jackie," I said.

"Should I stop?" Noreen asked again.

"No, no, keep goin'," I said.

I looked away as we rode past.

"What are you smilin' at?" I asked Noreen.

"I think he saw us," she laughed.

"Oh. And that's fuckin' funny?"

"He's just so *weird,* Danny. *Too* weird."

I came in when Noreen dropped me off at my house, took a shower, tried to go back to bed.

But I couldn't.

With a cuss or two I got up, got dressed, hiked back up to the corner where I'd seen Petey.

But he was gone.

The more I think about it, the more I think that's when Petey started getting cynical. And maybe it had more to do with me than it did with the YEA! Program. All I can tell you is, by graduation, a change had smeared over him. And when Sr. Agnes pulled some strings and made sure Petey got a $3,000 scholarship just the same (even though Petey had said he wasn't going to college), he had to get up and say something to the graduation crowd.

Everyone gave him a standing ovation when they called Petey's name, parents and teachers and everybody. Shunned him on the street but clapping quite nicely now. I think mostly everyone felt bad about what had happened to Petey, who he once had been. Only I could see—it hit me just then—that Petey was ten times the soul he used to be. And the courage of him. But I didn't want to think about that then.

He shuffled up to the podium with his eyes on the ground. Sr. Agnes handed him the scholarship thing, then kissed him on either cheek. She waved him to the microphone.

A hush fell. Petey's eyes looked out, then all around back and forth half-terrified. He turned red. He ran his tongue over his lips, the top one first, then the bottom. You could almost see in his eyes that he was thinking if it hadn't been for the accident, he probably would have been at the podium all day, accepting awards and scholarships, every kind of honor.

Then something like a grim smile settled on his face. He took off his ball cap and a disaster of sea-curled black hair tumbled out.

He grabbed onto the sides of the wooden podium. Then he leaned into the microphone, raised his eyes and spoke.

"Alexander Haig hastened to The Hague where he was m-m-met by a happy hag, who thought he looked haggard, but she h-h-hesitated to harangue as he was eating heinous haggis," he said.

Then Petey walked off the stage and went back to his seat. The silence that followed his words had all the ambiance of a funeral.

Almost didn't make it to the men's room in time. I kicked open a stall, took a few toots, but still it hit me, weeping, sobbing, so hard I started retching. What the fuck? Three graduation parties after that, maybe four, and by the time I crawled into bed at dawn the reason for my weeping, the memory of it even, had been pushed back to the mud, the mud at the back of my brain where I kept things.

That Must Have Been One Big-Ass Whack on the Head

A rather forgettable year later—Noreen working for Gillette now full-time and, Vesuvius-like, starting to make murmurings of marriage—me working for Uncle Bill, a plumber, when nothing else materialized, but knowing this wouldn't really work.

.And then, strange to say, a decision on my part: a billboardian one, I felt I was slipping away to some kind of permanent amnesia but the billboard on Broadway promised a way out: the few, the proud, in short the Marines. I was on my way to acquire a deck of smokes at the corner when I realized I'd left my Mister Green at home and instead I ended up going to Rotary Lottery and Convenience where they take ATM thingies. I stepped outside, packed my deck, lit one up, then looked up and there it was bigger than life: this close-up of the Marine guy holding a sword up to his nose.

I liked his haircut, admired the uniform, did some role-playing and thought how I wouldn't look half bad in that uniform and because of me forgetting my wallet I signed away the next three years of my life the following week.

"You made a d-decision based on advertising?" Petey gasped when I finally admitted my reasoning, after he pressed me no friggin' end.

"Well, I—"

"You signed up to go kill people for the next three years because somebody looks b-butch on a billboard?"

"They don't . . . Jesus gimme a break! I'm not gonna go kill people, Petey, that's not—"

We stopped because Mrs. Devaney, the neighborhood snoop—there were many vying for this title, but no one had the lift of the right eyebrow, the Mother Hearing, the gift of decisive verbatim recall, like Mrs. Mary

A Map of the Harbor Islands
Published by The Haworth Press, Inc., 2006. All rights reserved.
doi:10.1300/5677_14

Elizabeth Devaney—was approaching, two-wheeler shopping cart bringing up her ample rear. She was resplendent in powder blue tennis hat, matching Keds sneakers with a tiny opening in each pinky, a bright purple jogging suit, and wraparound sunglasses as seen on TV. We were on the corner of O and East Broadway. Me and Petey'd bumped into each other when I was coming back from a jog, I was trying to get in shape for boot camp. After the jog I'd stopped at his house to break the news to him. He was working for Sully's Moving Company a little and also nights and some weekends at the Animal Rescue League. Still had his paper route too.

But whatever he did with the money he didn't buy clothes with it. He was wearing cutoff navy blue sweatpants and a tie-dye T-shirt when I found him going up the road. Petey got all his clothes at the Salvation Army Thrift Shop, saying he didn't want to contribute to *human misery in a world full of sweatshops*. But even in these I couldn't help thinking how good-looking he was, what a figure he'd cut if he even half cared about that stuff. He had topped off at six feet, two inches taller than me, and was still in as good a shape as he always had been. I guess all the walking and swimming and chasing after dogs and God knows what kept him fit and lean. People that didn't know him, I noticed, strangers on the street, were always checking him out, so striking was he—it was only when his mouth opened and you got a fifteen-minute harangue on, say, the mistreatment of dogs at racetracks, the medical experiments being performed on monkeys, the motets of Hildegard of Bingen, you realized you were in for something far different from the average South Boston Joe.

Mrs. Devaney eased her rapid waddle down to a comfortable troll as she passed, like the pigeons on the Common slowing for each passerby, doubtful they would get fed but wanting to be ready for the pounce should any crumbs come their way.

Petey just glared but I smiled as she passed by.

"I understand you're going into the service," she threw back behind her out of the corner of her mouth.

"Yes, ma'am!"

"Good for you!"

I heard Petey groan in disgust.

"Pretty soon your friend there will decide to do something with his life too," Mrs. Devaney added.

"So what did *y-you* say when she refused to have the abortion?" Petey hiss-whispered when Mrs. Devaney was almost out of earshot. "What's the matter with her, she didn't enjoy the last abortion you made her g-get?"

What a wiseass he could be. Mrs. Devaney stopped so suddenly I feared for her long-in-the-tooth ligaments; then when nothing more was forthcoming she continued on her way as if for a wager.

"You're unbelievable," I said.

"Oh please, I did her a favor," Petey said, idly flicking crumbs off his ragged shirt. He'd been down at the beach feeding the seagulls. "I understand s-salaciousness is good for the c-circulation. But Danny lookit—I don't mean to be the one to b-burst your pretty pink balloon, but that's what soldiers do—they kill people and break things." He kicked at a small pebble on the sweltering sidewalk. "Why don't you want to be a b-builder? A g-giver? Don't you think there's enough killers in the world without swelling that rout?"

"They're not all—Christ, Petey look at my father, your father, everybody around here! They fought for freedom and—"

"Oh, was that what they were doing? I *would* ask my father about that Danny—but I c-can't, he's dead. From Agent Orange p-poisoning, even though the g-government is still fighting my mother over the pension. And your father hasn't s-said more than twenty words since he's been back, unless he talks to his flowers. He's a cipher, the poor b-bastard."

Mental note to self: look up cipher *when you get home.*

"Petey, you're taking this the wrong way—"

"Danny, here's an idea—why don't you just go to Broadway C-Costume and rent a Marine uniform and p-parade around in that for a while until you get it out of your system? Everybody would be a lot better off. That guy on the b-billboard's probably not even a Marine, he's probably some gym queen from W-West Hollywood who gets laid, re-laid, and p-parleyed because of the mileage that's given h-him. It's in his AOL profile n-no doubt, *I'm not a M-Marine but I play one on a billboard.*"

"What do you mean, a queen?"

"Jesus, Danny! I c-can't believe you're doing this! That's just what the elites want! Madison Avenue and the Pentagon have you right where they w-want you!"

"They do?"

"Sure they d-do! Why the fuck do you think they advertise in neighborhoods like ours? Make the working-class slobs aspire to fight their wars and protect their corporations so they can get richer, and you can have a-alleged societal approval and wear a uniform and come home in a box, or in a straitjacket, or missing an arm or a leg or b-both. When was the last time you saw one of those Marine billboards in Concord? Or Wellesley or N-Newton? *Be—all that you can be—go kill people—to make us riiiiiii-cher.*"

"Petey, lookit, I can't . . . I can never argue with you! You know more than I do about shit like that, about . . . about everything."

Petey crossed his arms and kicked at another pebble, hard like he was kicking a field goal.

"I just . . . I'm no killer, Petey, and that's not all they do. They help people too but you never hear about it. I'm not gonna kill anyone, I don't want to I mean, I just know I have to . . . I want to get away for a while. I have to think."

Petey's head snapped up at me.

"Your eyebrow just lifted like Mrs. Devaney's," I chuckled, pointing at him.

"Well and why wouldn't it? *Think?*" Petey repeated, dubiously. "A little l-late in the day for that, isn't it? Noreen won't like it at all if you start doing that. Then again, maybe you wouldn't be with Noreen if you started doing that—"

"Petey, let's keep her out of this, she—what's so funny now?"

"I saw her the other day at the bus smoking a butt," Petey laughed, "wearing her new f-full-length denim jacket and white hooker b-boots, and she looked like the Marlboro Man in drag."

"What's drag?"

"When a man wears w-women's clothing."

"That's gross, Petey. If it wasn't you I'd give whoever said that a backhander. I always stop her when she starts saying shit about you. I mean . . ."

"Ahhh," Petey smiled. "The truth at l-last! When I asked you why she always laughs when she sees me coming, you said it was b-b-be-be . . ."

"—because—"

"Because she thinks I'm funny. So wh-what does she say about me?"

"Petey, let's not fight. I just wanted to tell you. I wanted you to know before you heard it from someone else. Ask your mother, I just called for you."

He stopped for a minute. His eyes got bigger as he regarded me.

"You did?"

"Yup, I did."

Somewhat mollified, but still Petey was sulky.

"And when's all this happening?"

"I report to boot camp in two months."

"Well," Petey sighed. He held my eyes. "I guess it's better than you telling me you were g-getting married. That's what I thought at first." He paused, shook his head, looked down at the gutter.

"What . . . what is it, Petey?" I mumbled.

"Forget about it, Danny."

"C'mon, just say it, Petey."

He looked up again. The smirk in his eyes was gone and that other thing—whatever—was almost leaking from them.

"Alright, I will. Danny, I . . . I wish I could get you out in the islands for about a year. I'm not . . . not s-saying I'm better than you. I just feel I've been taught so much . . . given so much. Shown so much . . . so much I could pass on to you. You're not a killer, Danny. Don't let them make you a k-killer."

Such a longing of heartbreak in his eyes, I felt torn between wanting to say _I'll do just that,_ and wishing I hadn't told him. Wishing we weren't friends anymore.

"I'm sorry, Petey," I finally sighed. I didn't know what else to say.

"Danny, you're not stupid, even though I know you think you are. You're just uninformed. Nature abhors a vacuum and so all this other nonsense rushes into your head—they got you, D-Danny, they got you. And it breaks my h-heart." He turned his head away and looked toward the islands. He quick-brushed his eyes when he thought I wasn't looking. An ice cream truck floated by. Then an ear-splitting plane roared overhead.

When I looked over at the corner again, Petey was gone.

Two months later. A night late in September. Hot it was, very hot for late September, the last night of summer really. Balmy bye-bye. The next day it rained and roared and after that leaves and tenderness missing for six months. Maybe more as far as the tenderness was concerned.

A Sunday it was—a coleus Sunday, all mixed up and spangled. Can you see the pages flippin', like they do in Ma's old afternoon movies, the pages of a book, the pages of my story flipping, irregularly, in fits and gusts, like they're being blown by the ahhh . . . Winds of Time? A cheesy effect for these swollen-with-irony times, but I always liked that technique. The beginning of a good story and you can wiggle your toes under the blanket, a dark and portentous beginning like the twisting of a country road on a gloaming autumn night . . . as long as it's not _your_ story. So let them pages flip. Flip flip flip let's flip all the way back to September 27, a hot night at the colliding of summer and fall, both smells in the air rollicking.

I remember the exact date. I was leaving the next day for Parris Island for twelve weeks of boot camp. Like I say the plumbing job with my uncle hadn't worked out—he got to keep all the dough while I blew out all the shitty toilets and clogged pipes—and who the fuck wants to do that for the rest of his life? It's like cool for the first week or two—*Hey shit, I'm a Plumber! Look at my uniform! Look at this truck I get to drive! Look at this check I get every week! Wanna see my union card?* But then after a couple weeks you're poking your nose down that long drainpipe of life and you're saying *Holy shit, I'm a freakin' plumber,* and it doesn't seem like such a good idea all of a sudden when you never see plumbers displayed on TV or in commercials that aren't demeaning. *Hi, I'm Al the plumber, and next time your drains clog, don't call me! Get some Riddo!* Maybe if I had seen some sleek late-twenty-something woman, professionally dressed with legs up to her tonsils carrying a laptop in her briefcase and she was a plumber, maybe I wouldn't have felt so bad. Just because you're a critic of the way things are doesn't automatically make you immune to its influences. Its influenzas, as Petey would say.

Stop the flipping now. It's the night of September 27 and I'm saying goodbye to Petey, off to Parris Island in the morning. Bye bye Petey. September 28, I guess it was after midnight.

"Hey, c'mon, don't look so down, I'll be back."

I glance my hand across Petey's lean shoulder blades as we slide down O Street. A year and a half after graduation and slowly we've come back to each other again over the last few weeks, me going away and people starting to do their own thing now. Though I spend much of my free time with Noreen, there seems time again for Petey lately.

There's leftover dampness still on the inside of my boxers from where I've just cum, over at Noreen's house. I took her out to dinner and when I got back to her house over on West Sixth her family had this little going-away party for me. They had this red white and blue cake from Hanlon's with the American flag in one corner and the Semper Fi globe and anchor stuff in the other corner. It's one of the regular cakes they offer down at Hanlon's there's so many guys around here join the Corps. Then after the party her mother and sisters loudly announced their withdrawal to bed, and me and Noreen messed around in her pink room for a bit, and then she cried and got so upset she left scratch marks on my back on my bare skin with the new nails she'd just got that day down at Princess Nails. She didn't want me to go.

"Danny!" she kept saying, her face red. I was waiting for something more but nothing more after that. Then a minute later "Danny!" again.

I think she was waiting for an engagement ring or something, some kind of promise we'd get married when I got back, and truth to tell I had the ring in my back pants pocket, I'd cashed my last check from the plumbing job, $612.47 and the whole thing, practically the whole goddamn thing went to this ring I'd bought that afternoon at the Jeweler's Building downtown when all I really meant to do was just go in and price them just in case. Drive. Being driven. ASK US ABOUT THE 1/4 OF YOUR ANNUAL SALARY SHOPPING GUIDE WHEN YOU'RE READY TO PURCHASE THE RING the sign on the wall said.

Oh okay. Sure I will. And trying not to think of Petey's words. *They got you Danny.*

But something held me back at the last minute as I was saying goodbye to Noreen, something, and besides, I'd told Petey I'd meet him in front of his house at midnight and here it was quarter to twelve because it took me a while to bust my nut over at Noreen's, and I knew if I gave her the ring she'd make a big scene and wake up her pretending-to-be-sleeping family and there'd be sticky champagne in plastic cups or maybe her mother's Beleek and all that crap and I just didn't have the time. Funny how momentous decisions can be made or not because of other stuff that doesn't seem so important. Remember if you will the forgotten wallet, and Uncle Liam and *Did I leave the stove top on Petey I'm wondering all of a sudden like.*

But I had to meet Petey.

She didn't want me to leave, "You're leaving already?" How is it that some people you give the whole day, the whole night too and still they want more. You've reserved the whole day and the whole night for them and they begrudge the one hour out of twenty-four that you've reserved for this other person who is also important to you.

"Our last night together and you're spending it with *him!*" she wailed. "That . . . loser *weirdo!*"

I remained silent because Noreen and her sisters were in therapy now because of their dead father's abuse of them and *I need to be angry for a while, I'm supposed to get in touch and release my anger whenever I feel like it* and sometimes when I'd approach their back door wanting to drop in unannounced for a little afternoon delight, I would keep going, hearing them all releasing their anger at the same time even though it might just be a hairbrush gone missing they appeared to be fighting over. God knows, I didn't want to interrupt their recoveries.

"I knew you'd c-c-come," Petey says when he sees me. He spurts up from the shadows of his front steps, his smile the brightest thing this Southie night, brighter than the stupid ring. *What about a mother-of-pearl matching necklace?* the lady at the jewelry store had asked me, following me out the door, ready to bar my way seemingly. Please. My whole fucking paycheck wasn't enough for her, she wanted more too. Who the fuck's mother-of-pearl?

Shuffling down O Street now with Petey and why is it harder to say goodbye to him? We've been like brothers. We were always like brothers since first day in kindergarten when we met and it's hot and Petey's wearing a raggedy tank top and cutoff navy blue sweatpants that show his lean very hairy legs. He's got a very lean but somewhat muscled build now does Petey, working for Sully's Moving Company but his real vocation the caring for the dogs and birds of the world, Southie, the making of maps that no one will ever see I suppose. And very hairy legs for a twenty-year-old. Man-hair we used to call it way back when. No of course we're not the same person anymore if we ever were. There's been oceans of water swept under that bridge since but still we're friends, best friends, still very close almost like brothers me and Petey Harding though of course I don't see him as often as I used to. But more lately somehow.

"It j-j-just sucks," Petey murmurs. His hair is medium length and black, longer than most of us wear it around here like I say but that's Petey, and not just to hide the indent on the side of his head I don't think. It shines in the glow of the sodium streetlights and falls down into the sides of his face so I can't read his eyes walking beside me because he's staring at the ground as we shuffle along.

"I won't have anyone to hang with anymore."

"Naww, that ain't true," I say, even though I know it is.

I'm wishing I brought a change of clothes with me because I got somewhat dressed up for the dinner with Noreen, green polo shortsleeve and khakis and my loafers with no socks, because it's still like eighty degrees, the triple-deckers we slide by and brick storefronts selling butts and lottery and WE SOLD A TEN-THOUSAND-DOLLAR SCRATCH TICKET! are throwing back the day's heat, and for some reason I picture in my head going back to Petey's house, going back to Petey's bedroom where some of my clothes are anyway and changing and for some reason this image pops into my head of me changing from my khakis into some cutoff sweats while Petey lies on his bed and I half-tug at my boxers as I'm changing because a little of my cum has dried and is sealing my orange bush to my boxers, and you can still smell it a little in Petey's hot tiny bedroom, still with the Gandalf and Knights of the Table or whoever 8 × 10s and I hear Petey on the bed go *sniff.*

"What about Sully and ahhhh . . . what's their names at the moving place, Kev and Bri?" I ask. "What about . . . ahhhh . . . ?"

I hear a tenderness in my voice that Noreen would raise her eyebrows at. But see Noreen can take care of herself. Petey—I worry about Petey, always have. Okay maybe not so much lately, but more so tonight now that I'm leaving him. Why am I getting so emotional right now? Departures magnify things, like Petey's old Sherlock Holmes detective glass when we were kids. Put anything under it long enough and it'll burn.

"Sully?" Petey asks, throwing a hand on the bottom of his throat. "Bri and K-Kev? What are you, on cr-crack?"

Well he might say it too—we both know that.

He shrugs his shoulders, kicks at a dirty squished Big Fry box on the sidewalk from Burger King up the way. It takes a village Hillary says, but that's just something they say. If they really believed that or cared they wouldn't allow the cigarette-and-liquor billboards that instruct us from on high every waking day of our lives, the ads for blood-and-guns-and-drugs-and-soft-fuck movies, bars and poisonous fast-food joints at every corner. Marine billboards too I suppose, now that I think about it. I wonder if Petey was right about all that?

"We h-haven't hung with Sully in years anyways," he mumbles. "And . . . all those other g-guys . . . they were always y-your friends anyways, not mine. Never m-mine, Danny. Just you. Not since . . . not since w-way back."

It's true so I say nothing. I study him with the edge of my eye, the pot and drinking now, monosyllabic most times, cynical like I say, looking down, unshaven unshowered sometimes. Surly almost.

We're like mechanically without saying a word heading to the beach. It's where we always go. We like the water, we both do, we like to look at the water, just sit on the sand or the seawall and look at the water. When I can spare the time now. Maybe walk out to Castle Island and the Gazebo. We don't float out there anymore, don't run out there anymore either, haven't since we were kids one thing and another but still we like to look out there and Remember, not the days themselves but the way they made us feel, the things we believed in then.

We cross the Boulevard that borders the beach, light and lithe and sweaty-balled.

"I'll write you all the time, Petey."

Petey smiles for the second time tonight and it changes his whole face, always. He's got these dimples. Nice-looking kid when he cleans up. Dark Irish I guess you'd say. These golden flecks in his eyes. Have to get real close though. Like the best of him floating up to the surface from his heart.

"I c-can't really p-picture that but I hope you do," he says as we half-trot out of the way of a bread delivery truck. A warm breeze that smells like fruit gushes up from the shore and runs right through us. I hear Petey sniff deep, then go, *ahhhh*. Which is true.

We hop the seawall. We plunk down on the beach and draw our knees up and fold our hands over them and how many hundreds of times have we been here. We're staring at the Mister Mysterio dark ocean. After a while Petey turns to me. I see him watching me for a while.

"Danny—don't g-g-g-go."

The simple heartbroken murmur of this tugs at me the way Noreen's wails and screams could never.

I sigh, run my hand through my hair which is buzzed already, always buzzed. Oh, I talked Petey into getting his buzzed once four years ago when we were fifteen but he said he looked stupid with it cuz his ears stuck out too much and you could see the little indent in his head. One of the younger kids from the projects saw the indent and said *Cool dude, where'd you get that?* like it was a tattoo or something and Petey just laughed. I thought he looked great though, and like the rest of us but that experiment failed. He would always be different. He looked great but not like Petey—that was the only thing. He didn't look like himself if you follow.

"I just . . . we been through this all, Petey. I just can't be a fuckin' plumber for the rest o' my life. You know?"

No answer.

"You know, Petey?"

Petey's head jerks up but he throws his eyes out to sea and says, hard, "There's . . . there's oth-oth-oth—"

Then he smashes his left fist into the sand in frustration. He can't get the words out when he gets upset like this.

"Shhhh, shhhhh," I whisper, and I rub his back again, turn first, look. No one's watching right?

"Three years ain't so long, Petey. Think back when we were sixteen. That was three years ago already but hey it seems like yesterday, no? 'Member the day you finally got your license and you came by to show me? You turned and waved to me and smashed into Mrs. Flynn's Pontiac?"

Petey flings a handful of sand out toward the water, starts laughing a little.

"Plus you know . . . I mean . . . it's getting kinda hot around here and I should vacate for a bit. They busted Jackie Kilfoyle last week, I don't know if you heard."

"B-but y-you—"

"I know I know, I haven't dealt in a year and I been off the stuff too, but . . . I mean, I'm off the stuff thanks to you. But they're on a witch hunt now and they're nabbing everybody. There's no way they're gonna nab a Clean Marine when I come back."

It was true, I'd gotten kinda on coke a few years back and started doing a little dealing to pay for the shit and Petey was the one who got me off it. He smartened me up and when I got the cravings bad, we'd go down to the M Street Park and play one-on-one 'til we were soaked with sweat and my teeth stopped chattering and my mouth twisting. Petey wasn't too much into sports ever since the accident but when he played he flowed like water still. You just had to watch him. He didn't care but he flowed like water. Ran the ball right by me and me the all-star in the summer hoops league that year.

Those are both good reasons for joining the Marines, sick of plumbing and have to make myself a little less visible to the law, but the big one is . . . like I say I have to get away, have to get away and think, think things out. Before the door slams. I'd dream of it, wake up sweating *Slam!* Where is the door? What does it mean?

"B-but things'll . . . ch-change, D-Danny. You'll get m-married and—"

Petey turns to me and his lank black hair rustles a little in the licking breeze. His eyes go into slits.

"Did you g-g-give Nor-Nor-Nor-een a r-ring? An engagement ring? To-night?"

"No."

I say it flatly, looking away. I feel it pressing into my ass in my back pocket.

"B-but you'll get married and th-things will ch-change, they always d-do. They already have."

"They won't with us. Petey, look at me. They won't. I promise. You're like . . . we're like brothers and nothing's gonna change. Ever. I promise. Tonight I . . . I dunno, I really feel that tonight, Petey. I don't know why. Maybe cuz I'm going away but . . . I mean, I know the last few years I been a little not around maybe, but . . . we'll always be best friends. Always."

"No matter wh-what?" he asks.

"Of course no matter what."

He keeps staring at me from under his hair and I look away finally. Those eyes—

The moon peeps out from these slatty clouds and a bigger gush of warm air pumps in from the ocean. Now that it's come to it I don't want to leave, .don't want to go to no shithole down South and get yelled at all day by Yankee-hating southerners even though I hate the fuckin' Yankees and run fifty fuckin' miles before breakfast but I have to, I've made the commitment. Everyone would laugh if I didn't and how else you gonna get out of this town? Plus they already had the going-away party and everything. Half-eaten cake. Mawed. Mangled. It was melting into caricature when I left. *You're too stupid and poor for college so go kill for your country and corporations, why don't you.* Jesus why did Petey have to say that? But believe it or not, a part of me is glad he did. I mean, that's what this whole thing is about anyway, thinking about things—

Jesus I'm sounding like Petey now—

I pull a pint of Seagram's from my other back pocket and me and Petey swig it back and forth.

"I'm so glad you never got mixed up in the drugs, Petey. So fuckin' glad."

Petey nods his head, but he's still sulking.

After a minute he says, "I've got s-something. To t-tell finally."

I gulp and don't know why.

"Yeah? What?" I ask, too lightly.

Petey nods his hanging head, nods it quick-like.

"What?"

I find that my fingers are coiling around my shoelaces, tugging.

Petey hangs his head again. He's busy too—he's found a stick, teeny-tiny driftwood and he's running it back and forth in little diggy jerks across the sand between his feet, which are bare now that he's kicked his flip sandals off with the paint on top so he won't endorse any particular brand. *I don't want to be a walking billboard. Look at what one billboard did to you.*

"What?"

He looks up at me and his top front teeth are running across his bottom lip. He's scared. I see it in his moon-slashed eyes. With the hair hanging in them.

"What? What?"

"I'm . . . I'm . . ."

He leaps up so quick I jump. He stands with his back to me, looking out at the sea. There are little silver bands way out where the moon's bouncing off the water. I see Petey's hands, jammed inside the pockets of his cutoff sweats, ball into fists.

"You p-promise?"

His back to me.

"Yeah. Yeah, sure I promise of course. What is it?"

He lets out a gargantuan breath. Then he laughs, slaps his hands together and makes a fist.

"I'm really fine with it. Q-quite fine. I don't know why it's so h-hard to tell you."

He squats down with his back to me and starts tracing his finger into the sand. He's writing something. Then he stops. I hear him take another vast breath.

He stands up, turns around to face me, takes a step back. He folds his arms across his chest. His face is squirming. He grinds his eyes shut. Then a noise out of him and flash he takes off, goes running off into the mouth of darkness down by the edge of the water and fast as I am, I know I'll never catch him.

He does this sometimes when he gets too frustrated or when I piss him off unintentionally or whatever, just starts running but why the fuck does he have to do it tonight? Our last night together?

"Petey! *PETEY!*"

I vault up and hiss-yell his name but there's no stopping him when he gets like this.

I sigh, mumble a curse, wipe the sand off my ass, my fingers bumping the ring. Then I see it.

I'M GAY is written in the sand.

Five little letters but they flatten me. Five little letters and one fucking apostrophe but they come into me like a judo kick, like your mother just told you she's been turning tricks all these years when all along you thought she was waiting tables at the Blue Moon Diner, nights. I'M GAY, but that's fucking impossible I've known Petey all my life and there's no fucking queers in Sout—

Fuck.

FUCK!

A sudden thought: I wonder if he's told anyone else.

Because if he has, word like that you could whisper down on D Street and it would be out to Castle Island before you got the first sentence out of your mouth. And then of course everyone would wonder about *me*. Since I'm Petey's only friend.

Fuck.

To every thing, there is a season, and now it's time to get shit-faced. I turn around and stride off, trying to figure out what's the closest bar from where I am right here.

"*DANNNNNNYYYYYYYY!*" I hear from like half a world away, a wail, the cry of the banshee. It's Petey's voice and I block my ears so I won't hear it and dash across the Boulevard and don't stop running 'til I get up to Mulligan's, where everyone in the house is happy to buy a beer for a guy who's going into the Corps the next morning, as long as you listen to their war stories. The guy behind the bar is telling a story of the woman who shot at him for refusing her a drink. Twenty-odd years ago. Get me outta here please.

There are different kinds of drinking and now I am *drinking,* drinking with a purpose, drinking to get drunk like it's a job I've got to do and there's a wonderful purpose to it. No, better give me another. Sure, I'll have one more. *Hey Jimmy, c'mon get off the fuckin' phone and bring us another round over here.*

Petey is small now. He used to be big in my eyes, the unlocker of secrets, but now he's small and just another thing to get the hell away from here, and the last things I think of before I pass out in my swirly bed are, that it must have been one hell of a bash he got on his head and somehow it's all my fault still again and always. The way I called him before he got hit—Petey! The way he called after me tonight—Danny! Why are we still calling to each other? And what do we really want?

And, last: the realization that I have always known this. Of course. Always.

And loved him for it. Loved him anyways.

Bastard. I gotta get out of here.

Jesus, Petey.

Christmas Comes but Once a Year, Thank God

I'm still pretty cocked when the train pulls out of South Station the next morning. I kinda fall into my seat and despite my shower half an hour earlier I know I still smell like booze. Infinitesimal parts of me are oozing booze and the result of this is that I am giving off that kind of a reek. I take a dirty window seat and just happen to look out as the train starts spurting down the track in annoying fits and jerks and some lady's perfume behind me somewhere rises up as if its only purpose is to nauseate me. Not that I smell like a bed of roses.

A woman across the aisle *You're Kay O'Connor's boy, aren't you!* she says rather than asks and I deny it and instantly wonder why, and of course once you make that commitment you're stuck. Everybody lies. Nobody minds but I guess she's not a Morrissey fan and she keeps insisting, so I plunk on my Walkman.

I happen to get-me-out-of-here look out the smeared thick plastic uncleanable window and Christ there's Petey. It's Petey. Half-hiding behind a pillar, his bleary eyes riveted on mine. Must've followed me here. Maybe he's been following me all night. That would be Petey.

Petey raises his fingers. No other part of him moves just his fingers and then a little-kid scared wave of those fingers bye-bye, we going bye-bye now.

I leap up. Press both hands to the window, strain to keep seeing him. He dashes after me and for a while keeps up with the train while the tears stream freely down his face. Okay, my face too but I suppose I'm just a little freaked about leaving Southie for the first time in my life and everything.

Then he's gone, sliding into backwards, everything recedes and next stop Parris Island and it's easy to forget about home for a while, easy to forget

A Map of the Harbor Islands
Published by The Haworth Press, Inc., 2006. All rights reserved.
doi:10.1300/5677_15

about home and people and situations and shit. Hi how'ya doin' Danny's the name, South Boston, you? *GET UP THAT HILL YOU SACKS OF SHIT* two-day liberty next weekend and wow look at her with the big tits, no the one next to her and what not.

I wanted him to write first. I didn't want him to write. I dialed his number the eighth night there when I thought, I really thought—

I wanted him to write I didn't want him to write, I dialed his number in a wild Southern thunderstorm the second week I got there from this pay phone on base outside the rec center, dialed his number then hung up because I didn't know what to say without being able to look into his eyes, read his eyes.

I mean, what the fuck did he want to me say? What was I supposed to say?

Dear Petey,
The weather here is wicked hot.

Gee, that's profound.

I don't know if you know, but I've been sent out here to Camp Pendleton in San Diego. I'm a Communications Specialist.

Shows you the sorry state of communications in the military, I guess.

I found out today that Southie has contributed more men to the Corps than any other city in the country. But not this time around, I'm the only guy from up our way down here so far that I know, the rest of them are all southerners or from Texas or small towns in Utah or someplace without a coast and they call me "Yank" which I knew they would, also Jughead because of my ears of course, and sometimes Red, which shows quite the lack of imagination, no?

I stop as I write this and picture myself asking *Petey Petey who do you say that I am?* The way he used to ask me. I never have asked him that.

Sorry I didn't write during boot camp but I didn't know what to say. Plus they ran our asses off so much down there you'd fall asleep when your head hit the pillow.
Which were hard as rocks by the way, the pillows.

Now what.

This fall we were in Lebanon for a little while and then we went to Africa to give out food to these starving people and also we went to Iceland and the Mediterranean for training, but now I'm out here for a while. Petey, there's so much suffering in some parts of the world.

Duh. What I really want to write is that seeing this stuff affected me far more than I thought it would—that I'm afraid I'm not really as tough as I thought I was. Not that I ever thought I was tough really, but—

I'm coming home next week for Christmas, Petey. Just for five days. I'll be home Saturday. Hopefully we can get together. Your friend,

Danny

There. I did it.

Jesus Christ, I miss him. I hate the fuckin' Marines but it's like what am I supposed to do? What else can I do?

Nothing.

AN AWKWARD CHRISTMAS

I picture this title like it's boxed in a TV grid in the evening paper, in the *TV Guide* that comes in the mail wait for it every Wednesday like Mrs. Crimmins and she would check off the boxes of all the shows she wanted to see that week, *An Awkward Christmas, 7:00-8:00 p.m.,* just after the evening news and *Three's Company* reruns and just before *A Britney Christmas* or some fuckin' Hallmark vehicle for selling shit thing.

MA: Oh God Danny, lemme look at you. Frank, he's home! Cripes, the muscles on you and look how short his hair is, have you lost weight? Take his coat Frank, look at 'im, his uniform, get the camcorder Frank! I told you to have it ready! Danny dear, the cousins are on their way they're coming up from Milton just to see you, we have a little party planned tonight. Go out for a minute? What do you mean, we've been waiting for you for three months and I cooked you your favorite roast beef, a beautiful roast of beef, we got Grandma Flynn from the nursing home too just to see you and there's someone else in the parlor, I called her first thing I heard, I knew you'd want to see her—

DAD (Shakes my hand, feigns a jab to my shoulder but it's all mechanical still and his eyes still have that empty look): You look good, Danny. God you look good—

MA: Cripes Frank, don't shake his arm off, let 'im get his coat off for cripe's sake, Petey? *Petey Harding?* No he hasn't called, we don't see him around anymore at all do we, Frank? Noreen, he's home! Look at them, Frank, look at them, I think there's gonna be a wedding around here soon—

·NOREEN (Kisses me hard, she's crying and had her nails done again down at Princess Nails): Oh God Danny oh God oh God—

MA: She's got a big surprise for you Danny dear, you might as well tell 'im now dear, a nice ski trip for you two up to the White Mountains, a nice little getaway tomorrow and the next day, you'll be home just in time for the big party Christmas Eve, all the family's coming to see you, I even invited the Capellinis, what the heck Christmas comes but once a year, Frank, get me a cigarette and put on the kettle—

ME: Jeez Ma, I never skied before, I don't know how to ski—

MA: Well there's more to do up there than ski! It's your Christmas present from me and your father, Danny, a nice little romantic getaway, you kids have never been outta town, no no don't thank me just remember me when I'm old and bring me back some nice maple syrup, you can't get the good stuff around here, it's the same place your father and I honeymooned at a hundred years ago. Frank, go wheel Ma out here, go now, go, see if she knows 'im, you were always her favorite, Danny, and let's see if she—Frank, watch the cabinets I just waxed 'em, don't scratch her wheelchair on 'em and pull her shawl up for heaven's sakes—Ma! Ma! Look who came home to see you for Christmas! Ma!

GRANDMA FLYNN (Smiling and looking fixedly at Noreen): Sgh brsh shlmgh.

MA (Loud, loud): Over here, Ma, over here look who's home, look who came home to see you for Christmas, over here, Noreen dear just step into the parlor again if you don't mind you're distracting her, oh cripes Frank, get the door that'll be my sister's gang now and I didn't finish the bathroom yet, Noreen dear be a love and just wipe the toilet seat down with a face cloth and a bit of Ajax and hot water—never mind I'll get the door—

GRANDMA FLYNN: Shgh arghhh shhhgsh.

And so it went. Two days in New Hampshire where we got a flat and it was freezing rain the whole time and I sipped Seagram's and then fucked Noreen, hard, half a dozen times on sheets that smelled like Clorox, hard. Once she said *You're hurtin' me,* but she laughed when she said it, told me in the next breath she loved my red bush. She pulled on it with her thumb and forefinger like it was weird moss in the woods. Later I heard her whispering laughing on the phone to her girlfriends while I was in the bathroom *No nothing yet but we'll see,* course she was talking about the ring. She gave me a black leather coat with the green shamrock already sewed onto the collar, paid about 600 bucks for it cuz I'd priced them last year at (Don't Call It Macy's) Jordan's, a gold watch too maybe a sweater I forget now—finally got home, finally snuck out Christmas night from home, said I was tired wanna sleep in my own bed alone just once, we never get to sleep in, see, but out the window after midnight sliding down the icy drainpipe still if you can believe it, and I could always do this when I was a kid and I'm bigger faster stronger more agile now a Marine and sober too but nonetheless I slip half-way down and scrape my hands on the pavement, twist the shit out of my ankle. But Petey's not home, limping back and forth in front of his house, hucking driveway pebbles up at his dark bedroom window that's already cracked from one thousand other nights like this then finally knocking at the door at 12:22, what the hell I'm a Marine and it's Christmas and I've gotta see him, gotta talk to him tell him it's okay—sure I was pissed at first, shocked, but then you figger what the fuck, start missing him, he is my lit-tle bro after all, I mean kinda, maybe just a little messed up, probably just needs a good fuck to straighten him out and then you get wrapped up in all the changes around you, the missions, the training missions, and you marvel at what you've become, the beauty of your body, the focus of your mind, the beauty of the bodies all around you in a non-faggy way of course I don't mean like that, the beauty of the machines around you, your body is a lean white machine but all the while you make friends descend on ports a-whorin', distribute food to starving people in Africa go on maneuvers off the coast of the Middle East and see things you can't believe but still miss your family including your messed-up little bro, you start off thinking the folks at home are ignorant because they don't see this stuff, don't know anything but eventually that novelty wears off and you just wanna go home. Period. No matter what they fucking know. It's great to be home, but it can't be fully home without Petey. I know that now.

"Danny! Danny dear, you're home!" Mrs. Harding says, yawning and keeping the cat inside with one of her huge pink slippers. She wraps me in a bear hug and for some reason I start almost choking up—

"How are all in your care? Your mother?" she asks, but their friendship (if you can call it that) was based entirely on me and Petey's friendship and it didn't really survive the ages, kinda fell away as I got involved with Pop

Warner football and such in my teens and Ma got involved with the mothers from that group and hockey.

"She's good, good. You?"

"Ouf, one thing and another I'm worn out. But other than that no complaints do I make. Come in with you now and see the tree and we'll find a grand cup of tea for you."

The smell of the house, the clutter on the piano top, the 8 × 10s of the Harding boys lining the stairway, all the same, all the same—

There's a worldliness in Mrs. Harding's eyes when she hands me my tea that I haven't noticed before, a search in her look.

"So ahhh . . . is Petey home?"

"No. Out *flaneuring* he is as always. Youth doesn't care where it sets its foot and no mistake. Drink that tea now and do justice to that cake for God's sake. Went out a whiles back he did. Never tells me, God love him. He might be home in a minute, then again it might be when Apollo opens the gates of dawn for all I know. But you're more than welcome to wait, I myself must be off to the bed as I've been up since yesterday morning one thing and another. We had the boys and their families over earlier, God help us and I'm done for. I'll eat someone if I don't get some sleep. But I wonder now will you put on the TV and wait for him? He'll be over the moon to see you I know."

That look again and I squirm.

"Ahhh, I dunno. It's gettin' kinda late and I just got home myself more or less. How . . . how's Petey doing?" I ask, rising.

"God help us, Petey is Petey," Mrs. Harding says, walking me to the door. She pauses and looks again. She takes my hand in hers.

"I think he misses you," she says. "There was a bell in a church tower and its music wasn't very sweet. A second bell was added and didn't they sound beautiful together. I think that's the way with him when it comes to you, Danny dearest."

"Ahhh. . . ."

"But there's no tired ass like your own tired ass, so on that note I'll leave you, Danny dear, and a blessing on your road. Take those cookies with you and you'll be doing me a favor, I'm getting big as a house."

Looking at the old neighborhood with strange eyes now, but I'm leaving soon and I panic, wonder where he could be, why he isn't around, why he hasn't come looking for me—

A weird thing, coming home from Noreen's late the next night and a pickup truck parked across the street from the house, someone in it, drinking beer. I see the sparkling reflection of the Stuff of Life in a can through the icy windshield—that's not the weird part as you might see that on any given night round here, but as I slouch by I see that it's Donnie, Petey's older brother; awkwardness reigns but our eyes have sizzle-met so I can't just keep walking.

"Hey Donnie, what's up?" I mumble when he lowers the window. Of course he must lower the window and a gibbering late-night talk show chops out into the frost-spangled air, that and the strange acute awkwardness that has mysteriously plagued our interactions for years now.

"Brian," he says, my older brother who died.

This name issue might occur twice a year with those who knew him. Doesn't really matter to me but Donnie seems to become undone at this.

"S-sorry, sorry, Danny, Danny," he says.

He's a shingler, roofer, something, and the refuse of his latest job lies in a heap of permafrost in the back of his truck. But a permanent keenness in his alarmed eyes and, like Petey, sharp as a tack and misses nothing.

"The truck was overheating so I pulled over for a bit on the way home," he explains, tearing his eyes away.

"Will you come in?" I ask, the polite casualness of my tone nevertheless leaving room for a little something that we both realize translates as *I don't really mean this.*

"*What?*" he asks. Incredulously. Then quick he runs a palm across his face and smears back to seminormal.

"Thanks, no, it should be fine now."

His uniform is the de rigueur tradesman's, faded jeans splotched with plaster stains, work boots molded to the feet, gray hooded sweatshirt and a mustard-colored work jacket unbuttoned. The hair is redder than mine and workman-messy at this hour, workman-messy probably five minutes after he leaves the house in the morning.

"How are the kids?"

"Ahhh . . . fine, fine."

He is truly, inexplicably stupefied. The inside of his truck is a disaster of empty Marlboro boxes, rumpled old newspapers on the passenger floor, numberless Dunkin' Donuts coffee cups, a dog-eared atlas *Metro Boston and Its Surroundings.*

"How's the Corps?"

"Alright. I was ahh . . . looking for Petey. I was just over at the house again, your mother said he was out somewhere. Haven't seen him have you, Donnie?"

"Not tonight, no," he answers bluntly. He's staring straight ahead, his right knee bouncing so much the truck has a bit of a shimmy to it, *Ram-tough* though it is.

"That's good though, you're looking for Petey," he adds, nodding his head rapidly.

Whatever!

I recall the ingenious games he used to invent when he'd watch us for Mrs. H while she *stole forty winks:* Treasure Hunt down at the beach where earlier that morning he had buried a tennis can full of nickels and dimes and chocolate; Dragnet, where we'd have to roar through town finding such S-B oddities as a copy of the *New York Times,* the location of a Protestant church, an earthworm of at least four inches length. A yeast to our imagination he was in those days—well, Petey's anyway—and never the same when he came back from the service it would seem.

"Well," I fake-yawn. I shove my hands in my pants pockets and shiver a bit. "Gettin' cold so I guess I'll head in."

But the worst is yet to come. As Donnie continues his rapid nodding and starts up the truck, and I lean back, my eyes slant to behind his seat where the barrel of a rifle, maybe a .47, pokes up its evocative presence.

I don't gasp, nothing gives me away, but still Donnie turns and sees what I've seen. I don't believe it's possible for him to get any redder than he already is, but in fact it is. He lets out a deep breath, snorts a laugh, looks me in the eye with that fierce blue intelligence and woe and says, "Every Marine a rifleman, Danny," and drives off, and me half-forgetting he was in the Corps himself.

"What a fuckin' town this is," I mumble as I climb the stairs.

Next morning:

MA: We're taking you out for breakfast, Danny, the whole family, they're waiting for us down at the Farragut House—surprise!

ME: Oh, ahhh, wait a minute, Ma, I gotta go out for a bit. I wanna see some of my old friends. My plane's leaving at one—

MA: Go out? Where? We already made the reservations! Your favorite place! Who's more important than your family? You haven't seen your friends while you've been back? We'll drop you at the airport after breakfast, I already packed up your stuff—

ME: I gotta see Petey, Ma.

MA: We're late already, Danny, don't upset me with my high blood pressure, what good's a farewell breakfast if the guest of honor isn't there?

ME: Ma, I haven't seen Petey—

MA: Petey? I didn't even know you still hung around with him. I told him you were all tied up—

ME: Petey? You told Petey that? When did you see—

MA: Oh the poor soul came by some day I don't know a few days ago when you kids were up in the mountains, I told him all about it, away for a romantic getaway, you couldn't wait to be alone with Noreen, I guess I forgot to mention that, I thought I'd mentioned that—

ME: What did he say, Ma?

MA: Oh the poor thing I could never understand him anyway, poor thing he still stutters huh? Said something about the beach or something where you going? Danny, where you—

ME: I'll be back, I'll meet you down there—

MA: Jesus Christ don't upset me like this—

But when I got back to Petey's house his mother said he was at work and when I got to Sully's office, the moving company Petey worked for, Sully said they were on a job down the Cape. They wouldn't be back 'til tomorrow. He was pissed at Petey, said Petey hadn't come in to work for three days and Sully called him this morning, woke his mother up and said *If he don't show up today he'll be out of a job,* and no, there was no way I could get in touch with him. They were on the road.

"He's been showing up shitfaced a lot too, fuckin' hungover all the time," Sully said, shoving a honey-dipped into his mouth. He slurped coffee and the noise of it pissed me off no end.

"Go easy on him, Sully."

Sully looked away when his eyes met mine. I suppose I was glaring. Fucking Sully. He couldn't carry a feather up a flight of stairs without losing his breath and he drove his workers like the fucking flail of the Lord.

I was just in time for my farewell breakfast. Noreen brought her parents even though her mother had a cold.

MA: Mrs. Butler came and she has a cold for heaven's sake, aren't you glad you came now? And aren't you at all ashamed that you were late?

ME: No Ma, I'm not, I went to see Petey because Petey is my family too.

When I got back from Christmas there was a letter waiting for me from Petey, saying he knew I'd be busy with my family and all but he would meet me down the beach, he would meet me at our spot down on the beach at midnight any night I cared to come, he'd wait down there every night while I was home and if I wanted to I could find him down there, he'd wait for me, he wrote, at the Place Where the Land Meets the Ocean, and Please Come Danny and *Do Not Fail Me* underlined at the end. Final sentence,

I have been wondering [sic] the shoreline, staying close to the place where the land meets the shore, and I have recommended you to them, to all the things that swirl down there, and they have whispered back your name.

Whatever.

I wrote right back, told him what happened, told him I didn't get the letter 'til I just got back, told him Ma had managed to book my every minute while I was home and there were some things the Marines didn't train you to deal with like these Irish mothers.

I didn't hear from him. I wrote again. Finally I called him. Once. Twice. We talked. It was cool. He sounded drunk. I finally got him to believe me about Christmas. He could be pessimistic like that.

"I'm coming home in June and I'm not telling my family," I promised.

"J-June," he mumbled, like I said the year 13,000.

"I'll see you then. Okay, Petey?"

"O-okay. It'll be a dis-May. I'll be full of dis-May all May."

"Huh?"

"Figure it out, Danny. I'm sick of doin' your mental legwork."

He laughed.

"Whatever."

"You p-promise? June?"

"Yeah, I promise. Hey, you been drinking, Petey? You sound—"

"Ahhh, f-f-forget about it, D-Danny."

"How's your ahhh . . . garden comin'? You still got your garden over there on the West Side, Petey? You still makin' those maps?"

But Petey laughs again and reminds me it's winter.

"It's always f-f-fuckin' winter here," he says.

Not All Double Dates Are Made in Heaven; Some Come from Another Place

I wrote Noreen. I had this plan right, a night plan. What do I mean by that? Just this, the kind that comes at night lying awake when the car light shadows ghost-flow across your ceiling and a bit of boner goes up and down but you couldn't be bothered, somewhat horny not really, a little tired. Thoughtful like. The plan: Noreen had this cousin. Nice girl, suburban girl. Pleasant, wouldn't-say-shit-if-she-had-a-mouthful-of-it type, loves horses and bunny rabbits, very generous at Christmas with the nieces and nephews, came from Milton. Lace curtain. Would go out new car shopping on President's Day weekend.

Her junior college was having this prom. She needed a date. Petey needed a girl, that was all. The math of it, eureka California. I set the whole thing up. Nice double date. Ma freaked when I showed up at the door. Told her I didn't have no time, *No don't make any plans Ma, I'm back on Official Military Business.*

I should've stayed at a fucking motel. The headache of her, God bless her. *Official military business my ass,* I heard her say to Dad.

I met Petey at midnight down at the beach my first night back—after I did the nasty with Noreen, then begged off for being sleepy, time difference and all. She didn't realize it worked to my advantage, three hours earlier out there. I blessed the patron saint of Southie's Geographical Ignorance as I whistle-walked to the beach, the swinging gait of the just-got-laid.

I crossed the Boulevard. One or two errant joggers out, a few teenagers down the way—

—And then Petey. Sitting on the seawall, staring out, the breeze puffing his hair.

A Map of the Harbor Islands
Published by The Haworth Press, Inc., 2006. All rights reserved.
doi:10.1300/5677_16

I froze. Big lump in my throat. He turned as if I had called him, turned quick. I was ten feet away.

What the fuck? I got all choked up. He came toward me. Not a smile, but his eyes like saucers. Walked right up to me. His eyes going back and forth between mine. Biting his lip.

I don't know how it happened but we were in each other's arms next, holding on as if for life. Me crying if you can believe it. Couldn't stop anymore than I could figure it out.

"Oh God," Petey muttering in my ear. "Oh G-God, Danny." Squeezing harder when he felt the wetness of his shoulders. He pulled away to look at me like he couldn't believe it. I understood, couldn't either.

"A m-miracle," he whispered, coming back into me, "a M-Mother of Mary miracle. A Mother of Mary Miracle in the Merry Month of M-May. A Merry Mother of Mary Miraculous Miracle—"

"It's June, Petey, and I catch your drift," I said, and then we both laughed 'til we were gasping.

We had a few beers. I was able to regain control, come back to my normal Southie self. I can't remember what we talked about at first. That look edged back into his eyes, the little-kid look, the way he'd smile and stare. Petey. My bro Petey. My best friend. A little messed up, apparently confused of course but still my bro kinda.

The sea was an ooze and a whisper that night. No moon so you couldn't see the ocean, had to sense it and didn't we, all around. Not a word out of Petey about the moon coming up over fuckin' France or whatever, just smiling/staring at me with those big eyes then look away quick. Then look back again.

"No moon, no man," Petey said just when I thought he wouldn't, unpredictable as always.

Contentment settled down on our shoulders. You could feel it resting there. This was home again. That guy who said you couldn't go home had been right up to this point. He didn't have a Petey waiting for him poor bastard.

Petey wanted to feel my muscles. He wouldn't tell me at first—the beer made him.

"W-w-want to," he shy-said, pointing at my arms, squeezing with his hands like he was doing that deaf-talk stuff. The Golden Boy and look at him now and my heart aching and I wondered why.

"O-okay?" he asked.

What the hell, I rolled up my T-shirt sleeve and popped him a big white fuckin' jarhead bicep, let him find his thrill on blueberry etc. It was a guy thing not a fag thing, we'd done shit like this all our lives. His fingers came slow at me, like Holy Communion.

We both jumped a little when he made first contact. You wouldn't think a guy could touch so tender. This sound out of him—

"First Encounter B-Beach," he said at last, about five minutes after I finally pulled away.

Whatever.

"That's the name of a b-beach down the Cape where the Pilgrims first saw the First Peoples."

"What First Peoples?"

"The Native Americans. The Indians. Pesky Injuns as you probably call them in the Marines. That's what they'd prefer to be called now, Danny, First Peoples."

Petey always heard things like this first. I wondered how.

"A rose by any other name," I said.

Petey raised his eyebrows and his head jerked back. He pointed a half-finger at me like a TV comedian. "Quoting S-Shakespeare, is it? You learn that in the M-Marines? What'd they have Shakespeare 101 a-after Introduction to Assassination Class?"

But his eyes were teasing, joyous. "People should be ca-called what they want, Danny, no?"

"I guess. Who do you say that I am, Petey?" I heard myself murmur.

A slice into the night all of a sudden and everything quick-different with my words.

I couldn't decide if I regretted saying them or not the moment they left my mouth. It wasn't like I wanted to say them, the bastards just flew out on their own, when I wasn't looking as it were. It must have been the dark, that's all, the dark down here by the beach, the beers. The name thing, that had triggered this old memory, the way Petey used to ask me.

I couldn't read his eyes in this nonlight. I was leaning back on my palms against the warm sand. There was something that kept us both stuck-still.

"I . . . y-y-you . . ." Petey began, a series of false starts. He looked at the ocean, then quick looked back. Then finally, in a whisper, "Are you playing with my head, D-Danny? Don't, pl-please don't."

Silence again. I found I was peeling the label off my bottle of beer.

"Forget about it," I said, and this deep breath came out of me. Silence again for a few more minutes until Petey jumped up so fast. *"Let's run!"* he cried, our old thing, shoveling a wave of sand in my face with his bare left foot, and I chased him all the way down to Carson Beach, almost, I'll catch him finally for once and me in this great shape I thought, him laughing ahead of me, stopping, taunting daring, extending his hands, then taking off again when I almost had him. Bastard!

"Wh-whatever it is they learn you in the Marines, it isn't *speed,* huh?" he panted at one point and I stopped, cried out in quick pain, grabbed my back as if I had pulled something—then tackled him when he froze, instant concern inundating his face.

"They teach *trickiness,*" I laughed. "They teach *mastery!*"

"Sneakiness!" Petey yelled, thrashing like an alligator. "D-deception!"

We rolled around in the damp hot sand until I found myself on top of him, my knees locking down his thighs, my hands pushing his wrists against the sand, grunts and laughs and the snatching of breaths. Him looking up, me looking down. Panting the both of us. I could feel the thud of vibrant Birdy bumping through Petey's wrists. He went limp, but somehow at the same time tightened up.

Petey's mouth was open. His eyes open too, and something in them— not dis-May. Definitely not dis-May, the opposite of dismay. He closed his mouth, wet his lips, looked away half an instant, looked back at me. Something in his eyes that I must look at, look for—what was it?

"Danny," he said. Not a question.

How to say how it is, when you feel it's just you yourself now, finally, in some situation, you yourself finally after all these years—like you're ten, like you're forty, eighty, doesn't matter, just you yourself now finally, like that one second right before you fall asleep when you see yourself as if in a mirror and say *huh*—

At the leaning angle of me, my dogtags shifted, slid out from under the neck of my T-shirt, fell into Petey's face.

A little inrush of Petey breath.

"I . . . dr-dreamed of these," he said. "You know why they give you two, Danny? D-do you? So if you die, they take one and shove it into your mouth, they stand it up behind your front teeth then sh-shove down hard when you're dead. To identify you. When they ship the body back."

Petey's face scrunched up and he looked away. This tightening in his jaw. I could feel the taking of a huge breath in him beneath me. It lifted me somewhat. I eased up a bit to make it easier for him.

"How do you know that?" I asked. I was still leaning over him, my hands on his wrist. Why? I don't know.

"I r-r-read up on it, after you left. When you j-joined up. I had to r-read up on it. Danny, I had this dr-dream after you left."

I remembered a dream of my own just then. As a child it came twice, maybe three times: in this dream I'd wake and find there was a cornucopia horn streaming down at me from my ceiling—and brilliant ocean moon shining through the winter watery windowpanes. A blast would sound out of this horn, then all this money would come pouring out, spilling onto my bed, all around me, all for me—not Washingtons and Lincolns, not Grants, but outlandish money, thousand-year-old doubloons and pesetas, rubbed-bare silver in the shape of Communion Hosts—heaven's money, a treasure meant only for me—

"Wh-what was your dream?" I asked, and my voice cracked, my pulse quickening when it should be loosening now, slowing—

Petey looked back up at me and I heard myself gulp. Now his eyes like mirrors, and me and one smeared star in them—

"Well," he began. "I . . . I was m-made right again."

His eyes wandered back and forth from me to this Other Place, as he re-membered it. "I mean, right in the eyes of the w-world. No stutter. Straight As again, scholarships everywhere Harvard and fr-friends who enunciate and so many t-tickets out I could take my pick."

His voice so soft now. The only thing I wanted to hear.

"Uh-huh," I encouraged in a whisper, looking down at him.

"It was in this big hall I was, and thousands of people had come to see it, and I was a m-man and perfect and talented and flu-fluent. And everyone kept coming up to me, a little tenta-tentatively because I was the Man now, my future Golden, and shaking my hand, and congratulating me—but all along there was s-something else—something else, Danny, and I didn't know what but I was so p-perplexed—and then I looked into my right hand, and . . . . ahhh . . . there were d-dogtags in my hand. They were . . . y-yours."

Petey looked away. His body heaved and contracted beneath me as he si-lently wept. I turned my head to the ocean in an attempt at being polite, giving him some time—finally—

"Petey, lookit, don't worry, nothing's gonna—"

"Not through," Petey said, shaking his head.

He swallowed hard again. He sniffed hard, clearing his nose. He looked back up at me.

"And then I knew what I was l-looking for. It hit me, l-like my name: you, Danny. You . . . weren't there. I think everybody in the world was there except for y-you—you know how it is in a dream. And I started asking everybody, but they didn't know, hadn't seen you, hadn't heard of you. *Who?* they kept asking, *Who?* and finally I said I had to leave, had to f-f-find you, and then this silence, big biggy silence, all of them staring, and they wouldn't let me, they said if I left it would all be taken away again, every-thing, *You'll be a stuttering nothing again!* they said, and I said I didn't care, don't c-care, let me out let me out, *Ungrateful!* they said, *Get out, go,* threw me out, and then I'm on the beach, Danny, here on the beach, me myself again and you in the distance Danny, and I . . . I w-weep I'm so glad, rub the sand, pour it over my head so glad to be back."

His body trembled again beneath me.

Sometimes me and Noreen would see these sad movies, and I'd tighten everything up so I wouldn't cry. It reminded me of a submarine movie when they're getting ready to dive and they seal and screw everything up. That's what it's like.

Some time went by. Finally we stared at each other. Petey had finished talking. The ocean whispering, moving, doing its mysterious thing twenty yards away.

"Oh God, Petey," I said. Something fell onto his chin and I didn't realize it was a tear of mine at first.

I jumped up, jumped off Petey.

"Wh . . . what's the matter?"

"Nothing. Come on, I'll race you back!"

Petey got up, but halfway back when he hadn't passed me, I turned around and he was just walking.

We cracked open another when we got back to our spot at the beach. I remembered with an odd sinking feeling what I had to tell Petey.

"Ahhh . . . Petey, listen. I want you to do me this favor. Would you do me this favor, Petey?"

He gulped, got nervous, reached for his beer.

"Would you, Petey boy?"

I put a little plead in my voice, knew he wouldn't be able to deny me.

Looked up at me but his head still lowered, hair hanging into his eyes.

"Anything. You know it, Danny. A-anything, Danny."

"Great. Cool. Okay, Noreen's got this cousin see, this girl. Tricia. Tricia Butler? 'Member her?"

"No."

"Nice girl. Nice suburban girl from Milton. Goes to that girls' junior college down there, Aquinas or Fontbonne or whatever it is. She ahhhh . . . well, the thing is . . . her prom's tomorrow night. Very nice girl."

"I'm h-happy for her," Petey said. Cautiously.

"Well the thing is, ahhhh, I'm bringing Noreen, right? And I thought maybe, you know it might be kinda fun if like . . . if like maybe you could—"

"No. No w-way."

"We'd be going too. Me and Noreen I mean. You know like . . . like a double date."

When I looked over at Petey he was staring at me. Even in the dark I could see the hurt on his face.

A deep sigh out of him.

"Great t-timing, Danny."

"Huh? What do you mean?"

"Oh okay, play d-dumb."

"Will you come with us or not?"

Petey started laughing.

"What are you on, Danny?"

"C'mon, I said you would."

"No w-way, I hate that shit. I had to go to a p-p-prom once with my cousin Claire and it s-s-sucked."

"I know it but I already said you would. C'mon. For me. This'd be different anyways cuz I'd be with you."

"You trying to c-cure me? Don't b-b-bother, it won't work."

Silence for a bit. Petey pounds the sand with his fist.

"Is that wh-what this is, about *curing* me? Cuz if it is, I—"

"Ahhh, no, course not. I just . . . I just . . . I mean, you never . . . you never been with a girl, and I just thought . . . I mean, how do you know?"

Silence.

"How do you know, Petey, if you never been—"

"How do you know you're not g-gay, if you n-never been with a guy? Or maybe you b-been with a guy and decided it wasn't for you. Is that it?"

"Don't be fuckin' wise. That's not . . . don't fuckin' say that."

"Why not? It's the s-s-same thing. Don't you fucking come h-h-home here all butch-bossy and shit just cuz you went through b-boot camp and have a gun and shit and think you c-can—"

"It ain't the same fuckin' thing at all! What do you mean butch-bossy? I ain't being bossy—I'm just sayin' it ain't the same thing! It's like if everyone, I mean like ninety-nine percent of the world, went through life without getting pleasure out of hitting themselves over the head with a frying pan, and then that other one percent is like into it, and I'm just trying to get you to stop hitting your head with the frying pan and you're like trying to get me to try it instead."

"Oh is that what I'm doing?" Petey asked. "When exactly d-did I d-do that?"

"You know what I mean."

"No, I don't. But what if you were b-born with that fr-frying pan in your hand, huh? Wh-what if? And what if the only thing you could d-do with it was hit yourself with it? And then you found out it wasn't a frying pan at all, but a . . . a . . . when you m-m-met someone else who had a frying pan you discovered when you put the two of them together they weren't frying pans at all, but wings? W-wings, Danny. When everyone else st-stuck in the m-mud?"

He'd give you a headache sometimes, Petey, and me never remembering you couldn't argue with him. Like a nun, you'd never win. Nuns got 2,000 years of experienced dogma behind them and all you got is the Hersey squirts from too much beer the night before, and Petey . . . Petey has everything he has. Everything.

His head down now, sulking. Drawing a circle around himself in the wet-concrete sand.

"Okay, lookit, Petey, I don't . . . I don't wanna argue here. I just . . . you might have a good time. You know?"

Silence.

"You know?"

"At a *prom?* W-wouldn't."

"Seriously, how do you know?"

"I know. I f-fucking know."

"Alright, so you know. But just do it for me anyways, will ya? You never have to see her again. Just go tomorrow night. I said you would. We'll get to hang together. Okay? Please? For me? How long am I home for and it'll be a little more time we get to spend together. She won't have a date otherwise, the poor kid."

"She's a f-fatty?"

"No no, not at all. Just a little shy maybe, and her school's an all-girls school. But she ain't fat. Big-boned. She doesn't know many guys is all. She grew up protected, like. You know that suburban thing."

"So this w-w-wasn't your idea?"

"Ahhh no. No. I'm just helping Noreen out. And her cousin."

"Noreen can't stand me. I c-c-can't picture her setting this up. She'd ask Charles Manson before she asked me."

"Ahhh . . . what do you mean? She likes you Petey. C'mon. Say yes. For me. For me."

I picked Petey up first the next night. I hadn't seen him dressed up since his brother Timmy's wedding years ago. His black hair was like parted down the middle and he was fresh-shaven and he looked great. He could've been a model I bet. It's true that his dress pants were a little short and he was wearing white socks, but other than that he looked great. You could forget how good-looking he really was, the way he slouched around town quiet unshaven wearing all that baggy shit and a ball cap yanked down to his nose, keeping his eyes on the sidewalk.

"Lookin' pretty sharp there, kiddo."

The green sea eyes, black lashes around, black eyebrows black hair. Smooth white skin freshly shaven, lovely. Handsome. Petey.

"You t-too. What's th-that c-c-cologne?"

"I dunno, some shit. Noreen got it for me. Hey ahh, what's up with the flood pants though?"

Petey looked down. The pants were even higher now that he was sitting down in the car.

"I g-g-guess I outgrowed them."

"Yeah well . . . you don't got any others huh?"

"N-no. No others. Form follows f-function, dude."

"Whatever that means. No ahhh . . . dress socks either? Like black socks?"

"I could only f-find the one of them."

"Well . . . "

I looked at my watch. There wasn't really time to swing by my house and pick up a pair for him. Plus Ma was home and she would have nothing to add to the situation but chaos.

"Whatever. Don't worry about it."

"I'm n-not at all. Maybe you better n-not worry about it."

"Whatever. Alright, c'mon, cheer up, you're not going to a funeral here."

"You s-sure about th-th-that?"

"Sure I'm sure. This girl's pretty. Really pretty."

"Oh. That's n-nice." Petey folded his arms. "What dif-difference does that m-m-make?"

"You never know. Relax, alright? She's at Noreen's house, we're gonna pick them up now."

"They're not gonna take p-pictures and all that bourgeois shit, are they?"

"Well I mean . . . I don't know. What's boozjwha mean? Maybe a few. I mean, that's like the ahhhh . . . the custom. You know? They like all that shit, girls."

"I h-hate it. I'm gonna stick out my tongue. Make faces. Expose m-myself maybe."

I laughed, but I oddly remembered Petey's pregame ritual from the old days, when naked he'd bless his uniform—invincible then and look at him now—

"It won't be that bad," I said, checking my look in the mirror.

"Don't bother yourself, Danny, you look b-beautiful," Petey mumbled out the window. "A thing of beauty is a boy forever."

Sarcastically? Who knew, these days. I still blushed though and turned the radio louder. Petey started bouncing his knee. I was going to offer him a swig of my Seagram's to calm him but it smelled like he was already there.

We got to Noreen's and I parked and shut off the car.

"Can't you just b-b-beep for them?" Petey asked.

"Beep! No, you don't just *beep* for a fuckin' prom! Don't be a meathead! C'mon, we gotta go in."

"M-me too? Why?"

"Just come on!"

Petey groaned and got out. Mrs. Butler, Noreen's mother, was peeking out the front curtain and we heard her roar, *They're here!* as we ascended the stairs. I could feel the press and swell of my glutes, my hamstrings as I took the stairs two at a time in my tux pants. I liked that feeling.

Mrs. Butler was staring at Petey and through her glasses her eyes looked bigger like an owl's.

"Take a p-picture why don't you, it'll last longer," Petey mumbled as he hunched by her, but I quickly changed the subject and told Mrs. Butler how lovely the house looked. Someone had pinned a pink balloon to the end of the stair railing.

We had to wait, the girls were upstairs still getting ready, you could hear the boards creaking. Gambol-thumping was occurring. Noreen's mother asked us if we wanted something to drink, boys, but you could tell she was just being polite, there was never a thing in that house. I think they lived on Diet Pepsi water and celery—that's all that was ever in that fuckin' refrigerator. At least whenever I looked.

"I'd die for some J-Jolly Olly Orange," Petey answered from the couch, where he was way scrunched down and his legs spread and arms akimbo.

"It's just a joke," I explained to Mrs. Butler. Who was not laughing. A celebrity gossip show blared from the TV and Petey shook his head at it.

"What's happening in the real world? What's number one at the box office?" Petey asked Mrs. Butler, putting an urgent breathlessness into his voice, and I gave him a quick elbow in the ribs for him to knock it off.

The girls came down the wooden stairs in their uncertain high heels and the sound recalled woodworking shop in high school, or maybe the Clydesdales, all of them, going over a Vermont wooden bridge. The ever-ready Mrs. Butler already had the black plastic camera clutched in her ample fist. Petey's head was slumped in his hands. I stood up, kicked him to do the same. He did and shoved his hands halfway to the South Pole down his pockets. The girls' perfume and hairsprays reached us before they did, falling down the stairs like dueling waterfalls and their marriage not a happy one. Petey sniffed and made a childish noise of disgust *icky stinky cukka.* Noreen sailed around the staircase bend first like the *Constitution* when they tow it around the harbor every Fourth of July. She was an old salt at this prom stuff—we'd been to tons over the years. Her blonde hair was done different tonight, all shaggy-layered like, another cousin Debbie McQueeney down at the Hair I Am! beauty parlor being the perper-traitor no doubt. *It looks funny,* I heard Petey whisper behind me where he was hiding, *R-Rod Stewart in a dress* and I tried not to laugh. Her cousin Tricia brought up the rear shyly, stealing Elly May Clampett glances at Petey. I guess she was a little bigger than I remembered. I presented Noreen with her corsage, then remembered in panic I'd forgotten to tell Petey he needed to get one for Tricia, it just fucking slipped my mind.

"Ooooohhh," Mrs. Butler murmured, her shaggy brows sinking to half-mast as she up-and-downed Petey. "There's no corsage for Tricia, Peter?"

"Not unless you g-got one on you, and it's Petey," Petey mumbled.

"That figures," Noreen hmmmmphed, and her and Petey exchanged looks that were not fraught with cordiality.

"Jeez it's all my fault, I forgot to mention it," I said, stepping between them and slapping my palm against my forehead as if I really were as dumb as I hoped I looked. "Petey doesn't have too much experience in this stuff."

"I wonder why," Noreen snapped. She was staring at Petey's white anklet jock socks. One of which had a red stripe going across it. It looked like his ankles and shins had gotten a lot hairier in the last year.

"It doesn't matter, it's okay," Tricia smiled. For a big young lady she had a very tiny voice. I could tell she liked the way Petey looked. He looked really handsome. From the shins up.

"It does too matter," Noreen said. She thrust her corsage at her cousin. "You have mine. I've gone to enough of these things anyway, and it's your prom after all. Your very first prom. This is my elev—no, my twelfth."

"Oh Jesus!" Petey laughed, turning his head away.

"No really it's okay," Tricia said, but Noreen's mother on tippy-toes was already pinning it on Tricia after staring at Petey and figuring out he wasn't gonna do it.

"Besides it's the wrong color anyway. I said *cream.* This is *white,*" Noreen announced with a loud sigh to no one in particular. She could sigh in such a way that the bangs on her forehead lifted up.

"Sorry," I said.

"It's okay," Tricia said.

"This is Petey Harding," I said to Tricia. I'd met her a few times before on holidays and shit. Nice girl, lovely girl. Maybe a little bigger than I remembered.

"Hi!" Tricia gushed. I noticed her fingernails were tiny and pink with pinker little half-moons on them. Just funny things you notice, especially where they didn't really match her hands like.

"Petey, this is Noreen's cousin Tricia Butler."

Petey mumbled something and looked at the floor.

"Hi!" Tricia repeated, even louder.

"Pictures out back, now," Noreen announced, and I assumed everyone heard Petey click his tongue against his teeth and blow out a big sigh of universal unmistakable annoyance. I know I did.

We all trooped down the front steps—Mrs. Butler made five—then turned and marched off to the backyard, the girls clicking against the cracked asphalt walk, Noreen with conviction, Tricia a little unsteady like she'd been at sea for a few years. Noreen's stride was long-legged and that meant she was pissed. The tang of fresh chemically treated red mulch rose up and mingled with the girls' perfume. Noreen's mother had covered the scraggling flower beds along the side of the house that never grew nothing anyways with about a foot of lumpy mulch. Noreen's mother had this little roof thing out in the backyard next to the Blessed Mother statue, under which she kept the trash cans so they wouldn't get wet, but the trash cans were gone and in their place was this white plastic arch thing just for the occasion, which reminded me of Petey's *for an occasion* joke. We crammed into that and it started wobbling a little like it wanted to get loose and screw down the street but was stuck. I could see on its side it had a sticker that said O'SHEA RENTAL that someone had tried to pick off with their fingernails but it was one of them sticky ones that you just can't. The early evening was humid and the autobody shop behind Noreen's house was blowing off clouds of spray paint smell that floated into the yard then fell to the ground, fat unseen blimps that mingled with the girls' perfume and Petey covering his mouth and nose. Petey was taller than me but Tricia was taller than Noreen even though Noreen kept insisting she wasn't, and you couldn't fit four abreast under the tippy arch and there were Logistical Problems as we would say in the Corps.

"I can't see you, sweetheart, Tricia's blocking you," Noreen's mother sang out from behind her camera.

"Sorry," Tricia said, scooting down a bit and looking spraddled, like she was going to start doing the limbo.

"She's taller than you, honey, switch places."

"No she's not, it's just the heels."

Noreen prided herself on her height. *Sexy? Sexy?* she asked me sometimes. She'd just stop in the middle of the room, throwing her hair and chin back, one hand on her hip.

"Sorry," Tricia said, spraddling more and Petey laughed out loud.

"Why don't I get the kitchen bench and the two of you can sit on that and the boys behind?"

"There's no room in here for the bench, Ma. Just take the picture."

"Well I know it honey but I can't see you sweetheart. Let me run quick and get that bench."

"The bench won't fit, Ma."

"We haven't tried it dear and I think it might."

"The bench won't fit in the *fuckin' arch and I want the fuckin' arch in the picture!*" Noreen hissed between clenched teeth.

"Noreen!" Mrs. Butler gasped. Petey laughed again.

"Sorry," Tricia said.

"If you laugh one more time Petey Harding I swear I'll scratch your eyes out!" Noreen said.

"She always liked me, h-huh?" Petey asked, turning to me.

"Stop it, both of you," I said.

Finally I stood in the back with Noreen in front of me and Petey stood in the back beside me with Tricia in front of him. Except Petey had to go up on tiptoes cuz Tricia was bigger than him too, bigger than the lot of us. That fresh suburban air I guess and three squares a day will work wonders.

"Put your hands on my shoulders so everyone will know we're together," Noreen said to me out of the corner of her smiling mouth. Tricia half-turned to see if Petey would do the same thing to her but no way Jose. Tricia had her hair done up in these ringlet piles like Marie what's-her-name that got sent to the guillotine. She seemed to have allergies as she sneezed right when the first three pictures were being taken and we had to keep doing them all over again.

"Sorry," she said.

I still have one of those pictures in my wallet, moist and rumpled and sniffing of leather. Tricia looks like she just won the lottery. Noreen is posing but her neck veins are sticking out like ripcords, and I'm pie-faced because at the last second Petey put his arm around my back, and for one second me and Petey were going to the prom. Petey could be wise like that sometimes but there was really no cause for this. His arm slung across the back of my waist. The fingers dangling below. A good firm grip. I look like I'm in pain.

The pictures made us a little bit late and the traffic sucked on top of it heading down the Southeast Distressway to Milton. I wanted to take the shortcuts through Dorchester/Roxbury but Noreen said it always depressed her to drive through there and besides what if we got a flat in a n-word neighborhood and herself in her prom dress.

"An irresistible sight for the sex-crazed l-locals, I'm sure," Petey mumbled from the backseat, and words followed but there's no need to recount them here.

So when we got to Tricia's school in the piney hills of Milton, ten miles and twenty worlds away from Southie, they were just serving the chicken Diane—we'd missed the first course. Noreen was pissed because she was planning on eating only the fruit cocktail, as she was dieting again. She nagged Tricia into going out back into the kitchen and seeing if we could be served our fruit cocktail, but to no avail, though I'm not sure Tricia even asked, she was kinda shy. She introduced Petey to a few of her girlfriends and God bless Petey, he dropped the puss he'd had on his face all the way down here and acted like he really was interested in Tricia. He could sense she was usually the dateless one, and if Petey was anything he was a compassionate soul, recall if you will the frogs and dogs, except I haven't mentioned the frogs yet but I will. If I remember.

"What are you Tricia's *cousin* or something?" some bitchy girl with big tits and matching nose and attitude asked Petey when Tricia was out of earshot.

"No, just her Friday night fuck buddy," Petey answered with a pleasant smile, though that was probably going too far.

The Mother Mary O'Sullivan Auditorium of Tricia's school had been transformed into the Casa di Fiori for the evening by the prom committee, of which Tricia was the treasurer, and she took pains to explain the red-and-orange intertwined crepe paper running criss-cross around the ceiling, the electric candles with the orange lightbulbs, and a fake fireplace with rotating logs in each of the four corners that had been donated, the placards said, by Benniker's Buy-Rite Hardware Store in Milton Square. I thought it a curiously chosen motif for the middle of a heat wave. I could feel my whitey-tighties bunching up in my sweaty crack already and not even dancing yet.

"Casa di Fiori means House of Fire," Tricia explained. "We were here 'til almost *midnight* last night!"

"You can t-tell," Petey said. Noreen gave him a dirty look but didn't say anything as she was busy with her cocktail, which she had swiped from a girl at the next table when they got up to dance.

"What's this supposed to be, h-hell?" Petey whispered to me but I poked him in the ribs.

We finished our lukewarm deep-fried dinner without incident to the strains of Skip Whitaker and His Strings, then this other band came out and they were a tad livelier but still semi-octogenarianesque, and after every song the lead singer called out *Is everybody happy?* and everybody roared, but me and Petey laughed at the goofiness of it—how suburban. We went to the men's room at one point and this weird thing, in between the men's room and ladies' room there was this picture, a framed print, of three fat baby angels swirling around a flower, and in fancy writing it said PEONIES, A GIFT FROM HEAVEN, but the writing was so fancy for a minute I thought it said PENIS, A GIFT FROM HEAVEN, until I looked closer.

A little later Petey was making his third run to the bar when I intercepted him halfway.

"Hey ahhh Petey, I think Tricia is just wondering when you're going to ask her."

"Ask her wh-what?"

"To dance, duh."

Petey clicked his tongue and sighed.

"Ask her if 'never' works for her."

"C'mon."

"Danny, you know I don't d-d-dance."

"Yes you do! You used to dance down at the beach when the storms came. The full moon and shit. I saw you all those times."

Petey made a repelling gesture with his hand.

"At least you could dance with her once."

"No way! Did you see the s-size of her f-feet? They're canoes."

"It's just the shoes is all. All dress shoes look big."

"They're a s-size fifteen if they're an inch. She must'a got 'em at a dr-drag queen store. My b-big toenail just grew back, I don't want to lose it again so q-quick."

"Just once. C'mon, it's her prom, you have to dance with her. What's a drag queen store?"

"I don't have to d-d-do anything."

"Do it for me. C'mon. Please Petey?"

"When are you g-g-gonna do s-s-something for me? I'm always doing shit for y-you."

"Just ask me," I said.

"Okay, I'm asking. L-leave me be."

"C'mon. You're gonna bring a girl to her prom and not dance with her? She'll never get over it at all!"

"Not m-my problemo."

"Petey, c'mon! All the other girls are watching!"

He stared at me, sighed, staggered back to our table, then walked up to Tricia and said, "M-may I have the pleasure of this d-dance?"

Petey bowed so low he lost his balance and half stumbled against the table.

"What a class act," Noreen snorted, grabbing onto her wobbling Sex on the Beach.

"Look who's t-talkin'," Petey slurred.

"I don't know what your problem is, Petey," Noreen said, "but I bet it's hard to pronounce."

Petey made a face at her, then asked, "If I throw a stick, Noreen, will you g-go away?"

"For Christ's sake you two, stop it," I said. "Can't you try being nicer?"

Petey looked at Noreen and smiled.

"I'll try being n-nicer if you'll try being smarter."

Noreen opened her mouth to retort, but Tricia floated up from her seat like a pink May moon and off her and Petey stumbled to the dance floor to trip the light fantastic. She towered over Petey I noticed. She seemed to be growing by the minute, like the toys you throw in the toilet and they swell up overnight. And by trip the light fantastic I do mean trip. I watched as Tricia whacked Petey's shins once, twice, thrice, and stepped on his toes innumerable times, oblivious if one judged from the sublime look on her face. I thought of Mrs. Harding's oft-repeated but heretofore obscure *Never give a sword to a man who can't dance.*

"They make a lovely couple," I said to Noreen. Petey was so handsome and I was having a little hope.

"Yeah, too bad he's a fag," Noreen slurred, lighting up a butt. She'd only had two and a half Sex on the Beaches but she could never hold her booze when she was dieting.

I felt like she'd punched me in the stomach.

"Excuse me?"

"You heard me."

"Who says he's a fag?"

"I says."

"How do you know? He's . . . he's no fag."

"That's what you think. I can tell. Female tuition. He stares at your ass like it's an ice cream cone when he thinks no one's looking. I'd watch my bum if I were you."

"And I'd watch my mouth if I was you. He's like my fuckin' brother!"

"Oh. And what the fuck am I?"

Thirty seconds into this conversation and I was already picturing Noreen with duct tape on her mouth. That had to be a new record.

"Don't start. Just drop it will ya, here they come."

The local yahoo bucks were resplendent in navy blazers and pastel pants and Top-Siders with no socks. The only thing they were missing to complete the picture of the spoiled and pampered perfect preppy Sons of Commerce was that white shit they put on their noses when they're out in Hingham Harbor fucking around on their daddy's sailboat. The black or red hair and sky-blue eyes and peeling sunburned skin proclaimed that they could be nothing but Irish, but for all of that their patrician ways and overheard names—there were any number of Skips and Chips and Brads—made them anything but.

"Might as well be Guineas," I said to Petey when the girls were in the ladies' room. One of them later, this big drink of water with a seven-foot Kelly-green tie, was a little too free with his eyes when all the girls got up to do the electric slide. They took a walk all over Noreen whose breasts were, I admit, always a little jiggy when she danced.

"Look at that fuckin' douche bag over there," I said to Petey.

Petey lifted up his head and looked but didn't say anything.

The jerk said something to Noreen as she left the dance floor with Tricia, and she said something and smiled a little but kept walking, and then he put his hand on her forearm. I was over there before I could even think about it, but Noreen dragged me back.

"Don't ruin Tricia's prom, it's her first one."

"What'd that loser say to you?"

"Nothing, he's drunk. C'mon, forget about it. Dance with me."

We danced, but this goon gathered with some of his yahoo friends on the edge of the dance floor and I waltzed-or-whatever Noreen over there nonchalantly to see if he would have the balls to say anything in front of me. When he saw me closing in he turned to one of his loser friends.

"You know what the sign says down in the shithouse?" he said, goofy-like.

"No, what?"

"Flush twice, it's a long way back to Southie."

I popped him under the chin before he even turned back around from geek-laughing with his friends, and he went down with me on top of him. There were about six of them though, and someone, or a number of someones, was kicking me while I pummeled the big one. I could hear Noreen screaming, and a few nuns came over and tried to break up the fight by clapping (not like applauding, but like clapping once STOP IT that kind of clapping, which never in history stopped nothing) and then I heard intermittent howls of pain, and I turned my head to see Petey biting the calves of the one who was kicking me. Somehow the ceiling crepe paper came down, and when it did 1,000 orange and red balloons that weren't supposed to fall until midnight and the last dance dropped down slowly, surreally.

"Oh no!" I heard Tricia sob, lifting her Atlas arms up like she might push them all back to the ceiling. "Oh no!"

When the smoke cleared his friends dragged the big loser out of there. I got up sore and kicked, but somewhat flushed and pleased, and especially glad that Petey had pitched in for me despite his pacifist yearnings. Noreen though was red-raging furious and Tricia was guffaw-sobbing and Petey was already back at the bar for another.

The nuns requested that we leave.

"We're shocked a lovely girl like you knows such hooligans, Patricia," one of the nuns said to Tricia on our way out.

"Sorry," Tricia said.

"We didn't start it, they did," I said.

"Those fine young men have been at several of our dances and there's never been trouble before," the nun said back. "Do the math."

"Whatever," I said. I kept walking. What are you gonna do, argue with a nun? But my face was smarting red—the ol' They're-from-Southie-So-They-Must-Be-Trash thing. Still there's worse things. You could be a harmless little twit consumer full of irony.

When we walked outside there was a magnificent sunset, Petey said, but of more immediate concern was the group of about eight of these Fine Young Men leaning against a few spoiled-brat cars in the parking lot, their arms folded.

"Oh shit," Petey said, following my eyes. "The swains have a-g-g-gathered."

I didn't know what that meant but I said to Noreen, "Gimme your cell phone."

"Why?"

"Just fuckin' do it!"

Tricia's sobs had become hiccups.

Noreen fumbled in her purse amidst her cigarettes and lipsticks and hairsprays and perfumes and handed it over. Like forty-seven clowns getting out of one teeny circus car, I could never figure out how she got so much shit in her tiny purse thingie.

"I'm gonna make one call and have forty maniacs wit' baseball bats down here in a minute," I yelled across the parking lot, holding up the phone. "You'll think you died and went to hell."

"It'll take them some time to get down here, shit-for-brains," one of them yelled back.

"*Some time,*" I mimicked, laughing. Talk about geeks.

"Boys! *BOYS!*" one of the nuns called from the portico, clapping again. "I just called the police. They're on their way. You've already ruined our prom, so please leave. Please leave now."

We got in the car and took off. No one followed us or said anything, so that was the end of that.

The roads were twisty and smelled of woods and you could hear crickets above the sound of Noreen's flared-nostrils breathing and Tricia's occasional whimper/hiccup/oh-excuse-me's from the backseat. Now, fighting, like sex, is one of those occupations that you don't just do, you must also talk about it afterwards. So I began to wax lyrical about the good account- ing me and Petey had given of ourselves during the altercation, despite dis- concerting odds. But Tricia started crying again and Noreen kicked me in the right shin. I changed the subject to the many strange things that could give rise to fisticuffs, drawing on experience, what pitcher started the sev- enth game for the Red Sox in the '75 World Series, the color of Timmy Concannon's sister's house before it got painted. No one had anything to contribute to this line though so I gave it up.

Looking in the rearview it looked like you could've fit a couple of area codes in between Petey and Tricia. Petey started hiccupping as if it was catchy.

Driving along and I felt bad the night had gotten so fucked up and ru- ined. Then I thought of a way it might be salvaged. I took a turn up this one road, then made a left at the next intersection and headed up to this place me and Noreen used to go parking at, when we were teenagers, this Blue Hills Reservation place.

"Where you think you're going?" Noreen inquired beside me.

"Ahhhh, nowhere. Nowhere special. Just for a little drive."

"You're crazy, Danny, if you think I'm putting out. Not after what hap- pened tonight. No way, buster."

"Quiet, they'll hear you. I'm doing it for them."

"Good luck to you and the Red Sox," Noreen said. "Remember what I told you."

Then she bounced her two hands limply on her wrists, which must have been her fag imitation. I glared at her to make her stop.

The summer night was *girdle-sticky* as Mrs. H would say and moonless and woods closed in around us as the road climbed higher and snaked around and through the reservation and I started getting a Pavlovian boner. I pulled off into a little dirt place not too many people knew about and wheeled the car around behind these trees and a sign that said RESERVA- TION CLOSES AT SUNSET, so you could see if anyone else was coming in. I shut the car off and lowered the windows all the way down, but kept the radio on low.

"Ummm . . . what are we doing here?" Tricia asked timidly, kindly, curi- ously, from the back.

"Ahhh . . . it's just such a nice night out, I thought we'd pull over for a minute. Smell the pines?"

"Mmmm, lovely," Tricia said.

"I hope I don't get my allergies or asthma," Noreen said glumly, staring out the window and lighting up a cigarette.

"My fifth grade science class took a field trip up here once," Tricia said. "But we had to go back because Debbie Sheehan needed to use the bathroom."

"Oh," I said after a minute. I couldn't think of anything else to say. That evidently had been the alpha and omega of Tricia's story.

Fighting always makes me horny so I slid my hand up through the convenient slit in Noreen's dress, and then along the inside of her thigh. She grabbed onto it to stop my further advance but didn't move it away.

I looked in the rearview and saw that Petey had passed out.

"Hey Tricia," I said. "Wake Petey up."

"Oh. Oh, I don't know."

"Go ahead. Ask him if he can smell the pines."

"Oh I don't know. Are you sure?"

"Sure I'm sure. He wouldn't want to miss this. He loves the outdoors. Pines and shit."

"Well . . . okay. Petey? Petey?"

"Mmmmph."

"Petey, excuse me, can you . . . Danny wants to know if you can smell the pines."

Tricia slowly inched closer to Petey. I could hear the crinkling of her things, her pink things. Miraculously, I could see in the rearview that Tricia had a small piece of pineapple from the dinner stuck in the middle of her corsage, like it was not only flowering but fruiting as well.

Petey opened one eye and looked around groggily. When he saw where he was, he sighed and shook his head in discouragement. Then he turned to Tricia.

"Huh?"

"Can you smell the pines?"

"No. All I can smell is p-perfume."

"Sorry," Tricia said.

"Bastard," Noreen mumbled. We were slouched down making out in the front by then. I was particularly horny tonight. Noreen lifted up and stared into the backseat at Petey.

"What are you l-lookin' at?" Petey asked her.

"I'm trying to picture you with a personality," Noreen said.

"Shhhh," I whispered, pulling her back, pulling too the fly of my tux pants.

"Nice p-perfume, Noreen," Petey shot back. "How long did you m-marinate in it?"

"Stop it you two," I called. I pulled Noreen back down to me. We scooted lower in the front seat and Noreen reached up and twisted the rear-view mirror so they wouldn't see her reach for my hard dick, bobbing and throbbing out of my dress pants. I worked my hand up further 'til I felt her moistness with my fingers through her pantyhose. She moaned quietly and closed her eyes. Yeah baby.

"Can you p-put NPR on instead o' this stupid conformist m-music?" Petey called from the backseat.

"Bastard," Noreen mumbled again.

"Sure," I say. I hit the second button and Petey's station, as I always called it, is on. I go back to what I was doing, try to ease Noreen's head down onto my fat boy. A snort-laugh sneaks out—can't help it. Her new hairdo *does* make her look like Rod Stewart.

"What's so funny?"

"Nothing baby, nothing, c'mon."

"No, not here. They'll see. They'll know."

"No they won't. C'mon, just for a minute. Just lick it a little."

"No, they'll know. Tricia doesn't know about that stuff."

"What are you kiddin' me? We're born with that, no? If Petey whipped his out she'd be on it like a duck on a June bug. C'mon."

"No!"

Noreen wouldn't provide head but started jerking me off instead, carefully. She'd gotten new nails again that afternoon at Princess Nails and could only use her fingers, not her fingertips. Then I heard Petey in the back, being a wiseass again, chanting some stupid thing from when we were kids:

> Oh when the weather's hot and sticky,
> That's no time to dip your dicky—
> But when the frost is on the p-p-pumpkin,
> Aye, that's the time to d-dip your dunkin'!

"He's so crude," Noreen says.

"Never mind, I'm almost there baby. C'mon, faster."

"Oh shit," Petey says from the backseat.

"What's the matter?" Tricia whispers.

"I don't . . . f-f-feel so well."

"What's the matter?" Tricia repeats.

"I think I'm gonna p-pu . . . I think I'm gonna throw up." He sounds like he's ten again.

"Asshole," Noreen whispers.

"Quiet, he'll hear you. C'mon baby. Faster."

"This is stupid, Danny. I feel like I'm milking a cow and them in the back listening."

"They can't hear you," I said, turning up the radio. Some nerd with a twangy Midwest accent was interviewing a famous bug expert. "C'mon baby, don't stop the train before it reaches the station."

"Oh shit," Petey says from the back. "Unlock the door, Danny."

"Uh . . . uh . . . okay, uh, wait a minute—"

"C'mon, open the f-fu . . . open the d-door! I'm g-gonna puke!"

Petey makes a retching sound and I jolt up and hit the unlock button. It wouldn't do to besmirch the Dadmobile. Petey vaults out of the car and flies by us, but not before turning and looking down into my seat. My dick is red and sticking straight up and my legs are spread and my pants and sweaty briefs are bunched up down by my ankles. I see Petey look down as he goes by. I don't try to cover it with my hands.

"Shit," I sigh.

"That's it," Noreen says, retreating to her corner and yanking herself together. "Let's get outta here. He's ruined the night."

"For Chrissake Noreen, he's sick," I say. I pull up my pants, shove my stiffy back into my underwear, zip and buckle up. I open the door.

"Where you going now?"

"I'm gonna help him. He might need my help, it's dark out there."

"What, you gonna puke for him? He just drank too much, serves him right."

"Oh and you never got sick from drinking! I'll be right back."

"Christ on a crutch, are you his friend or his mother!"

I get out and shut the car door. Noreen rolls up the windows. I hear her screeching about some bug that flew in.

"Petey . . . Petey! Where the . . . where are you? Petey!"

No answer. The sound of retching. I follow it, about fifteen yards into the woods. It's hard to see in these suburbs. Petey's on his knees, puking into the grass at the foot of an old tree. Dribbling down his chin it is. Not so good. The Golden Boy Straight-A student perfectionist that was going to be bright-eyed President.

"You okay?"

"Uhhhh. Oooooo."

"It's okay, I'm here." I put my hands on my knees and bend over a little. "I'll stay with you."

"Oooooo. It's n-not okay. Nothing's okay."

"Sure it is, Petey, everything's okay. You just drank too much is all. Everything's okay."

"No it isn't. N-n-nothing is."

"Oh stop. What do you mean?"

"There's n-n-no one like me in the world. I'm all alone. You d-d-don't like me the w-w-way I am. You're the only one knows and you d-d-don't . . ."

Petey hurls again. I cringe and get queasy to hear it, then toughen myself up, remembering I'm a Marine—I'm not supposed to be squeamish.

"Shhhh, not so loud. 'Course it's okay. 'Course I like you. The way you are I mean."

"No you d-don't. This was all your doing, Tricia told me. You set it up. You l-l-lied to me."

"C'mon, don't get like that. I was . . . I was just trying to do you a favor."

"There's n-no one like me! *There's n-n-n-no one like m-m-me!*"

Petey's moaning the words and his voice is all bubbly and waily. He starts thrashing around in the dirt, keening.

"Quiet, Petey, c'mon! C'mon, you wanna have every cop in this hick town down here? C'mon, Petey, Petey, don't—"

"THERE'S NO ONE LIKE ME! I'M ALL ALONE! I'LL AL-AL-WAYS BE ALONE!"

Petey's getting hysterical and I don't know what to do. I flop down beside him and reach my hand out to him from behind, then stop.

"Petey, stop! Quiet, c'mon! The girls'll hear you!"

"Oh, we c-c-can't have that, can w-w-we? We can't have them knowing your b-b-best friend's a f-f-f—"

"Petey, shut up, c'mon, stop it! Quiet! There's . . . there's people like you, what are you talking about, there's tons of 'em around."

"Wh-where? Where the fuck are they? Not like m-m-me! Not like . . . us!"

"Keep your voice down, will ya? That's not true! Don't be a fuckin' meathead! What about those movies? They have people like you in movies now."

"They're fuckin' g-g-gay. They're not like me, not like us—"

My eyebrows bunch in confusion.

"Well I thought you said you were . . . ahhh . . . gay."

The word tastes funny as it spills out my mouth. I notice how shaggy the tree bark is right in front of me. Rough. Wild.

"Not like them. I'm n-n-not fucking witty and . . . gayish. I'm not gonna b-be anybody's comic relief. Telling them what they oughta do to their apartments. I'm not like anybody!"

He's drunk and making no sense.

"Well listen to me, Petey, we . . . we had these two guys in the Corps right, they threw 'em out for screwing around together. They weren't . . . like witty or whatever."

In fact one of them was the toughest guy in our battalion, though I don't tell Petey that—I still haven't figured that one out myself.

"Where the fuck are they n-now? Wh-what am I s-s-supposed to do, walk to f-fuckin' Alabama or somethin'? Plus they wouldn't understand m-me, or the o-ocean. My m-maps."

I don't tell Petey either that one of them shot himself with his rifle the day before his court-martial. Every Marine a rifleman—

"It d-d-doesn't fucking matter anyways!"

Petey was nearly screaming now. But from the car I hear the vague thump of *chick-a-boom chick-a-boom* and I know Noreen has put her dance music station back on so that's some relief—they won't hear us.

"What do you mean, it doesn't matter? I thought you said—"

"They're not . . . they're n-not . . . like us! They're n-not . . . n-not . . . you."

His words make me freeze up.

"What?"

"They're n-not . . . you," Petey says.

He twists his head and looks back at me.

"You," he says again. "Y-O-fuckin' U, Danny boy."

He lifts his head defiantly higher and mumbles, "You're the only one I w-want. The only one I'll ever want. I guess you're gonna keep playing dumb until I spell it out for you. There's s-something so good in you deep down, Danny. You don't even know it. We belong to each other, Danny. Too bad the universe forgot and made you a dumb-ass m-malleable breeder."

Malleable. Petey's helped me decipher words based on their roots. That must mean male-like, manly, masculine—I guess that's a compliment. But Jesus, what he's just said!

All I can see in the dark is his eyes, swollen with something, shiny. A roll of saliva tongues down from his italic mouth.

Petey makes one more retch sound, then stops. It appears his vomiting is finished.

It's very quiet now in the woods here. Not a relaxed quiet. There's a lonesome cricket off to the left, that's about it. No wind goes through the trees. *If I was you I'd watch your bum.* Noreen's bitchy words jump back to me, gain credibility.

See it's one thing to have your best friend, someone you've been with all your life, tell you he's . . . he's . . . different like that. It's altogether another to hear him say that he . . . that he . . .

"I'll be in the car," I say.

"W-wait. W-wait a minute, D-Danny—"

"We're leaving now. Stay here or come, please yourself."

"D-DANNY! D-don't g-go!"

"Where's the pick of the parish?" Noreen asks when I get back to the car. She's reapplying her CandiApples lipstick in the vanity mirror. The smoke from her Eve 120 cigarette fills the car like Pittsburgh.

"He's in the woods."

I slam the car door.

"What's the matter with you?"

"Nothing, what's the matter with you?"

"What was all that yellin'?"

"Nuthin'. He . . . he's just drunk."

I roar up the car, flip on the headlights.

"Is he coming or not?" Noreen asks.

"I dunno."

"Well where is he?"

"I don't *know!* Jesus Christ, who are you Sherlock Holmes with all these fuckin' questions?"

"Don't talk to me like that! I just asked a simple question—"

"Well give it a rest, will you?"

"Sorry," Tricia says from the backseat.

I blast the horn.

No Petey.

"Fuck him, I told him we were going."

"Serves him right," Noreen says as I peel out.

We drive in silence to Tricia's house. I'm so mad I can feel the blood thudding in my ears. I have this temper sometimes, this thing inside, waiting. Noreen stares out the window beside her. Tricia's in the back, quiet as a tree.

"I'm staying over here tonight," Noreen says when we get to Tricia's house.

"Fine."

"I'll call you tomorrow and hopefully your humor will have improved."

"Fine."

"What are you gonna do now?"

"I dunno. I'll see you later."

"Sorry," Tricia says as she gets out of the car. Noreen slams her door.

I hate when people slam my door.

Deeper, Danny, Deeper

I'm up to Florian Hall, almost to Southie, when I stop. The anger's hissing out of me but there's still enough to flush my face.

Fuck.

I pull over into the breakdown lane on the Expressway, put my hand up to my forehead. Jesus Christ.

"Fuckin' ass*hole*," I mutter. I pull off at the Neponset exit and turn around. He's liable to get himself run down by a car or something on the way home. I don't want that on my conscience.

Why him? I wonder as I'm coming back into Milton, why *him?* There were ten of us in the gang growing up, though it was always me and Petey that were closest, ten of us and where are the others now? Sully turned out to be a jerk, Bunso Burns went into the Big House, Jackie and Timmy—I don't know, we just ran out of things to say to each other. Kev died of an overdose God rest him as did Sean, though everyone said Sean was a suicide but we all knew better. Mike and his wife moved out of town, Chris went into the service, like myself—

But why Petey? Why still Petey? Why are we still close? And him a fa— a queer too? What's up with this?

Cuz he's special. Always been special.

I love him. Love him like a brother.

What did he do tonight that was so wrong? What was it? Told me he loved me. Told me he loved me, and so I deserted him. Told me he loved me and I ditched him in the woods ten miles from home shitfaced might as well be a hundred. Loser I can be.

I picture him stumbling along the road, feeling hurt cuz I screwed on him. Staggering maybe. A car sweeps round the corner like in one of Ma's old black-and-white movies—

A Map of the Harbor Islands
Published by The Haworth Press, Inc., 2006. All rights reserved.
doi:10.1300/5677_17

I've never been a weepy drunk but I start filling up now. Step on it.
Petey—

In ten minutes I'm back in the woods, pitch dark now, crickets going
nuts. How do these suburbanites sleep nights with the racket? I jump out of
the car, my eyes jag around, then I see him. He hasn't moved an inch, still
on all fours. I start running at first, clumbering through brush and branches.
Then I stop, slow down, pluck a stalk of grass and shove it in my mouth—
I'm a Marine for chrissake. There's no need to be dramatic.

"Hey, uh . . . Petey."

No answer.

"I came back, Petey."

Zippo.

"I came back for you, Petey. See?" I squat down a little.

"Don't bother. Lemme d-die here. I w-wanna die here."

"Don't be a meathead. C'mon, I'll take you home."

"I have nothing to l-live for."

I squat down further.

"Don't be a meathead, 'course you do. You're fuckin' twenty years old.
You'll look back on this night and laugh someday."

"No I w-w-won't."

"Sure you will. Petey, you're so smart and have so much to offer the
world. I think you'll change the world someday, Petey, with all your . . .
ideas and stuff. C'mon, let's go."

"Where's the others?"

"I brung 'em home."

"Oh. G-good place for 'em."

"Now now, be nice."

It's quiet for a bit and we both relax a little. I know he's glad I came back,
but I know with his pride he can't say that yet. Thank God he's okay, thank
God thank God—

"The night was not entirely s-successful," Petey mumbles.

I start laughing a little, can't help it. What a funny little customer he is,
the odd way he says things.

"Nah, don't worry about it. What are you gonna do? I . . . I should'a
known better I suppose."

A long low whistle of a faraway train sifts through the June midnightness
and the sound comes into me, happiness on one side, sadness on the other.
Maybe it reminds me I'll be leaving again tomorrow. I look down at Petey.

"I love that s-sound," he says. "Away-ness, away-ness. Next tr-train to Happy Land, all aboard."

A stray shaft of moonlight leaks out from the clouds. It finds the side of Petey's downturned face as if it's been looking for it. It lights up his black hair, the glimmer of the side of his eye. The eyelashes, too long for a boy.

It's quiet and still in the woods here, another world. Somewhat peaceful, now that I think of it. Different, this world. I sit down on an old stump beside him. A contented resignation—only better—sifts down upon us. Upon me anyways.

It's not like me but I look up. The stars. Wow. Maybe three times as many as me and Petey saw the night we went to his alley, like a drive-in to heaven. It's not like me, but now it is, for Petey has left his mark upon me. A gentle swipe that's dribbled all the way to my soul. Trickle-down enlightenment.

I'm a different man because of Petey, no other way to say it.

"Petey," I whisper. "Look up. Look at the stars."

Petey doesn't move, being stubborn a little. But I know what he wants. He wants to be coddled a bit. He's nursing his wounded pride after I screwed on him and made him do this tonight. That's okay. I can coddle him.

I get up, take a reluctant look at my suit, take off my jacket and lay it on the ground. I lay down beside him on the pine-needled ground.

Petey shifts over a little to make room for me, rolls over on his back.

"Your s-suit, Danny," he mumbles as I scoot in closer.

"Ah, the hell with it," I sigh. "That's what Chinese people are for."

"What an unlovely r-remark. Danny, don't say that."

"I'm just kiddin'. My best friend in the Corps is this Asian kid—"

"You're making it worse, Danny. But I know you're that Irish, your jokes are conciliatory b-bouquets.

"Well, what are you gonna do," I sigh. I mush closer to Petey.

Like a dog, a shudder goes through him as he lets go a deep breath.

"Look at them, Petey," I say, staring up at the stars. A little breeze waffles through the leaves over our head, swaying them, like they're a fanfare to the show.

"Mmmph," Petey says. He lets go another deep breath. I start laughing a little.

"What's so f-funny?"

"I don't know if it's funny or not," I say, "but I was just thinking. I play this little game now in my head sometimes. Like I pretend I'm looking at a video of my life, and I see myself in the future. Like when I was in Lebanon, and if I had seen a video of me like the year before, and watched me being in Lebanon, I would'a said, *Wow, look at me! Where am I? Is that a Marine uniform I'm wearing? Who are those people I'm with? It looks like I'm in the Mideast! What am I doing there?* Follow?"

"Yeah."

"Well, I was just thinking if a year ago, when I was in Lebanon, if I had seen a video of us tonight, lying here in the middle of nowhere, looking up at the stars, I would'a said, *Wow, what's up with this? Me and Petey, lying in the woods! What are we doin' there? How'd we get there? Is that monkey suits we're wearing?* You know what I mean? It would'a been kinda hard to figure it out, I guess."

"Mmph," Petey agrees.

A wave of something protective for Petey sweeps over me. I snuggle into him a bit. I feel his body tense up.

"It's okay," I whisper. "Just relax, Petey."

Another deep breath out of him.

"O-okay," he sighs. I feel his body lean into mine. He shifts his head onto my shoulder.

"Is th-that okay?" he whispers. He sounds like he's seven.

His voice breaks my heart. For the second time tonight I choke up, though I'm able to hide it. I turn my head away for a second.

"'Course it is, Petey."

I wrap my right arm around his shoulders and pull him into me. His head settles on my chest. My arm runs down his back, then comes across our waists where I join it to my other hand.

A sigh of ecstasy comes out of him. A feeling of comfort inundates me.

For the first time, an appreciation of Otherness rises up in me. All my life I've been the man in the street, the boy next door, the kid next to you in class, suffocatingly normal. Never stepped off the sidewalk, never had to. Just like everybody else.

But now I picture cop car lights sweeping in here, flashlights, cries of shock and alarm—*Yeah, we got a situation up here in the woods—Two men. Lying together. And him a Marine*—

Is there anyone in my life that would understand what's happening here? For once, my turn now, I taste the fruit of Otherness, of Polarization (though I don't know that word yet either), of what-it-must-be-like—to be one of those the world in its ignorance calls freaks—

Fuck them.

We stay like this for a bit, my heart at ease. We've been still long enough for the crickets to have come back full force, their sound a sweet sprinkling to the night, like when the priest hyssops the congregation with holy water. A deep peace settles over this place, the moon flickering through the shadows. I begin to hear variations within the crickets' songs—there are other voices within the voices, peeps and calls, whispers and plaintive little coos— it strikes me as eminently reassuring, and also somewhat surprising, given our collective greed, that these unseen nightly troubadours have managed to keep their show on the road all these millions of years; that they can still find unbulldozed pockets to do this in.

The odor of Petey rises into my nostrils, mingling with the wood smells. To tell you the truth there's a bit of sour vomit tang on the edges of this Eau de Petey—but this doesn't even signify. We've seen each other at our best, and worst. It's Petey smell for sure though. How else to describe a unique aroma without comparing it with others? But lemme try and pick out a few strands of it—one of them is definitely the Outdoors, like when an apple-cheeked little kid comes in from playing all day on a cold winter's evening; Petey's Garden, by which I mean when we'd dig it up every spring and it was black and wormy and fertile smelling from all the leaves and grass and doggy-do we'd bury in it every fall; Strawberry Ice Cream, his breath, always; and something else—sweet, faint, now-you-smell-it-now-you-don't— like fresh-cut grass—

A warmth from his body seeps into mine and this smell of Petey rises into my nostrils like when Ma used to make her almond-cinnamon rolls of a Sunday morning.

I shift my eyes and see that Petey's are closed. A sublime look I've seen shining on his face before—but not for a while: the day we spied Cozy Cove for the first time; when the full moon climbed out of its ocean nest all those nights; when he won the Holy Name Society's Young Man of the Year award a month before his accident. Petey looks like he's filling up, like at a gas station. Can almost hear the dinging as the numbers fly by.

I take a deep breath. I don't want to ruin the moment, but there's something I need to say. I'm not really sure what that is; but for once I trust my tongue.

"Petey," I whisper, his ear maybe an inch away from my mouth. "It . . . it feels like . . . wicked like . . . home when I'm with you. Home."

And it does, too.

He cuddles into me more, throws an ankle over mine.

"H-h-heaven."

I study Petey, his face. Gentle and kind it is, like him. A heart as big as his head. Bringing home stray dogs and birds. A healer. A talker to the sea. While I felt too honored almost as a kid, pre-accident, a little dubious in an I-Am-Not-Worthy way that he was boring me's best friend when he could've had anybody, I realize the post-accident version of Petey is even rarer. He doesn't belong with me—he belongs with gurus on mountaintops, with that guy Thoreau on midnight discoursing rambles; in non-smoke-filled backrooms with Jesus and Gandhi and Martin Luther King, drawing up plans on how to heal the world and all its people—

And yet—here we are. And in knowing that Petey would have no one else but me by his side now, I *do* belong with him, by virtue of that.

Jesus, talk about lucky. Talk about being gifted. I pull him closer and sigh.

We stay like this for a while.

I study him again.

Petey is gentle and his hair looks so soft in the moonlight. Like a girl's, when you think about it. Petey is like a girl—

I reach over and touch his hair. It's soft, I knew it—

"Your hair is softer than a girl's," I whisper.

He jumps, pulls away.

"Don't d-do that. I'm no girl."

A car swipes by on the not-too-distant parkway, its headlights like scared ghosts of animals dashing through the woods—they slice on us for a moment and I sit up. I kinda snap out of it. Though I may know now what it's like to feel Other, that's no guarantee I'm ready to be seen as such, stand in that brave rogues' gallery.

"Alright then," I sigh, standing up, stretching, brushing off my suit. "We should go. Let's get outta here."

Petey raises up on one elbow.

"Wh-where?"

"I dunno. Home I guess."

"I know it but I don't w-w-wanna go home."

"Well okay, we'll go for a little ride then. Where you wanna go?"

"I dunno. I w-w-wanna run away."

"Well c'mon, let's go back to the car anyways. These mosquitoes are eatin' me alive and you're ahh . . . you're kneeling in your puke there, Petey."

Petey gets up—I half pull him. We flounder back to the car. I have my arm on his shoulder, and he's staggering a little. His baby-blue bow tie is all wrangled to the side, like he's a package and something went awry with the delivery somewhere. Lost. Refused.

"Wait a minute," I say, leaning Petey against my car to keep him from falling.

I snatch a bunch of leaves from a nearby tree and start wiping off Petey's puke, from his sleeve, one of his knees. His chin. He freezes.

"Relax, kiddo," I say.

Not a job I especially relish, but you don't think twice. I spit into my hand and use the saliva to finish matters under his chin.

"Nuthin' wrong with you that a little oil o' Danny won't cure," I say. Petey's eyebrows leap up.

"What?" I ask.

"N . . . nothing. Th-thanks, Danny."

It sounds like he might start blubbering any minute.

"Anytime."

His eyes are like saucers.

I open the car door for him and gently slide him down to the seat. I shut his door. I'm feeling very protective of him right now, doing the shit I do for Noreen. I go around to my side, open the door, get in. I shut my door, don't slam it. I hate when people slam my door. I reach underneath my seat for the bottle of blue Winterfresh Listerine I keep here for when Noreen gives me head in the car. She always wants to gargle afterwards. She says I taste like the boys' gym at the Y down there.

"Here, Petey, you'll feel better."

Petey takes it but he can't figure out the child-proof top so he gives it back and I open it for him. He takes a big guggle, swishes it around, tilts his head back and gargles. "Gargoyle gargoyle gargoyle," he mumbles as he does it. Funny, Petey. Just when you think.

I lower his window with my button and he squirts blue out the window. I watch him as he does it. His movements are seamless, perfunctory and efficient. Unlike Noreen when she does this. His ejected stream is an arcing arrow. Noreen though, she'd have to open the door and lean down almost to the street to do this, spraying shit all over hingdom come, making muttered exclamations of . . . well, not disgust exactly. More like a chore that's completed now.

The crickets start up again. The moonlight sneaks out, brighter; brighter still. I almost wait for a noise, a seeping blare, to correspond with the brightening. The moon's never this bright in Southie, just one more streetlight really. Bright here though, and the darkness around it of course all the denser.

I lower the rest of the windows. Petey jumps a speck at the whirr. I turn on the radio, looking for the Sox game. It was on earlier, but now the AM station's resumed its former broadcasting, which is like Bible stuff I guess. This choir is singing a song—

> There is a balm in Gilead
> To make the wounded whole.
> There is a balm in Gilead
> To heal the sin-sick soul . . .

Pine smell and the scent of nearby unseen water drifts into the car, mingling with the voices of the singers like they're marching over a hill to Alleluia Land or something—these folks always sound so *strident,* no? I reach for the dial but Petey grabs my hand halfway.

"D-don't, Danny. Leave it on. I always l-liked this song. Ma'am used to sing it to me."

"Okay."

I sit back. I'm very relaxed and in no hurry. But it's weird—I start getting tense too. I feel good about what just happened, feel that Petey and I have had some kind of breakthrough—though he still looks like he's been slammed over the head with a two-by-four. But something else nips at me—

"D-did I . . . Danny did I j-just dream what happened back there?" he asks.

"Oh Petey," I say, extending my right arm. "C'mere."

I hug him, right there in the front seat. When I let go we're right beside each other.

But the thing is I can still smell Noreen in the car. But Petey's next to me. I become . . . aware of him. Aware of how there's . . . no one else here. I don't know how else to describe it. There's this shift from what happened in the woods five minutes ago, where I was all about peace and bliss and innocence—

"I can . . . hear you breathing," I say, before I know what I'm saying.

Petey kind of freezes again, then says, carefully, "That's always a g-good sign."

Petey here beside me, but I can smell Noreen. I remember how my clammy bare ass felt against these slickety leather seats just an hour ago, when she was jerking me off. I still haven't gotten my nut off yet. I start getting hard. I feel sweat gathering in the secret places between my whitey-tighties.

The holy song continues, which kind of pisses me off because it's not the mood I'm in right now. Jesus, won't they ever finish? Twentieth verse, same as the first—

"G-Gilead is like the Promised Land," Petey says, sounding very far away. "The land of Never-Never. When Ma'am would sing it to me, I used to think, if you lived your life the way you wanted to, the way you were s-s-supposed to, why would you need an escape? A N-Never-Never Land to dream about, when this world here is already a dream? I decided that Skovo, when He/She whispered B-Bible thoughts into the people who wrote its ears, that's what was meant. That l-love and justice c-can make this world into a Gilead. And that's not the only Bible the Lord/Lady Skovo gave us Danny. The wind going through the trees is a Bible. The look of a homeless dog's eyes when he first allows you to cuddle him. The look in a dying person's eyes if you hold them."

Petey pauses. He's getting philosophical now and me getting harder.

"So I d-decided, Danny, I'd make my life a Gilead, so I wouldn't have to escape."

"Ahhh . . . yeah. I know it."

I shift around a little so my boner isn't quite so uncomfortable—pants are too tight though. It reminds me of how we'd stuff big ol' Aunt Claire into the back of Ma's little Tercel cuz *I ain't ridin' in the death seat in no foreign car.*

"But when I grew up," Petey says, like he's talking to himself, "I s-saw that my mother was right."

Petey sighs a deep sigh, pushes the lank black hair off his forehead.

"This isn't no Gilead, this f-fucking life."

"Ahhh . . . yeah, I know it. You're right there." I try to remember what we're talking about. Who's Gilead?

I shift around again. I'm starting to sweat, from the inside out, like. Something comin'—

"Nice here," I say.

"I g-guess." Petey shrugs. "I'm still a little . . . a little c-confused I think—"

"Ahhhh . . . yeah. Quite a night. I'm . . . lookit, Petey—I'm . . . sorry. Sorry about tonight. Tryin' to fix you up and everything."

I turn to look at him as he turns to me.

"That's . . . o-o-okay. I think . . . I th-think I could almost live on . . . live on what . . . j-just happened. Almost."

Whatever, but what a jerk I'd been. Petey was right. I hadn't accepted who he was. What a jerk. How shitty this must be for him. He didn't ask for it. And here I was trying to fix him up with—

"Ahhh, lookit, Petey, I won't do it again. I swear to you."

"That's okay, D-Danny."

We sit draped in cricket silence for a bit, the air sprinkled with Petey forgiveness.

"You're such a . . . Petey, you're such a good person. I . . . mean that. You are."

I turn to look at him again.

I can see just the outline of his face, his hair, a gleam where his eyes are, the bow tie gone awry. It's dark, but the moon spangles the car, reflects around a little bit. A pine sigh runs through the open windows. It lifts Petey's hair again, that girl's hair. Just a little. I shift in my seat. I hear something and don't recognize for a minute the thudding in my ears. The seat's hot. Ditto with my pants, the places and spaces contained within my pants. I recall an hour ago, when Petey looked down through the window at my stiffy.

Damn I'm hard. I can see that girl-soft hair hanging down. I can picture it hanging down on either side of Petey's face as he puts his mouth down there, I can picture this. Jesus Christ I must be shitty still. But a blow job's a blow job, right? Doesn't really matter who's doing it and that hair, that soft girl's hair—geez, I must be drunk, horny as hell when I'm high. Doesn't make me a fag and Petey would love it, no? Long as he—long as he doesn't get the wrong idea—long as we both remember who we are—

No don't! Don't!

But this is something once started can't be stopped, so I lift up on the seat a little and pull down my fly. Like I'm watching someone else, shocked at my own ballsiness or whatever this is, I yank my pants down to my thighs, keeping my cling-damp underwear on. My dick springs up under my white Hanes like a punching-bag clown, and thuds against my belly. I think I can almost hear the quiet smack of it.

A certain smell infiltrates the air.

"Wicked hard right now," I say, but a quiver to my voice, a bo-jangles. I feel like the first time I looked at a girlie magazine, deliciously, innocently wicked. When we were thirteen, fourteen—Petey was never there—but once in a while there was like this six-month period where we'd go over

Timmy's house on Friday nights, watch wrestling, watch the Bruins me and Kev and Timmy and Sully, and then Timmy would break out one of his older brother's porn tapes and we'd whack off, watch it and whack off, and once or twice we whacked each other off, no big deal and kids' stuff—

.   I snatch a quick sideways glance at Petey and his face resembles nothing more than when he got hit that night, right after he got hit but before he fell. The thwack of him, two-by-four behind the head look—

—A part of me wants to run into the woods now, run, keep running, everybody, all this energy now and a rapid thumping all over as something inside roils—

No big deal and doesn't make me a fag, I've fucked Noreen about 1,000 times and other girls too, lots, ports o' call and what not here come the Marines—

"Look how hard that fuckin' thing is right now," I say. Does Petey hear the quiver in my voice? Fuckin' quiver—

I notice my voice sounds almost the same as when we pick up girls in juke joints. That's good, that's what I want—but that fuckin' quiver—

But how else is it supposed to sound? What would happen if I just said it, normal voice? No not that, never that, but the blood ka-thunking in my ears the way it would the first few times with Noreen, how hot, how I thought I might drop dead, the sizzling thrust of everything—flushed, jagged, moist. My mouth goes dry, my knee starts bouncing—

Petey freezes. For a second I get like coke-paranoid, thinking everything's frozen up in time, but then this noise out of him, a squirm of a noise—

"Look at that, P-Petey," I say, an oft-given canned speech as if my mouth is still working on autopilot, but something else, unknown being born within—

Petey's head turns. I see him gulp. His eyes look down at it and it gives a leap, as if his eyes were fingers. I look at it too as if it were someone else's—

Petey looks back up at my eyes. It's dark. I can't tell what they're seeing—I look away—

"C'mon. C'mon, Petey. Do it. You know you want to."

I lift my ass up and slide my scudding briefs down to my ankles in sweaty yanks. I lean forward, reach underneath, and drive the seat as far back as she'll go. Petey's body jerks back as the seat goes flying. He puts one hand on the dashboard to steady himself. I notice it's shaking, his hand.

That smell gets stronger. The air wraps around my groin, licking. Holy shit—

"Yeah, look at that thing. You want it. Go ahead, suck it."

I'm staring straight ahead as I say the words but I'm keeping a good peripheral peep on Petey.

He runs a hand through his hair, looks out the window, looks back, looks down, looks forward again.

"J-Jesus Christ," he whispers.

He shakes himself like a wet dog, like he might be dreaming. He joins his hands together and cracks his knuckles, a gesture I've never seen in him before, like you came home and your mother was smoking a cigar. His head jerks up and he stares at me.

"What . . . what's going on here, D-D-Danny?"

The quiver is catchy. It's in his voice now too—

But what else is there? Heartbreak? Hope? Both? What the fuck *is* happening here?

"Ahhh . . . look at that fuckin' thing. I . . . ahhh . . . didn't have a chance to do it with Noreen, so . . . c'mon, c'mon. C'mon."

Petey freezes up again, then covers his eyes with both hands for a moment. Groans, grunts.

"This . . . oh J-Jesus. What are you doing? It isn't h-how I p-p-pictured it would be."

A part of me, not the ka-thunking in my ears wild now but some other part, decides the best answer to this is no answer at all. I want a blow job, that's all. I'm almost twenty-one and I want a blow job, Petey the only one here and there'd be time later to think about this. Or not. But another part of me is weeping over this—

Petey's breath is coming faster now and his body tenses up, a jackknife ready to spring—

"O-okay," he says, but he sounds like a little kid again. He shifts closer to me, looks at me for a second as if for guidance but I've got nothing to say now. Couldn't even. He looks down again. There's a blob of moonlight gleaming on my thigh. I slide into it until the upright throbbiness is illuminated therein. The shadow of it blacks out a long slice of my thigh. I think of when we learned Stonehenge in Sr. Claire's history class and would laugh if my heart wasn't pounding like this. Breathe now. Breathe—

Petey reaches for it, his hand passing in and out of moonlight on its trembling way—I close my eyes as his fingers encircle it and a noise comes out of me that I wish hadn't. His fingers gather round it, softly, tighten, softly, and we both jump at the touch. My eyes pry open on their own and I see his mouth falling open, not in preparation but in dumbfoundedness. A strange image pops into my head, the first day of kindergarten, the first day I saw Petey, smiling like he'd been waiting for me—

Petey's fingers don't stop trembling as they tighten further, or maybe it's me now, impossible to guess where I end, and him beginning—

"Oh G-God," he whispers, to himself I think. A writhe jiggles through his entire leaning body and spreads into mine. "I n-n-never knew, n-n-never knew, how could I have known . . . oh God!"

He leans in closer. A gasp comes out of him then he whispers, "Birdy!"

Oh Jesus in heaven, don't let him get weird on me now—

"Ahhh . . . I know it," I heave. "Just . . . go ahead now. Quick. Go."

He's staring up at me, the mouth all open but still I won't look down at him. His smell is magnified now twenty times, four hundred times—

He leans his head forward and lowers it down, slowly like a lunar landing. An animal sound comes out of him, something, neither whimper nor growl. His hair falls down and brushes my thighs, my nuts, electricity. I knew it would feel like this, maybe didn't know I'd be writhing so much—

I hear him sniffing. He draws in my scent—oh God—

"What does it smell like?" I mutter, again regretting the words instantly. Whatever filtering process I possess has shut down for the night—

He's trembling so much he can barely answer.

"Oh G-God D-Danny," he says, his voice quavery like through water. "I d-dunno!"

He whisper-wails the words.

He breathes in again. My eyes shut. "Like l-l-life," he whispers. "Like you t-times ten, and L-L-Life. Birdy."

I squirm, my eyes open again because I'm feeling faint. I don't know why I should be feeling faint now. The blood thudding away in my ears—

Something soft and wet and tender encircles my dickhead. His hair on my soft/hard white belly short-circuits a universe inside me.

Petey's entire body is shaking except for his right hand and his mouth.

"Ouuuuuu," comes out of me. Again I wish it hadn't, wish it didn't sound so . . . so like some part of me I didn't know about, so I add quick, "Yeah, go ahead bitch, suck it."

Petey freezes. His lips are halfway down me. Freezes but he's still shaking—

I raise up my hand and reach to touch the back of his head, pull back, then go ahead and do it. I push his head down. He resists.

"C'mon," I whisper, my voice like a rollicking wave. If I could stop this now maybe I would.

Petey springs back up and away. He scares me. I lurch back, hit my head on the ceiling.

Petey retreats to his corner.

"What?" I mumble-pant. It's all I can get out of me. I won't look at him.

"I'm not your b-b-bitch, D-Danny," he says.

I hear a big sigh come out of me.

"Yeah, well . . . okay whatever, you're not my . . . you're not. C'mon though, c'mon. Just do it."

"Okay," he says, but his voice different now. "But I w-want you to kiss me first, Danny."

"What?"

"You heard m-me. I want you to k-kiss me first."

He turns to look at me, and a wiseass curl to his lip. But his eyes strange, vital, something huge at the back of them—

I can't speak for a moment for the loss of breath. Then—

"Yurgh! You gotta be kidding me! You're kiddin' me, right?" But even as I say the words something vast and sad opening up inside me—

"And w-will you do me afterwards, D-Danny boy? Will you suck mine afterwards, Mr. Cl-Clean Marine?" Why is he being so derisive now?

"Forget about it, forget about it, I don't know what I was fuckin' thinkin'. You got me all screwed up."

"Yes, it was my p-passionate advances," Petey chides, but there's a bitter sarcasm to his words.

I pull myself back together, zip and buckle up. I have to stop for a minute, ease down, catch my breath, ease down, ease down—

I lurch the seat forward and fire up the car. I peel out, spin gravel as I'm backing out—

"Ooo, t-tough guy," Petey says, his voice full of scorn. And something else I can't pinpoint—

Fuck you, I think. I almost say the f word—the other one—in my mind but then I don't.

What a disaster.

We don't say anything all the way back to Southie. Petey looking out the window, doing something with his eyes. When we get to the rotary there's a big fiery car crash and they got the Boulevard shut down, so we slide up Old Colony instead, right underneath the CROWN ROYAL and SALEM LIGHTS and THE FEW, THE PROUD, THE MARINES triple billboard, all wavy and glary from the car flames beneath. Petey cranes his neck to look at the Marine billboard pointedly and thoughtfully as we sweep by, his finger on his chin speculatively.

What a wiseass.

We reach the West Side and navigate our way round the Jersey barriers .and detours—it's all screwed up over here from the Big Dig—then finally come up *Oh-wow-surprise* at a place I've been to before.

I idle the car for a bit as this memory punch smacks me. I turn the car around and blast the high beams out into this little trashy abandoned lot. A tangle of briars and weeds six feet tall turn lacy under my car lights and the sodium streetlights above, the dance and sift of these lights together.

Something goes sad within me, like a meal souring. I know where we are.

Petey purposely won't look out the window now and that's all he's been doing the way home.

I clear my throat and he jumps a little.

"Ahhh . . . you . . . don't have your little garden over here anymore, Petey?"

My voice has back-to-normaled. Thank God.

Petey looks up and out. Silence.

"Your little garden? 'Member? You don't have it anymore?"

"N-no."

"Well . . . why not?"

"I j-just don't, is all."

"When did you stop? I thought you still did this. Why'd you stop?"

"What are you, Sherlock Holmes with all these f-fuckin' questions?"

He must've heard me and Noreen fighting while he was puking. Wise-ass.

"Whatever," I say.

I cluck the car back into drive and we pull away.

Five minutes later we're in front of Petey's house.

"I want you to do me a favor, Petey," I say, slamming the car into park but not shutting off the engine.

"Another f-fucking one?"

"Yeah. Exactly. Another fuckin' one."

"What, don't tell no one you w-wanted me to s-su—"

"Yeah yeah, well that goes without fuckin' saying, Petey." I try to take control of my breathing. "That ain't it but that goes without saying."

I mean what the fuck, this is Southie, Petey knows that. Keep your fuckin' mouth shut is all. Many a man's tongue gets his nose broke so keep your fuckin' mouth shut.

"Don't fuckin' mention that anymore—alright, Petey? I was drunk, big deal, no big deal—"

"Yeah and I always want to eat p-pussy when I'm drunk, happens all the time—"

"SHUT THE FUCK UP, PETEY!"

Petey jumps again and stares at me.

I won't look at him. You can't hear anything for a bit, just a seethe in my nostrils. After a while I calm down but remain silent. I reach into the back, grab a beer. Petey jumps again at my sudden movement, almost like I'm going to hit him.

"Oh please, as if," I mumble, answering his thoughts for once rather than the other way around.

We don't know it at first, but then we both notice I think a shifting at these words. Our postures unlax a scoonch.

"So . . . s-so what's this other favor?" he murmurs after a bit.

He sounds so depressed. Deflated.

Still I wave him away.

"C'mon, t-tell. Whaaaawhat is it?"

"Awright."

I turn to him. I almost pause, his eyes like open wounds, like Mary's eyes in the *Pieta* if you could crawl onto her lap and peek up into them.

"I . . . I really want you to quit drinking, Petey. I'm worried about your drinking and I want you to quit. You drink too much and the way you drink . . . it's fuckin' mournful, Petey. You shouldn't drink alone and you do."

"Okay Dr. Joy Brown," Petey says, slumping back into his seat. "That's none of your b-beeswax."

I feel like I've been slapped.

"Oh? Bullshit! Did I say that to you when you got me off coke?"

"That was d-d-different."

"No it wasn't. How was it different?"

"It j-j-just was."

"Petey, listen to me. I . . . I don't . . . if you can't do it for yourself right now, just . . . just do it for me. I mean I don't know what I would do if . . . I mean . . . just do it for me, okay?"

Silence.

"Okay, Petey?"

"I'll think about it, D-Danny boy. In the meantime is there another brew in the back w-with my name on it?"

"DON'T MAKE ME FUCKING MAD!" I scream, slamming my fists on the dashboard.

I really must've yelled—a second later the front light floods on and a bathrobed Mrs. Harding shoves her red-tangled head out from her garden porch into the night. I must've woken her up and her with the night off seemingly.

I couldn't figure why I was so mad—

Petey was staring at me with his mouth open when I finally looked over at him.

"You n-never yelled at me before like that, D-Danny."

"Yeah well I'm . . . I'm sorry, Petey, I just—"

"Is that you, Petey? What's all this consternation? Is it having a contretemps you are, at this hour?"

"Yeah it's me, Ma'am. N-nothing, we're just . . . we were just talking out here. Go b-back to bed, it's okay."

"Who's that with you? Oh hello there, Danny dear! Well be quiet for heaven's sakes, you're waking the echoes. Edna Quinn next door will eat you if you wake her. How was the promenading?"

"Ahhh, f-fine, fine. Good night, Ma'am."

Petey turns back to me. I won't look at him. I'm picking at the leather grip around my steering wheel.

"What's the m-matter with you tonight, Danny? It's like some . . . crazy dr-dream when you're feverish or something."

"Nuthin', what's the matter with you? Nuthin', I'm just . . . I dunno I'm in a weird mood or something. I'm . . . I'm sorry about the yelling, I didn't mean to yell but I just . . . I'm serious about that, Petey. I'd really like you to think about that, about your drinking."

"Alright I will," he mumbles. Humoring me?

"I mean it doesn't make you a bad person, Petey. You're not a bad person. I mean you're like the most beau—I mean, you're a great person, Petey, but it's like a disease, it's nobody's fault, 'member how the nuns told us that? Like a disease in your genes, and I mean with your father and all—"

"I s-said I'd think about it!"

"Alright fine."

Silence.

"Alright. I gotta go."

"A-alright."

"I'm leavin' tomorrow. I . . . yeah, I gotta go back. Tomorrow."

"I thought . . . you are? But I thought you were h-here until . . . I thought you were here for a week almost?"

"I changed my . . . naw, something's come up, I gotta get back."

Things are too fucked up here, crazy. I have to get back, get back and think. Or not—

Petey turns his head and stares at me again. I won't look at him now, don't know what will happen if I look at him—

"I'll write to you," I say, keeping my eyes on a car about a quarter of a mile up on East Fifth, a van, a grayish silver van and the streetlight over it swiping an orangey brown blob on its roof.

Petey sighs, straightens himself up, gets out. He shuts the door. He doesn't slam it. Just closes it, like a bureau drawer he's finished with. Something leaps up inside me, clutches at my throat—

"Petey!"

He jumps again, leans against the car, puts his hands on the roof of the car.

"What?"

Now what?

"Petey, let's not . . . if I'm going tomorrow I don't want to go away mad. You know?"

"I kn-know," he mumbles. Sniffs. Goes to wipe his nose with his sleeve but it must still be puke-smelling. He yanks it away quick.

"Just . . . Petey, just remember . . . just remember when we were lying in the woods. Remember that part about tonight, okay?"

There's silence for a minute. Then Petey lowers his head into the window.

"Danny," he says. "I . . . I don't think I was ever h-happier. How could I f-forget?"

"Petey, 'member when we used to—"

An odd voice inside cautions *Don't look back! Don't look back!* but nothing to withstand the flood of memories now, a veritable Memorare here in my front seat, him standing outside—

"Petey, 'member when we used to sneak out when we were thirteen, fourteen whatever, we'd sneak out at night and run to the beach, sometimes all the way out to the island, we wouldn't say anything but we'd laugh, laugh just to be running, just to be alive just to be to . . . together, just run and laugh and the moon on the water and . . . and those times? Do you re-member those times?"

A shifting outside of him. Can't see his face again. Finally, with difficulty: "Yeah. Yeah, 'course I r-remember."

"I—"

"'Course I remember, D-Danny, that's where I l-live now."

A sigh.

"So what th-though?"

"Well . . . I dunno. I guess . . . it's just that . . . there was nothing wrong with the world then."

Silence. I shut off the engine.

"And remember the night we took the *Argo* out and we found that big turtle, stranded? In that net or whatever? Crying kinda? 'Member how it was crying and we set it free, we cut it free and carried it back into the ocean?"

"Yeah but we were c-calling it the *Little Andy Foley* by then, after that l-l-little kid that dr-dr-dr—"

"Drowned."

"Yeah." A pause. "So wh-what?"

"I dunno, I just . . . I never felt more alive."

The tang of the salt air, the swirl of the sea all around doing weird night stuff, small boats big boats medium boats drifting past, stories and histories of their own, on their ways to anythings and everythings, red lights green lights fore and aft and us racing them out the causeway and Petey talking to the sea and the sky and the islands and the gulls and me opening up the box that was my life then—

"Petey, listen do you wanna . . . do you wanna do that now? Can we just do that now, just run? Just fuckin' run out there? I got sneakers in the trunk and we could—do you still have the *Andy?* 'Member whenever we'd take it out there you'd say those words, those weird tour guide words just as we were leaving Pleasure Bay, you'd say those words and—Petey, you know what? I still remember those words."

"Wh-wh—"

"I do, listen, you'd say *Danny and me, Danny and me, Danny and me and the sea*—"

I hear something like a gasp come out of Petey—

Bobbing out of Pleasure Bay, the islands on our lee:
Spectacle, Georges, Gallops, the sun-wash on the brine—
Castle Island where Skovo danced a bear-dance in bear-time.

The Golden Boy has chosen, I know what I will be—
Danny and me, *seanchaí*, Danny and me and the sea.

"Let's do that now, Petey, let's do that now," I say. "Let's run down to the beach and go swimming or something, run out to Castle Island, anything—can we do that now?"

I turn and face him. I can't see his face, just his body from his neck to his thighs cuz he's stood up again and leaning against my car. There's a grass stain on one of his suit-coat sleeves, a little puke on his shirt that I must've missed. I stop.

"I'm too dr-drunk," Petey mumbles. All the sadness of the world in his voice. "And it was always *swumming,* not sw-swimming. Once upon a t-time."

This pit opens up before me, of what Petey's life has been the past five years, the utter aloneness, the waiting—a shiver runs through me and I pull back, can't look—

We don't say anything. I want to say everything to him but don't know how. So we both say nothing. For seven minutes and thirty-seven seconds, according to the digital dashboard clock, one of those clip-on ones. Right next to the air freshener dangling from the radio dial. The longer this silence goes on, the more it signifies, I know, but I don't know what that is. Don't know anything anymore—

"What do you want from me, Petey?" I hear myself ask him.

Petey snorts.

"C'mon, tell me. I can't seem to make you happy anymore. I try, but . . . "

I'm asking because I want to make him happy . . . but somehow I don't think it comes out that way—

"You really w-want to know?"

I think about it and realize I don't, not really not now, too late though—

"Yeah."

"Everything," he says. He squats down and leans his face into the car again. "Everything, but m-mostly I want to go out to the Harbor Islands with you. I want to go out to the Harbor Islands with you and w-watch the sky with quiet eyes. Forever."

Jesus—I got to get out of here—

"Petey, lookit—"

"D-Danny?" Petey says at the same time.

"What."

"I just . . . can we . . . t-talk about that for a minute? About . . . what al-most h-happened?"

"When what almost happened?" I stall, picking at the steering wheel again.

"When we . . . when you w-wanted me to—"

"Oh, that. Naw, forget about it will ya? It was no big deal. I was just horny and shit faced, that's all. There's nothing to talk about."

"I know it, b-but—"

"End of discussion, Petey."

My voice sounds colder than how I really feel.

Another long silence.

"Alright," I finally say, stretching, feigning a yawn, "I gotta get going."

"Wait," Petey says.

"What."

"I want . . . I want you to d-do *me* a favor, Danny."

"Huh?"

"My t-turn now. I want you to do me a favor."

"What?"

Petey stands up. The shadow of his lean body falls into the car, across my lap.

He opens the door and gets back in, slipping a little. He shuts the door, carefully.

"I know you like that," he explains intermittently.

"I do. So what's this favor?"

He cracks his knuckles again, won't look at me.

"I w-want . . . I w-w-want you to say . . . "

He makes a grunt noise, runs both hands through his slicked hair, looser now after the night, the nonsense . . .

"I know it isn't true," he says, still looking forward, "I m-mean, not the way I want it, but . . . I want to hear you say it anyways."

"Say what?"

"One thing. J-just one thing. But first . . . f-first . . . I want to tell you something. Danny, listen to me. I want you to know that . . . I m-m-made a choice that night. The night of the g-game. I heard you."

He turns to me.

"When you c-called to me. I heard you."

"Ahhh . . . what game?"

I won't look at him.

"Don't you say that, D-Danny O'Connor! Don't you say that to me! Don't you d-do that, it does you no credit."

We both hear something jagged come out of me. A breath, a writhe—

"Sorry," I croak. For chrissake there's a tear runnin' down my face—"Go on."

"I . . . I knew the ball was coming to me, but . . . you called to me."

I can't answer for a minute.

"Oh Jesus, Petey, I just wanted to warn you, I swear to Chr—"

"I know that, Danny, I know that," Petey soothes. He reaches out shyly, head hung down and touches my forearm, in vise-lock now, both my arms across my chest. "I know that but I'm not through. I w-want you to know that I made a choice. You called to me and I . . . I turned. I did. What else could I do? What else c-can anybody do when they hear the voice of the b-beloved? Calling to them?"

There's something suffocating about the night now, something inside too that begins to rip and tear apart—

"Even then, D-Danny," Petey whispers. "Even then when I was still . . . n-normal."

Jesus Christ. How does he get to me like this?

My voice is all jaggery when I say, "This . . . favor. What's this favor?"

I find now that my hands are on the steering wheel, turning white in a death grip.

I fumble for my beer and gulp down the rest of it.

"*I love you.* I j-just . . . want to hear it once. How . . . you would say it. To m-me. What it would s-sound like to my ears. Inside me. H-hold onto it, I will. That and how you held me t-tonight. I think that could change my wh-whole life. Just to hear that."

I gulp. Loud like in a commercial.

"Just w-want hear it once, Danny. Like Miss Havisham I sometimes have s-sick fancies."

Something flashes inside me and I bang the dashboard again.

"Alright that's it, get out. This time I mean it."

A car alarm goes off up the street and a spooked pigeon swoops down from a billboard.

Petey laughs. His body recoils a little, like we're boxing—

"Deeper, Danny, d-deeper," he says. "Twist that knife a l-little deeper why don't you."

"I mean it, Petey, get out. I gotta go and you're . . . you're fuckin' with my head."

"Your *head?*" Petey says.

Fuckin' wiseass.

Then he gets out and, this time, slams the door.

Trouble Man

My plan is to beat off when I get home from Pete's Place, where I closed the joint with the new best friends of the drunkard (I didn't have too much to say to them but they *understood* me), then pass out and forget about everything. I'm good at this. I've done it before. I sneak into my house as quiet as physics allows but Ma, an element of chaos in any immutable rule of the universe, still hears me, and nothing will do but to put on the kettle and lug out the two cakes she's spent that evening making for me.

We sit at the kitchen table across from each other, something writhing inside me. I beseech saints to make the phone ring, send a long-lost cousin to the door, but it's 1:17 in the morning and my prayers aren't in vain, only ill-founded.

"So, how was the prom? You had a great time I suppose."

"Ahhh . . . "

"It was wonderful, wasn't it."

"Well, to tell you the truth Ma it was kinda a bu—"

"Danny, you've had a drink or two, *phew!* But I s'pose it's a special night. I'll remember 'til the day I die my own prom from St. Cecilia's. Is that a big enough slice for you dear? Danny, your hands are shaking!"

"Just . . . I had the AC on high in my car."

"Oh. Well be careful, you don't want to catch a chill in this weather, those summer colds. Where was I? Oh, my prom! I hadn't met your father then—he was off in Vietnam still. Willie McAllister took me, do you remember him? Five boys in that family and one handsomer than the next. But divils all. Oh, what a night it was! The lilacs were in bloom and I wore a sprig of them in my hair. Remember nights like these as long as you live, Danny. You'll bring them out and smell them like flowers when you're old like your poor mother here. Wipe your mouth, dear."

A Map of the Harbor Islands
Published by The Haworth Press, Inc., 2006. All rights reserved.
doi:10.1300/5677_18

"Yeah. Well actually Ma, the night was kinda a bust—"

"Noreen outshone the moon I suppose."

"Ah . . . yeah."

Rod Stewart in a dress—

"I'll want some of the pictures for the mantel, tell her mother. She loved the corsage of course?"

"Uh . . . "

"See I told you that off-white was wrong for her. Blondes want white, Danny, it's their best color."

"Ahhh . . . yeah. Actually she was kinda upset—"

"So speaking of white—when are you two gonna tie the knot? Girls don't like to wait forever you know, Danny. I've been meaning to have this talk with you."

"Ahhh, I dunno. Look, Ma, I'm kinda tired—"

"You know I haven't told you this yet dear, but listen, me and your father have been putting a little extra by whenever we can for you. Now it's not a fortune, but enough for a big down payment on a nice little place nearby. Just to get the two of you started."

"Ma . . . you . . . you have? Jeez Ma, I dunno what to say, I—"

"Oh it's as much for me as it is for you two. Us, I mean. You're all we've got, Danny dear and I want to be close to my grandchildren when they come—"

Come—

"—A nice little place over on the West Side. I've already looked at a few places, just to see what's available. With that Betty Regal, your father's second cousin. I don't know if I told you but she's selling real estate now you know. Doing quite nicely for herself too from what I hear, which is always a pleasant surprise where that side of the family's concerned. 'Course the market's going crazy so I suppose a trained monkey could sell homes nowadays. Maybe tomorrow we could look at a few places. I mentioned that to Noreen, if she could take the day off tomorrow—"

"You did? You . . . did? When?"

"Oh she called around midnight from Tricia's. I must say it was very respectable to get those two girls home at a decent hour. Parents notice things like that, Danny. Danny, do you feel alright dear?"

"Ahhh . . . wait a minute Ma, I wish . . . I wish you . . . hadn't said anything—"

"And why not? You *are* going to marry her, aren't you? Everyone's been asking when."

"Well I—I dunno, I mean, I s'pose so but—"

"Dating her for almost ten years and—"

"Ahhh . . . seven, Ma."

"—What else could you have in mind? I don't want to be ninety when my first grandkids start coming. You know we had you so late, Danny, I'll be sixty next year and think of yourself while you're at it. There's nothing but trouble for an unmarried man in his twenties, Danny, nothing but trouble and no mistake. An unmarried man is a dangerous man, Danny, remember that. He's a Trouble Man."

The curtains fluttering and outside, waiting, throbbing quiet, is the heart of this summer night and I want to leap into it, the syrupy holiness of it, the wild shagginess of that tree's bark and the wild shagginess of us all. If I scream into the night maybe I can survive this rising storm inside me—

"You listening, Danny?"

"Well I dunno, Ma, I . . . you know I always thought it would be kinda nice to ahh . . . I dunno, just have a little time on my own for a while . . . I mean, maybe get a little . . . get a little place for myself or something when I get back and figger things out—"

"A little place for yourself! And why in the world would you want to do *that?* Here, try the chocolate, dear. What are they teaching you in that Marine Corps? I never thought that was such a good idea to begin with! A little place for yourself! I never heard of anything so ridiculous! And who would cook for you and clean for you and—"

"I guess I'd have to do that stuff for myself."

"How much have you been drinking tonight, Danny? You're talking foolishness. Here's Noreen now, who you've been dating for ten years—"

"Ahhh . . . seven—"

"—Waiting by the hour for a ring. You know? Maybe after we all look at a few places tomorrow we could go into town and take a look at some rings. Just look at them. Just you and me, I mean, the Jewelers' Building, we can surprise Noreen later and wouldn't that bring a tear to her eye. My eye too to tell you the truth. Would ease my heart, Danny."

I look up at her. She's in her nightdress, the little pink satin bow tied up at her throat, her fingers playing with the edges of the plaid flannel placemat in front of her. She looks up quickly. There's a tight smile on her thin lips but her small eyes are full of fear.

I take a deep breath.

"Why? Why would it ease your heart, Ma?"

"Why?" she laughs, rubbing the mat a bit more strenuously now. "Why *wouldn't* it? To have you settled, dear, just to have it all settled—"

"Have what settled? What do you mean?"

"Don't . . . Danny don't upset me about this, please, please please please please please don't upset me—"

"Well I told you Ma . . . Ma didn't I tell you I was kinda tied up on this trip? I don't have much ti—"

"What could be more important than your future? You want to go off shooting pool when—"

"Shooting pool? Who said anything about shooting pool?"

"Well isn't that what you do with those idle friends of yours and what else could you have in mind? It won't take long. 'Course you can't touch the East Side now, but once you've got some equity built up in a few years, you kids could move a little closer—what's the matter, dear? You don't like that cake?"

"No, Ma, the cake's great, it's just that I . . . I mean . . . well, Ma, I don't even know if Noreen and me . . . I mean I dunno if . . . I mean . . . "

"You don't know what?"

"Well I mean marriage is such a big . . . big step, and I . . . "

"The girl you've dated all your life and you don't know yet? What's the matter with you?"

"Well . . . nothing. Nothing's the matter with me I don't think, I just . . . maybe . . . I'm not ready yet I don't think. Just . . . I'm not ready."

"Never mind not ready!" Ma leaps up and grabs the sponge from the counter, then plunks back down and begins wiping the three crumbs off the table. Scrubbing really. "Every man says that, Danny dear, it's just male nature. If . . . if every man waited 'til he was ready the race would've expired a million years ago. You just leave it to me, Danny, I'll arrange everyth—"

"No Ma, don't."

"What?"

"I said . . . I said no. Don't. Not yet. Please. Thanks, but—but don't arrange anything. *Anything.*"

Ma grabs the dirty plates and teacups, marches over to the sink in a wordless huff.

"Ma, c'mon, I . . . I do appreciate it, but . . . "

Silence.

"I just . . . I'm sure, I'm sure we . . . I mean I'm sure we'll *probably* get married some day, but I . . . it just doesn't feel like now is the right . . . "

Silence.

I get up from the table and walk over to the sink. The floor seems uneven, dangerous. I try to kiss Ma good night on the cheek but she turns her head as I do and sniffs.

She's crying. I've made my mother cry. What a loser. What an ingrate. And in her state too. She's putting away every penny she has so she can give it to me for a house, and I've made her cry. I've made my mother cry, and Noreen's mad at me and disappointed, and I can never seem to make Petey happy and he's getting weirder by the minute and he told me tonight that he . . . and I actually asked him to . . . I actually *wanted* him to—

I slink up the stairs with a headache, a Birdy-throb headache. I pee and think about drinking a quart of water before I go to bed. Some old rummy down the corner told me a few years back that if you drink a quart of water after a night of drinking you'll wake up with much less of a bigger head, but I don't want to be peeing all night. I just want to sleep and forget about everything, but a stab to my thoughts tonight and the drinking hasn't helped at all—

I watch my pee color the toilet water, and I think about all water being the same and touching each other and whatever the fuck Petey used to say about it, and maybe I should pee in the sink instead as it doesn't make a difference. Nothing makes a difference and you can't outrun your fate. I tiptoe into my bedroom and close the door as I hear Ma out in the parlor pacing like a thoroughbred before a race. She's putting on some all-night talk show on the hi-fi. I turn on the little sailboat lamp on my night table. I sit down on the twin bed and it goes *squeak* and why this need to roar now, to wail. I pull off my dress shoes, sniff them lightly. I always do that all my life, raise one up to chuck it across the room into the half-open sliding door closet, half of which has Ma's winter stuff in it now but I refrain at the last second. I don't want to wake Dad up. My black dress socks with the red paisleys I do chuck though. One makes it into the pink plastic laundry basket in the closet. The other catches on the rim and stretches open like a tongue. I get up, hang my suit coat in the closet, take off my pink tie and white shirt. The pink tie goes on the tie rack—my parochial school blue plaid tie is still hanging there too—and the shirt goes into the laundry basket.

I hang up my black pants. My white briefs I slide off. I run my hands along the bristly buzzed top of my head, a nervous habit I guess but better than that thing I used to do with my mouth, still do sometimes on certain occasions. But it feels good. It reminds me of who I am. What I am.

A Marine. I'm a Marine now. It's gonna be alright. I'm a Marine.

What the hell does that mean?

But why wouldn't you want to be a builder? A giver?

I step back so I can see myself in the mirror over my bureau, flex my white bicep to show off the new Marine Corps tattoo I got last month in Norfolk on a weekend liberty. I don't exactly remember getting it to tell the truth but here she is and she looks bad-ass, but for a second . . . just for a second I get this picture in my head of cattle getting branded, cattle getting branded and there's a long line of other cattle waiting to get branded stretching off to infinity. The cattle that have already been branded are marching up a ramp and getting prodded into a train car that's on its way to a million individual nice little places on the West Side with a Noreen in each one, bitching about how hard life is cuz she has to go to PTA and then a Tupperware party down the street after that and she's exhausted as the kids were fussing all day, and me silent in the La-Z-Boy wanting to smash things up with my baseball bat and that can't be right.

What the fuck is happening here?

I continue looking in the mirror. I half turn around.

Wow, what shape I'm in. The mounded blue-whiteness of me. Tufts of red hair where they're supposed to be.

But what of that.

I haven't shown the ink to anyone yet, except to my Corps buddies of course. And Petey, who said I was wearing a UPC symbol meant for someone else, whatever that meant. I sit down on the edge of my bed. I don't mean to think but thoughts come at me anywise. I roll onto the floor on my back, throw my legs up onto the bed. Beads of sweat announce themselves all over my body. I wonder if I make myself puke will I feel better. Something gargantuan and monstrous stirring inside me, trying to wake up and eat me—

Never mind never mind, sleep sleep forget, think of something else, anything—

There was a library that I walked by in Norfolk that weekend, the weekend I got my tattoo, a library and I told the two guys I was with Smitty and the Duke to meet me in half an hour. I had to do something. It hit me quick like that. There was a little branch library on West Broadway when I was a kid, and Aunt Alice (Dad's aunt, my great-aunt, a nun) brought me there once and we got some books out and I got this feeling, this incredible feeling when I walked in, that the whole world was there in that library.

That's what Aunt Alice said anyway and she was right.

Aunt Alice. A bit of relief at her memory and *Help me, help me Aunt Alice, something awful's happening to me tonight—*

Aunty Alice a nun and a teacher but was retired by then and the only teaching she did was teach piano to this little old man every Thursday morning at his house down on Farragut Road. What was his name? What was it? A shrunken tottering old thing, used to be a man but instead of piano they discussed politics over tea mostly. He'd been in the IRA; she'd been to Selma. Talk about strange bedfellows. Or maybe not. After he died she put a green carnation on his grave every Sunday. She did some volunteer work too those days, but had been all around the world as a nun, working with poor people in India for tons of years, then Africa, finally Vietnam. The habit of sandals acquired there and this automatically made her suspect with Ma. She used to send me the stamps from Vietnam, old men with yard-long beards mostly, some of the writing in French. I sold them all to some shop downtown during my coke days. Aunty'd gotten arrested at an anti-war protest in Chicago or someplace like that and they did a big story on it in the Herald, 10,000 screaming longhairs that are all probably fat cats in Lexus SUVs now, and five nuns giving the peace sign as they were escorted into paddy wagons. Ma was disgraced and didn't like her to begin with like I say. *Miss High and Mighty, the Lady Pope* she called her, but it didn't matter because she died two years later. *See?* Ma mumbled to me on the way home from her funeral, which was cruel because Dad I think still heard her.

"Listen, Daniel," Aunty said the day she brought me to the library.

It was hushed and the wooden floors shone and smelled like they had just been waxed. The chaos and clamor of West Broadway, steps away outside the door waiting, roaring, eased into a muffle.

"What do you hear, Daniel?"

She always called me Daniel, no one else, ever. A name that implied Possibilities somehow but never since then. She always carried a black umbrella even in nice weather because *You never know.*

"I . . . I don't know . . . something. What is it?"

"It's the world, Daniel. The world. Ships at sea. History. Adventure. Science. Philosophy."

"What's philosophy?"

Instinctively I was whispering. I've always been very adaptable I think. This was a place where you whispered, in delight.

"It's the study of ways of living. How to live one's life. What to devote one's life to. What to believe in."

"I don't follow."

"I'll explain later. But look at all those books now! You can find out anything about everything here. And this is just a tiny library. But in some parts of the world, these are more books than they have in the entire country. This would be their most precious treasure if they had something like this."

"Why don't they then?"

"Well! They are very poor, some of these countries. And many of the people can't read. Reading is exercise for the mind, Daniel. Remember that. And a boat. A big boat that can take you anywhere."

A big boat to take me out to the Harbor Islands, but sure I'd get lost there on my own, foggy, murky, Petey and dangerous. Treacherous—

The way his hair sifted down onto my thigh—like the falling of something inevitable, leaves onto the soothed winter streets of things—No, don't go there—

We got a library card for me that day. It fit right into my shirt pocket. The dragon woman behind the counter demanded my birth certificate but Aunt Alice silenced her with a curt kindness that was efficient and blunt as a mallet.

I get up from the floor and pad over to my top bureau drawer. I roll it open, retrieve a little cedar box at the back beneath my BVDs too small for me now, folded, ironed. Ma likes to bleach and iron things. She cannot abide mess. Open up the box. Here it is still my library card, with my birth certificate and Social Security card and a few rubbers. Lubricated rubbers. The squishiness of them, their puffed-out packages pregnant with—how urgent fingers in a car might tear at the dotted lines—you might rip them open with your teeth as the lights of the Harbor Islands twirl through the windshield as you—

Boston Public Library. Still in its thick yellow paper sleeve. I think how if I died now, right now and I just might, these are my remains and what would archaeologists make of me 10,000 years from now? A once-used library card, rubbers, a birth certificate. A Marine tattoo. *The life they got laid out for you.* They would know nothing about me.

They would know everything about me.

I put the library card back. Ma never seemed to have the time to bring me there; Aunt Alice died, and when I got older I was too embarrassed to go there, even though Petey did a lot. He didn't care what the other kids said, never did still doesn't. Not unlike some. See everyone said it was nerdy. After a while the desire left me.

And then in Norfolk. It wasn't like I was looking for it or anything. We'd just docked and were rolling along amidst the brick warehouses and the smell of tar and seagull poop and things and rambling for the nearest bar/house of ill fame and someone said something about shooting pool and somebody else said something about getting some tats, and then I just happened to look up and there's this library. This beautiful sad building with flowers and cracked stairs, set back from the street behind a wrought iron fence in aloof embarrassment at its shagginess, or perhaps in pride like Petey.

I stopped. It was vital that I stop. I wonder if that's when the weirdness began with me. That black-and-white interior image of a dam and you can hear, you can't see but you can hear the water rising on the other side, hissing and rising—

"Hey ahhh . . . where you guys gonna be?"

"Say what?"

"Where you guys gonna be? I gotta . . . I gotta go in here for a minute."

"In a library? Shit, man, what you—"

"Yeah. I gotta . . . I gotta look something up. For my girlfriend. I won't be long, I just remembered."

The only weird things you're allowed to do when you're a guy are when you do them for a woman. Or apparently I thought so anyway.

"Pussy-whipped, pussy-whipped."

"C'mon, where you gonna be at?"

I made a Southern speech concession to get them off my ass. We don't say where you gonna be *at* up north you know.

"Dunno, dude. Look for the shore patrol and the paddy wagon, that'll be us."

"I'm offended by that ethnic allusion. But I'll catch up to your asses all the same."

"Poor bastard. We're gonna get you laid later by a big ol' sister though. You just remember."

"You won't never go back to the white shit once you had some o' that."

"I'll catch up to you later."

Libraries are like fast-food joints, I decided once I stepped inside. They're all over the world and they appear architecturally different—well kinda—but the product is the same. The feeling the same. Toxicity and catatonic despair under the harsh lighting in the latter, lonely old people, the Pompeii Pimplii of local youth; in the case of libraries it's the Hush, the Smell, the People Who Work There God Bless Them, standing up for the right to read books, with bad breath and ratty cardigans and ten bucks an hour when Peoria lowers the boom on the f word or men kissing, but Christian Soldiers Marching Off to War all well and good as long as we don't see the pictures of the dismemberment of children, disembowelment of the grunts and the retrieving of limbs from blood-spangled bushes twenty yards away. Not always but often greasy hair, ugly glasses, catastrophic posture sans abdominal six-pack. Lovely people.

There was no way I could take a book out or anything. I mean I didn't have a card and we were only in port for forty-eight hours and all that. Had to look around though. Maybe Daniel was still in there.

One of the reasons I had joined the Corps: my bedroom at home was a small box and Southie a small box and my life a small box—all these small boxes nested inside each other, Russian dolls, and you think the next phase will be something different but it isn't, the same thing only smaller. I wanted to see if I could maybe turn into something else, grow into something bigger though I had no idea what.

But the Marine Corps was becoming a box of its own.

I wandered through this arch and found myself in the children's section of the Norfolk Library. A string stretched out from wall to wall just over my head, hung with papers on clothespins showing a dinosaur with different parts of his body colored, one section for every book that had been read by different kids, some of their names big and important in crayon, others scrawled neatly in pencil so small you'd need a Petey magnifying glass to read them.

I smiled. I remembered that, those little book clubs for kids. Try and get you to read. Not from experience I mean, but I remember from that day in the Southie library with Aunt Alice.

It's warm in the room but lazy-comfortable warm, not stifley. Library smell pregnant with delight. An ancient ceiling fan swirls slowly overhead. Missing a blade, aren't we all eh? A large open window at the end of the room, its two panes tossed open, a large flowering tree just out back half leaning in. Its fragrance spritzes the room, irregular whiffy gushes and the intermittent drone of bees. The only thing I have seen so far in America that hints at graciousness, learning, enlightenment.

Except Petey of course. And Aunty Alice before him.

The window sill full-up with bright red geraniums in old damp-spotted clay pots and old newspapers underneath to save the wooden sill, which is a catastrophe already.

I think how if I had read more as a kid I might know the name of that tree. I think of Petey and his naming/claiming things and I name the tree the . . . the . . . I can't think of anything.

"Can I help you?"

Halfway around and look. A pleasant-looking young man with a nice smile and longish hair like Petey's is behind a desk to my left. He has a southern accent but it's seen some work. I think of what we found in Grandma Flynn's attic when we cleaned out her house—*How to Lose Your .Accent and Speak Proper English.*

"They still do this, huh?"

I jerk my head upwards to the reading club papers.

He smiles and nods.

"I'm glad," I say.

"Can I help you find anything?" His earnestness borders on the catechetical, God bless him.

"Just looking around. Just . . . I'm on shore leave and this reminds me of . . . someone."

"I could tell by your uniform."

"Oh yeah," I laugh, looking down. I have my Class As on. Duh.

"Feel free to look all you want."

"Thanks."

I wander around, looking at the posters and featured books and I have to confess half of them look interesting and exciting to me even though they're children's books and I think *Wow I must be wicked ignorant.* Especially enticing are the ones on a polished mahogany table in the corner with a curvy sign against the wall behind it that tells us MAY IS PIRATES AND THEIR GOLD MONTH! On the table about two dozen books, *True Tales of Buried Treasure! Jean Lafitte: Pirate or Hero? Walk the Plank, Mary!* and the like. Front and center on the table are three copies of *Treasure Island* by Robert Louis Stevenson, which even I've heard of. I pick one up and leaf through it and spend some moments in the land of What Might Have Been and learn the meaning of a word I'd heard once or twice but never knew what it meant when applied to something other than Chinese food—bittersweet.

Beneath the table there's three or four big boxes full up with used children's books for sale, one dollar a pop. All proceeds going to the Norfolk Children's Library New Book Acquisition Fund. I'm very tempted to rifle through them—every Marine a rifleman—but what would my buddies say when I met up with them again? *These are for my girlfriend—Treasure Island? The Mystery of Captain Kidd's Treasure?*

In the far corner there's a circle of children and their mothers, listening to another woman in a chair with a Mother Goose hat and a long red pleated skirt reading aloud from a book. Her posture miserable, a chiropractor's dream but her face sublime.

Not too far away at a long wooden shiny table there's a little kid sitting by himself, his chair turned to the circle beyond him, his chin in his small plump hands. He's wearing scuffy sneakers and one white falling-down sock on one foot and no sock on the other. He's staring at the story lady, trying not to stare at the same time. Nose running unchecked.

There's a black metal rack next to him that looks like it should be holding lunch-size bags of Wise Potato Chips but no, kids' paperbacks instead. I walk over and pretend to browse, then realize all the books are different titles in this girls' series, *The Baby-sStters Club.*

I turn around.

"You don't like this story?" I whisper.

The kid—he's about seven—looks up at me with eyes too penetrating, a tart old person's eyes.

He makes a shruggy face but doesn't answer.

"Sounds like a good one to me. You're not interested?"

"Not especially," he says in a very Southern accent.

"You like being here alone?"

He looks down at his sneakers. He starts swinging them against each other.

"Sometimes I do, and sometimes I don't."

"That's just like me," I say. "And today is one of those times you wanna be alone?"

"You talk funny, mister."

"I'm from a funny place."

"No, I don't especially care to be alone today."

"Well why don't you go sit with the other kids then?"

He continues to watch his sneakers.

"How come?"

"How come is they all got their mommas with 'em."

I turn and look at the circle. It's true.

"And where's your momma this morning?"

"Out doing the errands. She drops me here sometimes."

"Oh. She's not . . . working, is she?"

"No sir. She works nights, rubbing men's sore backsides."

"Oh. How do you know that?"

"I seen her once when she didn't know."

"Well good for her. I can tell you there's a lot of sore backsides in this world. I have a friend . . . my best friend's mother works nights too. She makes candy, she works at a candy factory."

"Really? Does she bring him home candy?"

"Not really anymore. When she makes the candy bars though she always leaves a little pinch on the bottom, and if anyone ever buys that brand of candy bar in her presence she grabs it and says, *Oh look, look now, one of mine!*"

"I hope her hands is clean," the kid says.

"Oh. Yeah. Ahh, would you excuse me for a minute?"

I go up to the guy behind the desk.

"Would I be stepping on any toes if I sat with that kid for a while listening to the story? He doesn't want to join the others cuz he's alone."

The librarian smiles.

"If you can get him to sit with you. I've tried before."

He looks over and shakes his head.

"How often does she do this?"

"Two or three times a week. I guess she's got nowhere else to bring him. We're not supposed to allow that but we don't say anything. Some of the other mothers don't like it though."

"I bet. Thank you."

I walk back over to the little boy.

"You know, I'd like to ask you a favor. Can I do that?"

"You can ax me anythin'."

"Well, I want to hear that story but my hearing isn't so good. I need to sit close and listen to it. But I don't want to sit alone over there, everyone's got someone else to sit with. Would you mind sitting with me?"

He works his mouth for a bit, picks his nose quickly then looks up and gives me the eyes again.

"H'it's a story for children, mister."

"I know it but I wanna learn it, in case I have children of my own someday. I can tell it to 'em."

This seems to satisfy.

"Well," he says.

We drag two chairs over and join the circle. One mother looks up and smiles at me, as does the story lady. Another woman stares and then inches her and her daughter's chair farther away from us.

When the story hour is over fifteen minutes later, I take the kid aside and pull out my shore-leave wad of twenties from my pocket. I show him two of them.

"Here. This one you split between you and your momma. You can get treats and she can get whatever. The other twenty here I'm gonna give to the librarian guy over there, and you're gonna pick out twenty books from the little book sale over there. There's a couple o' big boxes over there on the floor. You can pick out twenty of them. Just for you, to bring home."

"Twenty!"

"Twenty. Because reading . . . because books can . . . ahhhh . . . "

I struggle to remember Aunt Alice's words.

"You see that tree right there?"

I point out the window.

"Yessir."

"If I read when I was your age I bet I'd know what kind o' tree that is. But I didn't, and so I don't. Reading makes you strong. It can give you . . . a whole lot more choices of what to do with your life. What you can become like. The courage to be your own man maybe. It opens up the whole world to you. But most important of all, it gives you something of beauty to hold on to. Now you gotta promise to read every one of those books."

He considers this with a furrowing of his eyebrows.

"Thanks mister. I will. You don't like bein' a soldier then?"

"Uhh . . . I dunno. Sometimes I do I guess. But if I'd read when I was a kid I would've had other things maybe I could've done instead." I pause. "No, actually I don't like it."

"My daddy was a soldier."

"Oh. Ahhh . . . where is he now?"

"He had to go away."

"Oh. Okay. Well, I gotta go now too."

"Umm. Well . . . thanks, mister."

"No problem. But you read all those books, that's the deal. And don't ever be ashamed of doing stuff alone."

I walk over to the librarian, explain the situation, and give him the twenty.

I'm halfway out the door when the little kid comes after me.

"Mister, wait."

"Yeah?"

"That there tree's a magnolia. Ev'ybody knows that."

Well, almost everybody.

A magnolia. It was a fuckin' magnolia tree. What difference that can make at this hour I don't know. But the memory of this has stilled the beast within so we are grateful to God who brings joy to our youth.

I pull back the covers and get into bed. I pull the sheet up to my chest, stare at the ceiling I've stared at all my life.

I snap out the light.

I find I'm not so horny anymore. I rub the softness of my nuts by rote but my dick's splayed flop onto my bush.

I realize you can beat off 'til the cows come home but it doesn't really get you anywhere.

I roll over and try to sleep, careful not to roll too far—there's an abyss just beside my bed.

But I can't sleep.

I have to find something out.

This question is plaguing me.

No, you're not, of course you're not, forget about it, go to sleep—

But I won't be able to sleep until I find something out, answer this question.

A plan takes form. I know this place, see. This place where things happen—

I lie there for a bit, then toss back the covers, sit up on the edge of the bed.

Jesus in heaven, can I do this? Can I not do this?

I get up, stretch, pull on maroon shiny gym shorts, a sleeveless Notre Dame athletic shirt, my sneakers. This being my armor, I'm normal, jocky, malleable.

Still it's got to be the most courageous thing I've ever done, sliding down the drainpipe, grabbing my bike from out back, walking it one block down the street so Ma won't hear the squeaky chain of it. I can bike ride to this place, right down the street.

I'm there in seven minutes. Down at this beach, the last one in town before you hit the rotary. A parking lot, looking out onto the harbor, the Harbor Islands. My heart is thumping but the thought of the Harbor Islands out there comforts me. As does the thought of Petey. Thank God. Again. Bestest. Always.

There are cars parked here. With their lights out. I forget exactly which one of my friends told me about this place. What happens here. Said it with derision, he did. Men in the cars. You can see the glare of a drawn-in cigarette, the flash of eyes. Waiting. Sometimes people get out of the car, walk to another car. Or take a walk along the shore. In the shadows. Behind the building here.

I pull my ball cap lower. I ride by a white pickup truck that I recognize. Can't be. Is it? Yes! A fireman, two blocks over. Married, three kids. Well well. Who would'a thunk. Somone needs to be a little more discreet, I would suggest. Then again he is backed in.

I drive my bike behind the building, let out a deep breath. There's someone leaning against the building. His ball cap's slung low too. Doesn't look familiar but then again he might by the light of day. I walk by him. He nods. I walk past him, take up a spot a little further down against the wall.

I lean my bike against the wall, lean my ass against the still-warm wall. Slouch a bit.

Out of the corner of my eye I see him grab the crotch of his cutoff dungaree shorts. So this is how it happens down here. I do the same, feeling my thing like slack rubber between my legs.

He comes walking over. He's nervous—I can tell. He's about my height, my build. Maybe twenty-five. A wedding ring glimmers on his left hand. He stands in front of me. There's a light smell of beer on his breath. Why wouldn't there be?

"What's up," he mumbles. Just the trace of a brogue? Hard to say. He hesitates, then reaches down, puts his hand on my groin over the soft nylony material of my gym shorts. Oddly, I'm not shaking. Nor am I hard. Nor am I turned on. I'm not turned off, not repulsed, but I'm not turned on. But best to make sure.

I return the favor. I reach down and place my hand on his thigh, where the flesh meets the edge of his shorts. Oh, the places you'll go, as Dr. Seuss noted. I move it up and for the first time in my adult life feel another man's dick. Granted it's through his shorts, but the ocean in front of us, sighing contentedly in the summer night, might as well be the widest Rubicon I've ever known. How do I know about Rubicons? Petey of course—how do I know about anything? But this is different. For once I'm doing something on my own, finding something out about myself on my own.

"Take it out," I whisper.

He pulls down his zipper, takes out his dick. It's sticking straight out. I put my hand on it. I feel the throb of it, the Birdy of it. It feels interesting, different, odd—

—But it doesn't really turn me on.

His hand worms its way up my shorts, finds my nuts. He pulls on them. His hand is very warm. It feels good, but no more than if I were doing this myself.

He pulls my shorts down, drops to his knees. His hands are on my thighs, running up and down. Feels good too, but again—like I'm getting a massage, doesn't matter who's doing it. I feel his hot breath on my groin. Then he gathers my soft dick up into his mouth.

We stay like that for a minute. I can see now that he's a few years older than me, but not much. Good-looking guy. Somewhat familiar. I touch his shoulders, start thrusting easily back and forth. But again I'm people-pleasing. I'm hard now but who wouldn't be? Everything from this night comes at me, and I watch it shatter as I close my eyes, pull out of him, then bust my nut.

Before I know it his hands are on my shoulders and he eases me down to a kneeling position. The sand is warm. I remember thinking that. Something warm and fleshy and fragrant—as well as flagrant—bobbing around my chin.

Oh boy.

A thing of beauty is a boy forever. I guess Peteyisms are forever fated to pop up in my life at the appropriate moments.

Finally I pull myself up gently, slowly.

I look into his eyes.

"I can't do that," I whisper. "Sorry."

He looks away, wipes his hand across his wet mouth. He puts things away. He's about to move off when I touch him again. I put my hands on his waist. He looks at me, a bit of surprise in his eyes.

I pull him into me, hold him, hug him. He hesitates at first, then puts his arms around me.

This feels beyond wonderful.

Never be ashamed of who you are, I want to whisper into his ear, but I'm a stranger here, and I'm too embarrassed that it might be patronizing.

His body tightens, then relaxes again as we continue to hold each other. Someone else walks by, looks, then keeps going. I feel a great communion with humanity. I feel a strength inside me I haven't felt before. Why is that?

In a lifetime of playing it safe, I've taken a chance. I've learned something about myself. There's still something else I've got to figure out, but I've learned something about myself tonight. I feel a weight come off my shoulders.

My companion rests his head on my shoulder. Finally he pulls away, nods, then vanishes into the darkness by the water's edge.

I get back on my bike and pedal home, but not before I stop at the City Point Beach, me and Petey's beach all our lives, further down, and sit for a while. Thinking. I think and I think and I think, but can't find the exact answer I'm looking for. But I believe that it will come in time. What makes me think this, I can't say.

I go home and sleep like the dead.

"I do love you, Petey," is the last thing I say to the ceiling.

19 W ◇ E

A Boy or a Girl?

"Training mission? Whaddya mean, training mission? I thought you were gonna be here until the weekend!"

"I did too, Noreen, but ahhh . . . something came up. I have to go back. Right away. I'm . . . leaving in an hour."

A *silencio profundo* from the other end of the phone, like Consecration during Mass and the itch of you when you're young, the need to cough, the urge to roar—

I batten down the mental hatches—only when you're hungover—

"Your mother said . . . did she tell you what she told me, Danny? Last night? When I called you at midnight?"

"Ah yeah, she did, Noreen, and I—"

"Well I took the day off today, thinking we were gonna go looking at places! We're not? Now you're telling me we're not, is that what you're telling me?"

"I gotta go back, I told you. And . . . I mean . . . lookit, Noreen, my mother spoke out of turn. You know how she is."

"No. How is she?"

"Well, I mean—"

"What am I supposed to tell the girls at work now? When I called in sick this morning I told them all we were going out house hunting today. They're having a friggin' *cake* for me tomorrow at lunch! What am I supposed to tell them now?"

Noreen's a secretary at Gillette and her voice breaks.

"Lookit, Noreen, you know how Ma is. You know, I mean she's always . . . always arrangin' shit. You know that."

A Map of the Harbor Islands
Published by The Haworth Press, Inc., 2006. All rights reserved.
doi:10.1300/5677_19

263

"Let's keep your mother out of this, Danny. This is between me and you. Don't you hide behind her! What you're *really* telling me is you don't want to get married. That's it, right? Isn't that it?"

"Ahhh . . . no, no, I ain't sayin' that. I do think though . . . I just think . . . "

"What ARE you thinking, Danny?"

I'm thinking how censuring her voice is. Also, that I should've taken the old rummy's advice and drunk that quart of water last night. Two quarts.

"I just think that I . . . that we . . . "

Ma's hovering in the kitchen pretending to dry dishes so I pull the phone around the corner to the dining room and shut the door.

"Yeah? I'm listening, Danny."

"I just think we ought to ahhh . . . wait. For a little while. Don't you?"

"Wait? Wait for what, doomsday? The market's going crazy, and here we are with a golden chance to pick up a little house—*they're handing it to us on a freakin' silver platter!* And you're saying no, and there's nothing wrong with a free house so it must be me! You just don't want to get married to ME!"

"Ah . . . "

I have my hand on my head and I realize it's the same shell-shocked pose my father's had for 99 percent of his life so I quickly put it down and scratch my nuts through my boxers instead, rearrange my baseball cap.

I start getting pissed. I haven't once even asked this person to marry me and here I am explaining why I don't want to get married—

"I don't even have a job Noreen, have you thought about that?"

"You can get one when you get out of the service. I have a job."

"That's not gonna pay the mortgage."

Mortgage!

"Well I got some stashed away too you know, I'm doing my little bit. And how many times, Danny, have I told you, haven't I told you my uncle can get you a job over at the pharmaceutical plant? Where he works? I've told you that a million times."

"And do what, put tiny little white pills in the little glass bottles all day? I don't wanna do that for the rest of my life."

"That wouldn't be all you were doing—you'd be raising a family too. Isn't that what you want to do? Get married and raise a family? They have great benefits over there. Or you could do something else—being a veteran you could get on easy with civil service—the post office, the fire department . . . "

In my mind I try on a quick litany of futures as if they were ill-fitting hats, ironically all uniformed, one seeming more wrong than the next.

She starts crying.

I don't want to commit myself because . . . because I've got a headache. And I have to get away and think—there's still something from last night I need to figure out—

—And who the hell wants to make decisions when they're other peoples' decisions, not your own?

But what the hell will I do with my life if I don't get married and have kids?

And why do I have to make this decision when I'm twenty?

"Isn't it? Isn't that what you want to do, Danny? Get married and raise a family? What else is there to do?"

"*SHUT UP!*" I roar.

"You shut up! You go to hell, Danny O'Connor!"

She hangs up and devil a soul could blame her. I click down the receiver, start counting, *one, two, three, four, five six seven . . . ring.* She does this, we do this, this is the dance we do sometimes.

"Hello," I say. "Sorry."

"Hello."

I don't know what to say.

"Danny?"

"I'm confused, Noreen," I finally say. I tell the truth.

"About what?"

"Ahhh . . . pretty much everything. Noreen, listen. . . . "

I start sweating.

"I don't know who I am or what I want. I . . . have a pretty good idea of who I'm *not* . . . but . . . I'm . . . I've got some thinking to do. I'm confused. And . . . I'm a little afraid too. Afraid to do anything until I figure stuff out."

There's a long pause.

Now, when you tell the truth, one of two things happens. People either become almost violently angry, or they also tell the truth. Petey, the exception to this rule like most others, Petey lives his truth, doesn't just talk it. Petey *is* his truth but his stories full of embellishments.

Noreen senses that I really am telling the truth, not just putting her off with this . . . this *construct* I've somehow become, to use a Petey word. There's a long, coming-down sigh at her end of the phone.

"I am too, Danny," she says.

My eyes narrow and I strain to hear her over the phone.

"You are?"

"Yup. Me too."

She lets go another big breath.

"Oh God," she says.

"Ahhh . . . about what?"

"I don't know . . . everything too. Maybe I'm more scared than confused."

She pauses and sighs again.

"What are you scared of? I've never seen you scared before."

"Oh please. Danny, listen, I . . . oh brother. In my better moments I don't want to force you into anything you don't want to do. I . . . I really don't. I really don't want anything from you that you don't want to give me . . . freely. I mean, what good is something if it isn't given freely, right?"

I think it's been about three years since Noreen and I have had this kind of conversation, where we step out of our roles for a minute, stop jockeying for position.

"Ahhhhh . . . I'm listening," I say.

"Danny, I don't know what comes over me. I guess I'm afraid of being . . . alone. But then I think . . . I think . . ."

"What?"

"I think I've never really been alone my entire life, and I . . . really yearn for that sometimes. To see . . . who I might be. Who I might be away from this place and everyone in it. But also . . . it must be fear, Danny. Where does this come from, this fear? You know? Do I just want to get married because everyone else is and it's what I'm supposed to do and I'm afraid to be alone?"

My ego takes a small hit and my eyebrows leap up, but still I know what she means.

"I know it," I say. "Do you think . . . Noreen, listen, do you think you even know yourself? Because sometimes it's like . . . it's like my whole life has been laid out for me and I feel like I'm trapped, like no matter what I do or how far away I run, I'll only go so far or stay stuck in a certain . . . track? Rut? And come back in the end to where I started? Like a yo-yo snapping back? Like I'm wearing the personality that was handed to me? You know what I mean?"

"Yes. God yes, I do know, Danny. Tell me about it, stuck in the secretarial pool, *Oh she's a Southie girl* and they won't have anything to do with you by day, but at the office parties they're all over you like a new suit cuz they think you're easy if you're—"

"They are? Who is? You never told me that."

"Oh please, Danny, grow up. You're the king of not telling so get over it."

This is undoubtedly accurate so I say nothing.

There's a silence that isn't uncomfortable. The idea of Noreen being someone I can talk to—*really*—is new and exciting and a little frightening. Okay, a lot frightening.

I'm way bent over on the card table chair in my intensity, the metal cold against my bare thighs so I scoot my boxers down a little. Fortunately they're the big-ass baggy kind—which are fashionable now which is why I bought them. Have I ever done a thing that wasn't prescribed for me? Yes, actually last night I did several—

"You know, Noreen, that's really why I joined the Corps, I just had to see if . . . to see if there was anything out there for me. For me, alone like. You know? It wasn't like I was trying to get away from you per se, you know?"

Noreen mmmms in understanding.

"Danny, listen, that therapy I got from my father's abuse? It was like—I had to be tough and strong and not let anyone know how scared I was. I was the victim, Danny, afraid of everything. But then the therapy got me thinking that I wasn't a victim anymore, once I turned eighteen. Maybe I could have some kind of life. I was happy about that for a while, but then I couldn't think of anything I wanted to be, and then I'd get so nervous when I thought I might end up alone."

"Mmmm."

"Do you know what I was going to do?" Noreen asks after a minute.

"No what?"

She laughs, sighs. I can see: her blonde bangs lifting up with her breath; something at the end of her eyes that is solid, good, the look I see sometimes when I catch her looking at me when I wake up—

"You're going to think I'm such a loser, Danny."

"No I won't. I promise I won't."

"It's the oldest trick in the book and a lousy thing to do . . . but I was gonna do it anyways."

"What?"

"I stopped taking the Pill last week. I was going to . . . oh Danny, you must think I'm such a jerk, but I . . . I stopped taking the Pill last week and I was gonna try and get pregnant so you'd have to marry me. Isn't that awful? I've always so looked down on women who do that."

Thank God we argued last night—but another part of me pulls back a curtained tunnel, and beyond, there's a threesome on a ballfield, picnicking, playing catch, a little someone trying to hit a Wiffle ball with a big fat plastic bat as red as his jiggling cheeks—

A gasp comes out of me and I cough to hide it—

"I can't believe I just told you that, Danny."

"Ahhh . . . well, I guess I haven't exactly . . . I guess like . . . committed to you really. I guess when you don't know if you have a thing or not, you'll do anything to try and get it."

"You're right, you've really left me hanging, Danny."

"You're so agreeable when I admit I'm wrong. But, Noreen, listen, I'm really glad you told me. I . . . admire you, and I thank you, for telling me."

I know Noreen so well I can even read her silences. This one is of shock, and pleasure.

"Noreen, do you ever wonder what your life would've been like if you . . . if we I mean, if any of us . . . had grown up somewhere else? Like Concord or some fuckin' place? A lawyer or something for a mother, a doctor for a father?"

"Oh my God, hello, there was this state senator woman. Do you remember her? Wasn't from here but used to come to the St. Patrick's Day parade every year, always wore tweed suits. Tall and . . . I don't know, like . . . indomitable. So sure of herself. A three-named person and I can't remember now. I used to pretend she was my mother and how she would . . . do you remember her at all?"

"I don't think so."

"I used to pretend she would . . . what would be the word . . . *advocate* for me. Help me with my homework. Stop my father from hitting me. Call colleges to make sure I got in. Pick me up in a new white station wagon and— get the bastard. Danny, I was raped once."

"What?!"

"I never told you but I was. When I was fifteen. Almost sixteen. That was . . . what was it, two years after we started going out. About a year after my father died."

"Jesus Chri—Noreen! What do you mean? Is this a . . . you're not joking?"

I vault up from my chair, catch a glance at my dumbfounded face in Ma's hutch cabinet.

"I wish I was. I was . . . walking home from Patty Flanagan's house and this guy, I don't . . . I don't know if he was walking or if he came out of a car just ahead—I can never remember that. I've dreamed about it so much I can't really separate what happened from what I've dreamed happened. He just . . . it happened so fast, but it was still like slow-motion, like I was watching this happen to someone else. He pulled me up this alley and . . . the next thing I knew I was on the ground and his hands . . . his hands like stones on my shoulders, pressing me down—"

Her staccato rapidity comes to a breathless halt.

"Noreen, I—I can't believe this! How come you never told me?"

She takes a deep breath over the phone.

"Hold on, Danny, Ma's just leaving." She covers the mouthpiece and mumbling back and forth. Then I hear her shut her bedroom door. The click of her Bic tells me she's lighting up a cigarette.

"Hi. Why didn't I tell you? I don't know Danny. I think I was . . . I thought that I would, and then . . . I think I thought you'd get so mad you'd want to kill him and no way to find out who he was. But now I think I was . . . ashamed somehow. Too ashamed to tell you. I felt so dirty."

"Ashamed? How could you be asha—"

"That's a common reaction, Danny. You just feel so . . . you feel a lot of things, so many emotions. It's like spaghetti strands all tangled up and it takes you a while to sort them all out, but . . . and then the police . . . hold on, lemme get an ashtray."

Whatever next? I stare at myself in the hutch, study my expression, don't change it. *Hello, who are you in there?*

"Hi."

"Hi."

"It took me a year to report it, and then they sent me to this counseling place at the hospital once a week. I skipped the first few times but finally I went when I locked myself out of the house by accident. That really helped. It was the year after it happened when I . . . when we first . . . when you and me first started . . . you know. I thought maybe it would . . . blot it out or something. I didn't want to wait forever and have that be the only . . . association I had with . . . uhmmm . . . with that kind of thing. Not that I associate them together now, Danny. Not at all, apples and oranges. Violence and love."

"Do you . . . Jesus Christ Noreen, do you have any idea who—"

"No. It wasn't anyone I knew. It wasn't anyone around here I don't think. It was a Sunday night and I was walking back from Patty's. It was raining out."

"I can't believe how calm you sound about it. You might be . . . giving a book report."

"Well . . . my hands are sweating anyway. If it was last night I would've been bonkers telling you. I don't know what happens to me, I just get these rages—"

"Oh sweetheart. I don't mean to sound flip. I just can't believe . . . I just can't . . . "

I find that I'm gripping the phone so tight my fingers are turning blotchy. A curdle of rage rises within me. I picture baseball bats, not the red fat plastic ones—

"So what were we saying?"

"What were we saying? When?"

"Before. Before I just told you about . . . what happened to me."

"What are you kiddin' me? Noreen, you just tell me—Jesus Christ—"

The same cocoon of light and healing, protectiveness, that I mentally ensconced Petey in after his accident settles over Noreen, and me standing guard over this image, but a throb of rage inside—

"Just . . . just gimme a minute here. Are you . . . you're sure you're okay? You got counseling and everything? Jesus Christ—"

"I haven't dreamed of it for about two years, so I guess that's a good sign. But . . . I don't think you're ever really the same after something like that happens. I think about that sometimes. If I turn a corner quick, or walk out on the street and there's a guy right there, I still . . . get a little twitchy."

"Why wouldn't you? I wish you had told me though."

"Oh, that's what we were talking about."

"Excuse me?"

"That's what we were talking about. Earlier. About . . . like who we might've been if we grew up somewhere else. Had a different upbringing."

"Ahhh . . . okay. Do you . . . do you want to talk about the other thing anymore?" ·

"Not particularly, Danny. Do you?"

"Ahhh . . . no, no, I guess not. I just . . . I'm sorry Noreen. I'm really sorry. If there's anything I can ever do . . . anything you . . . I mean, if you ever . . . if you're ever like not in the mood or something or want to talk about it or whatever—"

"Danny, listen to me." Another deep breath. "I always wanted to tell you this, but I couldn't without telling the other thing too, which I always put off. You've . . . made touch good again for me. I can't think of anything that . . . I mean the counseling was so good, the police. You hear a lot of horror stories about rude police and *What were you wearing* and all that awful stuff, but I have to say, the police, the detective who questioned me, the counseling . . . they were all so wonderful. Couldn't have been better."

"Well . . . I'm glad of that anyway."

"But no, that's not it. I started telling you . . . you were the one who . . . I mean, so many times, you've been so tender, Danny. What I want to say is . . . you've made me okay again with . . . all that stuff. You . . . you always—well, most of the time—make me feel safe, and loved, and . . . beautiful. When we . . . whenever we . . . do that."

I have to put the phone away from me for a minute. I feel like my face might break from how tight I'm keeping my jaw, the sting in my eyes.

I clear my throat.

"Thanks," I mumble.

"Thank you, Danny. I mean, not that I have anything . . . I mean, anyone else to . . . compare it to. But I don't need to. I mean you've . . . you're the . . . only one, Danny. But I couldn't—I can't imagine it being any better. I can't . . . imagine myself with anyone else."

Her silence after this indicates a similar response would be appropriate.

"Ahhh . . . "

"Oh, you're going to tell me?" she laughs. "You're going to tell me if you've ever been with anyone else? People want to know that, Danny, no matter what they say. I won't lie to you and say I wouldn't like to know that."

"I . . . "

Ports o' call and so forth and . . . this uninvited remembrance: Petey's hair, the moon and stars on Petey's gleaming hair last night, on my white hairy thighs but forget about it, shit faced, nothing really happened, horny, the little head ruling the big one—

"You're the only one," I say. Careful of my tenses.

"That's good to hear, Danny."

I strain to hear disbelief in her voice, a trace of sarcasm, can't be sure—

No one says anything for a minute.

"But I wanted to say something else about that other stuff, Danny, what you were saying. About being other things in life."

"Oh right. Yeah, go ahead."

"I mean, if Ma had ever told me there was other things I could be, besides a secretary and a wife and mother. Not that those are bad things. There are so many people at work who judge you for your place in the pecking order, I've totally gone over to the other side. The nicest person in the whole building is this old black guy who buffs the floor. He might be the wisest too. But

I think about that stuff once in a while, what else I might have been some-where else—not out of envy, or look-what-I-am-now, because that doesn't really change you. I'm not talking about that kind of growth. Like Mr. Sullivan, when he won the lottery. Remember? He bought that place down on the water and a boat and all those cars, but he was still angry. Mr. Sullivan, you know? And then Rita Murray—"

"What about her?"

"I saw her a few months ago downtown. Her car was the same and her job was the same, but she was different. You know? Just . . . different. Whole somehow, I can't describe it. That's what I'm talking about, not to better myself for the sake of bigger things, faster cars, but . . . my life. Me."

"You sound like Petey now."

"Do I?" Noreen laughs. "Maybe I should start stuttering."

"That wasn't nice, Noreen."

"No you're right, it wasn't. It was awful actually. I don't know why he bothers me as much as he does, I'm sure he's . . . harmless. But no, the change I'm talking about is . . . I mean, for my own sake. Seeing how far I could go. I almost hated my sister Maura growing up, because Ma always told me how smart Maura was, how she was like the smart one. You know how we've always struggled to get along, me and Maura."

"I thought it was five girls in the family and one bathroom."

"Well, that didn't help. But last month we met at Jen Taylor's shower, me and Maura, and she told me Ma always told her I was the pretty one, and she should plan on a career because no one would probably ever marry her, because she wasn't pretty enough like me, and she'd always hated me for that."

"Hmm. Not so good. I think you're very smart, Noreen."

Certainly it had proved very difficult to fool her over the years.

"Yeah right! They call me Mrs. Einstein down in the secretarial pool."

"If they don't they should. Or Noreen. What about . . . do you ever think about if we'd gone to a school where we might've had a better chance to get into college?"

"I try not to," Noreen says. "I try not to look back and think about that stuff. What's the point, you know? But . . . I mean, like what happened with my mother and everything, I mean what she told me . . . and then my father, violent and everything. I could use that as an excuse up until I was eighteen Danny, but I can't anymore. I'm twenty now and . . . the rest of my life is up to me. I can't let her opinion of me be my opinion of myself anymore."

"A lot of it is she's just old-fashioned maybe," I say.

Silence.

"So what do we do now, Danny?"

"You mean . . . what do you mean?"

I stand up, start pacing the room. Ma's knickknacks wobble on the hutch.

"I mean about our . . . future. Me and you."

Back to that again. But why wouldn't we be?

"Ahhhh, I dunno. But you know . . . I think the first thing we have to do is take this pressure off ourselves. I mean I still got almost two years left in the Corps anyway and . . . I mean, I guess there's no mad rush, right?"

"No. I don't know. I guess not. It's my stuff anyway, I guess . . . I just wish I could get away for a little while and think, Danny. Do something different for a little while. Be someone different. Like what you're doing. I so envy that, that's probably why I get so mad. Oh God. I was such a jerk last night to Petey."

"Well . . . it takes two to tangle."

"I think it's tango but you're right. But I mean . . . I know how important he is to you and everything. He just . . . I don't know why he gets me so mad. I think I'm just . . . mad at myself, for feeling . . . so dependent on you for my happiness. That's what the therapist says anyway."

That was a mouthful.

"Ahhh, well, okay. And ahh, you're right, he *is* special to me," I say.

"Maybe that's why, probably just my pettiness or jealously."

"Hey, you could be a lady Marine."

"Ha ha."

"No seriously, you should do something. You can, you know."

She laughs.

"What's so funny?"

"When you talk like that, Danny, I don't know whether you really love me, and want what's good for me so much you'd be willing to maybe lose me, or whether you're just trying to get rid of me. It's the ahh . . . eternal battle, Danny. Self-esteem issues, no doubt. That's what they told me at the counseling anyways."

There's another pause.

"And then I think what the hell would I do anyway? I mean, I've been home all morning and I'm already bored out of my mind. Maybe it's this place. I don't know. I do know . . . I do know I love you, Danny. I really do. I . . . care about you. You're a good soul when you're not driving me nuts.

You . . . make me feel like home whenever I'm with you. Well, most times. Proms excluded, I guess."

Home. How I felt when I was holding Petey last night—but not really how I felt when we almost—when we—

"I love you too, Noreen," I say.

I mean it when I say it. I would not have meant it last night.

Another pause.

"Ahhh . . . Noreen, lookit, can I see you before I go?"

"What time are you leaving?"

"I dunno. Two-ish I was thinking, there's a plane at two. And ahhh . . . can I tell you something, Noreen?"

"Yeah."

"I don't . . . there's no . . . there's not any training exercise. I just . . . I just really need to get away and think. Ma's drivin' me shithouse. I can't seem to think when I'm home here."

"I figured as much."

"You're not mad at me?"

"Well . . . maybe a little. I'll get over it. I . . . guess I can sort of see where you must've felt a little . . . pressured. You're not mad at me for my . . . little scheme?"

"No. Ahh . . . is your mother home?"

There's a pause and I feel a shifting within my boxers. I rejoice over this, like something that's been broken's whirring back to life.

"Yeah but she's going out now, she told me so."

"Ahhh . . . okay. I'll be over in about half an hour. Okay? I'm just gonna hop in the shower."

Noreen giggles, the way she used to.

"Okay. If she's . . . if she's gone by then I'll leave the front door open for you."

"Ahhh . . . okay. Maybe ahhh—"

I have to sit down on one of the dining room chairs as my woody is blossoming exponentially—

"—Maybe you could ahhh . . . be waitin' for me like . . . in your bed. Pretending you're—oh no, never mind."

"No, tell me!"

"No, forget it."

"Just because I told you about . . . getting . . . raped, Danny . . . I'm not a nun. Tell me."

"Are you sure? I don't wanna be like . . . I dunno. Joe Insensitive Caveman."

"Why change now? No, just kidding. Go ahead, what? Pretending what?"

"Like you're ahhhh . . . asleep."

"Oh, I see. We're in that kind of mood."

"Why, you aren't?"

"No comment."

"And ah, Noreen . . . what will you be wearin'?"

"You'll just have to come over and see now, won't you, Danny boy?"

"Well," Noreen says an hour later. "That's . . . okay, Danny."

"That's never happened to me before."

"Actually it has, Danny, once or twice when you were all coked up. But it's okay. It's just . . . nice to be here with you."

I was doing fine until I remembered last night, what I had done with myself last night, what I allowed someone to do to me last night—

We lie in silence for a bit. I hear our hearts slowing down. I pull her into me—the way I pulled Petey into me last night.

I begin to look for something within this time and space with her.

"What are you thinking, Noreen?" I ask after a bit.

"You really want to know?"

"Sure. Why not. Yeah."

Noreen's stray hand is rubbing my shoulder.

"Well, Danny . . . since you really want to know . . ."

She lifts up her head and faces me, her long hair swirling against the skin of my bare chest.

"What?" she asks.

"What what?"

"A shiver just went through you. Are you cold? Do you feel alright?"

"I'm . . . fine. You were about to tell me what you were thinking."

"I'm wondering why your skin's so soft."

"Ahhh . . . excuse me?"

Noreen laughs.

"I mean, it's true! You wouldn't believe how much lotion I slather on every day. Before I take a shower, after I take a shower, before I go to bed. Night lotion, day lotion, aloe vera, vitamin E, shea butter . . . and your skin's still softer than mine!"

I snicker, sigh.

"Especially here," Noreen says, rubbing my ass. "Like silk. I love the little red peachfuzz on it. I'd kill for this skin. What's so funny, Danny?"

"Nothing. It's just not the thing a guy wants to hear when he couldn't . . ."

"Danny, forget about it! It's true though, I'd kill for skin like yours. And you don't do a damn thing to it except abuse it and get tattoos on it."

"Must be the genes. Either that or the Oil of Old Lady I use."

"Good genes," she smiles.

Oh boy.

The conversation stalls. I'm plucking at her hair as she lies with her head on my chest. Petey's position from last night.

"I better get going. My plane's at two."

"You're still . . . going back early then."

It's a muttered statement rather than a question. I just shrug my shoulders.

I get up, extract my clothes from here and there around the room, pull them on. Noreen stays in bed, pulls the covers up. I am acutely aware of her eyes on me, her mind on me.

"When are you coming home again, Danny?"

"I dunno. Christmas I guess."

"Christmas," Noreen murmurs. "Six months. A long time."

I don't say anything.

"Are we . . . we're still . . . going out though. Right, Danny?"

"Yeah." I turn around to face her. "Yeah! Of course, why wouldn't we be?"

"Alright, don't get pissed, I was just asking."

"Why wouldn't we be? Just because I couldn't—"

"No, no, I just meant like . . . after what we talked about earlier. This morning. I guess I . . . I don't know where I stand with you, that's all."

I sit down on the edge of the bed and lace up my boots. Noreen pulls the sheet up to her shoulders.

"Just . . . let's just keep it like this. It's the same as it's always been."

"With no commitment."

I don't respond. I finish dressing.

"Sorry," I say. I kiss her lightly, on the mouth. I can smell myself Down There on her lips. Our eyes lock together again. It seems a host of information is exchanged in this look, but its language is indecipherable to me. I picture a vast stream of computer gobbledygook rattling away. Going somewhere, the home office in Dayton. At last Noreen nods her head, barely.

Again, I turn away first.

I pull on my T-shirt and turn as I'm leaving the bedroom. We stare again. She's pulled her sheet further up.

"Bye."

"Bye, Danny."

I'm halfway down the stairs when she calls me back. I wince, stop, sigh, then climb back up the stairs. Slowly.

"Danny," she says. Crying.

"Noreen, what is it? What's wrong?"

"Danny, I . . . I . . . Danny, do you think . . . I know we had that talk this morning and everything, but I just got this awful feeling . . . but do you think . . . maybe we should just go out and elope tonight and get married?"

She pulls a corner of the paisley sheet up to her eyes and wipes tears away. Then she covers her face with the sheet, embarrassed at what she's said.

Oh boy. I rush over to the bed.

"Hey hey, don't be embarrassed," I say, pulling the sheet down a little. "You can tell me anything."

But when the words come out of my mouth they sound phony.

"Listen Danny," she sniffles, dropping the sheet a little. "I know you've got a while left in the service and everything, but life is so . . . it's so uncertain, Danny, and . . . and we do care for each other, so much, I know that. It might work. We might have a chance."

I'm standing over her. Her hands are tugging at mine. I squeeze onto them.

"I'd never . . . I'd never cheat on you, Danny, or anything like that and . . . and . . . I'd really try to make it work. I really would. I just . . . I'd even be nice to Petey for you, Danny. I don't want to lose you! I don't, and I just have this feeling . . . when you were walking down the stairs I just had this weird feeling—"

Soon I'm on the edge of the bed, slumped, and I'm crying too. I can't figure out who I'm crying for, me, Noreen, Petey, maybe all three—

"Danny, I don't know what it is, but I just have this feeling if we don't do it now . . ."

"Noreen—"

"You know those crazy things I get? Like right before my father died and everything? I just have that kind of feeling now, that if we don't . . . if we don't do it now . . . when I heard you walking down the stairs it was like you were walking out of my life forever and . . ."

She's sobbing now and I've never seen her so sincere, so . . .

"Noreen, I—"

"Sometimes you just have to take a chance, Danny. I'm willing to take the chance, to say that I'll try to spend the rest of my life with you. Are you willing to do the same with me? To spend the rest of your life with me? To grow old with me?"

More than anything, I wish it isn't dread I feel at hearing these words. And yet some part of me senses she might be right here, about now or never—and a profound sadness is born at this possibility—

"Noreen, I just . . . we been through this already, I just don't . . . d-don't think I'm ready . . . I've got . . . I've got . . . something to figure out."

There.

I said it. I wait for the other shoe to drop—

"What?" Noreen whispers. "What is it?"

I pause. My back is to hers.

Noreen, I long to say, *I . . .*

But I can't do it. I was brave last night in my trip to the beach, braver than I've ever been; but maybe I've used up all my courage for the week—

I wait for Noreen behind me to touch my shoulder, to hold me, to offer me some comfort. I stare at one of her prom shoes from last night, half sticking out from under the bed.

I wait in vain. When I turn around her eyes are dry, and they flash off of mine.

I don't think I've realized up until now how much pride Noreen has. How much these last words have cost her in that pride—

I know I have to answer now—

I take a deep breath. I feel it again, the same way I felt it a year and a half ago the first night I left, the ring in my back pocket, jabbing into my ass. I've brought it over today because . . . because . . . just in case I—

A sudden compression of time and space and something comes into me, unusual, the realization that ordinarily waits years to appear, as if I'm looking at this moment from a vast distance, but still having it within my power to change my fate. Scrooge seeing his life as a young man rather than an old—

—And also the weighty presence, as if we're not in this room alone at all, of Ma, Southie, half the world waiting now—

I close my eyes and decide that whatever comes out of my mouth now will have to do: even I stop to hear myself say, "I'm . . . sorry Noreen. I love you very much, but I'm just not ready now. I need to figure out who I am and what I want."

A stopping, then a stirring, then a whirring. Something leaves the room and now it's just the two of us again.

"I'm sorry," I repeat. I sound like Tricia last night.

"Forget about it. Don't . . . miss your plane, Danny."

I take a deep breath, get up from the bed. I stop at the door and turn. "I'll write."

She nods her head, grimaces, runs her hand through her hair.

I stop outside at the bottom of her stairs. I take a deep breath. A neighbor I know is across the street and I wave, say hi. I love that about this place.

What I have to figure out. I know it now. Couldn't tell it to Noreen but I know it now. Doesn't mean I'll figure out the answer soon—

But at least I know the question.

What a freakin' question. But a relief here as well, some kind of comfort—

I dash over to Petey's on my way to the airport an hour later. He's at work moving furniture, no answer and I don't want to keep knocking and wake up Mrs. H. I look around for something to write a note on; but as I do, in one of those twists of fate most of us don't believe in, I hear someone coming up the stairs and it's Petey.

"Hey."

He stops. Bristles up a bit, on his guard.

"Oh, hey. I was just . . . just looking for something to write a note to you on."

"You look . . . is that your u-uniform?"

"Oh. Yeah."

"I didn't know if the c-circus was in town or what."

"Ha ha."

"Looks g-good on you though." He up-and-downs me. For once I don't look away or feel offended. "But it's really not you, Danny."

"Well if you don't want to be a Marine, don't join then," I answer back.

I tense, waiting for the other shoe to drop again—I don't have to wait long.

"Maybe you'll be the next one on the b-billboard."

"Yeah, maybe. Maybe you'll join up then if I am?"

"Keep d-dreaming, Danny. But it does look good on you."

"Oh, thanks. You get to fly for free if they have a spot. How you doin' today?"

Petey shrugs, rubs the back of his head.

"Okay, I guess. You?"

"About the same."

And then we can't help smiling at each other.

"I ahhh . . . have to get going or I'll miss my connecting flight. I have like fifteen minutes tops."

"Ahhh . . . okay."

"But I . . . I wanted to say something, Petey."

"Ahhh . . . okay."

I jerk my head in the direction of the front porch. Petey's black eyebrows lower, then he scampers up the stairs, holds the door open for me. So much in his overloaded green eyes, can't even begin to tell you.

We take seats opposite each other on Mrs. H's plant-stuffed porch. The light is limey, ethereal. Petey's bouncing his knee and playing with a petal. His eyes dart between the petal and me.

"What I . . . what I wanted to say is," I begin.

I clear my throat and Petey jumps a little.

I look down and see that I'm bouncing my knee too.

"Yeah?" Petey asks.

"What I wanted to say is . . . I . . . I'm not . . . see, the thing is, I'm not . . . like you are, Petey. I mean, in so many ways, I couldn't be. You're . . . you're a one in a million. I mean . . . what I'm trying to say is, I'm not . . . like gay. Not that there's anything wrong with that at all, at all. But that doesn't seem to be the way I'm . . . wired."

I pause.

"I don't think."

Petey freezes, mid-petal twirl. *I don't think.*

I take a deep breath.

"But . . . I . . . I do know something, I . . ."

My eyes seem to narrow. I feel hot all of a sudden, cold—

"I do love you, Petey."

Petey's not moving, not even taking a breath it looks like. Even the sea breeze has stopped to hear this.

"I do," I repeat. I take a deep breath. "Petey . . . look at me why don't you."

I take off my sunglasses. He raises his head. His mouth's open. His eyes are ruffled oceans—

"I love you, Petey." I don't qualify it. What I'm not saying is the most important thing of all.

Petey snaps his hands together so I won't see them shaking. He's knee-bouncing furiously now. He looks away. His jaw tightens. He gasps. He tries, but he can't stop the tears that start running down his cheeks. His eyes turn into green fire.

I lower my head but stand up. I open my arms to him. He falls into me. He's so wide at the shoulders now—when did that happen? I lower my head onto his shoulder.

"D-Danny," is all he can say into my ear.

"Always," I whisper back. His hold tightens on me.

"Bestest," he says. He's shaking so hard we're both shaking.

"Shhh, shhh," I soothe.

I break us apart.

"I really have to go. I'll miss my flight."

"I know," he says.

He pulls me back into him and we hug again.

"Take good care of yourself," I say.

"I w-will, Danny."

"Promise?"

"Pr-promise."

There's so much to think about on the plane ride back to Camp Pendleton.

Almost too much. But at one point as it darkens in the skies over the Midwest, I catch my reflection in the window.

I nod at it.

Whether it's a function of maturity or the work I've decided to do, beginning last night—asking some questions and acknowledging some feelings—I'm becoming someone.

Danny O'Connor.

No, Daniel. Like Aunty Alice called me. It's a sound that's full of possibilities.

The Marine Librarian

After reporting back to my CO, then cashing in my unused vacation days for something longer down the road, I go back to the unmarried men's barracks and say hello to the boys. They want to know all about my trip home, what I did with my girlfriend and how often.

For once I don't embellish, nor do I describe her as being little more than a receptacle for my sexual desires. I also tell them of my best friend Petey, and the quality time we spent together. It doesn't feel quite the same when I leave the room. There's some kind of shift coming; like most shifts, it doesn't come without a bit of pain, a feeling of emptiness and uncertainty.

I go back to my room and sleep, my remedy for everything. I awake at sunset. The weather is predictably sailboat-calendar-beautiful, but as the night descends with a wail I can almost hear, the Santa Ana wind blasts up dry and hot. There's orneriness in the air. A feeling that Big Things in the Sky are displeased about Something. I am reminded that Nature, too, has her bitchy moods. Heat lightning smears over the not-very-distant mountains to the east. My teeth are chattering and I can't say why—the heat tonight is dumbfounding.

I unpack and my clothes smell of Southie. TV won't satisfy. Neither will any of my music. I beat off twice but that doesn't get me anywhere, smoke six cigarettes, a lot for a nonsmoker.

I step out onto the tiny balcony and it seems shaky. A stray cat leaps up onto the railing, scaring the shit out of me.

I pull on my sneakers and gym shorts and decamp, stumbling down the stairs and outside so I won't roar. I burst through the glass front double doors. I'm outside. Now what. A dry-heave retch blurts out of me. It's got to come out somehow—

A Map of the Harbor Islands
Published by The Haworth Press, Inc., 2006. All rights reserved.
doi:10.1300/5677_20

Not knowing what else to do I start walking, like I'm moving away from a car wreck. Faster. I've never been on a hilly base in my life and Pendleton is no exception. The flat expansiveness opens up around me as I turn a street corner and my woe seems to spill out, trying to fill the corners. A big breath comes out of me.

The energy of the night washes onto me like penetrating rain. The evening is electric. I start walking faster.

Something starts to ease up. Sweating commences. Breathing deeply. I break into a trot, then a jog. There's a group of palms in the distance and I tell myself when I get there I'll stop, turn back. But when I get there I keep running. I'm in a groove now. It hits me that I'm *a-gro-ba*-ing, as Petey would say. Until a hundred, several hundred years ago we always did this, we nomaded, Petey said, and believe it or not I feel the people who did this beside me in spirit, Irish shepherds leading their flocks to the sea, Masai running for days to reach water. Everyone heading for Promising Land. What did Petey call it? Gilead, I'm looking for my Gilead. Aunt Alice again, right before she died I asked her what she missed most about being young. She didn't hesitate when she answered—*Oh running of course, what do you think?*

Faster. The sweat leaking down my sides, much the way it would scurry down pitchers of Jolly Olly Orange on Mrs. Harding's front porch on the dew-point doggy days of me and Petey's fourteen-year-oldness. And me and Petey squinting through the leafy green, writing our initials in the evaporation. Sweat drips convene at the end of my nose, hover for a moment—I give a shake and they spangle off, some of them splattering my bare thighs and knees. My calves are burning, crimping.

I keep going. I get whiffs of my sockless sneakers, postulate that I'll have blisters in the morning. I see the base gas station in the distance and decide when I get there, I'll turn. But when I get there I keep going. Our base is huge and I've never been to this section. Eventually there's another building about a mile off in the flat night—I'll turn around when I get to that. Halfway there I don't think I'll make it. A jeep o' jarheads passes by and toots cordially and this inspires. The landscape bounce-rises and falls as I jog-approach and it recalls a lumpy sea voyage. An ache for Petey-beside-me surfaces, then that too goes by the boards in the roll and breach and gasp of me.

"Birdy!" I gasp at some point. It's involuntary, like the dry heave was. Goddamn it, how do the tender win in the end? The defenseless? The invincible? *The meek shall inherit the earth—*

I reach the lawn of the building and stop, bending over, gasping, my hands on my soaked knees that are finally man-haired. My breath runs through me like a soothing hand. My mind empties, a deserted shore. I wonder what was burdening me, then recollection smears back. But—somehow their faces—Petey's, Noreen's, Ma's, the nameless guy from last night who sucked me off—floating up on some interior watery monitor—don't trouble now.

I walk back and forth across the lawn of this building, huffing.

It comes to me that my decision not to marry Noreen—at least not now—may not have been the right decision, but it was *mine*. It was *my* right decision.

A single man's nothing but a Trouble Man!

But this drifts away too. Somebody else's truth. Ba-bye. Poor Ma.

I feel an interior emptiness, a nothingness, which strangely doesn't trouble. Free-falling. I am nothing falling through nothing. I try to call to mind some of Petey's hundred Zenny sayings growing up, but me always half listening. He would be able to put a name to this, and, naming it, I would claim it. Is that what he said?

I flop my sweaty ass down on the grass, fall back, spread-armed spread-legged. The damp grass laves my bare back, or maybe vice versa. My sweat-wet right nut oozes out of my slicky nylon gym shorts. I leave it lay upon the grass, a dropped jewel.

I look up into the night. I squint, looking down through God's Time Machine. Petey again.

The half-moon is westering, lying lower on its back than it does in Southie. Or is it a different moon? Different moon, different man.

I'm half-surprised I don't start floating away, so empty do I feel. Unknown.

Okay. Let's have at it. Let's continue the process I began last night. Let's ask the questions. No running away. Deep breath.

Who do I say that I am? What do I say that I am? What do I want? What do I like?

I ask the questions out loud.

Then I lift my eyes skyward, but turn them inward at the same time.

"Guide me, oh Lord Skovo," I whisper.

Possibly the first honest dialogue I've ever had with God in my life. A profound longing seems to leap out at me. A sympathetic profound longing leaps back to this. I become aware of a strong desire to know God again, as I did as a child. If there is one.

I pull my knees up a bit, pluck at grass. Squeeze it within the folds of my fist. My right nut retreats to its hidden colleague.

What do I want? What do I like?

My mind sifts through a number of interior Rolodexes. Nothing.

Then, finally, *Well, I like running,* I think. *I like the way it makes me feel. That's one thing anyways. That's one for me.*

I'll start running, every day. What else?

I like Petey. No, I love Petey. If I said it to him, I can say it to myself. I do. I do love him. Despite all the years of my resistance and his otherness, it's still hard to say where he leaves off and I begin. There is nothing but delight and a feeling of home when I'm with him.

I think back again to prom night. I don't believe I'm gay, despite the experience down the beach. But I had no desire to reciprocate. Or was I just hedging my bets?

But never have I fantasized about being with a man. And when I . . . when I had Petey . . . do that to me in the car, when he . . . okay, when he started to blow me in the car—it felt strange, bad . . . unholy almost. And yet I wanted him to do it. Whiskey dick? Just one of those things?

But when I was holding him earlier in the woods—when we were side by side in the woods, holding each other—

—If that wasn't holy, I don't know what is. Have I ever felt so complete, so whole? So . . . home?

No. No, never. I hate to admit it, but it's true.

Another deep breath. But there is something soothing, liberating, in the truth—discomforting as it feels at first.

Maybe the other stuff felt unholy because I was hiding behind something—not being real with him, not being honest, using him.

This thought, too, strikes a chord of truth deep within.

Ouch.

At home with Petey—have I ever felt not at home with him?

Have I ever felt that way with Noreen?

I've felt good with Noreen, normal, comfortable, safe, sexual, satisfied—

But have I ever felt home with her? Have I ever felt with her the way I felt with Petey when I was holding him?

No.

Double ouch.

Okay, we're getting somewhere. I feel an exhilaration I've never known before, that one can actually reach in and know oneself, tinker with oneself, as it were.

There's one more question. This is the tough one.

It didn't feel right to have sex with Petey—but how would it feel to make love with him? To be really myself with him, not to pretend I was some whiskey-dicked, jacked up, super-horny Marine looking for relief just cuz the broads weren't around—

I cringe at the memory—how could I have done that to him?

But at the same time, something urges me to be gentle with myself, to forgive my ignorance.

I tighten my arms around my shoulders as a sign of this—

—But the tough question still remains.

I go there: I close my eyes and see it again, feel it again: the smell of the woods, the chanting of the crickets, the feel of Petey next to me, the well of feeling I have for him—

I see this morning, when we embraced, held on as if for life—which I guess we've really been doing all our lives, since the day we first met in kindergarten.

Who the fuck made these labels anyway?

Another yank of grass. I sniff it. Lovely. I concentrate again. I see myself pulling back my head from Petey's shoulder, but still hanging on to him, our arms wrapped around each other.

I pull back so I can look into his eyes—

I pull back in, so I can . . . so I can . . . bring my lips to his—

What would that be like? What would it feel like? To be me, and do that? To let him be him, and do that.

I hold the image in my mind for a long time.

But I can't find the answer. It doesn't repulse me, but neither does it drive me wild. But I do find that I am smiling.

Well, I guess you can't answer all the questions at once.

Dad built a garden wall one time, to ensconce his precious peonies in. I helped. At the beginning I was instructed to witness this wall-building, to learn it.

Get the first block right, son. Get the first row right and the wall will build itself.

Must've been the only kid in Southie called *son.*

Well, I've got three blocks now in my hands as it were; nay, there are four. Four blocks of truth: I have an urgent desire to throw out some feelers in the direction of Skovo, the Lord/Lady of the Universe; I like jogging; I love Petey; and the peace, the utter contentment, that I experienced with Petey when I held him in the woods the night of the prom—and again, this morning, when I left him—is a thing I've never felt with Noreen, or anyone else for that matter. That's four, four for me.

I remain where I am. For once in my life I remain where I am. I want to get up and plunge into the jiggly Distracted Life again, but I stay the fuck where I am.

Something writhes, but something else goes click.

I expect guilt at what I feel for Petey, but none comes. Why should it? It is what it is. Who couldn't help but love him? Can you be gay with just one person?

I stand up, vault my arms skyward. I bend over and stretch out my screaming leg muscles.

You'd never know it to look at me. I'm still 5'10", still red-headed, *An fear rua,* as Mrs. H is wont to call me, *the red man.* Still with the buzzed head and the jug ears, still seventeen freckles (Petey said) scattered across my nose and under my eyes. *Seeds, Danny,* he said once, *seeds to what will come later.* Still the pug nose, still the blue eyes, still one shoulder tipping lower than the other, *Like you're ready to charge someone,* Sr. Ruth Anne said.

But everything . . . well, something . . . is different. Changed.

It's not just feeling acutely at home here in this moment. Much more than that, though that's a big part of it. Not *here* as in Camp Pendleton, thirty miles north of San Diego; but *here,* inside my own skin. This moment and me in it.

I turn around, look around. I notice the sign on this zoysia lawn here, ten feet away from me, lit up with two spotlights shining from the so-green-it-looks-fake grass: Building 1224 Base Library.

The base library.

The stars laugh and the click kicks in, roars.

Dear Noreen,

Sorry I haven't written in a while. It's been super busy here. I called you the other night but your mother said you were out.

Thanks for the socks and underwear and cookies on my birthday, much appreciated—it'll save me doing laundry this weekend. Sometimes I go to the BX and buy new underwear and socks to avoid doing laundry—that's so welfare I know, but . . . there you are.

Sorry to hear about the snow, so early too, before Thanksgiving. I had a nice Thanksgiving, one of the guys here, Hector Nunez, has family not too far off base. His mother remarried a few years back to this Asian guy, and Hector brought three of us over there and we had a typical real old-fashioned Mexican-Thai Thanksgiving, with lots of relatives on both sides and a few rowdy Marines thrown in for good measure. It was a hoot and a half and I'll tell you more about it later, especially the turkey stuffed with refried beans and pad Thai. Only in America, no?

I was so glad to hear about your courses at Bunker Hill Community College—that's great. Your company's paying for them so why not? You said you felt like a spider, coming out of your corner for the first time in your life and throwing out strands and seeing where they might land—you said that was a poem you were studying or something. Well, I've kind of done the same thing out here. I didn't want to say anything until it came through, but I'm officially out of Communications (where I basically drove the radar engineers around all day and stepped and fetched for them) and am now the AMS (Assistant Media Specialist, whatever that means) at the base library. It carries the rank of sergeant with it so I've been promoted, which means I get my own apartment now in the unmarried guys barracks—a vast treat, and it's sure cut down on my drinking to boot. The place I was living in was worse than Animal House. Technically I'm still liable to go here and there if a crisis arises, but failing that I'm a librarian now if you can believe it.

I really love the job. So far I've put together one of those reading clubs they have for kids, for the kids on base, and also I've written a proposal to try out a mobile book van thing, like the one that used to come around when we were kids that almost everyone would boo because its bell made us think the ice cream man was coming. I visit the base schools here once a week and lecture the kids on reading, and also show them some of the new books we have at the library. When I ask them if they have any questions, most of the boys raise their hands and ask if I ever shot anybody and what kind of gun I use. It's funny but in a pathetic way, no? Also I need to get some more computers here too. I think that would draw a lot more people in, and also we need to make all the information about the benefits available to servicemen and women more available— especially the educational benefits. I've been thinking of maybe going back to school myself, maybe when I get out, though I have no idea what I'd like to study or anything. Besides that stuff, I also check books out and help people find stuff when the other people who work here, who are mostly civilian family members of enlisted guys, are busy or whatever. It's all new to me and I'm trying the best I can, haven't screwed up too bad yet, though I couldn't shut off the alarm one afternoon when my boss was out and that was pretty embarrassing—a colonel in the reading room was not amused.

Everyone with a higher rank than you is your boss in the military, but my immediate supervisor is this late-fifties woman Marine "lifer," from Clearwater Grass, Kansas—great name, no? She's very sweet, though she's got a temper, and has a kind of southern accent which I didn't think they had out that way but she's a little . . . set in her ways I guess you'd say. "My stars!" she's always telling me. "You want to change everything around here, don't you?" Her name is Lucinda V. Skewell, and when she answers the phone she says, "1224 Base Library, Head Librarian Major Lucinda V. Skewell here. How may I help you?" It doesn't sound funny when I write it but you'd have to hear her. She kind of looks like a tall shocked bird, and sounds like one too. She likes things her way and everything in its place. I've been so excited about different things I'm kind of running around like crazy, and I think I disturb her a little but I also think she likes me.

I'll tell you how it all happened. I think I told you a few months ago how I joined the library here. It was kind of slow at the time and whatnot and pretty soon Lucinda was calling me "our best customer" because of all the books I was taking out. As a matter of fact it was her who told me about the job opening in the first place. See, I was out jogging one night, the first night I got back here, and I just happened to look up and there I was in front of the base library. I didn't even know they had one. They were closed because it was around midnight, but I came back the next day and joined up and got a card and everything. I don't know if I ever told you this, but my dad's Aunt Alice, Sr. Alice, the nun, she joined me up at the Broadway Branch Library when I was a kid, and . . . I don't know, it did something to me. So I joined up at the base library the next day and started taking books out. On anything, anything that seemed interesting to me. Baseball books at first, war stories, junk like that, but then other stuff too. After a while Lucinda seemed to take an interest in me, and started asking what I was driving at, and I told her I basically didn't know anything but wanted to know . . . everything. She started giving me a book a week to read, then two, then three when she saw I was just plowing through them. She said she would start me off with what she thought were "The Classics" and then move on from there. She said make a note of every word I didn't understand and look it up, but the lists of the words I didn't know were almost as long as some of the books themselves, so we took a time-out and she gave me some books on improving my vocabulary, and also gave me, as a gift, this big fat dictionary that took me about two hours to carry home it was so heavy.

Anyway Noreen, it was like this door opened.

Aunt Alice said that reading was exercise for the mind, and I've found, like the running I'm doing now, the more I did it, the more I wanted to do it. And words, the way some writers make magic out of words! Some phrases just seem like jewels to me, and I go around the library hearing their music over and over in my head. After a bit Lucinda invited me to join this book group they have here at the library, where every Tuesday night seven or eight people get together in the conference room and pick a book to read. Each week somebody different gets to pick a different book, and then the next week everybody sits around and talks about it. What's even better is when some crisis arises and someone doesn't finish the book in a week, and everybody laughs at the stories. They call me Junior as I'm the youngest person in the group, and the only active-duty guy in it. There are two women Marines (who I think are a couple), three retired guys who live off base, and four wives of enlisted guys. They're really nice people, and you find out not just about the particular book you've read that week, but also about people and places you never knew of or dreamed about and the crazy funny ideas and lives we all have. One of the retired guys was actually at Pearl Harbor, and later was a prisoner of war in a Japanese prison camp. One of the women is Vietnamese and spent two years in a refugee camp for boat people, and two years before that in a reeducation camp, where she was kept in a metal grain-storage shed and every night the rats would come in. When it was my turn to pick a book, I picked one about the

Irish Revolution, as that was one of the topics I've become interested in, and most of them said they loved it, they had no idea, and I said I know, even many Irish don't know their own history.

Anyway, about five months after I walked through the library doors for the first time, Lucinda told me she wanted to speak to me one day when I came in. She brought me into her office and shut the door. She told me to sit down, then folded her hands and told me about this job opening at the library. She said her assistant Jocelyn was retiring, as her husband was transferring overseas for a year-long TDY (a travel assignment) and would I be interested in applying for the job? Noreen, I couldn't sleep that night. Lucinda helped me study for the test, and they had to post the job opening, but she said she'd put the postings up in places where no one could see them, and also give me her highest recommendation. Well, five weeks ago it all came through, and I've been working here since. Hard to believe but true. I took some ribbing from some of my friends out here but that was to be expected and somehow I seem—I don't know, immune to all that now. It's been a whirlwind since then, and I hope that excuses my lack of communication. I'm really happy, Noreen.

The best part is the nights. "I don't believe I particularly care to work nights," Lucinda says, so she's on 0800 to 1700, I'm on 1300 to 2200. She used to have to work nights because her assistant was a mother and needed to be home afternoons and evenings. The library—oh, that's 8 to 5 for her and 1 to 10 for me. The library closes at 9, and then from 9 to 10 I do whatever paperwork Lucinda doesn't get to (which isn't much) and also restack returns and go through the catalogs and recommend what new books we might get. Lucinda said the first time I did the WARF (Weekly Acquisition Request Form) I exceeded twice the annual budget for new books! We have an audio-visual room here at the library that Lucinda insists on calling the music room, which is the only form of rebellion she allows herself. Otherwise she's as by-the-book as they come. They have a couple of different stereos in there, so people can listen to music on headphones, and one of them is really kick-ass. There's not too many CDs but tons of records, most of them like symphony stuff. The first few nights I blasted this rock station all over the library, but then that got old soon and didn't seem to fit with a library, so I started playing some of the records we have here. There's thousands of them. I just started at A. It's like some kind of door opens, and you walk into a room and find it goes on forever. I just never knew. It's not just music, there's hundreds of records where people recite poetry and stories and whatnot, and I listened to one the other night called "Crossing the Ravine," by some mystery writer, narrated by that Vincent Price guy. Well, it had me double-checking all the windows and door locks and looking over my shoulder on my run home.

It's about four and a half miles from the library to my apartment. I take the base bus over to work but change into my gear and run home when I'm through work. There's so many things crowding my brain it's like I have to. And then there are the books. Noreen, it's unbelievable. I have no idea where all this reading is taking me, but I wonder if you feel the same way with the stuff you're reading for your classes? Like you're growing? Changing? Seeing the world in color for the first time?

Remember that conversation we had the last time I was home, where we did the What If thing? I really feel like my What If is turning into reality.

I'm writing this letter on one of the computers here at the library and it's way after 10 so I better get going. I have to check all the doors and finish this report I'm running for Lucinda. Another thing—I'd hardly ever seen a computer before, and they kind of intimidated me at first, but now I'm the computer expert here if you can believe it.

Now the bad news. Since I just got this job, I'm kind of the low man on the totem pole, and I won't be coming home for Christmas, as Lucinda is going to her sister's in Florida. I know that stinks, but what can I do? If it's any consolation, my next visit home will be longer.

I'll call you again soon, and hope all is well. Thanks again for the birthday stuff.

Love,
Danny

Okay so I've withheld a little.

I didn't write Noreen that I'm actually looking forward to Christmas: I'll be in charge of the library for a week, and though I'm nervous I'm also anxious to show Lucinda and everybody else that I can handle the responsibility.

Still, I'll miss home, Christmas—though last year could've been better. I'll miss the family, the hush that comes over all of us at midnight on Christmas Eve, Dad's reading of *A Christmas Carol* the seven nights in a row before Christmas, the cousins the next day, the singing of the carols in the parlor after dinner, the feeling of family, the joy bursting out of the holly-and-balsam-festooned Gate of Heaven Church, when, for at least twenty-four hours, it seems the whole world has taken into its collective heart these simple words: *Peace on earth, good will to men.*

Petey was the one I felt worst for—he'd been really looking forward to my visit home. I'd been too—sort of. I knew what I had to do the next time I saw him. I would do it—so help me I would.

But if I could delay it a little—and, really, in this instance I had no choice—then I would. I guess change is a process.

So I stayed on base for Christmas—faux Christmas I called it, 72 and sunny—but things at the library couldn't have gone better.

I often wonder, what would have happened if I had gone home that Christmas? Would I still have lost Petey?

21

While You Were Gone

Dear Danny,

Greetings from the planet of South Boston. Now listen to me like you never listened before. As S-B's plenary potentate and Emperor of Mysteries, Whispers and Winds, I—I mean, We—have recently annexed some lands and waters at the Eastward, and We are pleased to announce that the Ramifications of South Boston now extend from the Broadway Bridge, all the vast way to a point just west of the Blasket Islands, County Kerry, Republic of Ireland.

We were urged to take this course of benign snatchery by a delegation of seagulls, mackerel, dolphins, sundry whales, starfish, harbor seals, petrels, crabs, and others, in light of continued degradation of their habitat, to wit, there was another oil spill in the outer harbor last week, Danny, and said creatures floated up dead ashore.

It was a silent but most convincing representation of their case.

So, like many a sovereignty before us, a-gobbling we have gone. In fact that spirit figgers prominently in our Battle Cry (though not our National Anthem, which is more peaceable than nostril-flaring), which is titled "Here We Come A-grandizing," which is sung to the tune of "The Wassail Song." But don't go getting nervous, Danny, don't worry that you're about to be deployed to the western North Atlantic to die for, err, Freedom: We are pleased to report that the proclamation of said annexation—which occurred at the rear of Castle Island last Thursday afternoon—was bloodless and unopposed.

My—I mean Our—most trusted councillors and ministers—Fergo the Seagull; Mister Mysterio the Water Rat; and Bluto, Buttercup, and Felicity (my latest stray canid adoptees) have strenuously advised, urged, and otherwise nagged that We proclaim to the world the boundaries of our new annexation, in the same way that countries report new borders to the United Nations.

We thought that only right. No doubt you will read a full account of these new acquisitions in the *Times,* the *Guardian,* the *Christian Science Monitor,* the *Observer,* and the other papers you and all other governmental employees peruse daily in your attempts to better serve We the People; but since you accompanied Us to these Lands and Waters at the Eastward on one of Our first exploratory missions some years ago, aboard the *Little Andy Foley,* We thought you should be first to know.

A Map of the Harbor Islands
Published by The Haworth Press, Inc., 2006. All rights reserved.
doi:10.1300/5677_21

Therefore we aver, avouch, and otherwise bray that these new borders are defined as follows: From a point at the rear of Castle Island, said point now being henceforth forever known as the Pepperminty Coast, our new borders extend east-northeast through the Tropic of Afternoon Kindergarten across the Sea of Seven Spanish Angels, skirting the Point of Lost Ribbons but including, we hasten to add, the sea isles of Concepcion de Sancta Mavroules, Scintillation, and Grod, all the way in this same general direction (which we retain the right to change at our slightest caprice) to the Isle of Unopened Packages, specifically to a point some vague miles beyond the Mountain of the Merry Meeting Which Suddenly Turned Dour, at the north of said Isle; from that point due east, along a secretive, ever-changing, dubious, and undisclosed line to the Bay of the Sharp Retort on the Island of Trixie McFeeley's Bingo Windfall; hence southward through the Sea of Danny's New Haircut (you got a haircut one time freshman year Danny that was so very beautiful, and I would be derelict in my duty as a cartographer if I didn't memorialize this through the millennia) to the Straits of Republican Innuendo Wildlife Sanctuary, including the John Muir Shopping Mall and the Bushmill Oil Fields located there; hence westward through Inky-Dinky-Parlez-Vous, Miasma de Mustafa, the Plain of Surpassing Ambition, and other liquidy landmarks, back to said Pepperminty Coast, including Upper Kitty Carlisle and the briny islands of Cat Wants Out, Suspicion, Dingelberry, and Suddenly Last Tuesday Morning As You Were Doing Your Poopsters, including, it hardly bears mentioning, the Jo Anne Worley National Seashore.

Enclosed you will find a photo of Proclamation Day, when we officially annexed these lands; feel free to distribute these to the media, since, astonishingly, no representatives of same showed up, despite being invited. I suppose they were trepidatious about being in our Imperial Presence.

I remain, by the Holy Grace of Our Hermaphroditic Friend and Creator Skovo,
Your Plenary Potentate Friend,
Petey Harding

Enclosed with Petey's letter is a black-and-white snapshot, taken down at the beach, showing a blurred Petey, from the rear, running back to a spot where three sitting dogs await him—one incredibly diminutive (Bluto no doubt), one savage-looking (Felicity, I'm sure), and one the size of a healthy heifer (Buttercup, in all probability). A seagull with one foot gone missing lists to the starboard beside the dogs; another blur at the far right end of the photo, circled in red ink, has written underneath it

His Majesty's Sage Councillor Mister Mysterio the Water Rat proved camera shy on Proclamation Day, and thought it best to scurry on off. Too, We apologize for the less-than-crystal-clear depiction of His Majesty Petey Harding, but His Majesty overestimated the duration of the royal camera's self-timer device, and as this was the last exposure (the greater part of the Royal

Budget being currently earmarked for dog food), we thought it best to send this along as is.

The next day a more accessible letter arrives.

Dear Danny,

Thanks for your letter last week. You write such letters now, Danny—I remember the first few you sent me (like every six months) when you first were in the Army [No matter how many times I tell him it's the Marines, Petey still calls the whole experience "In the Army"] and they were full of misspellings and usually had chocolate cake smudges (and what looked like boogers?) on the edges of them and so forth. Not that it ever bothered me. But you write so well now. Remember when "sweating like Danny O'Connor trying to write" was a local proverb?

Danny, I've something I want to tell you. I didn't want to say anything at first, until I was sure. But now I think I can tell you without jinxing myself.

But first I want to set the scene like you do in your letters.

Okay, so I'm sitting up in my bedroom. You remember my bedroom.

Ahhh, yeah, Petey, I do—

I've rearranged my furniture, and now I have the desk up against the window, because it's winter still, even though the calendar says spring, and if you remember you can see the ocean in the winter from my bedroom window. If I look hard, Danny, I feel I can almost see Janet Birchfield up in her weather tower. That doesn't mean much to you, but remember when I got the ham radio set after my accident, and I used to delight in listening in to the world? Every now and again, based on the vagaries of winds and sunspots and electromagnetic diarrhea, I could sometimes pull in this tiny 200-watt radio station from away down the coast of Maine. They played wonderfully erratic music—Beethoven's Ninth, followed by a James Taylor song, then something New Agey and abstruse, then like maybe a less-than-well-known Ray Charles song when he was in his country-western phase (or "the country and the western," as my mother would say). It was all beautifully unslick, and though they weren't exactly amateurs you had lots of pauses and sometimes things would drop and clatter and they would laugh and explain what it was. They frequently shot the breeze when they changed shifts. They were in no rush to fill every nanosecond with rapid, monkey-mind gibberish; they had interesting Down East accents. The news and advertisements were great, as was the Farm Report every morning at five; but what really struck me was when they would do the weather. They were in a farming and fishing area, so they reported on the weather lots, a couple of times an hour. "And now," they would say, "let's take a look at the weather. Let's go to Janet Birchfield, live in the WXXX (or whatever it was) weather tower."

And then this nice woman would come on, sounding a mite tinny and wind-whipped, but oh-so-earnest, and she would give the weather, including winds and knots and tides, sunsets and moonrises and what have you. Then she would sign off by saying, "This is Janet Birchfield reporting live from the weather tower." Anyway, I liked her, and I used to think of her being in this tower at the edge of the sea, this old stone tower like the ancient round ones you see in Ireland. It's got a little balcony at the top and she comes out from time to time like a cuckoo clock to make her observations—not with meteorological instruments, not with Geiger counters and barometers—but with her nose, eyes, and ears—and her elbow, which broke in two places when she was thirteen and throbs now when the pressure is falling. She's dressed up like Enya or something in all this Druidy drag, the sea winds streeling through her long black hair, and she has a wicked old spyglass that belonged to her great-great-grandmother, who sailed the seven seas. (Though not the Sea of Seven Spanish Angels, unless I am gravely mistaken.) She scans the beach, the ocean, the skies, with her glass: has the latest tide deposited glumps of seaweed on the beach, or has it snatched everything in sight? What direction are the starfish facing? Do the islands offshore look sharp as glass, or are they wrapped in a tulle of mists? It is these things that inform her prognostications, which are remarkable in their accuracy.

Anyways, one time I pulled the station in, and to my shock, horror, and disgust it had been gobbled up by Clear Channel Communications, and was now "EZ 99," or something, playing the same catatonia-inducing ten songs over and over, love themes from vacuous cineplex movies for the most part, interspersed with slicky ads from national chains, and then big fatty loudmouth blab shows at night, angry, angry, telling people whom they should hate now. No more farm report; no more wonderfully weird mix of songs; no more locally produced shows and ads; worst of all, no more Janet Birchfield reporting live from her weather tower.

Bastards!!!!!

I often wonder what's happened to our Ms. Birchfield, how she has weathered the sea changes wrought by the corporate world's acute overeating disorder. Sometimes I think she's still there in her lonely old tower, making dulse tea, sighing as she stares at the sea, noting her observations in her large leather-bound double-folio volume, which is covered in a deep sea green—and then once a month going on a crying jag and getting shit faced inside her Spartan lighthouse bedroom because no one wants her reports anymore; she's taken a cashier's job at the new Wal-Mart out of necessity, and she's saving up her pennies to buy her own radio station—and she looks with ironic eyes at the dispirited customers who happen to mention "Cold today, huh?" But alas, you see her pay is so low and her heating bill so high she caught pneumonia and she has no health insurance and that's wiped out her savings. She's taken up smoking out of boredom and frustration, and has been seen more than once down at the new dive in down, Appleseeds, a national chain that recollects happier, simpler times that never existed. Like Mrs. McGinty next door here she likes the Misty 120s—she runs one hand through her raven tresses, tilts her head back, and dreams of starfish coming in from the cold of full-moon seas as she exhales zephyrs of blue smoke out of her mouth while the jukebox blares out "Achy-Breaky Heart."

Such songs should never be played in Maine, she thinks.

Or maybe the weather tower was owned by the radio station, and was included in the sale, and it's now, after its recent vinyl renovation (during which they gave it a bit of a tilt) Pisa on the Penobscot, complete with mini golf and microwavable pizza "just like Mama used to make." It's attracted quite a crowd thus far. Just follow the fat ladies up Route One in the Vanagons with the American flag decals on the back. Ms. Birchfield has been booted out and is now living in a trailer park and she had to pawn her lovely Enya wear—but wait a minute, Danny, maybe I'm making her much less proactive than she really is—possibly she's led a boycott to keep Wal-Mart out of town, has set up a ham radio station where subscribers can still hear her weather lore, and in the evening becomes an avenging angel, sabotaging the new 50,000-watt EZ 99s transmitting towers.

I'll have to get back to you on this, Danny.

Anyways. Today it's a cold day—the sun is warm, but there's a fresh wind rattling things, a clean sweeping of things to get ready for spring. I just finished cleaning my room. Right near the top of my window there's a bright band of light, shimmering and waving. That's the ocean. In a little while I'll take my walk around Castle Island and listen to the conversation of the waves. It's Sunday afternoon, just home from roaming and the roast beast dinner we had afterwards down stairs, which of course I didn't partake in. We have a visiting priest from Ireland at Gate of Heaven for the next six months, and he stays with us on the weekends—he's from one village over from where Ma'am was born, and they know a continent of people in common. He's a very nice guy, Fr. Kiernan Ó Ghrádai (O'Grady but he spells it the Irish way and why wouldn't he) oldish, maybe 65, and a beautiful voice that he raises in song at the drop of a hat. He served for a time in Baghdad where the Christian minority there celebrate the Chaldean, rather than the Roman, form of Catholicism, and this he has imbibed, so there's a bit of a mystic to him. He recites Rumi in a way that brings a hush to the L Street Tavern, and that place hasn't known silence since Kennedy was shot. And his stories! We've had a lot of good talks, and I've told him all about myself, over time.

Anyway, what I wanted to tell you was that on Halloween Day I gave a present to myself—and though it was my doing, I really don't think I would've had the wherewithall to go through with it if you hadn't come back to me the day you left, and told me what you told me. I know on the surface it would appear we love each other in different ways; but I think, at its core, all love is love, and I can't tell you how good it was to hear you say those words to me, Danny.

Anyway—on Halloween Day, I attended my first AA meeting. Danny, like my father before me, I am an alcoholic. But now, after almost six months of attending meetings every day, and sometimes twice a day, I can say that I am a recovering alcoholic. And though there's a lot of emotions pouring out of me right now, and a lot of stuff I'm dealing with, I don't think there's been this much hope in me since I was a kid. I'm even planning my biggest garden yet over on the West Side this year. The things that used to give me pleasure are coming back into my life again Danny. Tenfold. Jolly Olly Orange and so-forth, Mavroules de Sancta Concepcion and the like.

Anyway—Fr. Kiernan last month told me about some AA meetings where most of those in attendance are gay guys like me. Young and old, rich and poor, judges and doctors and priests and bus drivers and carpenters and everything else you could think of. I was incredibly nervous, Danny—so Fr. Kiernan offered to take me. Well, he did, and he brought me to the second meeting too, and now it's part of my regular routine of meeting-attending. It's still an AA meeting, and as such a lifeline to me—but now I can talk about some of the issues roiling inside me, and find understanding and empathy.

What a difference that's made, Danny—I don't feel half so alone as I used to. I've made some good friends there—and believe it or not, I hardly stutter at all now when I talk in the meetings.

There's this one guy in particular I've become friendly with, from my Wednesday night meeting. His name is Paul and he's an unbelievably nice guy. He's a few years older than us, 26, and has been sober for three years. There's four or five of us that go out to eat after the meeting—Paul is one of them. He's somewhat tall and lanky, quiet. He works in a drug rehab place and also makes cabinets for a living. In his spare time he drives through small towns in Vermont, Maine, and New Hampshire, looking for old falling-down barns made of chestnut wood—which he says is the best for making furniture. He has amazing hands. He doesn't even know it I think, but he's always running his hands along wood, like in the restaurant or at the meeting. It's like his hands have a love affair with the smoothness and the potential of wood. I know it sounds weird that I should notice that. Anyway, like I say he's kind of quiet at first, but there's something really good and whole there—like the earth. And when he smiles—

I guess this must sound like I have a crush on him (it still feels a little weird to confess these things to you, Danny, but it's important that I do, it's an important part of me recovering from the shame I felt for so many years) and maybe I do. And to tell you the truth, Danny, for once it feels good to have these feelings, and not like I'm barking at the moon. But they encourage people not to get involved in a relationship until you've been a sober a year. I can't see exactly why, but I believe the people who tell me this. Right now, the most important thing in my life is staying sober—one day at a time. I'm eating better, sleeping better, and living better. There are still times I feel a little lost, but I'm definitely finding my way, Danny. And in so many ways, a lot of that began when you said those words to me. I hold those words to me so often.

It's all about love, Danny, really. For so many years I was ashamed at what I felt, ashamed by my desires—and now I see them in such a different light. The Lord/Lady Skovo made all, and all that is made by Him/Her is good. Our sexuality is a gift, Danny, not a gaffe—and that goes no matter whether one is gay or straight or something in between. As you probably have noticed, I've spent a lot of my time on this earth studying its beautiful ways—what a paradise we've been given, Danny. When I think about cloud formations and tidal surges, midnight moonlight on the water, icebergs and giraffes and blowfish and mountains, deserts and savannahs and oases and stars and starfish, buffalo and fire ants and the way Mrs. McGinty next door caresses her cat every morning on her front porch—if there's one word for all of this, Danny, it's diversity. Skovo is a child-creator, always playing, always trying new things—and inviting us to celebrate this and join in the fun. This other stuff—this insistence that we all look the same and act the same and love the same—strikes me as powerfully UN-Godlike. And so many people suffer, Danny, with shame because of these other people's rejection of God's creation.

So I've taken to plastering some homemade posters all over town—"Celebrate God's Gift of Homosexuality," "God Has Always Made Lots of Adams and Steves," "Thank a Gay Person for Not Contributing to Overpopulation," "Like Leonardo? Cherish Tchaikovsky? Admire Alexander the Great? ALL GAY!" stuff like that. I've put them up on school doors, in front of churches, on telephone poles in front of corner markets, down at the fire station, covering them in layer after layer of wicked sticky cellophane tape so they're almost impossible to take down. And for every one that's defaced or spray painted over, I put up ten more.

As you can imagine, they've caused a bit of a ruckus around town. Fr. McCarthy gave a sermon about it last month, that these posters, "Do not exactly reflect the teachings of the Church on this matter," but then Fr. Kiernan later that weekend preached that while the posters may not reflect current church teaching, everyone should ask themselves whether they might nevertheless reflect Christ's teaching, to love one another and to refrain from judging. He observed that many times in the past the church has erred on various matters, and that, being a human institution, it is bound to err still today. A number of people clapped when he said that, which is very encouraging, Danny. He has a lot of balls. He gave me some literature from the Society of Friends, the Quakers, that says the same thing—how homophobia is a sin that rejects God's creation, and how all God's children have been blessed with the gift of sexuality, and it matters not whether they be gay or straight—and it was so wonderful to read an official church teaching that lifts up, rather than denigrates and shames, a significant part of God's children. It makes one very tempted to abandon our own church, Danny, but too many good people before us have taken that route—like the Elves leaving Middle Earth—and that just leaves the unenlightened and judgmental to run things, so I'm not going to do that. For fifteen hundred years my ancestors have been in this faith, and this is a powerful gift they have handed down to me. The Faith of Our Fathers and Mothers wasn't always this judgmental Danny—for several hundred years, Celtic Christianity celebrated people, life, the earth, the animals, the seasons, and the Glory of a God of Love and Mystery and Life—in fact, there's a movement afoot to revive the best of this ancient and powerful tradition, and reinvigorate a church that has in many ways fallen asleep to God. So I'm trying to do my part. I dance on the parapet of Castle Island when the moon comes out to celebrate the joy and beauty of living, to affirm my own place in the miracle and joy of living—and I distribute these posters to spread God's healing message of love. If only one shame-filled person sees these and takes heart, and changes their thinking, then it is a very good thing. I will stop doing this when the schools and churches in this neighborhood start proclaiming this same message.

God bless you, Petey—twice the balls this Marine will ever have and who would think that in this crazy backwards world. Yet there you are—I'll be saluted and feted from one end of town to the other when I come home, the brave Marine, and Petey'll be lucky if he doesn't have the snot kicked out of him.

Surprisingly, Ham Bone Kelly reportedly stopped someone from tearing down the poster I put at the corner of A and Broadway, if the local rumor mill is to be believed. Who would'a thunk it from Ham Bone, but maybe one of his nine kids is gay or lesbian.

Besides the ocean, God, Danny, do I love those Southie nicknames! I love the humor of them, or their dead-on accuracy. I'm not talking about the cruel ones, like Pissafloor Cronin or Animal Head Ed O'Brien. And I so miss the laughs we yucked when I used to point out to you the irony of people's names in town. Remember? Old Doctor McFeeley, who used to give us our "cough" physicals during the first gym class of every year—and old Mrs. Meaney, the nicest lady in town? What about Rita McSorley, with her face so pretty she's a model now? Debbie Priestly, who's doing time in Concord House of Correction for doing in her grandmother, Billy St. John, who did the stickup at the First National, or Officer Kevin McGurly—the self-styled toughest man in town?

So, when are you coming home again? I missed you at Christmas, and I miss you still. Write when you can. I'm going down to Castle Island now, Danny, to take my walk, then I think I'll lie on my back on the grass and build castles in the sky, to wit presidential palaces for our newly acquired kingdom at the eastward. As this suggests, I am resisting the Great Epidemic of the Modern Age—no, it isn't cancer, or TB, or even AIDS, though all of these are horrific scourges—I'm talking about the Silent Killer: Productivity. I intend to be totally unproductive for the rest of the afternoon and evening. I will contemplate that wise old Spanish proverb—"How lovely to do nothing, and then rest afterwards."

Write again when you can. In the meantime I will keep your health and well-being in the weather tower of my heart.
Your Friend,
Petey Harding

I have to laugh—Petey still signs his full name whenever he writes to me—but at the same time, what an ache, to be there with him on the grass, staring up—why does this seem like a vision of heaven to me now? The slow-motion part of a Hollywood film when the main character, heretofore befuddled, looks at the other leading character and finally gets it? And how many times have we done this, and half the time me bored, picking at a scab, listening to the Red Sox game—

And good for him for doing what he's doing—who else but Petey.

But I fear what might happen to him if certain people catch him in the act.

I bring Petey's letter to work with me, and read it again once I lock the doors at nine. I'm happy for him, so happy—I actually start tearing up a bit .on my run home.

But that night I can't sleep, and when I do, I dream I'm in one of Ma's old black-and-white movies. It's foggy and Casablanca-ish, and as the fog lifts a bit I see that Petey is on one Harbor Island, and I'm on another, and we are waving as his island slowly drifts away into the mist.

Petey's not home when I call him the next night. Or the next. Or the next.

I finally get him over the weekend, but he's running out the door and only has a few minutes to talk.

"When are you c-coming home, Danny?"

I smile. At least that hasn't changed.

"September, Petey. I'll be home in September."

"If this were a musical this would be when I'd break into song, Danny. 'See You in September.' When?"

"The fifteenth to the twenty-seventh. Almost two weeks."

"I c-can't wait, Danny. I can't wait. Danny?"

"Yeah?"

"There's something I've got to tell. I was g-gonna write it but I really wanted to tell you in person."

"Oh. Ahh, okay."

Tingle-time. Uh-oh—

"I don't know if I should tell you now or wait 't-til you get home."

"Ah . . . tell me now, Petey."

"Ahhh . . . okay."

I hear Petey shut the door in the dining room after he's pulled the phone in there. I can see it all, smell it almost. In the Moria of my innards, something wakens and stirs. How I long to be with him this moment—

"Danny, I . . . okay."

I hear Petey take a deep breath. I can see him twisting his finger around the phone cord.

"Danny, I had a lot of anger at you over the last few years. I realize that now. I'm sorry. That was wrong of m-me."

Oh, is that all! Thank God!

"Oh Petey—don't worry about it! You don't have to—"

"Shut up, Danny!" Petey hiss-giggles. "I'm trying to do my ninth step, lemme finish!"

"Okay, sorry." I pinch my nose the way we did when we were kids. "Go ahead please."

"I . . . resented you, because I . . . I loved you so much, and you didn't re-turn that love in the way I wanted you to. I was a-angry with you for n-not . . . being like me. And I really resented you for that. That was so wrong of me."

"Oh Petey. . . . I . . . can see how you would do that. Don't beat yourself up for it."

"I'm not, really—I'm just gaining a lot of clarity and I want to . . . just cl-clear that slate, Danny."

"I could've been more sensitive to that. I . . . I think I must've known that deep down, how you felt . . . about me. And . . . if I were a better person, or was more enlightened back then—"

"Oh Danny, d-don't expect more from yourself than you were able to give," Petey says. "We've absorbed so many wrong things."

"I know it, Petey. I just . . . I guess I was afraid, that's all."

I swing my feet off my desk, sit up straighter. The library's been closed for fifteen minutes now, but what I really want to say is I feel so close to Petey, really start aching for him—

"But I'm not anymore, Petey. Afraid I mean. I'm not." This realization hits me as I say the words. "And Petey? I'm really proud of you. I mean the AA stuff and all. And I know your dad would be too."

"Thanks, Danny. Oops, there's my ride, Clyde."

"Okay, I'll let you go."

"September," Petey says. "The eagle shits on the fifteenth."

"Excuse me?"

"Donnie told me that's what D-Dad used to say before he died, when Donnie and the others would bug him for money. Pester him for p-pesetas. Dad worked for the city then, the g-government, and he used to say, *Kids don't bother me go ask your mother, the eagle doesn't shit 'til Friday.* Meaning his p-payday of course."

"A banal truth expressed in succinct language," I say.

Petey snickers.

"I love it when you talk smart to me, Danny. It p-pays to increase your word power. Speaking of which, Ma'am is taking tai chi now down at the Curley Center and getting more p-politically correct by the hour—she's calling that lovely old rug in the parlor the Asian rug now, instead of using the O word."

"The road to enlightenment was never without its bumps."

Petey pauses.

"Jeez, Danny, I'm going to have to start having tofu and bran on my cereal to keep up with you, sp-speaking of enlightenment. That library job is m-making you a veritable W-Webster with the vocabulary! Alright, I gotta go, Dictionary Breath. Jolly Olly Orange over and out."

"Goofy Grape gettin' outta here."

Horny. Unbelievable. Out of nowhere. How long has it been? Was it . . . wow. Last summer, with Noreen. The last time I've been with someone. Why is that? It's like I've put myself on hold until I . . . figure things out.

There's no need of that though.

I get up from my chair in my office at the library and there's a tent springing up out of my pants. It feels good to walk around the library with it, the friction as I walk up and down stairs, checking windows, setting the alarm, turning off lights.

"Uhhh," I moan at one point. See I let myself go until I can't stand it anymore. But I see my sexuality more as a means to an end now, rather than an end itself. It's a vehicle to take me into the place where I can express that part of me with the one I love—

See, it's really that "Home" feeling I keep thinking of—

And I'm not afraid to think of who gives that to me anymore.

Well, sometimes.

It's been two weeks since my last talk with Petey, and I'm counting the days, counting the nights, until. See, I've been thinking. Playing really.

Nine to ten every night, the library's my own, in here alone with all the wisdom and frivolity of the ages. My own personal salon. The erudite smell of them in their tulles and togas. Poe and Hawthorne's frilly silk cravats under their haunted gazes. A blousy Edith Piaf recording trilling through all three floors and me with my legs crossed at the knee. The hush of the stacks, the whispered eurekas as they all announce to each other the birthings of new ideas. The Children's Hour, I call it, my nightly perusal time from nine to ten, when the child I am attempts to become an adult, tries to wean himself off the pap I've fed myself all my life—others' pap mostly—and replace it with the murmurings of Aristotle and Gertrude Stein, Milton and Harvey Milk. One week I believe we are our ideas; the next day, our desires; the night after that, the way I always hook my right leg over the edge of my chair when I sit naked at home in the chilly blush of the computer light and beat off. Or the green grassy smell that comes out of me after a run.

Or am I my compassion, as I begin tutoring this one kid every Wednesday afternoon, a ten-year-old who hates books, he says, when all along I know it's just that he can't read yet?

Listen! I tell him every time we meet. We stop and pause inside the main foyer of the library. *What is it that you hear, Stephen?*

Or is it the unknown thing—*the fire in the head,* as the ancient Irish bards called it—that makes me wake up early this particular Tuesday morning, one of my two days off a week, to be one of the first at the base exchange's annual plant sale, 25 percent off, and fill every filtered-light corner of my apartment with ferns and orchids? And in the mornings when I awake, they greet me and the slanting morning sun with a fragility so invincible it's plaintive?

I'm all of these, and then some. And the more I become, the more I realize that I was not nothing before this process. And so many little roads of thought that I tiptoe down now—you can almost see the signs flashing at the intersections of the various electronic runnels of my brain: *Petey was here.* No surprise there, but still it's ironic that I had to join the Marines to learn this, to learn all about the Kinsey Scale, to read and understand Kierkegaard. (In fact a quote of his rests above my shaving mirror, soddening by the week but still legible: LIFE CAN ONLY BE UNDERSTOOD BACKWARDS, BUT IT MUST BE LIVED FORWARDS.) And to learn to be totally okay with what happened one early morning after a swim at the base pool, when a fellow jarhead and myself jerked off together in the sauna: slowly, luxuriously, and so ritualistically that one almost wanted to summon Margaret Mead in to take notes and ask questions. But God knows the poor dear's glasses would have fogged—and us hidden behind the anonymity of our goggles, the only words exchanged being my, *No touching, man,* when he reached a drippy pumped forearm, his vein-throbbed fist, in my direction. But I couldn't have said the words more tenderly if I had said, *Kiss me now, darling, take me, you fool!* I have to laugh later that night when I write in my journal, and draw a little sketch of the new and improved Marine billboard in Southie, the one right above Rotary Lottery and Convenience, cheek by jowl with the Salem Lights babe and the Crown Royal ice cubes—the latter no doubt replete with subliminal skulls and fervid couplings. Yes, the very same billboard that lured me into the Marines in the first place, though I shudder to admit that now.

But my own redesigned billboard—unapproved as of yet by the Ad Council, but based on my own experience—shows two blurred jarheads naked in a sauna, sweaty with suggestion, while in the foreground we have horizon-scanning, earnest (like Che) depictions of pioneers in various realms of art, literature, and science. The Marine-red text blares: COCK, KIERKEGAARD, AND KAVANAGH: ONLY IN THE MARINES. Hey, it works for me. The few the proud etc., is so five minutes ago, no?

We have a Lilliputian play corner in the children's library downstairs where the little darlings can take a break from reading. We offer them building blocks, dolls, teddy bears, Chutes and Ladders—and toy soldiers. Well what do I expect, this being a military installation, not a touchy-feely play klatch in Berkeley or Cambridge. But still. Indoctrinating the open eyes and hearts of our young to the business of killing rankles.

What the hell's happening to me?

When I casually bring this up to Lucinda, her head jerks up from her current task at hand, and she looks more than ever like a startled bird—to be specific, an emu, I can be specific now and that there tree was a magnolia—and asks, "Daniel, what exactly is wrong with teaching our young people that freedom isn't free?"

Uh-oh. One of those.

"Nothing," I say. "I myself believe that children and guns don't mix, and I wonder if it may send the subconscious message that might makes right, and violence is the way to resolve problems." I pause, almost surprised to hear myself. I didn't grunt in answer, then crawl away to nurse resentment, my previous life's MO when confronted with an opinion different from my own.

"Why, *Danny!*" Lucinda gushes, beaming from one edge of her spatulate face to the other. "What a mature, intelligent way to express yourself, and engage a contrasting opinion without a personal attack! I commend you!" She walks around the front corner of the main counter and pecks me on the cheek. "Well done!"

Anyway, it was about a week later when I began kidnapping the plastic green soldiers. Not all at once of course, but in twos and threes, and reassigning them to the demilitarized zone of my top desk drawer. Within a month they had all gone missing and no one, i.e., Lucinda, the wiser.

But the point is, I sometimes take them out at night and play with them, right on my desktop. The game's evolved over time, and this is what it looks like as the summer wanes: the majority of the troops are dispatched on my desktop, broken up into a right flank, a left flank, and a main body. They are being led by three generals, each in a chauffeur-driven jeep, each scanning the horizon with binoculars. In my game, one of the generals is Ma; one is Fr. McCarthy; the third is Noreen. Off a ways and near the edge of the desk are two soldiers. One of them has a bit of the rebel about him—he's not carrying a gun and he's looking over his shoulder. He looks a little like Petey. The other one has a rifle in his hand, but it's lowered, and he's looking bewildered.

Like me, that soldier will be going home in a month for a few weeks. One of the first things he's planning on doing is going to visit his best friend—the gunless soldier, the rebel—when his flight gets in at 11:15. It'll be midnight by the time he grabs his luggage and gets out of the taxi in front of his friend's house. The stainless steel smell of the airport is disgusting when he's leaving, but liberating and welcoming when he arrives home.

I've borrowed one of the tiny dollhouses from the children's room to add realism to my little play.

The rebel soldier I put up on the third floor, in his bed. You can't really tell but he's reading by candlelight. Or drawing a map. Something.

The stars are out.

The first soldier walks up the front stairs of the house. He takes a good look at this house, the Harding house I'm calling it just for the sake of the argument. Light gray with black shutters, an enclosed, plant-ridden front porch and a green front door. But that's not the half of it. What's happened there. Who lives there. The swirl of lives and living, the wild winters, the purr of summer nights. Footsteps and whispers.

The first soldier gets the key that all his life has lain under the doormat of his friend's house. He unlocks the green door, slips inside.

The smell will hit him first, the Harding House smell. I hold my soldier in my fingers and he pauses when that smell hits him. Hard to describe it. Warmth. Love. A whiff of the sea, but not to the point of dampness. A lingering aroma of Irish soda bread, hot from the oven, pulled apart with ravishing buttery fingers.

The soldier breathes deeply. He's not nervous at all, even though all the other soldiers and generals are watching intently to see if he follows orders. Or not.

I leave my toy soldier like that for one night, in the parlor of the doll house. The next night, I push him up the stairs, passing all the 8 × 10 Harding boys in their high school photos. His friend the rebel soldier will be the last, at the top of the stairs. Dressed like the ragpicker's son. Couldn't have cared less in those days. The hair every which way. Making a face, for chrissake. Still beautiful. Those green eyes. Invincible in their vulnerability I now realize, like my orchids.

The top stair creaks. As it creaked when we were five. As it creaked when we were eighteen. Blessed be your life, if you're still creaking a stair when .you're twenty-two that you creaked when you were five. Connections. Connections still connected.

The rebel soldier's mother is at work on her night shift.

I make the first soldier take a right at the top of the stairs, passing the bathroom on the left. There is a hardwood floor here, that red scatter rug in its midst. Last door on the left at the end of the hall. The rebel soldier's room. The oak door.

My first soldier stops at the door, composes himself. This is it. He's had orders all his life about what to do now, but for once he's listening to himself, listening to a Higher Authority. The generals behind their binoculars begin to sweat.

He turns the handle, slowly and carefully. I see this on my desk, his friend in the bed the other side of this door. Sitting up, reading.

The first soldier opens the door.

The rebel soldier looks up at his friend. He's reading by candlelight. As he's done all his life. Anything and everything. *Secrets of Medieval Herbalists; The World of Owls; Trees of Eastern North America; Sayings of the Desert Fathers; Egyptian Tarot Cards; Tap-Dancing Your Way to Sublimity.*

"Danny?" he'll say. Not surprised though, not really.

"Petey," the first soldier says. He smiles. Maybe. "C'mere to me." I reach my other hand into the dollhouse and lift the rebel soldier from his bed. He's wearing pj's, just the bottoms.

"Danny," he'll repeat. He stops in front of his friend. Smiling, goofy-shy, overjoyed, overwhelmed.

The first soldier opens his arms to his friend.

They hug. The warmth of his friend, from the bed.

They'll hold each other. The first soldier feels that again, that being Home feeling, the thing that started this all. Although really it started in kindergarten when you think about it. But I mean, started this new thing. Made him think. Made him start thinking. Unafraid now. Unafraid of the other soldiers and generals. Couldn't care less.

Home.

But see, the first soldier already knows this. Already knows how it feels like home when he holds his friend.

What he doesn't know is—

How he will feel when he does what he's come here to do.

They hug for a long time. Finally I pull the soldiers back just a little. It's air conditioned in the library so I feel a little surprised when a bead of sweat rolls off my nose and plops onto the desktop.

I bring the two soldiers together again.

"Petey," the first one says. "Petey, close your eyes."

The second soldier's mouth falls open, just a bit the way it does. You can't see it but it does.

He closes his eyes. His bottom lip is quivering a little. The first soldier tightens his grip on him, pulls him closer. Stops for just a minute when their faces are maybe two inches apart.

And then I put the lips of the two soldiers together. Softly, softly. But this time the first soldier brings all of himself into this. He's not drunk, isn't high. He's not all horned up and looking for relief. He's not hiding behind the construct that he never really was.

He isn't thinking of someone else.

They kiss—

Jesus Christ, but they do—

And then the first soldier pulls back.

He knows now.

I lift my soldier up to my face.

"What do you know now?" I ask him, in the heart-thudding silence of my office. It's way after ten and time for me to be out of here.

But he just looks at me, his face Mona Lisa mysterious.

And the generals and other soldiers are still watching, intently.

22

Peter, Paul, and Mary

"Keep the change. Thanks."

"Thank you, mon."

The taxi crawls off. I watch his red lights smear down the street. I look up. The stars are out. Check.

I'm early. We had a mighty tail wind from west to east, the elements conspiring to bring me here faster thank you.

I turn, set my bag down on the sidewalk. It's five minutes past eleven. I fold my hands across my middle, look at the Harding house.

The night is calm and so am I. Sort of.

The front porch light's on, as always. Filtery light seeps out from the porch, limey colored from Mrs. Harding's plants, heartbreakingly effusive now in September's swanny song.

I take a deep breath, finger the two plastic toy soldiers I have in my right pants pocket.

"Can't get enough, eh?" the security guy at the airport joked when I had to empty my pockets just before boarding.

"Oh yes, that's it," I laughed back. *If only you knew.*

I walk up the stairs. Someone's left the mail on the top step. I pick it up, then get the key under the mat. The porch door lock still sticks a little, but I pull back as I turn the key and the door swings open.

The porch is even more overloaded with frilly green than I thought. I can't help smiling.

Just for luck—or something—I pluck a red geranium blossom and stick it in my lapel. I've got my Class A dress uniform on. Tan chinos and shirt, tan tie, green coat. Funny hat. My perusal of history has taught me one thing—one can't be a soldier without the funny hat seemingly.

A Map of the Harbor Islands
Published by The Haworth Press, Inc., 2006. All rights reserved.
doi:10.1300/5677_22

I open the heavy green door and step inside. I breathe deeply. Bingo, there's the smell. I've done this so many times. Signing the olfactory guest book as it were.

Not only does the house smell of Mrs. H's soda bread, there's a generous hunk of it in plastic wrap on top of the microwave. I can see it from the parlor and it calls to me. On a crystal plate. I approach. *Boys, help yourselves*, is written in Mrs. H scrawl on a note beside the bread. I take her at her word, and cut a slice. God bless her acumen for sensing I'd come right here this night. A marching band couldn't be a better welcome.

Delicious. Try getting Irish soda bread in San Diego.

Home.

I put my nylon duffel bag down on the living room rug, yes the Asian rug, then ascend the stairs, saying hi to all the Harding boys. I stop at the top step. Petey. I shake my head and smile. Then I gulp. Skovo, be with me.

I stop in front of his door. I take off my cap, scratching the back of my head, just unbuzzed this morning for the occasion. My hair is getting Petey-longish and if I didn't work at the base library I'd never get away with it.

Well. Here we are.

Twenty-nine sweaty palms wiped on my pants and how is it that every moment of my life has come down to this? Back to where we started? Not a circle exactly—more like an ascending spiral.

There's no light coming from underneath, not even the flicker of a candle.

I take a deep breath. Into the breach. I turn the handle, open the door, slowly.

A bit of light smears into the room with me. My heart leaps up—a lump in the bed, facing away from the door, cocooned in covers, Petey.

I say his name aloud though I don't mean to, "Petey."

I close the door behind me. There's that lovely click. Wait a minute until my eyes adjust. The smell of him like heat rising in a cold room. Clean. Earthy. Petey.

He's sleeping—it's not the way I pictured it, but maybe . . . maybe better.

I slip off my shoes, one at a time. Put them down at the side of Petey's bed, beside his sneakers. Then the sight of that hits me. What it looks like. What it could mean. How this could be repeated ad infinitum.

Just four shoes beside a bed, but what it signifies.

I walk softly to the other side of his bed. I blur by the small mirror over his bureau and catch a sideways glimpse of myself. I stop and turn. In the half-dark, my reflection could be a recruitment poster, so set is my face, so determined. *Cock Kierkegaard, and Kavanagh* but I'm nervous now and not in the mood for irony. Perhaps knowing yourself is one part not knowing yourself and two parts determination.

.   .   There's about three feet of space between Petey's bed and the wall. I infiltrate this space and occupy it. Beside his bed, his little nightstand. There's a medal hanging from the lamp there, *Six Months of Sobriety*. God bless him. Reborn. Look out world.

I'm standing beside his bed now, at the head of his bed. I squat down on my haunches. My right knee cracks, as it always does.

I stay like this for a bit. I can hear Petey's breathing, soft and easy. Birdy breath. I look down to the end of the bed and see that both Petey's ivory feet have slipped out from the covers. One foot has a sock on, one is without. I can't say enough how this is the quintessence of Petey. The baby toe on the unsocked foot has a tiny Band-Aid on it.

I turn my head and study his face. My head's about a foot away from his.

I'm not too too nervous until I think—what if I do like it? What if it does . . . speak to me? What if this kiss turns into . . . into everything?

I hadn't thought of that before.

I might wake up in this bed in the morning. What—

What exactly would we do here?

I feel my face flush.

I check to see if there's some kind of nether reaction to this, but there isn't. Still can't tell at all if this is what I want, what I need; but ready now finally at last to see.

Now for it.

I bring my face to Petey's.

The eyes closed, the black lashes and hair spilling into his face. Him looking sixteen in this light. I know, I knew him at sixteen.

I tilt my head a bit, half close my eyes. I lick my lips, once, twice.

I come in close. Until I can go no closer. My nose brushes his. Oh Jesus—

One more deep breath. Here we go. I close my eyes then place my lips against his. The feeling of falling as I move in. A gentle fervid scudding in my ears.

I am kissing Petey Harding.

The first thing I notice is the softness of his lips. Their tenderness surprises. There's a sweet fecund smell coming out of him—you see the mouth's a tad slanty-open and awry. I place my arm carefully on top of the ruffled mound that is his shoulder, and pull him closer into me. I leave one world, enter another.

I kiss Petey. I am twenty-two years old. I have known Petey for seventeen of those twenty-two years, and now I am kissing him. I am a Marine, and I am kissing my best boyhood friend. Half the world and maybe more would recoil at this, but it feels like the most honest thing I've done. I almost laugh at the realization that I've never been more a Marine than now—leaping into the dark unknown of Petey Harding's mouth, for Truth, Justice, and the American Way of being who you really are.

Petey groans, stirs, moves onto his back, pulling our lips apart.

I leap up—there's still enough of me that's chickenshit.

But he remains sleeping.

Okay, okay, relax, he didn't catch you.

I recoup a bit, take my hat off again, run my hand along the top of my scalp.

What do you feel? How did that feel?

I don't know. I don't know. It wasn't long enough. My mind was spinning. It felt good. I don't know.

Why did I think this would answer everything?

I unbutton my top shirt button, loosen my tie a bit.

Maybe this would work better if I woke him up, started from the beginning. Or maybe I should put myself into a more sexual mood, take off my clothes, get myself a little excited. This is partly about sex, but it's about so much more than that too.

I take off my jacket, place it over the chair in the corner. My chair. The old tipply green chair that my ten-year-old non-bum squirmed in when Petey would do his ritual dressing. There's a lot more of me that's bum now, and still squirming it is too.

I squat down again. Very carefully, I watch my hand move onto the edge of Petey's bed. He's lying flat now. I study his face. What would it feel like to see this all the nights of my life remaining?

It would feel good, comforting, safe. Home.

But to make that happen, I'd have to do more than just stare at him. I know that.

My hand slowly rises up, moves under the covers. My fingers come to rest on a place at Petey's side, where the waistband of his pj's meets the hard-soft firm flesh of his side. Slowly, my fingers move over. A part of me wishes Petey could stay asleep while I . . . do things to him. But that, I know, is a cop out.

A memory snaps back at me, doing this to Petey while he was in the hospital.

No, I can't do this while he's sleeping. When I was a child, I thought as a child. . . .

Best to wake him. Involve the all of him in this, as I am trying to involve the all of me. Do I have the balls to do that?

Whether I do or not, I must.

I step lightly back over to his doorway. I half turn and knock on his door behind me.

He shifts a bit in the bed.

I knock again, a little louder.

"Petey? Petey!"

He stirs. Itches his nose with his right hand.

"Petey! Petey!"

He opens his eyes.

"Wh—Danny?"

An almost overwhelming warmth punches into me—it's all I can do not to jump onto the bed with him.

"Hey! It's me, Petey! I'm home! Home!"

"Oh, Danny, wh—Danny!"

He sits up, blinks his eyes, stares, smiles. A thousand emotions smear across his face.

"Danny? Is it really you?"

"It is! I came home! I'm home! Surprise . . ."

Okay, this is more like it. More like how I planned it. Tell him to get up now, tell him to come here—

"Sorry to wake you, Petey, but I came right over—I . . . I haven't even been home yet!"

"Danny!"·

Petey rolls over and snaps on the light on his bed stand. There's a blue lightbulb in it. He squints when he looks back at me, laughs. Half his face is rumply-red with pillow smudge.

"Come here, Petey," I say. I try to open my arms up but somehow I can't, not quite yet. There's a difference between thinking of a thing and doing a thing—

Petey tilts his head a bit, then pulls back the covers and slides out of bed. He looks great, better than I've ever seen him. The hair is a bed-sodden disaster, every which way. Blacker, if anything, and his flesh whiter, more solid—

He gets out of bed and stretches, still smiling ear to ear. I am too, can't help it. Finally I open my arms.

He comes into me and we hug. I knew it would be—his body is bed-warm. The smell of his flesh is like the earth, that first night in early April when it wakens. I close my eyes, and, to my embarrassment, a deep, almost purr-like sound comes out of me.

"Welcome home," Petey smudges contentedly, his voice still sleep-sodden. I open my mouth but I'm struck dumb.

"I had the funniest dream," Petey mumbles into my shoulder.

It feels odd to be touching the bare warm skin of his back. My fingers are tentative at first, but then they relax, move across his shoulder blades and his back like they're devouring a map.

At least my fingers don't seem confused.

"What was it?" I ask.

"Danny, you're shaking!" Petey says, pulling back a little and staring at me funny.

"I am?" I ask.

"Like a l-leaf! Look! What? What is it?" His eyes narrow and he looks at me appraisingly.

"Just . . . glad to . . . I don't know, just . . . what was your dream?"

I'm shaking because I think I know now. I want to try it anyway—can't leave this room without trying it—a tingling on my chin like right before you get into a fight—or steal home—

"I dreamed that . . . oh, never mind." He grimaces and raises his eyebrows. "Do I have bad breath?"

We're still holding onto each other. Petey leans his head back on my shoulder.

"Ah, no, you don't."

"Great to see you," Petey mumbles into my shirt.

"Vice versa. Tell me. Your dream."

"I thought . . . someone was kissing me," Petey says. He laughs again into my neck. "I thought it was . . . Danny, I have some news for you."

He pulls his head back and stares at me. The smile hasn't grown any darker. Now for it, I can tell Petey anything—

"Yeah? Well I . . . I got some news for you too kiddo. Ahhh . . . what's yours?"

"Danny, you sure you're okay? You're still shaking—"

"I'm fine, fine, just a little . . . strung out. Long flight and all."

"I can't believe you came here first. But anyways, Danny, listen I . . ."

Petey looks away, looks down at his toes. When he raises his face back up it's as radiant as the day a butterfly came to his garden.

"Danny, I'm in love."

"Ahhh . . . what?"

Petey's eyes go back and forth between mine. Their light is fierce with joy.

"Can you believe it?" he asks. Looks like he won the friggin' lottery— I hear the breath leave my body like a punch to the gut. I cough to hide it.

"Ahhh . . . who's . . . who's the lucky man?"

Petey sits down on the edge of his bed behind him.

"It's Paul, that guy from AA."

Petey smiles again, puts his lips together like he's almost a little embarrassed, tilts his head down but keeps his eyes on mine. My arms flop to my sides.

"Ahhhh . . . Paul."

"I mentioned him in some of my l-letters. In fact I thought it was him when you woke me up. Do you want anything, Danny?"

"Uhm . . . well, actually I'd like to . . . uh, no. No, I'm fine."

"I'm freezin'," Petey says, scooting back up the bed like he's ten years old. He pulls the covers up to his chin, then slaps his hand on the edge of the bed.

"Sit down, Danny, take a load off."

I comply. Numbly. I start laughing.

"What?" Petey asks, half smiling.

"Nothing," I say, but I can't stop laughing.

Petey raises his eyebrows.

"It's just . . . good to see you," I say. "Ahhh . . . tell me about it."

"Well," he says, smiling again. He runs a hand through his hair. His eyes dart around the room.

"We're taking it kind of slow. I still only have ten months of sobriety, and they say you should wait a year before you get involved with someone, but . . . I don't know, it just felt really right for b-both of us."

There's a light shining in this room, and it isn't the small sailboat lamp on Petey's nightstand with the blue lightbulb. It never pays to leave Life, Others, Fate, out of your plans—

"That's . . . that's great, Petey. Really . . . great."

And now of course I ache to get under the covers with him, touch him, kiss him—

—Just to find out? Or do I know now? Now that's it been withdrawn from me?

"What ahhhhh . . . what does he do? Tell me about him."

I'm glad I'm sitting, don't think I could stand now—how is it that my whole life for the past few months has been all about this? How did that happen? And now—no wait, it hasn't been all about this. Mostly, but not entirely: I still have the library, my reading, my dreams of going back to school—even though all of that seems devoid of its joyous fuse right at this second—a relationship can be such a fucking cul de sac of your own development sometimes, no?

"He runs a drug rehab program at one of the hospitals," I hear Petey saying when I tune him back in, pride stringing the beads of his words. "And he's a cabinetmaker too. Danny, he's such a good person. And believe it or not, he also keeps bees."

"Bees?"

"Yeah, he's a beekeeper on the side. He's got two hives in his b-backyard in Jamaica Plain. Danny, it's fascinating! You can't imagine. . . ."

Petey goes into a five-minute spiel on the lives of bees. I can't help but smile, drowning in his excitement as bees to—

"—And sometimes, Danny, when I'm over there we just lie on the grass and stare at the sky and watch the bees come flying back at sunset. We emptied the hives this past weekend and got almost two hundred pounds of h-honey! Oh, wait a minute—"

Petey leaps up from the bed, dashes over to his bureau, and hands me a jar of honey before he gets back into bed. It's pale, rich, gleaming—the skin of his body—

—A tremendous sadness hits me. But I smile.

"Woodley Hall Honey?" I read, from the jar. I'm pushing my voice up on tilts of happiness that sound like they may collapse from their insincerity any second—

"That's the name of his little honey company. His house has these cool woods in the back and he's put in a water garden and waterfall and has a little patio out there where his friends come over a lot at night and they all nicknamed it Woodley Hall, so that's the name he gave to his little honey business."

"Well, that's . . . that's great." This guy sounds like a real asshole.

Petey's eyes go off somewhere else, and the smile on his face softens. When he turns back to me I'm staring at him. He colors up a bit.

"Sorry," he says. "And ah, speaking of sorry—Danny, lookit, I want to say again how sorry I am I was mad at you all those times."

"Ahhh . . . what times?" My voice is getting leaden—

"When you were going off with Noreen. Now I know . . . now I have a better idea of what that's like, to . . . have someone." He lowers his voice. "My God, Danny, I never knew."

It still might not be too late, a voice says.

I reach over to him and take his hand in mine.

We stare at each other. The smile fades from Petey's face.

His eyes grow larger. I see him gulp—

"Petey, lookit—"

But what kind of a selfish asshole would I be to do this now? To, to . . . use him like this. My own private little guinea pig, and me still not knowing—

"Congratulations, Petey," I say, shaking his hand. "I'm so happy for you. It . . . I have to say it agrees with you. You look . . . great."

I look away first.

"What is it, Danny? Is everything . . . okay with you?"

"Yeah. Yeah, 'course it is. I'm home now. Everything's fine."

"How's things with Noreen?"

"Ahhh . . . okay I guess. I think . . . we're supposed to be having this talk. I think . . . I think I'm at . . . I think we're at, I mean, some kind of crossroads in our . . . relationship. She, ahhh . . . she's been seeing someone else a little."

Petey's eyebrows jump, but he still can't hide the smirk that comes into his eyes whenever Noreen is mentioned.

"She *has?*"

"Yeah. Well, we had this talk a few months ago. I mean, I hadn't been home in so long and all, and . . . you know . . . we both decided while I was gone we'd kind of . . . maybe see other people a little. Just to be . . . sure I guess. I mean, neither one of us has ever really gone out with . . . anyone else."

"Wow. You know I saw her a few months ago waiting for the bus and she was actually nice to me. She goes to school now, huh?"

"Yeah. Full-time this year, she got a scholarship and everything. She wants to go to law school after she gets her degree."

"Wow. Good for her."

Petey starts laughing.

"What's so funny?"

"Sorry, Danny. I just had this image of Noreen down on the ground in court with her teeth affixed to a witness's ankle."

"Petey, you don't . . . stutter so much anymore."

"I know it," Petey beams. "Everyone says that. I still do a little but . . . I don't know, it's weird. I guess . . . I guess I've never been h-happier. I s'pose that has something to do with it. After . . . after like what you said to me and everything, and getting sober, and talking about, being able to talk about all the shit I kept bottled up for so long. And then Paul and all . . . I just feel so . . . I dunno. I have to pinch myself sometimes."

I almost close my eyes at the ache in my heart. Now my tongue grows eager, profligate. I want to tell Petey things, tell him everything, all the ideas swirling around in my head, my new vocabulary words, these new ideas springing up, my dreams, can't think of anything else I'd rather do.

But—

His last words seal my decision. Again, the Spirit of the Corps—you can't understand it unless you've been there yourself—rises up in me. To stow it away for the sake of another.

But at this same time, now that I realize I won't be . . . doing anything with Petey tonight, I understand that so much of what I want now in life seems to be contained within this room. Like the full moon rising, gleaming brighter, as the sun sets. Grabbing for it as it rises beyond my reach. Human nature? Just wanting what's been withdrawn? Well, maybe a little. But not entirely.

"If you want to stick around for a little while, Danny, you might get to meet him," Petey says, sitting back against the headboard and yawning.

My God, he's handsome.

"Ahh . . . Paul, you mean?"

"Yeah," Petey says. "He . . . stops over sometimes after work."

Petey flushes up again. Oh Christ—

"Oh," I say, standing up so fast Petey jumps a little, "I don't want to like . . . intrude or anything."

"Intrude? Danny, stop it. I just . . . I'd really like you guys to get to know each other."

As if on cue, I hear the top step creak out in the hall. Shit—

There's a light rap on the door—shave and a haircut, two bits—and then the door opens. I'm glad I'm standing. Paul's eyes jump from Petey to me. For a moment his eyebrows bunch together. Then something like recognition flashes in them.

"Hey, Paul—" Petey begins, but at the same time Paul breaks out into one of the warmest smiles I've seen and says,

"Oh, you must be . . . Danny? Right?"

I nod and raise my hand to his extended one. A good strong grip. Did I think it would be otherwise? He's tall, about 6'1", with dirty blond hair medium length and bright blue eyes. He brings a spritz of the mid-September night's freshness into the room with him. He's wearing a brown plaid woolen flannel shirt-jacket, faded jeans, and hiking boots. Oh please, this is the fucking city, not Maine—

"Yeah, Danny O'Connor, and you're Paul. Nice to meet you, I've heard a lot of good things about you."

"Same here, Danny. Hey there!" Paul says, making a fist and lightly punching one of Petey's feet at the end of the bed. I can't help but watch the look they give each other. Oh Christ—

Keep your eyes to yourself! Get your OWN boyfriend! I hear in my head, dialogue from Ma's movie melodrama when I was a kid—

Paul plops down at the end of the bed, turns back to me.

"Yeah, Petey said you were due back tonight—he hasn't talked about much else lately."

The look again between them. Petey looks so happy I think he might burst.

"Oh, yeah, well, I just got back. Thought I'd stop and surprise Petey—"

He has no idea the surprise he was almost in for.

"I've been wanting you guys to meet for the longest time," Petey says, sitting up in the bed Indian style. "I didn't know it would h-happen so soon! My lucky night! Jolly Olly Orange!"

Petey and Paul laugh but I grimace.

"So you're a JP guy?" I ask Paul.

"Yeah," he nods. "Though someone's trying to turn me into a Southie boy with all this talk of the ocean. I've been over there for about three years now."

"Where from originally?" I ask. A petty part of me wants to dislike this paragon, this beekeeper, this worker of wood. But so far I can't—you can tell with some people—a good, good man, this Paul.

"Danny, grab that chair," Petey says, turning around and pointing to the green tipply one in the corner. Then he stops when he sees my jacket lying on it.

He turns his head back to me—

His mouth is open, the ol' Petey-whack look on his face.

His eyes shift, look away. Paul doesn't notice.

"Upstate New York originally," Paul prattles on. "Lived in New York City for a while before heading up here."

"You like Boston?"

"Yeah, love it. Even became a Red Sox fan!"

He points to the cap on his head.

"Even got Petey to go to a game with me last week."

"Really!" I say, laughing. "Hmph. That was more than I could ever do."

"You never asked," Petey says. I turn and look at him. His face has changed. Does he mean more?

"Hey, you guys hungry at all?" Paul asks. "There's this cool diner I know in Dorchester, open all night."

"Oh no, no thanks, I need to get going anyway," I lie. "Kinda jet-lagged."

"Ma'am's got soda bread downstairs she left for us," Petey sotto voces to Paul, and it's this more than anything—I gotta get out of here—

"Well," I say, rising. "It was . . . it was great meeting you, Paul. Hopefully we'll see you soon."

Paul stands up, shakes my hand again. "Sorry you have to take off so soon. Yeah, did you tell him about Saturday night?"

"Ahh, no, I didn't get the chance," Petey answers. Petey still looks like he's been thinking of something, but that look comes back into his eyes when he answers Paul. Ouch.

"I'm having a little cookout in your honor," Paul says to me. "Saturday night. If you're not busy. Just me and Petey and another friend or two. Can you make it?"

"Ahh, ahh, Saturday night, ahh, yeah, yeah I think I can make it." Shit.

"Great! Petey'll give you directions. See you there then!"

"Okay," I say, nodding and smiling. "Great to meet you, Paul."

"Same here, Danny. See you Saturday."

"Don't forget your coat, Danny," Petey says.

With feeling.

He reaches over and grabs it, then stands up from the bed and hands it to me.

Paul, facing Petey's back, lavishes his eyes up and down Petey's bare torso. Paul's eyes are full of softness, expectation—and clearly, love.

"Thanks, Petey. Great to see you."

"Same here, Danny."

I extend my hand and we shake.

"Call me tomorrow," Petey says.

"I will."

I make a little wave, then leave the room.

I shut the door *click* behind me.

I so want to listen outside the door, but I don't dare. I head down the stairs but can't remember that. I grab my duffel bag off the parlor rug and head outside. I stumble down the front stairs. There's a cartoon character I resemble now but I can't put my finger on exactly which.

I find that I'm shaking my head out on the sidewalk. I look up at the sky. It's gone gray. I push away a billion Petey memories.

I walk up to the corner, then an idea hits me. I have a need to . . . what was it Petey said the night of the prom? Dig the blade a little deeper. Like Miss Havisham, I occasionally have sick fancies and now I have a fancy that I should like to see someone make love.

I chuck my bag into some bushes, put a spell on it so no one steals it (an old Petey trick that always seems to work), then head down O Street. I hop the first alley fence I come to, then move down the narrow alley, stealthily. I stop halfway, almost beneath Petey's bedroom window. A breath vaults out of me.

I stand and watch for a bit. God, I must be one sick bastard.

The ache inside me becomes almost unbearable. I remind myself that if I truly love Petey, I should be happy for his happiness.

I convince myself that I am.

I shove my hands in my pockets and lean my back against the fence behind me. I start getting cold so I turn up the collar of my jacket. Time goes by.

He knows something now, part of me says. *When he saw your jacket over the chair, he knew you were the one that had been kissing him. You saw how quiet he got after that.*

I'm not going to sacrifice his happiness for my indecision.

Indecision? But then I silence the voice inside.

A light comes on quick from a different part of the house and stabs into my eyes. I duck. It's the kitchen.

If I move just a little I can see them. From the waist up. Petey and Paul— and it hits me now how well that sounds together—are standing by the kitchen counter, wreaking havoc on the soda bread. Petey still has his shirt off, but is wearing his old fluffy robe, though it's open. Paul is naked it looks like—being taller, the top part of his waist rises above the counter just a little. His nipples are large and fleshy looking, and swirled with hair. This is wrong, almost morbid, I tell myself, but I can't stop watching. They're talking and laughing. At one point Paul holds up his glass to Petey's mouth. They exchange a long look as Petey gulps milk. The look finishes in a goofy laugh. Then Paul pulls Petey into him. He traces a few errant drops of milk across Petey's mouth. I gasp, start shaking. They kiss.

I mean, they really kiss.

It's the first time I've seen anything like this kind of male bonding, except for once or twice in a movie, and I remember how everyone in attendance groaned and the men made noises of disgust. But then, I now realize, we all felt we had to. It starts raining, and the wind puffs up. I huddle up my shoulders. I can't stop watching. It's beautiful, they're beautiful. I dare anyone to tell me this isn't beautiful. The light around them. The kitchen light reflecting off their mingled hair, dark and blond.

Paul puts his arms around Petey and lifts him onto the counter. I notice now that I can see them in the reflection of the glass cabinet across from them. Paul is naked. Petey is as well except for the robe that's now wide open, spilling off his shoulders. Paul runs his head down the front of Petey, up and down, ravenous. Petey's hands wrap around Paul's head. Paul's head goes lower, into Petey's groin.

I find that I'm shaking again.

I run my hand down to my dick. It's there alright, but . . . well, not exactly at full tilt. But I've never felt so moved in my life. Or so devastated.

I pull some kind of semblance of dignity around myself and lurch home.

Ma is waiting up for me of course and it's great to see her. She wakes Dad up, and the three of us sit up until two talking and eating cake. Her last breakdown hooked her up with a very good therapist and now she herself is in a program for people who grew up in alcoholic homes.

Surely there must be a program somewhere with my name on it. It's the thing to do now apparently and no arguing with the results.

It's nice to have some form of love in my life that is unchanging, unchangeable. When Dad brings up Noreen, Ma takes his hand in hers, kisses it lovingly, then says, "Honey, I don't think there's a thing we can tell Danny. He's his own man now."

Dad smiles, nods his head. Me, I almost have to ask for the smelling salts.

"Have some more cake, honey," Ma says, sliding another slice in my direction. "I'm going to bed. I have yoga in the morning."

Under the Boardwalk, Down by the Sea

Petey calls me Saturday morning.

"I thought you were going to call me yesterday?"

"Oh, ahh, I tried, but there was no answer. I tried you a bunch of times."

I did, too.

"Oh sorry, I was in and out all day. Meeting last night. So what are you up t-to?"

"Just hanging, really. Went out last night to see some of the old gang."

"Have fun?"

"I guess," I say.

"You okay, Danny?" Petey asks.

"Yeah. Yeah, sure I am. Just a little tired."

"Wanna take a walk down to the island?"

I stop for a minute. For a second I'm back there, back to the day of me and Petey; then I remember.

"Uhm . . . sure. Okay."

"Alright. Fifteen minutes? Our place?"

Our place.

"Sure."

We meet down at the beach. The day is warm for September and brilliant, a gleam to the sea and sky that only early fall can infuse. I get there first, sit on the seawall. I see Petey trotting down Farragut Road, a medium-size dog in tow. His face lights up when he sees me, as always.

But this time everything's different.

Smiling at him as he crosses the street seems like the hardest thing I've done. But I am happy for him, I am. It's me I'm miserable for. He's wearing what one would deem normal clothes today: baggy tan chino shorts and a light blue sweatshirt. I sigh thankfully when he gets closer and I spy with

A Map of the Harbor Islands
Published by The Haworth Press, Inc., 2006. All rights reserved.
doi:10.1300/5677_23

my little eye that both garments are logo free. I realize this is pure pettiness on my part: I am concerned less for the people in sweatshops than I am for Petey, and whether he has changed that much or not. *My* Petey doesn't support sweatshops. *My* Petey would never turn his body into a walking talking billboard—

"This is Trotsky," Petey says, grabbing onto my forearm in salutation. "Self-explanatory I trust if you noticed the funny gait on h-him."

"Hello, Trotsky," I coo, squatting down and subjecting myself to a bombardment of face licks.

"He likes you," Petey says.

"But then again why wouldn't he?" I joke, still squatting. I put on my shades.

"Why wouldn't he i-indeed," Petey says, and, my pettiness again, I'm glad to hear Petey stutter. Not so good!

"Shall we?" I ask, tilting my head toward the island.

"I want to ask you something, Danny," Petey says when we reach the gazebo, the halfway point in our Pleasure Bay walk. There's been a thoughtful quietness about us today. And not quite as much bounce to Petey as there was the other night.

I tighten up. I know what it is. And I know what my answer will be.

"Shoot." I shove my hands in my pockets.

Petey stops, leans his arms against the chain-link fence, stares out at the Harbor Islands. Well, what better place than this to give him his life back? Trotsky obediently sits, and looks up with Petey with beseeching eyes liquid with adoration.

"I'm . . . I'll only ask you once, Danny. Just a simple yes-no q-question. It might sound stupid."

Petey turns quick to me, tiny-smiles, then looks away.

"Okay."

I sneak a deep breath through my nose.

We have to wait a minute until the Barrys walk by, Mr. and the Mrs. They extend their well-wishes at seeing me again. For the first time I can recall, Petey adds quite a bit to this conversation of rich, satisfying banalities.

"Okay," Petey says when they shove off into the wind. "I keep thinking—I k-keep thinking about something, and the more I think about that something, the more I think about . . . s-some other stuff. About . . . like, the night of the pr-prom and everything, and then . . . how you came back the next day before you left and told me that you . . . that you loved me."

Petey gulps. His eyes swell.

If he doesn't look at me—I pray to Mary, Ever Virgin, that he doesn't look at me—maybe I can get through this.

"Okay," he says, more to himself. He takes a deep breath. He keeps his eyes out at sea.

"Did you . . . Danny, the other night when you came into my r-room. You didn't . . . by any chance . . . kiss me? When I was sl-sleeping?"

"No," I say, immediately, decisively, staring out at the islands. We're both in fact staring out at the islands.

I don't even have to think about this. They teach you some good things in the Marines. Falsehood isn't one of them but nobility is. Sacrifice. I have nothing to offer Petey but my indecision and confusion.

I won't do this to him.

Petey nods his head. I put my arm around him.

"I'll always be your best friend," I say to him, coming in close to his ear. I want to stay like this but I can't. "I'll always be your best friend."

"Bestest," Petey says. He sniffles as he turns away and we resume our walk.

Petey is much more relaxed, or maybe resigned is a better word, when I pick him up for Paul's cookout Saturday night. He's wearing a navy blue turtleneck and light chino pants, and, incredibly, a whiff of cologne fills Dad's car as he steps inside.

"The Mr. O'Connor mobile!" Petey says, looking around.

"I guess I've finally arrived," I laugh.

"You look nice, Danny," he says, fastening up his seat belt.

"Thanks. You too."

Petey tosses a little knapsack into the backseat. His overnight bag I suppose.

This afternoon's heaviness between us seems to have blown away, and soon we're back to our old selves—laughing, Petey going on and on about something, being absurd one moment, shy the next. But there's something new here too—a self-confidence, a strength. We're both trying desperately to scratch out some new turf between us, to take and occupy a hill that belongs only to him and me. And we succeed, thanks be to God. Thanks to the love that glows between us.

As we pass through Southie, Petey points out the trees that are thriving now thanks to his tree personals, the signs here and there proclaiming the *gift of God's homosexuality,* the general location of his new secret garden on the West Side which he promises to take me to while I'm home.

Petey gets us lost, but eventually we slide up in front of a grand old Jamaica Plain Victorian that's been split up, Petey says, into three condos. A spectacular twilight of blue velvet and vermilion frames the sky behind the house. Two gaslights throw the front of the building into regal, welcoming repose. The landscaping out front is beautiful, wildflowers and exotic shrubbery and ornamental grasses. Rough stone steps glistening with mica twirl up to a grand double front door, painted plum. Pumpkins, cornstalks, and bright chrysanthemums and asters adorn the two sides of the door.

"Your work?" I ask.

Petey smiles, nods. "And Paul too," he says.

I nod. I made the right decision this afternoon. I could never compete with this. Petey deserves this. Plus I still drink. Not much but enough I presume to rattle the recovering alcoholic's mojo.

Paul opens the door before we reach it, smiling that Upstate smile. This time he and Petey kiss lightly on the lips and half embrace when they greet each other. I get the firm handshake again from Paul. Inside, his place is full of wood and books and plants and music, and the smells of good food. How wonderful for Petey. A place to heal, love, and grow.

After a quick tour—I look away as we sweep past Paul's bedroom, where Petey will spend this night in tangled wonder—we are brought down the cellar stairs and out back to the patio/garden area. There are three other people here, two women and a man.

"No!" the two women gasp in unison at something the man is saying, and then their eyes fall upon us as we appear.

The man is handsome, dark straight hair cut rather expensively, a black turtleneck and black chinos. One of the women is blonde and willowy with a fantastic laugh. The other is shorter with shoulder-length brown hair and a bright smile.

I'm introduced all round and they all stand up. Petey knows these people already and he hugs them all warmly.

"This is my best friend, Danny," he says when he's through, slowly, simply, proudly, with a flourish and a wave, and an arm around my shoulder. My eyes fill up despite my mortification, and I pray that the fading light hides this.

"Welcome home," the man says, gleaming a smile. If it wasn't for the softness in his eyes his grin would look flashy.

"Thanks," I say, sitting down at a round wooden table. Above our heads is a kind of trellised pergola, drenched in grapevines. About half of the grapes are a deep purple, the rest somewhere between green and purple.

One of the women, the brunette, is a military brat who grew up ten miles from Parris Island, and we talk about that for a bit. Paul scurries off, then comes back with a bottle of wine and glasses. He and Petey stick to apple juice of course, but the wine is poured out for the rest of us, which surprises me. The table we're sitting at is surrounded by a swath of lawn; beyond lies an amazing garden falling in layers. In the middle of this is the water garden Petey spoke of, a small pond with a waterfall pouring in at one end. The fading light picks up the shimmering gold of the fish bobbing in it. Behind are woods, and though one knows they can't be too large here in the semicity, the illusion is that they are. Paul's beehives stand at the border of the woods. In the crystalline late-September night air, the trees are utterly still, soaring, Druidic and numinous.

Petey must have thought he died and went to heaven when he saw this place. Garden torches flicker here and there around the yard, and the ones closest to the woods half-illumine bird houses and feeders in amazing shapes and structures, some with minaret towers, some like alpine chalets, some onion-domed like Russian churches that the full moon fell upon in Petey's dreams and visions.

"Paul carves them all by hand," Petey mumbles, seeing where my eyes are going.

Oh yeah, I definitely did the right thing. My last hobby was stamp collecting and I sold them all for coke dough when I was sixteen.

A string of blue Christmas lights embedded in the grapes glows from the underside of the pergola over our heads. Soon the air is rife with laughter and the smell of grilling meats and vegetables. Petey comes in and out, helping Paul, then running back to me to make sure, I know, that I'm okay. I discover that Margaret and Jackie, the two women, are a couple—after I ridiculously ask Brian, the man, which one of the women he is with. Duh.

"Brian's next time with a woman will be his first time," Margaret quips, putting her arm around Jackie, and then they coo in mock sympathy when Petey points out how red I'm turning. My faux pas is forgotten, and something comes out of the darkness and finds us, something of comfort and hospitality and openness. The faces around me grow brighter, and something inside flashes back in sympathy, and is met, and embraced. This kind of feeling can be hard to find in the Marines, only the deathbed and the sickbed bringing it, alas.

A chill freshens the air as the night progresses and several well-dried split logs get chucked into the chiminea just as dinner is served. The smell of burning, snap-crackling wood mingles with the aroma of food and the combination is, to me, almost unendurably poignant. The orange light caresses the faces of Petey, Paul, Brian, Margaret, Jackie—this all smells and looks like nothing else but the grace of God's love. Either that or a photo shoot for Smith and Hawken.

"I like to serve everything at once," Paul grins, weighing down the table with dish after dish as the crowd coos. The eats are covered with Irish linen dish cloths and this declares the love that has gone into this evening as much as anything—or Paul's anal-retentive, obsessive-compulsive side. Oh knock it off, I self-chide.

"Okay, what's the theme tonight?" Margaret asks, putting her hand up to her chin inquisitively. Our eyes meet and she smiles, leans forward. "Paul's always got a theme going, and you kind of have to guess it from the food he serves."

There are roasted Cornish game hens, piles of garlic mashed potatoes, a wild green salad in a honey-vinegarish dressing, homemade macaroni and cheese with wheat berries (Petey's protein dish, Jackie tells me), and three different kinds of homemade bread.

"Everything from the garden, I trust?" Jackie asks, raising one eyebrow.

"Of course," Petey answers smugly.

"You have cows back there?" Brian, next to me, asks. No one responds.

"Hmmm," says Margaret. "Homecoming?"

"Yes," Paul says, setting the last dish on the table, a steaming bowl of pumpkin leek soup. He remains standing and grabs and raises his glass. "Harvest and homecoming. Here's to Danny—welcome home."

"Welcome home, welcome home," everyone says, clinking away, and the smile on my face is almost as involuntary as the one when Petey first woke up the other night. I can't believe they would do this for me. Before we plunge into the food Petey says grace, in Irish; his latest foray down the road of spirituality is ancient Celtic Christianity, and for the first part of the meal he waxes poetic about the rites and rituals, the wisdom and vitality, the connectedness and love of the Old Ways.

He is as close to mesmerizing as I've ever heard him, and a wonderful discussion follows about what we all believe in. When it comes to my turn I request directions to the bathroom.

The food is eaten slowly and lovingly. Margaret and Jackie tell the story of the time they came to visit Paul one lazy August afternoon and Paul, his nose in a woodworking book, took a bite of his sandwich with a bee on top, and promptly danced around the yard for the next several minutes, gripping his mouth with both hands and completely unintelligible. Brian talks about how much he misses nights like these in California, where he lives now. There's some kind of dynamic between him and Paul, and I find out later they are ex-lovers from college. I don't at all feel like the odd man .out—surely these are some of the nicest people I've ever met. In response to their questions I tell them about my librarian duties and life in general in the Corps.

"And when are you out for good?" Jackie asks.

"Six months," I say.

"And what then?"

Out of the edge of my eye I see Petey turn and look at me.

"Ahhh . . . not quite sure yet," I answer, looking down into my empty wineglass, which Brian then fills for me.

The dessert is a homemade raspberry-chocolate torte, we're told. Written in white chocolate shavings is *Welcome Home Danny.* The more I look at and watch Paul, the more impressed I become with him, with all of them. By and by Margaret and Jackie have to leave. There's a concert they're heading to at a lounge in Cambridge, and they decamp with assurances they'll see me again. I would like that, to know women without the usual jockeying for position and sexual innuendo, or lack thereof. Petey and Paul clear the table. I try to help but am firmly reprimanded. Brian and I start talking, and soon our chairs are facing each other. He's half-Italian and half-Irish, though I'm not sure exactly how that comes out. He says he has a brother whose hair is as red as mine. Petey, momentarily back, talks about the Celtic blood that runs through almost all of the peoples in Europe, and how the Celts were in many ways the aborigines of Europe.

"He's something, isn't he?" Brian asks, nodding his head after Petey as the latter vanishes inside the cellar door again.

"Petey?" I ask. "Yeah. Yeah, you could say that."

I launch into a Petey-diatribe, bell-tower-ringing, for spacious-skying, map-making, then Petey comes back with Paul in tow, bearing steaming chai tea, and I drop the subject.

"Paul is just an incredible guy too," I add when Petey and Paul disappear once more, saying they forgot the fruit compote.

Brian nods, looks down, crosses his legs.

"Yup."

He looks back up at me, knowing what I want to ask.

"My company transferred me to California," he says. "A year and a half ago."

He leans back in his chair, plays with a tassel on the end of a grapevine over us. "We tried to do the long-distance thing but it just didn't work."

"Nice that you two are still friends though."

"Oh yeah. You know what they say. Boyfriends come and go but exes are forever."

No actually I didn't know that.

Is that what me and Petey are? Exes?

After the tea and fruity thing, the four of us really talk. Paul comes out with sweatshirts for all at one point. They have a great smell to them. Eventually our talk winds down. We're left in the afterglow of a night that is so much more than the sum of its parts. I decide to leave at the perfect moment—and before it becomes obvious that Petey and Paul wish to be alone now.

"Well," I sigh. "It's . . . getting late. I better hit the road. I can't remember when I felt more at ease, more . . . "

"At home?" Petey asks. Ironically enough.

I smirk and nod my head. Petey reaches out his two hands, one to me and one to Paul. Paul reaches out his hand to Brian, then Brian to me, and we sit like this for a moment, hand in hand. I'm alternately shocked and profoundly touched, a soothing hand dispensing an electrical jolt.

With a squeeze, we all release at the same time. I stand. Somehow in the past three days I have moved very far away from thinking of myself as a Marine. But thus far I have nothing to replace this with.

Petey and Paul and Brian rise up from the table, Paul with a stretch, a yawn, and an apology.

"He was up at s-six getting this ready," Petey says proudly, elbowing Paul lightly in the side.

I won't look at Petey. I don't want to embarrass him into saying that he doesn't need a ride home, though of course there's nothing wrong with that. And of course there's everything wrong with that too.

"I can't thank you enough, Paul. Really. I'm very touched by all you've done tonight."

"It was my pleasure, Danny. I feel like I've known you forever from all Petey's said about you. I know I'll be seeing you again soon."

I finally turn to Petey.

"Good night, Petey, and thanks for everything."

"Thank you, Danny," he says, standing up and embracing me. Oh God, don't let me lose it right here. My prayer is answered, relief coming in the realization, again, that I did indeed do the right thing in letting Petey go. I can't even imagine a better situation for him to be in right now, even if I can imagine a better one for me. Sort of.

"Hey, would it be an incredible pain in the butt to drop me off on the way home?" Brian says, also rising. I don't realize he's talking to me until I see Petey and Paul looking at me. I've duhhed for a minute.

"In California? Well yeah, that's a little out of the way," I joke. As it turns out Paul is staying with his sister in Dorchester, which is, in fact, precisely on the way home.

Petey and Paul are enclasped at the front door as we pull away. It seems I've been transported into the future—so much has changed in the three days that I've been home. Having the company is actually a good thing, and I find Brian a comforting presence, even though we don't say much.

We're barreling along on Gallivan Boulevard when I lose it, totally—no warning signs, no sudden aches. I just open my mouth to pass along a pleasant nothing and a sob spurts out instead. Then another, and another. I have to cut down a side street and pull over. Brian bolts up in his seat, turns and gawks, as well he might. A clean Marine having a mini-breakdown in his presence.

"Sorry," I manage to get out. These are choking sobs that kill on the way out. Eventually I just say fuck it and let them come out. It's such a release and, though embarrassing, I'll never see this guy again.

A tentative hand finds my shoulder and soon we are hugging.

"S'okay, s'okay," he soothes.

"Yeah, yeah," I answer.

A few deep breaths and the squall passes as quickly as it descended. I open my eyes and see the reflection of Brian and me hugging in the passenger window. I pull back, resume my seat.

"Whoa," I sigh. A strange something—between a hiccough, a laugh, and sob—flies out of my mouth, signaling the end of this.

I don't apologize. Brian looks out his window, looks back at me. His right knee begins bouncing. A brownish yellow leaf flutters down from the tree we're parked under.

I sling the car back into drive, bang a U-ey, pull back out onto the boulevard.

"It's the second left," Brian says quietly after a few blocks.

"Alrighty."

Brian looks ahead, then turns back to me, a man who has made up his mind. There's this sound of decision out of him, a half-grunt.

"You love him?" he asks. His eyes have grown larger.

"What are you talking about?"

"Petey."

I put my other hand on the steering wheel, open my mouth to lie, then say fuck it.

"Yeah."

I turn, regard him. His head has lowered a bit. There's an animal glow in his cheeks. The space between us seems to have shrunk. He looks different this close, the dark eyebrows more pronounced, the eyes, which were black earlier, ringed now in a hazel green.

"Can you keep—can I . . . I really don't want Petey knowing this. Or Paul."

"No problem," he says lowly. The stare of him.

I turn away.

"It's this house up here, the white one."

We slide up in front of a Cape, set back from the road. There are sham-rock cutouts on the green shutters. It's a very late fifties, suburban-looking neighborhood for Dorchester. St. Mark's Parish I think. In Dorchester you go by the parish, don'cha know. There's a Mary-on-the-half-shell in the yard next door, and someone's gotten an early start on their Halloween dec-orating. But Brian's sister's house is as loosely, lusciously landscaped as Paul's. A kind of enclosed welcoming area has been built out from the front door, a transom light over it. The front walk is not flagstone but real Quincy fieldstone. On both sides of the walk, a four-foot-wide border of perennials, of all mixed heights and textures, runs out to the street. Up against the house are holly and hemlock. In front of these, smaller shrubs mixed with annuals and perennials.

"Gives me something to do when I come home," Brian says, seeing what I'm looking at.

"It's very homely," I say, meaning to say homey of course. I correct my-self, shut the car off.

"So," he says. He unbuckles his seat belt and twists toward me. He makes that nervous tic sound of his again. The car, my dad's and ergo a big-ass 'merican one, shifts a bit as Brian does. He's a big boy, powerfully built. I was expecting something else?

"Petey . . ."

I sigh.

"In the beginning there was Petey. One of my first memories is Petey sit-ting in his tiny desk in kindergarten and me walking in the door. He was smiling at me when I looked at him. Like he'd been waiting for me. In a way we've been together since. You probably don't know this, but Petey was what you might call a child prodigy."

"How do you mean?"

I don't answer at first, thinking how he still is—

"The Golden Boy, that's what his nickname was around town. You know those kids—everything they touch turns to gold. Star athlete, straight-A student, polite, social—but without the . . . insight, I guess I'd call it, that he has now. That . . . penetrating way about him. He—had this accident."

No need to go into details.

"Anyway—I . . . I got involved with my girlfriend and all that, and in a way we drifted apart but in another way we never did. There was always Petey. Like there's always God or something. Always there. Always . . . different and . . . Petey. The last time I was home we . . . well, it seems like I was a different person then and maybe in some ways I was. But I . . . something almost happened between us."

"Something . . . physical?"

"Ahhh . . . yeah. But it didn't feel right. But—"

I turn to Brian, look into his eyes. Yes, I think I can tell him.

"The thing is, I . . . when I'm with Petey, it feels like home. That's the only way I know how to describe it. I just feel . . . utterly myself, utterly . . . loved. Unconditionally. The Harbor Islands, for years we went out to the Harbor Islands when we were kids, and . . . "

I decide to cut to the chase.

"I've been thinking about this a lot, the last year, how . . . I feel about Petey. I'm not afraid of that at all. Well anymore maybe. And I decided that when I came home this time . . . I would . . . I kinda had this plan that we would . . . that I'd—just so I could find out, I decided I would—"

"Sleep with him?"

There's a sound in the car. At first I don't realize it's a gasp out of me.

"Well . . . not . . . maybe. I couldn't really think that far ahead. I just thought that I would . . . kiss him. Kiss him and . . . just see what that felt like. See if . . . he was someone I could also . . . I wasn't sure if I could really be with—"

"So instead, you come home and find he's with someone else."

"Yeah. Yeah. Someone I wanted to hate really but how could anyone dislike Paul? Unless for the simple reason that he's so—unhateable."

I feel myself blushing. Well, whatever. I guess it's one thing to tell yourself something, another thing to tell someone else.

"Well, I guess that's one thing we have in common anyway," Brian sighs. "Hopefully it didn't show tonight."

"What didn't show?"

"I'm still—I still have feelings for Paul. I still love him and wanted to hate Petey. It's been nothing but all Petey all the time since they met."

"So why'd you leave, Paul?"

Try as I might, there's a trace of blame in my voice.

"When I got transferred to California I wanted him to follow me. Prove his love and all that. When I finally realized I needed him, I called him up to tell him I was chucking my job and my fabulous California lifestyle and coming home, and the first thing out of his mouth is this new guy he's met."

"You didn't tell him?"

"No."

A pause.

"And you didn't tell Petey."

"No."

Brian stretches his long legs out, leans back, sighs. He turns to me.

"It must . . . I can't imagine what that must be like, not knowing."

Brian's voice, he's closer now—it's syrupy is what it is. Uh-oh.

There's some kind of shift in the air—and I realize I am about to be seduced by another guy. Or at least, he will try to seduce me. A part of me inches closer to my side of the car but at the same time there's a tingle under my tongue.

"Do you . . . I mean, other than Petey do you ever find yourself . . . "

"No. No, I'm not . . . gay or anything. No offense."

Brian makes a face.

"None taken."

"But I might be . . . bi. Bisexual. Or at least when it comes to Petey. I don't know, this sucks."

Brian looks away first. He runs his teeth over his lower lip. His nose has a tiny bump in it near the top. Brian has balls. He turns back to me, waits until I turn to him.

"I think . . . maybe I could help you." There's a smile at the corner of his mouth. It's definitely not a leer.

I hear myself gulp.

"And you could help yourself while you're helping me?" I ask.

His eyebrows bunch.

"Sorry. Old Southie saying. We joke when we don't know what else to say."

"I don't want to be alone tonight," Brian says flatly.

There's something in the way he says it. *This is who I am right now. This is how I feel.*

I keep my eyes on a mailbox three houses up while I say, "I can't Brian. .It's . . . I'm sorry. It's not you, you're a . . . you're a great-looking guy."

I look at him. His eyes hold mine. He nods.

"Well. I understand."

"I wish I did," I mumble.

I insert my baby finger into my mouth, gnaw down on the nail.

"My sister and her family are gone for the weekend," Brian says. He leans forward, reaches into the back of his slacks. He takes out a sleek, unlumpy wallet. Extracts a card, hands it to me.

"Call me if you change your mind," he says. "I'm home until Wednesday."

He smiles weakly, gets out of the car.

"Nice meeting you," he says as he walks away. "Good luck."

"Same here."

"Thanks for the ride. And ahhh . . . my lips are sealed, don't worry."

"I appreciate that."

It might be four miles as the crow flies, maybe five, from where I am to home. But tonight it's a very long drive. When I get back to Southie I head all the way up the Boulevard. I turn around at Castle Island, then drive down the Boulevard again, the ocean a blacker mass beside me. Several miles more and I'm back down at the rotary. I turn around again, come back the way I came. We called this Boulevardiering when we were sixteen and first licensed, driving up and down along the margin of the ocean for the sheer thrill of it.

I pass a bank of phones huddled together in the night like they're cold. Brian's simple eloquence haunts me: *I don't want to be alone tonight.*

Neither do I, kiddo. I could always go to Noreen's, but—

She doesn't know that I'm home yet. And who knows if she's even home. And anyhow been there, done that, something else inside me tonight—

I drive by the phones but can't seem to drive by Brian's words. Too, it's impossible to be by the ocean here and not think of Things Petey, and then it hard-hits what Petey's probably doing now. Petey and Paul.

I close my eyes and moan at the pain I feel inside. I stop the car, swing over, turn around. I pull into a parking space right beside the phone bank. Four phones. Beside them, a bench, covered with a green-tiled roof. These line the Boulevard/beach area every hundred yards or so. I become aware that fifty yards down on the other side is the Carson Beach parking lot, where guys go to . . . where the guys go. Came here myself that night I did.

I don't want to be alone tonight.

The thing is, I've never felt so alone.

"Skovo, guide me," I writhe-whisper.

I reach into Dad's ashtray, where he keeps his toll change. I pull out a few quarters and dimes.

I get out of the car. It's midnight on a Saturday night. I'm about to do something I've never done before. I reach into my pants pocket, pull out Brian's card. BRIAN MURPHY, VICE PRESIDENT OF MARKETING. The company is called Accu-Pro or Accu-Comp or something and they are all about Designing Software Strategies for an International Clientele blah blah blah. I hold it between my thumb and forefinger. I bring it onto the bench with me beside the phone bank. If I do this, I will no longer be able to hide behind the love I feel for Petey in justifying my . . . longing, if a longing it is.

"I don't want to be alone," I mutter. We won't do anything. Maybe we won't do anything and just sleep beside each other. But how weird is that? I don't even know him. He's a stranger to me and—

I don't see him until I stand up on my way to the phone. He's walking out from the parking lot. A nylon windbreaker snapping in the wind. His head down a bit, hands jammed into his pockets. A baseball cap pulled low, jeans, sneakers. His medium-length hair breeze-blown.

He stops when he sees me, but only for a moment. But that's enough. I pick up the phone so as not to look like an idiot, so as not to stare. But I am staring.

He chooses an unseen path on the cement boardwalk and walks by me, but not without looking up as he passes. Our eyes crash for a second. His are swirly, scared. He's my age, maybe a few years younger.

"S'up," I say, the standard Southie greeting. He nods. The dial tone is roaring in my right ear.

He walks by the sheltered bench I've just vacated. He turns when he's maybe ten yards past it. I sense there is an abyss at his feet. He pauses. I nod at him. Why do I?

He stays frozen for a minute. Then he looks behind him at the empty night. He takes a long lean forward, then comes back in my direction.

He noiselessly sits down on the bench. At its far side from me. Takes off his ball cap restlessly, runs a hand through his hair, pulls the cap back on.

All in one fell swoop, a gesture he does often. He keeps his eyes forward, to the sea. He tucks his ankles under the bench. One knee begins bouncing.

I hang up the phone. I look at Brian's card again. A lick of restless sea air puffs it out of my hand. It falls to the ground, rests, then another gush-sigh laps at it and carries it some ten yards down the boardwalk. I don't give chase.

There's another invisible path before me as I walk toward him, a fork in the road actually. One path leads back to Dad's car right here, the other leads to . . . to. . . .

There's actually two benches here side by side, separated by an old green wooden post holding up the roof over the benches. There's rough graffiti carved into this post, initials and dates. I sit down on my side of the thin post.

His knee bouncing becomes furious now. He becomes aware of it, brings it to an abrupt halt. He's still looking forward, at the invisible sea.

My mind races along a corridor of pleasant little nothings, but some dignity within seals my lips. When I was a child . . .

He does the thing with his ball cap again. His hair is black, his eyes blue, the nose slightly pug. Irish as Paddy's pig. He turns quick and scrapes another look at me. I recall Mrs. H's words, how a child with one blue eye and one brown was snatched by the fairies when it was a babe. I wonder who's snatched this boy, fear in one eye, and some irrepressible fuse of desire in the other. More than desire. More than that kind of desire.

He slides down a little closer to me. It's the bravest thing he's ever done, I can tell. I slide up. Now there's just the post between us. He's still looking forward. He starts the knee bouncing again, then again abruptly stops. A party ferry boat slides across the harbor, maybe half a knot away. Its retro dance music bounces and chops across the water to us, sitting here in profound anticipation.

"'Come on Eileen,'" isn't it?" I mumble.

A quick smile splits his face, summons dimples. He does the hat thing again. An ache rises up in me. The world doesn't see those dimples I bet as much as it used to.

"D-Dexy's Midnight R-Runners," he says.

With a stutter.

I find my mouth is open.

I get up, smooth out imaginary wrinkles from my khakis. I walk by him, sit down right beside him on his other side. He's biting his lip, still looking forward.

I raise my right arm. He watches it peripherally as it goes around the back of him, comes to rest on his far shoulder. He jerks when I touch him.

"It's okay," I whisper.

His bottom lip is quivering. There's a smell off of him, beer. Of course.

I bring my other arm around him, pull him into me. A tsunami of tenderness rises within me, and I tell him what I should have told Petey years ago—

"It's okay, it's okay, this is how God made you. It's okay, you're so beautiful, so beautiful—"

A retch-sob cracks out of him. His arms encircle me, grab onto me. His cap falls off as we come together. I try to rub the trembles out of his young body.

"Oh Jesus," he whispers, and his words burn into my ears, sizzle.

A car roars by. He wants to break away but I won't let him. I think of the new recruitment poster that's been showing up on base lately, two Marines in full battle gear side by side, both toting guns. I shudder at how comfortable we are with this image, two men side by side holding guns. But put them holding each other and watch the shit hit the fan.

"It's okay, it's okay," I repeat, and then his hands are everywhere, and I know he must be with someone tonight or crash.

I pull him up, stand him up. I half push him down the beach. We're almost running. We duck behind the bathhouse, make for the wild sumacs growing at the end of the back wall. The fronds swipe my face as we duck into darkness. At some dark point we both stop as if it's been silently prearranged. Our choppy breaths entrain into one. I lean against the wall. He stands before me. We're staring into each other's eyes.

He takes the initiative and lightly pushes me against the wall, his hands on the front of my shoulders. His eyes, inches from mine, dart back and forth across my face. My eyes. My mouth.

"I d-d-don't know what to d-do," he chuckles in a whisper.

"I don't either," I chuckle back. "Just . . . do whatever you want."

And he does.

We both do.

Some minutes later my mostly naked body is thrusting back and forth and him on his knees before me. I don't know if it's the furtiveness or danger or something else, but when I bust my nut it seems the most intense I've experienced. But maybe they all seem that way, and us forgetting.

He's right before me and after a few squeal-like moans, I lean back against the wall and he, still sitting, leans his back against the red brick as well. Our breathing slows.

Jesus.

I expect some momentous sympathetic response from nature, as my own world slants and tumbles away from me, crashing.

But no, the breeze still puffs intermittently through the sumacs around us; the ocean twenty yards away sighs and laps. There's the vague tang of oil in the air, oil and sea breeze.

Of Balrogs and St. Brigid's

I lift and heave his bike into my trunk and give him a ride back to the West Side fifteen minutes later. Full of proselytizations and encouragements when we first met, I find that I'm tongue-tied now.

Sean—that's his name, he says after a pause and another tug at his Red Sox baseball cap—isn't shaking anymore, but I am. The pre-earthquake tremors I know so well, all that time in California don'cha know. I seem to have swallowed something jagged, unknown—all I can think of is when Pippin drops a stone into the well in Moria, and the Fellowship waits and waits for the inevitable crash of its landing as it plummets, deeper. Where's that crash? Whatever I swallowed, it's still falling and what kind of Balrog will it awaken from my depths?

But imploding is kindly waiting, while someone else is here with me.

"You can l-lemme out here," Sean says. Presumably we're a safe block or two from his house. He wipes the end of his nose on the sleeve of his thick gray sweatshirt, which I now see by the horrid 2:00 a.m. sodium streetlight spangle says BOSTON COLLEGE HIGH SCHOOL FOOTBALL. He's safe for the time being in his jock drag. Then again so am I—

While I can still half-think I jot down Petey's name and number and give it to him when I slide over to the curb. I throw the Dad-mobile into park but keep the engine running. I've gotta get out of here.

"Sean, I'm going back to California next week, where I live now. But listen, here's someone I want you to call. He's . . . gay. He's my best friend. He's one of the nicest people in the world. He's got a boyfriend who's also a nice guy. I want you to call him, tell him that you'd like to talk to him. Don't tell him where you got his number if he asks. Just say a friend. That's the only thing I ask of you—just don't tell him anything about me. Is that okay?"

A Map of the Harbor Islands
Published by The Haworth Press, Inc., 2006. All rights reserved.
doi:10.1300/5677_24

"Yeah. Sure."

I hand him the number and he studies it between rubbing fingers. What those fingers have just rubbed—

"He's . . . like us?" he mumbles, turning and looking at me. His blue eyes are lazy, casual, but really behind this hood they're like lasers, almost as blue as Petey's oldest brother Donnie's.

"Ahhh . . . he's gay. He can help you. Promise me. Promise me you'll call him."

"Alright."

For the second time tonight he smiles, weakly; then quick-nods.

"S-see ya then," he says, vaulting out of the car with a litheness so beautiful it hurts. One of the last jaguars on earth vanishing back into the night jungle and you know you'll never see the breath-snatching flash of it again. I want to call him back, tell him everything, empty my bank account so he can get counseling and move the fuck away from here and live in a house of flowers and birds and like-minded football buddies. But I can't. I begin imploding as he shuts the door and the bang of it echoes within me.

There's a pause as he hustles down the street.

Then the monster wakens.

It's fifteen minutes later—a fifteen minutes I'll never hopefully recall and wouldn't recount if I could. I still have Noreen's house key in my wallet and I find I'm standing at her front door, my breath coming in jagged rips. My hands are shaking, so much I almost can't get the key into the door of her house. I take off my shoes, carry them up the stairs to her bedroom. I softly pry open her door. Her perfume is different, lighter. Over a bentwood rocker beside her bed—new too—there's a pair of chinos, a black turtleneck sweater, a half-length tweed sportcoat. On the floor there's a pair of duck boots. She's gone yuppie and I begin to question my ability to perceive things correctly. Beside her bed on the nightstand is a pile of books, thick texts all in blue, black or red. On top of them is a pair of metal-rimmed glasses.

There's a million smells skanking off my body as I strip, some of them familiar, some of them as unknown as an exotic, incurable flu. I walk naked from her room into the bathroom, praying Mrs. Butler doesn't wake up but she never has in all the years I've done this. I rinse off quickly with a towel run under the sink's faucet. The idea of taking a shower right now, everything I would have to do, is beyond me.

I avoid myself in the mirror. I gag sympathetically when I see the toilet, but nothing comes up. I hunt for mouthwash, finally find it, gargle. I rub a bit of it on certain parts of my body. I pull my T-shirt and pants back on but my socks and underwear I strip into smaller pieces and flush them down the toilet. I just do. Whatever would Freud say?

When I get back into her room I let myself down on the edge of her bed. Slowly, slowly. Thank God thank God thank God thank God. Noreen. Perfume. A flannel nighty. I wait until my breath slows a bit. *He's like us?* but no don't go there, the muskiness no don't go there, the look in his eyes ditto.

"Noreen," I whisper, grabbing her ankle beneath the covers—can't wait anymore, "Noreen."

She sits bolt upright.

"Jesus Chri—"

I cover her mouth with my hand, which, I can only hope, is free of eau de ball-twang.

"It's me, Noreen, it's Danny. It's Danny. Danny. It's okay. I'm sorry I did this but I had to see you."

Her eyes slowly diminish in size and she begins to look less and less like an order of bloody murder to go. I slide my hand from her mouth.

"Jesus Christ, Danny! What are you doing here?" she hisses, shoving me in the chest. "You nearly scared me to . . . "

Her voice fails. I can feel my face quivering around my mouth.

She vaults up. "Danny, what's the matter with you? What the hell's going on?" She squints at the clock on the table beside her.

"I . . . I . . ."

What's the matter? Now there's a question—

The sobs, again.

"Danny! Jesus, Danny, what is it?" She gathers up bedclothes in her reddening fists.

I fall beside her on the bed. The smell of her hair, familiar. Safe, normal. The feel of her hands on my back, ditto. No, not the home I felt with Petey, but next door to home, down the street from home. Close enough.

"Noreen," I gasp, when I can. I raise my head and wipe my nose with my wrist. "Will you marry me when I get out next year?"

Dear Danny,
So glad to get your last letter—and the wedding invitation. Congratulations. Paul is still iffy about whether he can get the time off from work or not from the Center, but I've already made my arrangements with work, and you can bet I'll

be there at least. And, again, thank you for the honor of asking me to be your best man. What else can I say except congratulations?

After six months I feel I'm finally settling into Chicago—it's a huge city, Danny, and there's no ocean, but in a way I guess the lake is big enough almost to be an ocean. But it doesn't smell the same at all.

As I told you in my last letter, we're living in what the realtors call an "up and coming" neighborhood, read slum (all we can afford night now) but what a great mix here. I love it, and I've become very active in the local church, which as I wrote you has a homeless shelter/soup kitchen attached to it where I volunteer nights. About a month ago they offered me a full-time position there, so I've had to cut back my hours at the dog shelter—which is maybe just as well, we now have FIVE dogs at home, all from the shelter, and I think Paul will kick me out if I bring home any more. It's come to the point where he counts the dogs when he comes in at night and them bounding down the hall to jump on him/greet him. Paul is doing well at the drug rehab place, but it's really exhausting work, and since he's the ED (executive director) he gives it his all. But I think he misses home, and certainly misses his garden. Most of the time I'm too busy to miss home, between my work and the dogs and all, and we also have a Celtic Eucharist here on Saturday afternoons at the church, and I'm pretty involved in that program. And when I have any spare time at all I get on my bike and go exploring.

Well, time to get ready for my shift now, and I've a meeting after that. Just wanted to write and say congratulations, and I'll see you in a few months. I'm happy for you, Danny.

Your Friend Always,
Love,
Petey Harding

We had the rehearsal dinner at the Farragut House the night before the wedding. Ma was in high glory to say the least. She even hugged and kissed Petey, who came flying in just as the first course was about to be served. Without Paul. Which at least forestalled the inevitable *He's gay, Danny? Oh my God, so that explains it!* from Ma. Surprisingly enough, Petey and Noreen had more of a conversation than he and I. She even took down some numbers Petey gave her for various legal aid programs in Chicago that he said would give her all the information she needed for a few projects she was involved with at law school.

He looked good, happy, but there was more than one occasion during the night when my eyes met his across the room, both of us in conversations with other people, and if I didn't know Petey better I'd say there was a twist of sadness across his eyes. But then a smile would break out across his face, and he'd give me that little-kid wave of his again, the uplifted eyebrows, and we'd both go back to our conversations. The Flynn cousins were all there, and I hadn't seen them, or Noreen's relations, in years.

The night wound down around midnight, and Petey, who had rented a car at the airport—which somehow I found the most outrageous thing he'd ever done, in its banality—had to run to pick up his mother from her shift at the Necco Candy Factory, as he'd promised her.

"What time do you need me at the church tomorrow?" he asked.

"Ahhh . . . say eleven thirty. Eleven thirty, is that good?"

Petey held my eyes and nodded slowly.

"Your hairline's receding a little Danny," he said. Then he smiled again, gave me a quick hug, and vanished.

I'd been home for a year and four months, and most of that time I'd spent at our new condo, painting and papering, when I wasn't working at my new job, assistant head librarian at the Jamaica Plain branch of the Boston Public Library. It was taking me a while to get used to their system and the way they did things—so different from the precision-like smoothness of the military where a quick bark from Lucinda overrode even generals and made the world go round. But I had already received approval for a local writers' reading program at the branch, and I was hoping like hell it would be a hit.

The down payment for the condo—a 50 percent down payment—had been a wedding present from Ma and Dad and, not to be outdone, Noreen's mother had donated an equal amount for furniture and appliances. I was living at the condo, and spent most nights painting and papering, with Noreen's help on the weekends. She had really outdone herself in the bedroom. Once or twice we had almost done it at the new place, but Noreen always pulled away laughing at the last minute, saying it was bad luck to make love in the new apartment before we were married. So we'd wait until I drove her back to her place, as long as her mother was asleep, which she usually was.

I didn't know this new Noreen, though I was getting to. Well-read, opinionated, more laid back. Her eyes definitely on the future. In her second year of law school now and working part-time for a downtown law firm, doing research. Or, at least one eye on the future and the other on her studies, which she attacked ferociously, an unabridged dictionary at her side. She sometimes would clear off a space on the kitchen table, put her glasses on, and buckle down for five or six hours of studying while I busied myself with one chore or another, and when I'd walk by the hall and catch a glimpse of her at the table, I sometimes had to do a double-take. I had to not think of

Petey's words of several years earlier when Noreen had first started school. *I saw her with books at the bus stop and I thought she was out selling encyclopedias.*

We never fought, another change. She was more confident, more self-assured, and her tastes had changed not only in the clothing she wore, the scant makeup, but in the restaurants we went to now, the amusements we undertook during the few leisure hours. Museum trips, lectures. As she had been the prettiest girl in school, the captain of the cheerleaders, I sometimes, cruelly, wondered if she now wanted to be the smartest, the most achieving, in the new worlds she was being exposed to.

But it seemed she was a fitting match for the new Danny O'Connor. Daniel, actually, was what I went by now, though only outside my family and friends. That had been Noreen's suggestion.

It's 12:30 the night of the rehearsal dinner—or the morning of our wedding, depending on how you look at it—when I pull up in front of Noreen's mother's house to drop her off.

"Well," she says. "That couldn't have gone better."

"I can't believe how your cousins have all grown up."

"Did you see Petey and Tricia dancing?"

I laugh. "No, I missed that. Reminiscing about the double date from hell?"

Noreen shakes her head and laughs.

"There's been a lot of water over that dam since then."

She puts her hands in mine. I break away one of them to shut the car off.

"Still time to back out, Danny."

I cringe and jump at the unexpectedness of this remark. I turn and scrutinize her eyes, but they're laughing. Mostly. What an odd thing to say!

"Ahhh . . . and for you too."

Noreen raises one eyebrow, looks away. She does this thing with her hair now, she'll shake it, run a hand slowly, thoughtfully, through the top of it.

She stares straight ahead and says, "Danny, I want to ask you something. That night you . . . came to me. The night you asked me to marry you."

She looks down at my hand, which has *almost* imperceptibly tightened.

"Yeah?"

"Where had you just come from that night?"

She turns and stares at me frankly.

I look away first, up the street. It seems I'm forever doomed to look at a double row of parked cars in front of triple-deckers when the pivotal conversations of my life occur.

I open my mouth, then shut it.

No, I'm not about to begin this marriage with a lie.

I turn back to her, hold her eyes.

"Noreen, don't ask me that. Please. I'm . . . thinking about the future now. Believe me. Just . . . I swear, that's where my eyes are. Do you believe that?"

She opens her mouth, then shuts it. Her eyes shift back and forth between each of mine. Her mouth sets a bit, then she sighs.

"I do, Danny. I do. I just . . . sometimes . . ."

"What?" I'm rubbing her hands tenderly.

"Sometimes I feel there's this . . . little wall you put up. I never felt that before. Funny though, I don't feel it right at this minute. I just always want us to be able to talk to each other."

"I—"

"Maybe there's a place that everyone keeps to themselves, I don't know. I just always want us to be able to talk to each other, Danny. I mean, I don't want to be one of those people who colonize every inch of the person they're married to. I really don't want that, and I don't want that from you."

"You've changed so much, Noreen."

"I don't know if that's a compliment."

I laugh. "Well, maybe yes maybe no. I . . . you continue to surprise me."

"You've changed too, Danny. Sometimes I don't know you." She lets go another deep breath, then adds, "but I guess I have the rest of my life to figure that out. With a little bit of luck."

I lean into her, kiss her. In twelve hours I'll be married.

Noreen kisses back. I put my arms around her, pull her into me. There's a comfort here, such a comfort.

"Careful, Danny, you'll hurt the baby," she says, pulling back a little.

"Oh baby, I'm sorry."

I rub her stomach lightly.

"You still haven't told your mother?"

"No, I'm going to wait for about a month or so."

"Still so hard to believe," I say.

"I know it. I know it."

She places both hands over her stomach, folds them.

"Did you tell Petey?"

"Ahhhhh . . . no, not yet."

"He looked great, I thought."

"Yeah."

"He's . . . gay, Danny. But I presume you knew that."

"Ahhhh . . . yeah."

"He and his partner are doing some amazing work out in Chicago. I don't know why I never saw what a good soul he is."

"Ahhhh . . . Petey's an acquired taste."

He's . . . like us?

The next day, 235 people crowd into St. Brigid's Church.

Petey and I are waiting in the vestibule, me pacing, Petey biting his fingernails.

"I'm the one getting married here, Petey," I tell him.

"I know it but I'm w-worried about my speech a little bit."

"You'll do fine. It's all friends and family anyway. Nothing to worry about. But just do me a favor, Petey. Don't . . . you wouldn't get up there and say *Alexander Haig hastened to The Hague* and all that, would you?"

Petey's head lowers a bit but he holds my eyes. He has this way, damn him, of making the whole world fall away when he looks at me like that—

His voice is blown-glass brittle when he mumbles, "How can you even think that, Danny?"

I sigh, look away, crack my knuckles.

"Sorry, Petey," I mumble. "Just nervous."

We're quiet for a minute. There are squeals and booms in the congregation as people recognize one another.

"Danny?"

"Yeah?"

"I . . . really mean this. I wish you every h-happiness."

"Thanks, Petey."

He wants to hug but I can't, not now. The sadness and quietness of him this minute. Last night I had this dream that Petey burst through the church doors on a white horse, dressed up in a knight outfit, and he forsoothed and gadzooksed his way to the front of the church where he swept me up and denounced the entangling, bourgeois trap of marriage in particular and Western civilization in general.

That can't be too good but after all it was only a dream. And that was the old Petey. Nothing like happiness to dull your edge. But why not? He deserves it. We all do. And this will make me happy, what I'm doing.

I keep telling myself that.

The flashbulbs go crazy as Noreen, beautiful, beautiful, walks down the aisle. Oddly I think of a very expensive cake that you look at, too exquisite and icy to eat. But at the same time my eyes sting with the rush of years I have known and loved this woman. . . . Petey is beside me, but I can't look at him. I focus on Noreen, on Noreen and my new life, on the life Noreen is carrying inside her. Everything will be okay. I really believe that. I have to believe that. Petey's got Paul and I've got Noreen.

I close my eyes when I say *I do*. I have never been so fervent about any two words before. But it strikes me as I hear the words echo within that they are more a wish than a vow. Like I am still in the Marines and undertaking a mission that, I hope, I will succeed in.

The waiting room at Beth Israel Hospital is quiet, as it's three in the morning. They've got to do a C-section and I've been asked to leave for the time being, so I walk out into the waiting room and here's Ma, Dad, Mrs. Butler, Cousin Tricia, and two of Noreen's sisters, to wit Patty and Alice.

"C-section," I say when their heads leap up to mine.

"It's better that way," Ma says briskly to Mrs. Butler, and they launch into a hushed discussion of their own trials and tribulations of childbirth.

"It'll have a beautiful head," Noreen's sister Patty announces. I can't sit, so I pace. Patty and Alice get into a minor contretemps when Alice can't remember Patty's new boyfriend's name, she says, because she's on a new diet.

"It isn't lack of love, Patty, it's a lack of protein," Alice tells her sister reassuringly. It's less than an hour but it seems like days when a nurse pushes through the door.

"Mr. O'Connor?" she calls, and for a minute I look at Dad.

"Oh, oh yeah, that's me."

"You can come in now."

The nurse is smiling. Everything's okay thank Christ. Medical smells and Noreen's hair is plastered against her forehead and the sides of her face with dampness, and another nurse is wiping her down with a facecloth. Noreen is holding a small bundle wrapped in white against her chest. Tears are streaming down her face.

"A boy," she says, and I break down as everything inside me gathers up and rushes to what she is holding.

Dear Petey,

We've both talked about how we prefer real letters over e-mail, so I hope you'll forgive me not putting pen to paper and sending this electronic message instead. I'm typing with one finger and if there are any typos I hope you'll forgive me. I've got "Wee Jamie" as your mother calls him cradled here against my stomach and arm.

Petey, I know I must sound like every other parent in the world, so if you want to skip over my mush go ahead and scroll down a few paragraphs.

But I can't believe that I had anything to do with making such a beautiful creature. I'm glad you got the pictures of him okay, but I need to send out some more, because he's growing by the day, and I looked just a few minutes ago at the pictures I sent you last month and he's almost doubled in size, I'd say, and a real little personality is starting to show.

We've settled down into a little routine now and I can't believe he's such a good baby. We didn't sleep much the first couple of weeks as you know, but that's all behind us now and he's really on a pretty good schedule. He wakes up at fourish usually, and Noreen and I take turns getting up with him—neither one of us minds, believe me, and sometimes we both get up, and just can't believe God has blessed us with such a beautiful baby, and such happiness. Then he goes back until about six, which is when we get up anyway. Noreen goes off to work, and I drop Jamie off at my mother's, or Mrs. Butler's, they take turns. But he's all I think about for the most part all day, and I dash home on my lunch hour to check in on him, which Ma loves of course but I think Mrs. Butler resents. Too bad! She looks even more like an owl than she used to, but her heart is as big as her head, though you don't notice that at first. Noreen picks him up about four when she gets home from work, and then I'm home by five thirty, just in time to have a quick meal with the three of us before Noreen goes off to school. She hates leaving him at night, and frequently has tears in her eyes as she leaves. I used to think first-time parents who did nothing but hang out with other first-time parents and talk talk talk about their kids were so boring and lifeless, but . . . well, you can finish this thought on your own. Hard to believe it's been eight months, hard to believe that there was a time when Jamie wasn't in my life. I so wish you were here to see him, and see the changes that take place almost daily. He's smiling all the time now, and seems so happy. And every night, after Noreen leaves, I bring him out to the living room, place him on my chest, and sing to him, and he falls asleep breathing baby-breath into my face, and more often than not I cry at my good fortune.

I've been thinking a lot about something you said one time about love, how people say there are different kinds of love but you said there is really only one kind. I think you were right, because what I feel for Jamie makes me love everything, everyone, and he's worked such a miracle it seems on all the people around us—Ma and Dad, Mrs. Butler, Noreen's sisters—we have no end of visitors as you can imagine, and I'm afraid Jamie is going to be very spoiled.

Anyway, I could go on but you catch I'm sure my general drift. Work is fine. I've instituted a literacy program at the library and that seems to be catching on, and the local writers and poets series is really taking off. They're thinking about using it as a model throughout the whole system, so that's good. Things are fine with Noreen and me, actually wonderful since the baby came. I'm glad things are going well with you and Paul, though I think you're right, it sounds like Paul has to take a little more time off, or maybe you guys need to move to a different space, where he can garden or something. Anyway, are you coming home for Christmas? Please let me know, and if you do, please consider joining us for Christmas Eve (I know you'll be at your mother's Christmas Day if you come).

I love you.
As ever,
Danny

"Are you nervous?"

"No, no, not nervous."

Noreen tosses down her magazine, gets up from the living room chair, walks out into the kitchen.

"It just seems odd. Without Jamie here," she calls from the kitchen. There's an echo to her voice. Noreen kind of likes the minimalist look, but to me it's a little cold, what we've done here.

"I know it. But he'll be fine, Noreen. You know my mother's been dying to do this for two years now, take him for the weekend."

"I know. But after your mother's stroke—"

"She's fine now! And my father's there too."

Noreen sits down beside me, snatches the remote out of my hands.

"The game!" I protest.

"You and that game."

She places a hand on my thigh, flicks through the channels.

"Is the case on your mind?"

"Oh, a little," she answers abstractedly. Noreen graduated law school last year—cum laude—and landed a demanding job with an even more demanding downtown firm, the one she had interned with. One of the biggest. She was seldom home before nine now. I'd put Jamie in at seven, then Noreen would wake him up and the three of us would spend an hour together before putting him back to bed.

The phone rings and we both jump for it, Noreen getting it first.

"Oh, hi Ma. No, I'm fine. I thought it was Danny's mother. No no, but I'm sure they're fine."

Noreen takes the portable out into the kitchen. I click the game back on and nurse my acute ache for Jamie.

When Noreen comes back we make love on the couch. It's silent and perfunctory. It's been that way lately. There's a reason.

"I want to talk about that again, Noreen," I mumble into her ear.

Noreen sighs, gets up.

"Danny, what's the point?"

"Noreen, do you remember what you said to me the night before we got married? That you always wanted us to be able to talk?"

She sighs again, sits down on the chair opposite me. Starts dressing.

"Danny we just disagree on that, that's all. We've said it all."

"I just wanted you to know how I feel. I feel really strongly about this and—"

"I know how you feel. And you know how I feel, Danny. I just don't want to have any more kids right now. I do eventually, but not right now. I feel stretched to the limit as it is."

"You do?"

"You haven't noticed?"

"Well . . . maybe a little."

I shut the TV off and walk over to her.

"Is there anything I can do?"

"Oh Danny, you do enough," she mutters. She buttons up her blouse. She doesn't look happy. I notice there are bags under her eyes. "I'm going to take a shower."

She ascends the first few steps, then stops and turns.

"I don't suppose you've changed your mind about school?"

A chuckle floats out of me.

"What brought that up?"

She shrugs. "Well, as long as we're talking about things."

She lowers down onto the fourth step.

This time I sigh.

"No. No I haven't."

"But if you got your master's you'd move right up—"

"Noreen, I don't *want* to move right up. I love my job."

"Assistant librarian at the Jamaica Plain branch?"

My head snaps back a little.

"Ahhh, yeah, that's my job. You uhm . . . sound a little incredulous."

"Danny, it's just that I deal with people twenty times a day that are less bright than you are, that are really . . . *doing things* with their lives and careers. Really moving."

"Good for them. I'm glad for them."

"It doesn't bother you that your wife makes three times what you do?"

"Uhm . . . actually I never bothered to do the math. But no, it doesn't. Does it bother you?"

She's silent for a minute.

"I'm going to take a shower," she says, getting up.

"Wait a minute, Noreen—correct me if I'm wrong, but did I detect a note of . . . derision just then?"

"Well, Danny, what do you want to *do* with your life? You want that job all your life?"

I stare at her. There's a bit of a vein-throb on her neck. *Birdy*—

"I'm doing what I want to do *now*. With my life. With Jamie and . . . and you. In fact I love it so much I'd like to have a few more like him. I grew up an only child and I know how lonely that can be."

"Oh don't try the guilt on me again, Danny, please."

"Oh, is that what I'm doing? I thought I was expressing my feelings."

"Well it feels like guilt to me."

"Noreen, sometimes you seem like . . . like Stalin now or something, with a Five-Year Plan. When does happiness come in? Fulfillment? Enjoying what you've got?"

She groans and snaps back around. Her face is not a happy one.

"Danny, for your information it was *you* taught me to be like this."

"Oh?" I chuckle.

"That's right. When I was younger I built my whole life around you. Around my plans to get married to you. You took off for the Marines and left me with nothing, not even a promise." Her finger stabs the air as she says this, not right at me but in my general direction. "I told myself I would never do that again, become that pathetic girl waiting on other people's lives to make my own. I'm *so* over that. I'm smart and I'm talented and I'm going to do something with my life. I'm going to go as far as I can."

"Well, I wish you luck. You are smart and talented, and I believe you can do anything you set your mind to. And uhhh . . . where is this place, if I may ask?"

"Look, Danny, we're only twenty-eight. If I play my cards right I can make partner in three years and then really make a mark with the firm. It's true. I can't believe it myself but it's true." Her eyes roam off to Milton, to Newton, and for a minute she's gone. Then she looks at me, almost with surprise that I'm still here. "There'll be plenty of time, Danny, after that to have another kid." She pauses, then mumbles, "If we still feel that way. In the meantime you could go to school and . . ."

"And who would watch Jamie at night?"

"We could work something out. I could try to get home earlier. And there's always your mother or my mother, you know how much—"

"Noreen, I *don't* want our son brought up by other people, even if they are family. And I definitely don't want to miss my nights with Jamie. It's the best part of my day."

Her head snaps up and we stare at each other.

"Well, that's good to know."

She pads up the stairs.

That truth evidently angers her, though it doesn't seem to shock her. Not as much as it shocks me anyway.

"Hi, Jamaica Plain Branch. This is Daniel O'Connor, may I help you?"

"It's me, Danny."

"Oh hi. What's up?" I think this is the second time in three years Noreen has called me at work.

"Do you have anything major happening tomorrow? In the morning?"

"Uhm, I don't think so offhand. I don't know, let me check my book, hold on a minute."

"I can't hold, Danny. It's crazy here, but I'll call you back in ten minutes."

"Okay."

It's actually an hour later when Noreen calls back.

"Well?"

"Oh, hi. Uhm, nothing too important in the morning. A meeting later in the aftern—"

"Good. My mother called this morning and one of my cousins passed away."

"Oh Noreen, no, who—"

"Second cousins I should say. One of the Sheas. Michael, if you remember him, it's been years."

"I'm so sorry. Was he at the wedding?"

"No, his mother was though. We couldn't invite everybody."

"I'm so sorry. What happened?"

"They're saying drug overdose."

"What do you mean *they're saying?*"

"It looks like he . . . did something to himself." Noreen is typing away at her terminal as she reports this.

"Jesus. Another one. I'm so sorry, Noreen." There had been a spate of young suicides/drug overdoses in town lately. And not just the kids in the projects either.

"Anyway I've got the pretrial tomorrow morning and there's no way I can make the funeral. Gate of Heaven at ten, burial to follow, though the arrangements aren't firm yet. I'm going to try and stop at Cassidy's tonight for the wake on the way home if I can. Hold for a sec."

It's more than a sec, but her work is like that. I shake my head and stare out the large multipaned window to the back courtyard of the library. Another young suicide, the third in as many months.

How close did Petey come to this same fate?

"So can you make it, Danny?" Noreen asks when she comes back.

"Sure, I can go. Poor soul. I can't place him though. Was he the red-headed one?"

"No, I don't think so. There's five or six boys in the family and I always get them mixed up. Danny, I'm sorry, hold on again."

With an instantaneous click I am whisked once again into Muzak-world, complete with stolid encouragements that Hale and Dorr can assist me with my wealth management goals. Funny, I thought Noreen worked for a law firm.

"You never took me off hold."

I've been slumped over facing the other way for fifteen minutes, but sleep still eludes me; and it's not the night-light over Noreen's half of the bed. That's something I've become used to.

"What?"

I don't bother turning to face her.

"Today. On the phone when you called me back. I hung up after ten minutes. You put me on hold when you were talking about your cousin and—"

"I did?"

"Yes."

"I'm sorry, Danny. You know how crazy it gets there," she mumbles abstractedly. I hear the flick of a page as she moves on with her reading.

There's nothing like an election or, alas, a young death to turn out a throng in Southie. Even the vast granite confines of Gate of Heaven Church are swelled to capacity, and there isn't a face in the rout that is a shade less than mournful. It's the first bluster-cold day of fall—one always thinks the weather, rain or shine, means something specific on these days—and as I knotted my necktie earlier that morning the weatherman spoke of a second front that would crash through later in the morning, bringing even colder air with it.

Black cloaks and overcoats billow as the crowd streams into the church, heads lowered from wind and sorrow. A motorcycled contingent of Boston's Finest to escort and handle the traffic. A car drops a semidoddering white-haired man off at the front of the church to save him a few steps. He looks like a ninety-year-old Spencer Tracy. He walks carefully but deliberately to the bottom of the front stairs, turns, looks around, and then begins bawling.

His solitude is heartbreaking, and when I offer him my hand on his flecked sleeve he stumbles into me and wets my shoulder. It matters nothing that he keeps calling me *John, how could this happen John?* I am glad to be his John this morning.

Donnie's here, Petey's oldest brother. I see him through the crowd red-eyed already, alone again as usual. God bless him though for being here and I wonder what the connection is. Not the least of Petey's good deeds was bringing Donnie to a certain meeting of a Sunday two years ago when he was home for a quick visit, several hours after Donnie had been found more dead than alive down at the beach and so drunk he was hallucinating. Sober since, they say. Divorced too and back at home for a while as the distaff side got the house. Still doesn't miss a trick though—that much hasn't changed. His laser eyes pick me out and he nods.

Father James Sullivan, who was pastor of this church for thirty years and probably the most beloved man in South Boston, has been called out of retirement to perform the Requiem Mass for the Dead.

"Noreen couldn't make it, Noreen couldn't make it," is my mantra as I make my way through the crowd, answering inquiries. Once inside I realize too late that Noreen's family is up front on the other side of the church. I take one of the last seats available, behind beside among and in front of bereaved families I half recognize but don't know.

Sorrow falls down as the service progresses. Its weight grows unbearable. It occurs to me that I'm not just doing a half-hearted favor for the wife—I will be tugged at and tested this morning and me not prepared.

I am the only one, it seems, without a shoulder to lean on or a beloved to snatch the proffered Kleenex from. I am not even surprised that more than anyone, I ache for Petey by my side now. As comforting as the hand of God. But Petey's been gone these four years, off to Chicago when Paul's new job took them there.

Oh Petey, we need you here.

I do anyway.

The deceased's older sister strides up to the lectern to deliver the eulogy, her head hung, and the wash of empathy is like a tsunami, pushing her up the endless center aisle when it seems certain she won't make it. When she breaks down for the third time during her jagged speech, the sound of open sobbing is everywhere, popping off like mines around the church. Another family member, a red-faced brother with a quivering lip, eventually comes up to retrieve her when she can't go on. They crumple into each other. The eulogy goes unfinished.

After Communion we are invited by Fr. Sullivan, his voice sorrow-sodden but still tender as a child's, to walk by the closed casket at the front of the church, and say goodbye to Michael.

Everyone stands and makes for the center aisle.

I don't even know this Michael, may have met him once or twice over the years along with any number of Noreen's extended family, which is vast. But the swell of humanity pushes me onward—not physically, but emotionally. It isn't often we get to feel as one. Our grief unites us. The cattle shove to the front is a comfort, the bundling of people who ooze and bump into each other and do not spring back, as they would in, say, an elevator. Their smells comfort, their woolen and linen touches.

There are wheels within wheels in communities, and if nothing else South Boston is a community. As such I know every second or third person around me. We touch and shake our heads, lucky to be somewhat removed from the acute, catastrophic tragedy that has fallen onto the immediate family. Those poor souls are gathered in a shuddering black heap on the far side of the casket, quickly nodding their heads as individuals pass by whispering clutched condolences.

We shuffle ahead, and now I can see the coffin, the stretching and caressing and lingering of hands smooth or crabbed, blue white or red, on its radiant walnut surface. Filling up two pews beside the coffin are a dozen or so young men, old enough to have seen things but still young enough that they, by joint decision, have dressed identically in black suits, white shirts, and maroon ties. They are, somebody says, the football team this Michael once, in greener days, went out for long ones with. I imagine the phone calls yesterday that set up this touching testament, the growing consensus as Sully called Brian called Fitzy called Pinky with the black news. Or whomever. There is something in this simple gesture that breaks my heart the way the unfinished eulogy almost did. They are wild and inconsolable, half of them openly weeping, the other half with faces cemented in rigidity, though cheeks pucker and bottom lips quiver involuntarily. Mrs. Donovan the organist, who has seen, like Fr. Sullivan, too much tragedy, eases into _Ave Maria_. This is Gounod's, which he took from Bach. I know this because I am a partly educated person, because of Petey: Petey wanted to know things and eventually he infected me with the same bug, and now I work at a library, miss the bus stop sometimes because of printed-page Drama when I could and probably would be shoveling shit down at the docks, falling asleep afterward to comedies on the WB with a beer clutched in one hand and the remote in the other. Were it not for Petey.

We shuffle closer to the casket. Michael's high school portrait is atop the coffin. Even twenty pews away the smile of him is a dagger, the brightness of the eyes. *Tomorrow would have been his twenty-first birthday,* an older woman behind me choruses to no one in particular. *His mother already had the cake all put together.* And what will become of the cake, I wonder. Who will get the nasty job of throwing it out? It's these crises, as much as the arrangements and eulogies, that make up the real Rites of the Dead, and these must be faced alone. God help the one to chuck that cake.

Oh Petey—if anyone could have saved this young man's life it would have been you.

We shuffle closer. I feel something behind me, a sort of click on my neck, a pressure on the back of my skull. I turn around but then realize it's in front of me where I need to look. My eyes rivet onto Michael's picture. I feel my eyes blink rapidly. And then just as quickly they seem incapable of blinking.

For the second time in my life my vision telescopes. A fissure seems to run underground between me and the coffin. Those eyes, that smile. No—can't be—

But it is. Oh no—

Yes. Undoubtedly. Oh Jesus no—

Everything slow motions. I turn back but there's too many behind me, so I lurch past the coffin, pushing, can't help it need to get out, get some air. Don't make eye contact with the family, can't, push on push on, then march down the side front aisle to the side back door, open already and cigarette smoke puffing in from the crowd gathered just outside the doors on the steps. The smokers, jokers and wisecrackers and already someone is laughing and someone else spitting, but God bless them every one. How else to get through the first few days without the likes of these that have been and done and seen?

"Danny. Danny!"

A stepping in front of me, a blocking of my light and egress and it's old Joe O'Brien, the Mayor of Southie five years running now, a thing for names and funerals and if there's anyone he doesn't know in town they haven't moved in yet, and yearly the politicians scramble to walk beside him in the St. Patrick's Day parade. His webs are legion and golden.

Not just a thing for names, has Joe: an acute, almost Aristotelian noticing of people and things, changes of mood and the nuance of a raised or lowered eyebrow, and his *Jesus what a shames* to me end abruptly with a hamhand on each of my shoulders and a bit of a manly, old-school shake.

"Jesus, Danny, what's the matter? You alright?" but I can't even answer him. My ears involuntarily scoop up the surprised remarks of Joe and his cohorts as I half trot the hell out of here.

Home. Home.

Looking back, I believe it was at that moment that Noreen and I divorced; officially it wouldn't be for a year. We parted not necessarily by choice, but by the splatter-thwack of God's baseball bat, fate's absurdities served up in a heaping dollop that sodden blustery morning at Gate of Heaven Church. *Irreconcilable Differences,* our attorneys said, but only little Jamie heard the truth of it, the night of Michael Shea's funeral.

I was cried out by evening. Noreen was down at the dining room table cutting Gordian knots of legal corporate inscrutability with a determination and persistence I knew I would never possess, nor be able to congratulate her on her possession of same. *I could get used to you in a suit Danny,* had been the absurd first thing she had said to me upon her arrival home some time after nine. I didn't even bother to respond, though I could have by then.

I just couldn't be bothered.

Instead here I was in Jamie's room, my four most favorite walls in our condo. The navy blue walls with the half-moons and stars, a view of the ocean seven blocks away, a lovely purple orange glow from the teddy bear night-light. Infused in the darkened room I am with three-year-old boy smell. My story stool beside his bed, my shirt collar open and the tie askew as if someone had dragged me by it for the better part of the day—which indeed was the case.

Stooped on my story stool and leaning in, my right forefinger bouncing idly across the side bars of Jamie's Big Boy bed, occasionally straying in to finger a precious strawberry blond lock of wavy eiderdown. Noreen wants to cut it now that he's in pre-preschool; but how could you ever cut hair like that? A bit of a joke in the family, how devoted I am, but why wouldn't I be? *As innocent as a sleeping angel,* in Mrs. Harding's apt appraisal. Dad was a silent partner in our family growing up, his passion saved for his roses and Red Sox. Maybe Vietnam did that to people. Or maybe it was Ma.

But not here. Not me. How could I? The face white and facing me, the tiny Hummel mouth open, a red splotch on each cheek. The breath treacle sweet, milk sweet.

Even this close isn't close enough. I must lift and bundle him to me, pull him to me, oh sweet Christ rock him in my arms. He doesn't even stir.

"How ever to fathom it, Jamie," I whisper, stroking the inch-long pinky, closed into a pink fist. I shake my head for the 200th time this day. "You wouldn't be here, My Treasure, if it weren't for the man we buried this morning."

An eye for an eye and a life for a life?

I know I'm not the first to reject this kind of tit-for-tat justice when it comes to people's lives. There has to be a deeper answer.

Or, I don't know, maybe there isn't.

Over the next few weeks when Noreen idly asks what I'm thinking, *So far away and all,* it is this I'm pondering, though of course I can't share that with her. *Noreen, your cousin Michael—second cousin I mean. He told me his name was Sean. I had wild, animal, crazy sex with him and an hour later begged you to marry me because it freaked me out so much. And now he's dead by his own hand. And here we are with Jamie.*

In fact I take two weeks vacation from work immediately after the funeral—Noreen said there'd be no time to get away anyway for the next few years—and I think about this constantly, walking alone out to the island, alone along the boulevard, alone almost all the way to Carson Beach; and then back.

I walk, I walk, I walk.

Oh, I walk.

Mrs. Harding Has Her Say

Dear Petey,

Sorry it's been so long since I've written. I apologize, it's been a crazy year. Come to think of it, it's been about six months since I've heard from you, and I hope all's well at your end. I suppose you were waiting to hear back from me.

Anyway, Noreen and I have split up. There's no point rehashing it all; but there it is, and I took it pretty hard at first, which I hope will explain if not forgive my silence, and my not answering your letters in a timely fashion. Despite the fact that I didn't write, rest assured you are never far from my mind, dear Petey.

The important thing is we share joint custody of Jamie. Actually I have him all during the week, and Noreen has him weekends. She's very busy with her career. And other things. She's been seeing a man from her firm. I believe she was seeing him during our last few months together, someone from work, and I understand that she is engaged. But at this point that's neither here nor there. I will say that her love and devotion to Jamie have never waned. Things were okay between us the first few years after Jamie came to us, but then—we grew apart. That happens to so many, Petey—it would break my heart if that ever happened to you and me.

Again, I apologize for being out of touch, but the last year has been pretty rough. But not altogether without some clarity I suppose.

Thank God I have Jamie. He's not thrilled about the state of things, but at least he gets to see both his parents—and I have him all week. He's in first grade now if you can believe it, and "as cute a child as you'd see on a long day's walk," as your mother beamingly says when I bump into her. He's oddly precocious, and delights in making faces and imitating people. He has quite a wit on him for someone so young, and I have no idea where he gets that. I do think he'll be okay with all this—he's such a happy camper, and he's got so many people on both sides of the family who absolutely dote on him. I got the condo in the divorce, as my parents had more or less bought it for us anyway and Noreen didn't mind, she was really pretty good about things. She makes a truly amazing salary so perhaps that helps. My parents watch him in the mornings, I come home for an hour at lunchtime, and then MaryEllen Conroy (used to be Collins), if you remember her or her family, watches him 'til I get home at

A Map of the Harbor Islands
Published by The Haworth Press, Inc., 2006. All rights reserved.
doi:10.1300/5677_25

five. Ma is so good to him, Petey, so loving—she's changed so much since her therapy, and is nothing but benign now. She even asks for you on occasion.

Work is going fantastically well—Jamaica Plain (as no doubt you discovered when you were living there with Paul) continues to get funkier by the hour, and the local poets and writers series I started at the library several years ago has really taken off, and I now direct the program for the whole system of the Boston Public Library. It's become so popular we've expanded it into a number of various genres—gay and lesbian, Latino/Latina, poets and writers of color, etc. And each session is introduced by a popular poet from that particular group. They do a story on the program every spring in the *Globe* when we kick off that year's events, along with a horribly unflattering picture of yours truly— but somehow they always fail to mention that I'm a South Boston native and resident! I guess by osmosis I've written a poem or two or three myself. We had a poet from South Africa last spring and he did this session with the schools, and he was teaching the kids about meter and rhythm, and he marched around the classroom chanting his poems, using his feet to describe poetic feet, as it were, and that night when I went up and down the Boulevard for my evening jog it seemed his words just flowed through me, with every step; and then by and by over the weeks I started sticking my own words in their place. Anyway.

I don't tell Petey my latest saying above my shaving mirror. In California I had Kierkegaard, but this one's by Plato: AT THE TOUCH OF LOVE, EV-ERYONE BECOMES A POET.

So, that's what's going on here. I stopped by your house last Christmas to see if you had come home for the holidays, but no one answered, so I presume your mother was at one of the other houses and you and Paul stayed in Chi-cago, or maybe went to his folks. How have you been? And Paul? I'm sure you have lots to tell, so I can't wait to hear from you. Write soon, or give me a call. I love you.
Danny

A week later the letter comes back to me. Moved. No forwarding address on file. I try his number—something new, for some reason we both seem to prefer to communicate by mail—and the number's been disconnected. Fi-nally, an e-mail to his old computer address bounces back. While I can live without Noreen—fairly happily, as it turns out, certainly happier than our last years together—I can't apparently live without Petey, and every morn-ing upon awakening I resolve to contact him; yet each day brings its own cares and responsibilities, and I watch the morning light coming into my room go from delicately spring-spangled to densely summer-shaded, to stark February, and still I haven't seemingly found the time.

But then one particular September morning I awake, and there's an ur-gency about my desire to contact Petey that I dare not ignore. I call my mother and tell her not to expect me to drop off Jamie. I'm taking a day off, and he's got his piano lesson this afternoon anyway.

"Today," I whisper to myself in the shaving mirror. And then I stare deeper into my eyes.

"Who do you say that I am?" I ask myself.

"Mrs. Harding? Mrs. Harding?"

"Ouf, **Danny**! Danny! Look at ye now, come in outta that and set for tea!"

It kind of strikes me as Mrs. Harding up-and-downs me that I've quietly, imperceptibly taken on the starving artist look of my Jamaica Plain milieu: the gray jeans, black T-shirt, somewhat ratty sneakers, and you wouldn't leave the house without new ones when we were young. But as Petey sagely noted over a decade ago, why turn the beauty that is the human person into a walking billboard for companies that deal in miserable sweatshops? Or something like that. I think it was Einstein who said that wherever he went, he found that God had been there before him. There's hardly a bit of philosophy or polemic I come across that doesn't instantly knee-jerk a memory of Petey-speak back to me.

"I'm early to pick up Jamie from his piano lesson and I thought I'd just . . . I'm not waking you or anything?" But then I hear the shouts and laughter of children coming from the parlor as I step into the hall and Mrs. H shuts the heavy oak door behind me. Unlike poor Ma, Mrs. Harding hasn't aged much, and her wild red hair is still wild—loose and free and wonderful.

"God no, love, I've *retired*, Danny, if you can believe it. After forty years I thought it was high time, and now I'm trying to get away from the vampire routine—which I guess brings me right back to where I started, with this lot now! Wisha, if ten of yez will kindly shut up I've an old friend of your Uncle Petey's to say hello to. Sit down now and be stone-silent for a minute. Quiet as church mouses if you know what's good for yez."

Miraculously they comply, though the smiles on their faces sing loud and clear they know Mrs. H's bark is infinitely worse than her toothless bite. There are giggles all round as five all told scamper onto the couch, their feet dangling over the edge and their round faces tight with smirks. Three boys and two girls, four in what look like the end-of-the-day dishabille of parochial school uniforms, the last too young for school yet by the looks of him. I do a double-take at him, the youngest—he might be Petey's boy with that raven head of hair and the green eyes.

"This is Mr. Daniel O'Connor, your Uncle Petey's best friend."

"Who's Uncle Petey?" the youngest asks, and this causes more laughter.

"Who's Uncle Petey indeed! Has your mother not told ye about our Petey then? Nor your father? They'll come to grief for that when I get a hold of them! He's your father's youngest brother, like you and Molly there. That's his picture at the top of the stairs, so. Now say hello to Mr. O'Connor."

"Hello, Mis-tah O'Connor."

"Now say it in Irish," she instructs, with a wink at me. "I won't have them idling away their time Danny looking at that idiot box when 'tis Irish they could be learning."

"*Dia dhuit,* Mis-tah O'Connor."

"Danny, this is Maeve, Colin, Molly, Michael, and Christopher. Christopher and Molly are Donal's issue, Colin belongs to Eddie, and Michael and Maeve go with Sean."

"Why am I always last?" the Petey look-alike wonders.

"Because you're the most important," Mrs. Harding says expansively, to more laughter.

"Does anyone here know Jamie O'Connor?" I ask.

"I do, I do," they all say but the youngest.

"Who's Jamie O'Connor?" he wonders. "Why don't I know anybody?"

"He's my son. I think the rest of you must go to school with him."

"Alright alright, down to the rumpus room with the lot of yez now. I'll call you up for the tea in a bit. I want to have a still word with Danny here."

In a flash there's a burst of shoes clattering down the stairs, and Mrs. Harding shuts the basement door with a shake of her head.

"We'll have five minutes of sweet tranquility if we're lucky." She takes me by the hand and yanks me into the kitchen. "They all had day care after school or sitters, but with me home now I wouldn't hear of it, though I suppose I need my head thoroughly examined. But it keeps me out of Foxwoods anyway. Ouf! Those slots would tempt saints! It's the *possibility* of things, Danny, don'cha know. The lovely jingle-jangle of the winner. Though what would I do with the money if I ever won?"

The shining dishes on the hutch are still as pregnant with delight, the Blessed Mother Hummel still in its place of pride on the top shelf, the odor of fresh hot soda bread and Mrs. Harding's tea, the damp linen towels laid out on the stove rack drying, the kitchen window a smathering of herbs and the sun dancing through them and spangling on the old oak floor, polished to a pumpkin-colored gleam. The calendar on the fridge, ticked off with recitals and games that a grandmother dare not miss, the three-quarters finished morning crossword puzzle on the kitchen table that Mrs. Harding would never find the time to complete.

"Oh Danny dear, are those tears in your eyes?" Mrs. Harding asks, taking me by both hands.

"It's a good thing. Happy memories, that's all."

"Come on, come on, set now, the tea's on. Where's your wee Jamie today?"

I squish into the ancient Titian-red sofa that is the hallmark of the Harding kitchen. "Oh, not so wee anymore. A second grader if you can believe it. He's at his piano lesson."

"Yes, don't I see him now sometimes when I go to fetch the kids, and don't your mother and I have the grand talks! The proud grandmother she is now, eh? And doing well?"

"Doing great, thanks, both of them."

"And how's yourself? And who was that pretty little thing I saw you with last month out at the island, promenading?"

"Oh. That's . . . that was actually a few months ago. Just . . . this woman I was seeing."

"I shan't refer to that painful topic again, Danny dear, but proceed breathless to my next query: dear wee Jamie, and how he's doing and all."

I smile. "Wonderful. He's . . . making the adjustment well, I think."

"I know," Mrs. Harding oozes, rubbing my hand. "Well well well, make the best of it is all you can do. Aren't half of mine in the same postlitigious boat? Here, have another slice now."

"Are they? I've been out of touch for so long."

"Everyone's just too busy nowadays. To say nothing of being fraught with consternation. It's this unusual pace of life. Queer, I call it. In my village one had a whole tribe around, and one didn't try to get everything from a single person, like it is now, and everyone living so far away."

"Sounds like the way to go."

Mrs. Harding plops a tray between us and takes a seat on the other side of it. Steaming tea—Barry's of course—and several hunks of this morning's soda bread, lathered in "buther" that will have to be jogged off later.

"Speaking of far away, Mrs. Harding, where's Petey moved to? I sent him a letter six months ago and it came back to me. Has he left Chicago?"

"They have, they have, I'm sorry to say, further away of all things. California, if you don't mind."

Mrs. Harding's eyes wander around the kitchen, a habit she takes to when she's fishing for a topic to speak of.

"And where are ye living yourself now?"

"Mrs. Harding, what is it?" I stop midchew. "Did something happen to Pe—"

"Oh no, no, he's fine, praise to the God of good things. But . . . it's just that . . . well . . ." She sighs resignedly, looks me in the eye.

"I'm not saying I agree with it at all, but . . . well, Petey said . . . Petey said you might be coming by for his address and whatnot, but—"

"But what?"

"Well . . ."

She takes my hand again.

"Danny, he's a sensitive boy, and a good good soul, God bless him. Unlike anyone else, as yourself will speedily acknowledge. And people like that have their queer humors, so don't let's take this the wrong way."

"Take what the wrong way?"

"He doesn't . . . Petey said he'd prefer that I . . . not give you his address. Not . . . just yet. He wants . . . he needs some time out of touch, don'cha know, he says."

"Oh."

The next thing I know I'm standing.

"No no no love, it's not like that at all, Danny dear! Can't you see?"

She pulls me back down into the chair.

"See what?" I mumble.

She tilts her head and moves her face in closer to mine over the tray.

"I'll speak frankly love, and why shouldn't I? I always loved you like you were my own."

She clears her throat and picks up the bag of knitting that's never out of arm's reach. She has at the needles and the click of them recalls loveliness, if this moment itself is not lovely.

"He loves you, Danny. He's loved you since . . . well, after his own fashion since you were boys. *You* know that."

I feel myself not reddening. That's got to be a sign of progress—

"It's a case of him trying to make a go of it with this nice Paul lad. Like everyone else, the poor miserable creatures have their ups and downs. I think it's been hard for him, being away from home, and not having the things he's used to around him. The sea and all and what have you. But he's determined to give it his best, because as everyone knows Paul is a good man, and Petey loves him too I know.

"But, well, here's the way of it—he said he didn't hear from you in a while, letters unanswered and so forth, and it troubled him no end. He was beside himself. Snappy with Paul and not able to concentrate on his job and so forth, and calling by the day almost to ask had I seen you, were you okay."

"Oh no. That was when Noreen and I were—"

"Oh Danny, you don't have to make excuses love, my sister Aggie will tell you I'm the very worst of correspondents, delighting in receiving letters and loathe to reply. But the upshot of it all was Petey perceived that he was still . . . thinking about you too much and it was interfering with other things in his life. Issues, he said, it was giving him issues. We always called them problems and heartaches, love, but a rose I suppose. And so I think he's decided he needs a little time away for a bit, a little time out of touch. And that, Daniel O'Connor, is the truth of it. Though I suppose he'd have my head if he knew I told you. But I want you to know, love."

She looks at me and, perhaps seeing devastation in my eyes, adds, "It won't be forever Danny dear. Just 'til he figures things out. He just needs a little time is all."

I nod my head, stare down into my tea.

"You're not . . . angry at him I hope, Danny? Not inclined to simmering vindictive?"

I lift up my eyes.

"No. No, of course not. He's . . . well?"

"He is, well enough, busy with dogs and shelters and the homeless and God knows what else. Very active in the church, thank God. And something to do I believe with Native Americans."

"Well . . . that's good."

"Well it's not the Catholic Church exactly but something else again. But they sound like wonderful people and they must be doing something right because they're always getting arrested the half of them. Oh Danny, you look so sad!" She reaches over and tousles my hair. "Is it a big loss, love, so soon after your divorce?"

"I'll be fine, Mrs. H, I just—"

I think of Jamie, the job I'm crazy about.

"I'll be fine." I take her hands in mine and squeeze them and manage a smile. "I just miss him."

"As do we all, love, as do we all. Keenly, I hasten to add. If I were the type of mother who curried favorites among her brats, he'd be it." She pauses. "Donnie as well, but like I say I don't," she says with total sincerity.

We settle back into the quiet and ease that lurks at the back of the squishy sofa. My vanity, and something else perhaps, is mollified by the fact that Petey still . . . has feelings for me. He'll be back. Someday. And we'll be friends again. I believe that. I have to believe it.

"I've always loved your hair, Mrs. Harding," I say, solemnly, and we both laugh at my absurdity.

"This witch's tangle?" she wonders, attacking it with a kind of judo chop.

"Yes, I mean it. You haven't gone the South Boston blue bubble route like Ma and everyone else in town of a certain age."

"Hmmm. I'm not so sure *of a certain age* is flattering love, but I am pushing seventy and I don't care who knows it. To tell the truth and shame the devil, love, I always wanted to be one of those elegant ladies who wore their long hair up, and then brushed it out 100 strokes of an evening—or better yet had someone else do it for me who did not disresemble the phrase tall dark and handsome. But by the time I got to bed I was always too exhausted. And you yourself—you've kind of gone—what would it be— beatniky on us, is it?"

"Mrs. Harding," I say quietly after a bit, "can I ask you something else?"

"You can ask me anything love," she responds briskly, sipping her tea. She resumes her knitting.

"Uhm . . . do you know Joe O'Brien? You know him, right?"

"Old Joe? Ouf, I wonder who doesn't. He was the hand of God after Pat died, helping me with the insurance and veteran's benefits and all when I was at my wit's end. Triplicate and all that red tape. Yes, of course I know Joe, the Lord leave him his health."

I lean forward a bit on the couch. "I saw him . . . what, like . . . almost two years ago. At uhm . . . a funeral. Noreen's cousin died—"

"The poor Shea boy, God rest him and all those that are on the Way of Truth," Mrs. Harding interjects, shaking her head and dropping her knitting for a second to bless herself. "The only true tragedy in life, Danny, is when the young die before their time, and to take one's own life is—"

"Yes, exactly. Anyway, I—I was leaving his funeral and it . . . uhm . . . greatly upset me. It . . . I had uhm . . . met him on one occasion and . . . knew him."

"The Shea boy?"

"Yes. Anyway, I didn't realize that at first, that I knew him. I was only there because Noreen had asked me to go—she was tied up at work."

"Exactly, love."

"And when I was leaving the funeral I bumped into Joe O'Brien outside and he was . . . I think he was a little taken aback by how upset I was. I can't even remember what I said to him. I was barely coherent—"

I realize I'm twirling my black tweed cap incessantly. I put it down abruptly on my right knee and snatch a glance at Mrs. Harding. Feeling my gaze she looks up. Her eyebrows are furrowed and her large gray eyes, larger with her wonderfully unfashionable glasses, are washed with concern.

"Go on love. And please do go ahead and twiddle all you want, it doesn't bother me in the least."

"Ahh, well, anyway, when I was walking away from Joe and his little group there at the side door, I heard Joe say behind me *Jesus, poor Danny!* like he couldn't understand why I was so upset. And then someone else, this older woman I didn't recognize, said—at least I think she said, *Oh so close to home and all,* and then Joe said, *Right, right, I was forgetting.* I was walking away and I wasn't sure I'd heard them rightly. I was such a basket case I kind of forgot about that, but I think it's always been at the back of my mind, what they said. And now I . . . I'm sure that's what they said."

"Oh, and why wouldn't they say it, God love them," Mrs. Harding oozes, shaking her head again as she clacks away on her knitting. "Go on, love."

It's several moments before she repeats, "Go on, love," and when she finally looks at me she starts when she sees my face.

"Uhm . . . why would they say that?" I ask. I drain the rest of my tea. "That's what I wanted to ask you about."

Mrs. Harding holds my eye, then plops her knitting away and pours me more tea from the pot.

She wets her lips.

"Well, after what . . . happened don'cha know. Before you were born and all."

One of her bushy eyebrows lifts up appraisingly. There's this kind of electrical surge through my stomach.

"I don't . . . ahhh . . . what do you mean?"

Mrs. Harding leans her head in.

"You've . . . really no idea what they were talking about?" she demands. "What happened?"

"No. None whatsoever." I grab my hat again. "Mrs. Harding, what is it?"

She holds my eyes.

"You're not . . . joking, Danny dear?"

"Oh, Mrs. Harding," I reply, my voice jangling. "Believe me, this is no joke."

"Jesus wept," she mutters. "I'm shocked but not surprised. Wait a while, Danny."

She pushes up and off the couch with a groan, then marches over to the kitchen sink. She puts her hands on the counter and peers out the window at the diminutive backyard, the back of the Ferrys' house beyond. Her gestures do nothing to console me. On the contrary.

"I've made the most important decisions of my life standing right here, Danny," she mutters.

"What?"

She jerks her head as if she's made up her mind. She raises one finger, then storms over to the cellar door and calls up the troop from the basement.

"Hello, you lot—if anyone wants a treat, come up the stairs now in an orderly fashion and assemble in the hallway." The near-riot that follows is anything but orderly. After five minutes of ferocious promises demanded, and given, to cross only at the lights, to hold onto everyone's hand at all intersections, they're out the door and headed for ice creams at Sullivan's. They turn and stare at me before they go, itching themselves, wiping noses, and why wouldn't they? I must look like nothing less than a lump of dread on their kitchen couch.

Mrs. Harding comes back out to the kitchen, carrying solemnity in her wake, as she herself might say. Her eyes are large, vacant, staring at the floor. She doesn't come back to the couch, but stops at the sink with her back to me again. She begins fussing with her plants at the windowsill.

"Danny," she says quietly, picking at a few dried leaves on her potted herbs, "you're a grown man now, well grown, and I'd no more advise you than I would the man who built the Thames Tunnel. But . . . just the same love, I would strongly advise that what I'm about to tell you . . . well, it would serve no purpose at all now to . . . throw it in your mother's face."

She turns to me. A wafture of lemon balm and apprehension drifts in my direction. "In fact I really think it would kill her."

"My brother," I mumble, more to myself.

Mrs. Harding nods.

"Yes. Exactly love. Your brother."

"Please—Mrs. Harding—"

She sighs again and shakes her head. She retakes her seat beside me on the couch.

"Danny love, it's not my story to tell—but it is yours to hear, and you'll never hear it at home, God help us, if you haven't heard it by now. That much I can assure you. But you need to know it. So I think I'll have my say."

She does something with her lips and teeth, then nods her head again.

"Maybe you'll understand more when you hear it. But please, I'm begging you now, Danny, don't be too hard on your mother."

"If you could just tell me—"

"I will, Danny. But it's not a happy story and no mistake." She plops her hands onto her lap and folds them together. She wets her lips, not with relish.

"You know of course that your older brother Brian was born many years before you were, not long after your parents were married. I believe your mother was no more than eighteen, and your father perhaps a year or two older, when they had him. We didn't know them, but we'd see them at church. And once in a while if I stole an hour of bingo for the sake of my sanity I might see your mother there. And a beautiful woman she was too—full of life, wickedly funny. She loved dressing fashionably and made all her own clothes. She had a bit of a clique around her at all times and all the ladies wanted her on their church committees, holiday bazaars and what have you. Proud as Lucifer some said but I never paid that any mind myself. Before they were married people called her lot the Glamour Girls. I suppose in my own way I envied her—here I was always pregnant, my drumstick legs and flaming hair and looking like a lump of soda bread before it's tossed in the oven."

Mrs. Harding pauses, for breath and perhaps (I realized later) for a chivalrous remonstrance on my part. But any kind of polite discourse was beyond me at this point.

"But that's another story. Anyway, Brian was the same age as our Donnie, and when they came to be ten or eleven I suppose, they became great friends."

"I didn't know that."

"No? Well, I suppose why would you—though it's queer Donnie never said anything those times he would mind you and Petey. Well, I suppose he couldn't, the poor thing.

"Anyway." Mrs. Harding surprises me with a laugh and I jump. "They were great pals, always up to their eyeballs in trouble and shenanigans. Some of our best angels can be our worst devils. Many's the time your brother tarried right where you're sitting now. I know you _have_ heard over the years that you're the spit of him. So often, Danny, when you were young I would feel a clutch at my heart seeing you at the door or on this couch with Petey, and then it would hit me. By and by the shock of the sight of you went away.

"He was a grand boy, Brian was. A real character and a way about him. A bit of a temper too, and though you might resemble each other looks-wise you're entirely different people. Well, life went along as it does, and I was having children fast and furious then, and though I was friendly with some of the children's friends' parents, your mother and I . . . well, there was nothing bad between us you understand—we just weren't close. There were a whole lot of us from the old country and we more or less stuck together, and then my husband Pat God be good to him had his friends from Vietnam and so forth."

The phone rings. She looks up, then waves it off.

"If it's a disaster I don't want to hear about it. Well, Pat got sick, and me with all these children—but Donnie was a godsend. As he grew older he took on more responsibilities. And it seemed he and Brian spent more time than ever together. Ike and Mike, we called them, and Brian was as apt to show up at my dinner table as any of my own. They were—sixteen, and I was up to my eyeballs and Pat was dying, which I tried to hide from the kids, though why I did that I'm not sure—it was the way then I suppose. Maybe if I hadn't been so preoccupied I might have seen that . . . there was something going on."

"How do you mean?"

"Well, don'cha know . . . between the boys, so."

She looks me in the eyes frankly. I feel my ears flush up while I struggle to grasp her meaning.

"You mean . . . wait a minute . . . you mean . . . " I can't quite form the words. Every single thing in this kitchen—the stove, two old boots at the back door, the row of potholders, the cuckoo clock over the stove with a mind of its own—seems to jump out at me, to become highlighted in incredulity, shock—

"Yes, I do mean. I can't say I was all that surprised. Our Donnie was always different from the others—happy-go-lucky like the rest of them but at other times thoughtful, quiet. Deep, like. Sometimes I'd find him sitting on one of the stairs, staring up at the ceiling, and when I'd ask him what he was after he'd just smile and say he was thinking. Not the Chinese puzzle Petey became after his accident, but a thoughtful, strange little lad just the same. And a sweet and sensitive soul to boot.

"Brian you understand slept over quite a bit, and for his part Donnie would frequently spend the night at your house. What I'm saying is, Danny, they became very fond of each other. Very fond. I—one time I think it was Paul told me, *Donnie and Brian don't wear a stitch in bed and they wrestle under the covers when the lights are out and make funny noises.* I told him, *Don't pay them any mind, they're just being silly.* I suppose I knew then, but I had so much to think about, and I'd lie awake at nights worrying how I'd feed the lot of them when Pat died, as it was obvious he would."

Jesus.

"Danny—are you alright, love?"

Both my hands have decamped to my temples, the way distraught women in Victorian novels fly to tea at the imminence of crisis, so why wouldn't she ask that?

"Uhh." I nod. "Go on."

"Believe it or not, Danny, it didn't bother me. About Donnie I mean. Donnie and Brian. I knew he was as good a lad as you could ask for, special, and . . . like that, you know. Well I suppose to my way of thinking, I figured if he found someone like himself, then more power to him. I'd a brother is the same way back home, you see. And as far as my brother Liam is concerned everyone in the world knows he is—except for him. Apparently it runs in the family.

"I never said a word about it to Pat—I thought he'd not understand, nor did I want to upset him, not in the state he was in. I did tell Donnie one time at hospital if he ever had anything to talk about, he could surely trust me. His eyes roamed a bit after I said that, and then he looked deep into my own. You know those eyes he has, Danny, they'd startle Jesus. *Do you love me Ma'am?* he mumbled. *How can you even ask!* I told him. *Like the spring loves the sun!* and I hugged him then and there. *No matter what?* he said. *No matter what,* I answered. *I know you're special Donnie and never be ashamed about that. God made you that way for a reason.* And then both of us being melodramatic for a bit, tears and tissues and all that. I suppose that was our way of talking about it."

As shocking as this revelation is, I'm thrust back to the night on the wind-chopped beach when Petey wrote his message on the sand—the same astonishment hits me; and yet, and yet—I can't deny the bizarre realization that some nether part of me has always known this—just as it always knew this about Petey, even before he told me.

"Well . . . it wasn't long after that our Pat died, and me carrying wee Petey in my belly and not knowing it yet. I wouldn't have made it without Donnie—he was my rock then. And Brian too was a great comfort. But it was two months after, that tragedy struck us again. And this was even a crueler blow, and so unlooked for. Your brother."

Mrs. Harding suddenly yanks at her knitting again and takes it up. I don't realize at first she's crying, in her funny silent way, her face swollen and her throat gurgling.

I think, I should be crying too. But I can't seem to mourn someone I've never known—instead, a rage builds.

"So it wasn't . . ." I sit up straighter and lock my hands together. "Of course it wasn't a car accident."

She shakes her head.

"Not at all. Though that's what they told everyone. They . . . hushed things up more in those days, Danny. It was Fr. McCann took that ball and ran with it. He was a friend of your parents. You don't remember him of course but in those days they wouldn't even bury someone out of the church who . . . took their own life."

"Oh God, Jesus."

She reaches over and plucks my hand from out of my lap. Rubs it hard.

"No one knew, outside the immediate family of course. But in time the word got out, as it will. It was nearly a fatal blow for your mother, and why wouldn't it be, God between us and all harm. She was . . . away for a while after that, and when she came back she brought a beautiful new baby boy with her, you. And she clutched onto you like you were her hope of heaven. I thought . . . God forgive me but I thought she was . . . callous after that, airy. I had no notion. No notion at all, no one did. And the poor thing was on pills half the time as well. Lest she come to grief and do a mischief to herself. You see, it was she who . . . found him." She lowers her voice. "Down in the basement there."

It's some time before I can make answer.

"How . . . Jesus I don't even know if I want to know." I lower my face into my hands. "What was it?"

"Pills, Danny. But the worst part of it was—I didn't get this until much later, in fact not until Donnie gave up his drinking two years ago—that she had . . . your mother had surprised them together several days before. She just . . . apparently she just marched into your brother's room when he was with Donnie and . . . well, she couldn't handle it, Danny."

"Jesus Chr—"

"You mustn't blame her, Danny! It was the times then, the way she was brought up, the hate and bigotry she'd ingested."

"I . . . I . . . she flipped I'm sure."

"There was a gorgeous row, as you might imagine if you knew Brian. She barred Donnie from the house and tried to send Brian to some doctor. And at the same time Donnie was thinking he was being punished for what he was, by having his father die. Ouf, the suffering Danny! And for what? For what? Why?"

"Oh my God."

I'm lucky to be here in the Harding house. It's the second safest place I know. How to handle this? I can almost hear the *beep beep beep* as a vast eighteen-wheeler backs up, dumping 300 tons of rotting secrets on top of my head. I'm only sitting because I can't get up yet, can't run yet, run and rave and scream. My rage grows.

"Brian was resolute, though obviously it bothered him no end. He said there was nothing wrong with him, that she was the one who had things backwards. Then your mother put the house up for sale. She said they were moving far away and he was never to see Donnie again. For his part Donnie—well, Donnie didn't have Brian's gumption to challenge your mother—few did in those days. Donnie told Brian they shouldn't see each other anymore."

"Why?"

Mrs. Harding shrugs, lets out a vast sigh.

"You have to ask? Shame, fear. Guilt. All of it. I didn't know that at the time, Danny. If I did, I swear by Our Lady Most Merciful I would have called Brian and told him he could move in with us for as long as he needed to. I would have moved heaven. I would have beseeched him, implored him."

She's silent for a bit, crying again.

"But I didn't know. I rack my brains and try to remember those few days, those particular days—did Donnie seem upset? I ask myself. Was there a moment when he tried to steal my attention for a moment, and tell me about it? I don't think so. He said himself two years ago he didn't say anything to me because I was so overwhelmed, and Pat just dying eight weeks beforehand. But hardly a day hasn't gone by, Danny, when I don't ask myself, what did I do wrong? How was it Donnie thought he couldn't come and speak to me about that? He was always so good at hiding things. Concealing his feelings, going it alone."

I want to console her for she's crying again in her funny way, but all I can manage is a pat on her shoulder.

"It was three days later it happened. Oh Danny, you never saw such sorrow in the town. And your mother—I can't even imagine the guilt."

"It was her fault," I mumble, lifting my head. Implosion nips at me but I ward it off with an image of my Holy of Holies—Jamie's room tonight. I have to keep it together for Jamie. The night-light on, the story candle lit, boy smell and moon and stars and my precious son—I might be alright. I might be able to handle this—I have to be alright, for his sake—

"It was all her fault," I repeat.

"Well, that's one way of looking at it, Danny. But Donnie feels it was *his* fault, and as you just heard, I often think it was *my* fault—that's the thing with this kind of tragedy, Danny—it's not just grief we're left with, but guilt. One's bad and the other's worse. But who filled your mother's head with those ideas? No doubt she thought she was doing the right thing, protecting her son from something she thought would ruin him. And even if you do lay the blame on her, you'll acknowledge the woman has paid, and paid dearly. Too dearly. I can't imagine, Danny. To have to live with that. I can't imagine. It would kill me twice."

It's not until I realize I'm sobbing for Michael Shea all over again, that I realize I'm sobbing at all. Mrs. Harding pulls me into her and rubs my hair.

"There there," she says, over and over. "There there, Danny love."

There there. What do those words even mean?

But it's enough. For now.

"This shit has to stop happening," I mumble, after she's fetched Kleenex and more tea.

"It does. Danny, do you want something stronger? You're white as a hant, love."

"No, I'm fine."

Fine? Oddly I think of ancient Irish literature, how the bards, with a flourish, would string scores of adjectives after one noun, rhyming or alliterative, alphabetic or onomatopoeic; for in truth I am affected, afflicted, affronted, bitter, blasted, chafed, choleric, convulsed, dejected, depressed, disconsolate, ferocious, fiery, furious, hateful, heated, huffy, impassioned, incensed, indignant, heart-rendered, heartbroken, hurting, in mourning, in pain, in sorrow, melancholy, miserable, mournful, pained, piteous, plaintive, sad, sorry, sodden, tear-jerked, tearful, testy, woebegone, woeful, and wretched.

"I'm fine," I manage to repeat.

But then I think of Donnie and his silence, Michael Shea and his silence, and I roar, *"THIS SUUUCKS!"*

Not the eloquence that the bards possessed, but wonderfully expressive just the same.

Mrs. Harding snorts a chuckle through the sparkle of her tears.

"Keep that up, love, and you'll never die of an ulcer."

I get up to leave.

"Oh don't go yet, Danny dear, not yet. Please. Please." She puts a warm fleshy hand on mine and guides me back down.

"Sit with it a while with someone who understands, Danny. Please."

"What . . . aw Jesus." I look at my watch. "I can't Mrs. Harding, I have to get Jamie. I'm late already."

"Can I come with you?" Her meaty paw again seeks out my shoulder.

"No really, I'll be fine. The best thing for me now is to be with Jamie."

Or Petey, I can't help thinking. Christ, what a mess—

"I hope . . . I hope you're not too upset, Danny. Ouf, what am I saying, of course you're upset. You should be upset. I thought you knew all about it. Now that I think on it I'm not surprised you didn't. But he was your brother, and he died not because he was wrong, but because the world around him was wrong. And you should know that."

"This explains so much. My mother always hated me hanging with Petey—"

"Of course she did, Danny, and now you know why. Not only was it a re-minder of what had happened—she was no doubt terrified history would repeat itself. You can understand it all now, even if you can't quite forgive it. She, I'm sure she thought she was doing what was best for both of you. You, and Brian before you."

"What . . . poor Donnie. My God, what happened to Donnie?"

Mrs. Harding sighs again and shakes her head. I really have to leave so I grab my jacket.

"Well, I think you've seen that for yourself. He's never gotten over it. I knew of course he was devastated by the loss of his friend, but I never knew the all of it, never knew that he . . . blamed himself and all. That she had . . . caught them. He dropped out of school before they kicked him out. God forgive me, I had all I could do to make ends meet and it was beyond me, to heal him. I consulted a number of doctors, Danny, but before I took him to one I insisted they not try to change him, that they help him accept who he was. Those things have progressed in leaps and bounds thanks be to God since then, but believe me that was no easy thing to find thirty years ago. By and by Donnie went off to the service as soon as he could. He seemed . . . well, better when he came back. Though quiet and thoughtful. But I see now that he fought who he was, and when he got poor Rosemary pregnant he married her and that was that. I thought maybe the thing with Brian had just been, well, you know, kids' stuff or what do they call it, a *phase*. And then the drink took him, and why wouldn't it? But I think he's starting to come out of it at last. You should see the curtains I've made him for his new place. He's down on West Sixth now. A nice little place, if somewhat devoid of comforting furnishings at present. I must remember to stop by with some ferns."

.   .   Another tangled thread rolls once more unvexed to the sea—the twenty-five years of fierce stares I've caught Donnie directing my way. Why wouldn't he, and me *the spit of your brother,* as half the town tells me on a regular basis.

"That's nice, Mrs. H. Does . . . how much does Petey know about all this?"

"None of it, love, to the best of my knowledge. T'was only two years ago I heard the rest of the story from Donnie, and though Donnie always looked out for Petey when he could, I don't think he's ever told him. And it's not my story to tell Petey, it's yours, love, yours and Donnie's. What are you thinking, Danny?"

I laugh.

"Oh God, I don't know what to think. I just . . . it just has to stop, Mrs. Harding, that's all." I pause. "You know I don't even have a picture of him? Brian, I mean. I was snooping one time the way kids do, and I found a box of stuff in my mother's bottom drawer. It was in a pink box, Fanny Farmer candy, pink with a brown Easter rabbit on its cover. It was full up with Brian's things. Pictures, medals. Ribbons from a track meet. Report cards."

I close my eyes and shudder at the recollection as I zip up my jacket. "Ma was . . . I brought the box downstairs and asked Ma who they belonged to. She was watching one of her afternoon movies. She just freaked. Totally. It was . . . I was terrified but I was too mesmerized to run at first. I'd never seen an adult act that way before. I might've been eight, nine. I finally ran to the upstairs bathroom and locked myself in. When she couldn't get in she went back downstairs and started smashing stuff. Mrs. Harding, do you . . . you wouldn't happen to have a cigarette would you?"

"Oh Danny, you're not smoking and you a young father!"

"No no, I just . . . really could use one now. I quit when I was in the service."

"Well in that case I'll join you," she says, jumping up and pulling open a cabinet over the refrigerator. "I keep these here for emergencies. They're a day older than dirt but they'll do the trick." She opens the windows and lights up two of them, hands me one. "Have an ear for the door for God's sake, we'll have to be careful—if that lot comes home there'll be no end to the questions and the little ones can smell a misrepresentation a mile away. Anyway, you were saying."

"Oh, about the box. Well finally it got real quiet downstairs, about an hour later, so I came out of the bathroom, silent as I could. I snuck down the stairs and all I could see were her feet sticking out from the end of the couch. Her painted toenails. There was an empty bottle of liquor on the floor on its side beside her, and when Dad got home from work I was sent to the neighbors—I came over here instead—and by the time I got home that night Ma was gone. Visiting Aunt Ellen, Dad said. That was the first time I knew I even had a brother, when Dad told me that night. And he said I couldn't ever mention his name to Ma. He made me promise I wouldn't bother her about him."

"The poor soul. You really have to go?"

Before I can answer there's a tumult at the door as the five grandchildren return, and they come with drama of course—someone's dropped their ice cream cone because someone else pushed them and no one had the money to go back for another.

"There there, there there," Mrs. Harding soothes, squatting and taking Molly in the ample harbor of her arms.

They're the same words she soothed me with some minutes ago, for the death by suicide of my gay brother.

"If that's the worst thing that happens to you this year, Molly love, you'll be in pretty fine fettle."

Mrs. Harding winks at me as I stumble out the door, whacking my head on the screen as I do.

I guess I can't be too late when I walk up Mrs. Mulligan's five white and blue stairs, for I hear the clang of "Chopsticks" floating from her piano inside. I swore a month ago I'd do a mischief if I ever heard it again; but at this moment nothing's sounded sweeter.

"Hello, Danny." Mrs. Mulligan smiles when she opens the door, to a wash of clean-house-and-lavender smell. She looks like one of my archetypal librarians: the sensible shoes, the flowery shapeless cotton dress, the baby blue cardigan over the shoulders, the dubious posture, the thermostat set at a prudent 63 degrees. The eyes and smile that are nothing but benign.

"Sorry I'm late, Mrs. Mulligan, I got a little tied up."

"Dad! *Dad! Listen!*" Jamie yelps from the parlor, and once again we are serenaded. I write out a check, only making two mistakes as I do, which is something of a miracle considering the state I'm in.

Mrs. Mulligan starts when her smiling eyes come back to me, and I realize I've been staring at her with slit-eyed appraisal. I look down quickly. She's a sweet soul, but old, a product, probably, of her times. On the way up here, passing dozens of parlor windows, their shades exactly halfway down, the resolutions came in furious waves—I would declaim in the plazas, I would rave from the rooftops the evils of homophobia—but it's too late, I now realize, for the half of them. Either that or I don't have the balls. At any rate she's not the one I will begin my campaign with.

Five minutes later, when Jamie and I are walking home hand in hand, I clear my throat.

"Jamie, I want to tell you something."

He stops to look up, startled by the unintended sobriety of my tone.

"Is it bad?" he asks, the soft blue eyes dashed with woe. What Noreen does I can't say, but I've only chastised Jamie once, verbally, and it upset him so much he sobbed and twitched and ran into my arms.

"No," I laugh. I stoop and lift him up and his eyes vanish as the smiling cheeks bunch up. "Listen to me like you never listened before, Prince of My Heart."

The following Monday a letter's waiting for me in my mailbox when I get home from work. Quietly, but with intent. It's from Mrs. Harding.

Going through the mail is my first grown-up chore after Jamie gets put to bed nights, nine-ish; for he's home minutes after I arrive at 5:30 and I don't want to miss one second of my evenings with him: well and soon enough his friends will seem more fun to hang with than Dad, and forts (made from the sofa cushions); Treasure Hunt à la Donnie, Watch Ye Bean (piggyback rides on my shoulders and when we pass under doorways we both shout out "Watch ye bean!", Name That Tune, and our other diversions will no longer amuse.

But this can't wait. I walk it into the kitchen, snapping on lights as I progress from hall through living room and into kitchen.

I slit the card-size, butter-yellow envelope with a small steak knife—I want nothing to be damaged by my usual pawing procedure when it comes to opening mail. Inside is a scribbled note on pansy-lined paper:

Dear Danny,
    Hope all is well. I'm remembering you said you had no pictures of him. This is one of my favorites. This was a field trip we took out to the islands, and me chaperoning on no sleep, which will explain I'm sure the ill-humored retort I gave to Mrs. Bailey the science teacher, which enjoyed a certain vogue around

the school for some days. But that's another story. They were fifteen then, the boys.
    Look at them, Danny.
Slainte agus Beannacht [good health and a blessing],
Dottie Harding

From out of the note falls what must be a photo, folded in stiff white paper. My fingers twiddle the sheet against the Corian kitchen countertop and here come the booted soldiers thudding in my ears again. An interior Geiger counter whirs into action, telling me I should hold off, as this will prove no doubt to be emotional dynamite. But of course I can't. I take a deep breath and open.

Nestled in the paper's lightly lavendered innards is an old Polaroid snap. The years have smelted its colors into peaches and ivories; but nothing could douse the light blinding forth from the smiles that leap out at me.

Three teenage boys are edge-sitting on an old green bench, the kind with 10,000 years of jackknifed initials carved into them, and watch yourself or you'll be getting a splinter on the bum. The sea light is a collective radiant halo around them. Someone who looks exactly like me is on the left, though his facial expression is one I've never worn; something horribly sorrowful yanks at me, but I move on before it can devour. A beautiful young Donnie is in the middle; and a third young man I don't know is looking off to the right.

Baseball caps are yanked at ridiculous, facetious angles. Donnie and Brian have their arms around each other's shoulders. Donnie's in the middle of saying something, something wise by the look of it, for his mouth is puckered with the delight of delivering a good one. Brian is smiling. Brian is in bliss, the cheeks aflame with amber light. He looks a lot smarter than me. The third boy's presence is strictly ornamental, accidental. He's clearly out of the loop and very nearly out of the picture.

What really tells is the thing deep in Brian and Donnie's eyes. It's the same thing: it is simply the thing between them. A fierce strength, a wild, defiant joy, born of the life-giving secret they're keeping. You can even read their cocky astonishment; as if, _Why shouldn't we have the world, and each other, by the balls?_

It couldn't be more obvious—they are already young lovers.

A sharp inrush of breath at this.

Did Mrs. Harding see this just as clearly? Is that why she sent it to me?

The photo must be moved slightly away, to protect it from the teardrops, the nose sniffle. It must be set against the plant rack near the windowsill, to catch the light; no, on the refrigerator it goes, amidst Jamie's latest artworks; no, let us build a shrine, up in the corner of my bedroom, on the bureau between the crucifix and the candles and the pictures of Jamie and Petey.

I finally lay it away in a kitchen drawer, nestled in the midst of clean linen dishtowels for the time being. Jamie will be home any moment. But before I shut the drawer on them, I become aware of a wild exuberance in me, and as I continue to gaze at their faces I hear myself whispering *Yes! Yes!* as I pump my fist the way rabid football fans might, delirious at the prodigiousness of their victory, for one shining moment in time. Not all the powers of hell—or heaven, as the case may have been—could prevent them from being bold lovers, in a town where that love not only dare not speak its name—it dare hardly think its name. *Go! Go!* I hiss, as the tears sizzle down.

But knowing their history—by which I mean of course their future—the picture saddens too, as much as a photo of the Hanging Gardens of Babylon would, in its heyday, knowing it has been reduced to rubble, between that time and this, in the name of God.

That night Jamie gets more of a story than he bargained for.

"Hi Ma, how you feeling tonight?"

"Danny! Hi sweetheart. Wonderful. A little sore. Everything okay?"

Why wouldn't she ask that.

"Fine Ma, fine. Was it yoga today?"

"Physical therapy. That one was a slave driver in a precious life."

"Ahh . . ."

"Previous. Previous life I mean."

I can see Ma's wince of embarrassment over the phone.

Only in one or two of my remoter fantasies this week have I entertained the idea of blasting Ma, of locking all doors and letting a cosmos-large rage fall down upon her frail, lopsided shoulders. Control issues and ignorance, fear and bigotry—these character defects of Ma proved fatal for Brian, and very nearly so for Donnie.

But I have sins of my own ignorance to count; and God doesn't need me to police the universe. What a relief. And just now a wash of compassion juts into me for her. Thank God. Thank God. I tuck it away to pull out later—no doubt I'll need it.

"Ma listen, could you spot me for a couple of hours tonight? I need to go out for a bit."

"Of course, sweetheart! Haven't I been after you for ages to get out a little more, Danny dear?"

"You're not too tired?"

"Oh God no. Is the little angel asleep?"

"Yeah, I just put him in. That would be great. Want me to come and get you?"

"Oh God no, your father can drop me off."

I take a quick shower—a thoughtful one—and check on Jamie one last time before I head downstairs, to wait for Ma in the living room.

"Have a nice time, dear," she calls after me as I head out the door ten minutes later, and as I turn up my collar at the November nine o'clock chill I wonder if its Ma's recovery, or her age, that dissuades her from asking me what my plans for the night are.

I need a beer, just the one, for what I'm about to do.

I'm really okay with that. But still I find myself peeling the label off as I sip and ponder. There's a game on, two games maybe three, and a smattering of good talk at the bar, but here in my booth I remain.

Just the one and then I'm off.

It's dark and frosty when I leave the tavern. It's about a half mile walk to where I'm headed, which is perfect. Collect the thoughts. Not that there are that many to collect—I'm strangely calm.

I find the house in question with no trouble. The doorbell, the name, both are clearly marked, which doesn't happen every day. It's on the left side of a recently vinyled duplex. The front door has Indian corn dangling on it. I always liked that stuff. I straighten it out a bit. The wind's been playing havoc with it lately.

A bit of a glow comes from some interior room, but there are no lights on in the living room, which I can see through the front window here, through the slanty blinds. I look at my watch. It's 9:07—not too late for an unexpected visitor. But late enough for the mind and heart to go wandering down a little road of thought. We should both be in just the right kind of solemn mood for what we're about to do.

I'm still relaxed enough to wonder what he paid for this place.

The second ring summons the throb of feet, moving through the house to the door in a not-so-swift manner. Nor are they plodding.

The door pulls back a bit, sticks, then opens all the way with a bit of a wobble.

The head jerks back, blanches.

"Hi Donnie," I say.

For once I don't look away from the laser eyes. In fact I smile at him, and place my hand on his startled shoulder. "It's me, Danny. Can I come in?"

The Pepperminty Coast

"Dad! Dad! Let's run!"

I can't remember who started this running bit—me and Petey's old game—myself or Jamie. But it's a pattern with us now and we do it whenever he says, especially down the beach here at night. Third grade now, faster every day. A feyness all about him. Hates having his hair cut (my fault) and the golden-red curls fly out behind him when he runs, his preferred mode of transportation. Not at all unafraid to use his tongue—or his fists—when comments are made about his hair.

Must get that from his mother.

And yet big-eyed shy, sensitive, in front of strangers. Loves to imitate people, their walks and talks. And when a story mesmerizes him I have to contain my laughter, so wonder-whacked and funny-looking is his round white face.

We burst off down Pleasure Bay beach, our dog Buster making three; a stray that just showed up one night, pawing at the door and coming right in when we opened it as if we'd ordered dog-to-go.

I hardly have to slow myself to let Jamie win—he's getting that quick. He runs after a flock of seagulls and they squawk and scowl as they kick off into the sky. Jamie laughs at them, shouts out that he'd never hurt them.

It's building up to an almighty sunset, as vermilion and orange as the foliage on this warm October eve. Though the not-too-distant boardwalk is ample with joggers and walkers, Rollerbladers and rovers, the beach is empty at this in-betweenish hour, drippy with day and night. A thin time, as Mrs. Harding would say. A time when anything is possible.

Jamie comes back to me, arms airplane-wide, then opens a fist to show me a silver dollar he's found.

A Map of the Harbor Islands
Published by The Haworth Press, Inc., 2006. All rights reserved.
doi:10.1300/5677_26

"They come from treasure buried deep in the sea!" he whispers to me, his sea eyes agog.

"Who told you that?"

"They just do. Dad, is _Julie_ meeting us tonight?"

He says the name with a throaty breathlessness.

"Ahhhh . . . no Jamie, I don't think so."

"Oh. How come you don't hang around with her anymore?"

"Well, she . . . she got busy with her work and so forth."

Jamie purses his lips, tosses his head back, and half closes his eyes. _"That's an adult issue Jamie and we don't discuss that with young people."_ He's imitating Henry again, Noreen's new husband. The little rogue's got Henry's strident passive-aggressiveness down to a T. I have to look away so as not to laugh.

"C'mon Buster!"

He's off again, into the wall-less cerulean mist that is this shore at twilight, neither dark nor light but something of both.

Maybe I should chuck the dating for a bit. It seems as soon as Jamie gets to know them, things fizzle out. With a whimper, never a bang. I thought it would be easier than this, finding a woman who wanted to raise a family. Loving her. Wanting to love her. It occurs to me that the only two people I have ever truly loved in that _special_ way, I have known all my life: Noreen and Petey. And the love I had for Noreen has been replaced by a benign (well, mostly) indifference. It would have been somewhat easy to keep her in my life—but, as Mrs. Harding would say, I couldn't be bothered. It wasn't just the lack of desire to join her on her Fast Track, which was the name of her firm's program for its young executives desirous of upward mobility—at some dark junction our respective tracks had split, running off into other directions. Noreen's train is an express uptown; mine is . . . well, wherever it's going, it's taking the scenic bypass. The Magellan Route, as Petey used to call it, whenever we'd take the long way home.

Winters I join a nearby gym, located in the midst of the no-man's-land that separates the West Side from the trash-blowy edges of the Financial District. I'm an aficionado of its indoor track and it's there I do my wintry running—you see I lack Petey's meteorological hardiness. The place is remarkable for its members' varied town-and-gown demographic, as they used to call such motley social milieus. There are as many trash throwers and mailmen, waitresses and young hoods keeping in fighting shape as there are CEOs and judges. You're as apt to hear _Jesus Christ, Tommo did you hear? Fitzy won the Trifecta!_ in the locker room as you are the bloodless details of the latest hostile takeover of Xenigees.com, or whatever. Why is it all the latest startups have names vaguely recalling Greek battles? I say all this only by way of accuracy—while I hate running in the ice and slush, I *have* inherited, by osmosis I suppose, Petey's disdain for class boundaries and the objects and pronunciations that mark them. *That's fine!* As Jamie is apt to sneeringly say, imitating poor Henry again.

For those members less interested in the running track, there are running-in-place machines, and these the operator mounts like a pair of stationary cross-country skis; you press the start button and you're off, sluicing back and forth at a pace that would alarm Heidi, to say nothing of her grandfather. An industrial-looking black T-bar at the head of each machine accommodates personal stereos, iPods, landline phones, notepads, and, for the more traditional, a book or a magazine. Somehow it seems to me that the essential differences between Noreen and me can be summed up in our choice of running venues. In the semirare occasions that I see her at my gym—always a frantic hour before they close—she is availing herself of every choice on the T-bar. You could almost smell the grim determination dripping off her, were her gear not the very latest in wickish, sweat-free zylacron. Or whatever. Not Greek battles but the commanders of same. Sometimes I get a quick jerk of the head from her.

I'm sorry. Bitter? Who's bitter? After all I have no reason to be. Not for one instant do I even wish she were back in my life.

I just, sometimes, wish someone was. Anyone.

Well, maybe not anyone.

Jamie—well, that's a different story. In the same way that Petey extolled the junior-high virtues of island-hopping—all the world made to slap-dash two-by-fours through sun-spangled ocean water as a detriment to the rush to violence—I marvel at how such things as war, want, poverty, greed, and injustice can thrive like the proverbial bay tree, when such a miracle as one's child invades one's life. I have to admit that much of my dating has been directed by a desire to do this again—and again. Not only for Jamie's sake, so he won't be the only child I was—but for my own as well. Not a trait a majority of men are renowned for.

What else have I inherited from Petey?

That's a question as impossible to answer as what did I get from Ma. From Dad. What didn't I get? Where did this mole beneath my right armpit come from? The distribution of hair on my legs? The appeal that roads rising up to the horizon, ending at the infinite sky, have always had for me? The almost heartbreaking wistfulness that hits me when I hear beautiful words strung together.

I would have to say that if Petey affected me in any way—which obviously he did, and has—it was simply this: it's your life. Not only the life examined, but the life plumbed and spelunked and made magical, without regard to the thoughts, actions, pressures or judgments of others: an increasing impossibility in this world. It's only when you begin to taste the freedom of this kind of life that you realize how rare it is. What a gift you gave me, Petey. What a gift. A certain loneliness follows one inevitably in this life, like a dog; but in time that too passes and is replaced with a quiet joy, and the dawning of an idea: that the person, or thing, one has been searching for all one's life is oneself. Sans ego. Sans fast tracks.

The sky grows brighter with pinks and reds and salmons, and the ocean takes on a flat, silvery green varnish. A shimmering mist drapes the shore, and out of this mist Jamie comes running back. The energy of him. *He'd make coffee nervous, wouldn't he love?* as Mrs. Harding sagely noted last week at the M Street playground. Well, he'll sleep tonight anyway. As long as he gets his story.

"Dad! *Dad!*" He runs past me, then spins around with the airplane arms again.

"There's a man up ahead with a boat! He says he knows you!"

"There is, eh?" I ask. I squat down, put my hands on Jamie's shoulders.

Maybe from the Gavin House. I've been volunteering there since Michael Shea's death, serving on the board, implementing a diversity awareness program as we delicately call it. Basically we identify the gay or questioning kids and put them into a separate program with peers and facilitators from BAGLY, Boston Area Gay and Lesbian Youth. We still get the occasional youth suicide, but the epidemic seems to be over. At least for now.

"Mmm. And he knows all the names of the Harbor Islands." He drops his voice and says into my ear, "Not the regular names, Dad. The secret names."

"Really! Wow."

"He *does,* Dad!" Jamie blurts, pushing away from me. "He says this beach right here is the Pepperminty Coast."

For a moment I can't stand as Jamie's words hit me.

Petey. It can only be Petey. But no, it can't be—

"Ahhh—"

"He's waiting up there. He wants to see you. C'mon, Dad, let's run!"

"You go on, I'll catch up."

A part of me wants to vamoose in the other direction, but it must be a small part of me indeed as I find that I'm walking, my head down in haste. Then my eyes lift and go to the place where Petey is before I see him. How can they not? My eyes telescope right to the spot. Jamie runs into the mist, comes back to me, *C'mon Dad, c'mon!* then runs back to Petey. I keep my eye on the spot. A shape takes form, a small skiff, and then a man squatting behind it. Looking at me.

Petey.

He stands up. A beachball of a thing expands in my throat. It gets larger when I see the name freshly painted on the skiff in green letters: *Little Andy Foley II.*

"This is my dad," Jamie says when I join them, stopping about ten feet away.

Buster is giving Petey a cursory going-over with his muzzle. Wary from his years on the street, he nevertheless starts licking Petey's hands, wagging his brushy tail at the smell of a kindred soul.

"Hey," I say. How absurd. But what wouldn't be absurd?

"Danny," Petey says. His eyes are electric in this light, wormholes to ten other universes. His face is smeared with only about a hundred different emotions.

He's filled out a scoonch. He's barefoot, wearing light khakis rolled up to the knee and a forest green T-shirt that says LOS ANGELES HOPE HOUSE in white letters. He turns to Jamie.

"So who taught you the secret names of the islands, Jamie?" he asks. He squats down again, brushes the black hair out of his golden face. Thinner now, the hair, and a bit receding on the sides. Beautiful he is.

Jamie points at me while he stares deeply into Petey's eyes.

"Hey! We have your picture at our house!" Jamie cries, picking his nose while he says it. "I know who you are! You're Petey. My dad talks about you all the time."

"Hey, Jamie, how would you like an ice cream from Sullivan's?" I ask, before he divulges any more, for instance: the fact that we pray for him every night, or that *The Adventures of Danny and Petey* comprise the vast bulk of our bedtime story fare.

"YEA-ah! I thought you said we couldn't get one 'til Friday?"

"Daddy changed his mind. Here."

Jamie starts bouncing up and down on his toes, his tiny hand out and wiggling, his eyes bugged in affectation.

"Gimmegimmegimmegimmegimme!" he chants rapidly.

I give him a five and he snatches it and tears off. Petey laughs at him.

"Stay on the sidewalk, Jamie!" I have to restrain Buster so he won't give chaotic chase.

"He's got the life in him though, hasn't he?" Petey says, when I turn back to him.

"He does." I pause. "Who said that?"

"The Button Man," Petey answers. "I thought it was you. I swear to God Danny. That freaked me out."

"With the long hair?" I ask dubiously.

"You with a wig and highlights," Petey says. "Summer Blond or something. He's got a lot more energy than you did at that age."

I raise my eyebrows.

"Must be from his mother."

My eyes can't unstick themselves from Petey's face. He hasn't changed really, and yet in saying that I realize he is as unpredictable as the sky, the ocean; as much a part of my life—and as unknowable—as they are.

"Oh yeah, sorry about . . . I was sorry to hear about your divorce, Danny."

I shrug. Then pause.

"You were?"

"S-semi."

"How long are you . . . when did you get back?" I take a step toward him.

"Yesterday. I'm . . . back to stay. I'm starting up a drug rehab place."

He didn't say *we*. Of course I would notice that he doesn't say *we*.

"Great." I can't control the smile that's pulling involuntarily at the edges of my mouth. "How's—"

"We split up," Petey says quietly. "Year and a half ago."

"Oh. I'm sorry. What. . . ."

I let a gust trail my voice off as I realize it's none of my business what happened. Petey takes a step to me. He cracks his knuckles. My hands start shaking so into the pockets they go.

"It wasn't my life, out there, that's all," Petey says. "If your life doesn't find you, then you have to go find your life. Plus kids are still dying back here."

I nod.

I take another step, to him. My heart starts thudding. I'm not really listening. We're face to face.

"Do you . . . have some backers?"

"I do," Petey says, abstractedly. "The funding's all in place. Paul helped with all that. Now I just have to find some backers for my dog sh-shelter."

He's starting to look brittle again and a second ago he was invulnerable. Damn him.

"I'm still at the library."

"That's *good*."

"I love it."

Silence.

"Ahhh—" we both say at the same time.

"Go ahead," Petey says.

"No, what were you going to say, Petey?"

"Alexander Haig hastened to The Hague," Petey says, pushing the windy hair out of his face again. "But . . ."

He takes a step closer to me, looks down at his bare feet. Then back at me. A person's irises never change, really.

I don't know who opens his arms first. There's a mist, an orange gray glow against the horizon, the gentle lapping of things, and in the midst of all that Petey's in my arms, and I'm in his.

It's amazing, what we say in the great moments of our lives.

"Oh God, Petey," I whisper, and five years of sobs come chortling out. "Jesus. Danny. Oh Danny. My D-Danny."

Sublime that we're here—here along the Pepperminty Coast. But we could be anywhere and I'd still know it for what it is—home.

"Why are you hugging?" we hear after a very long time.

We slowly turn and see Jamie, lapping on a triple-header ice cream cone, all business.

"Why not?" Petey shrugs.

"Because we love each other," I say.

"Oh. Hey, Dad tells me *Adventures of Danny and Petey* at night. That's you, right? You're that Petey, right?"

Petey breaks off and squats down to him. Jamie's eyes cease their restiveness for once, and a bit of drool gathers on his lower lip as he stares back.

"I am," Petey says. "But maybe tonight we should *live* a story rather than just *hear* a story. You know what I mean? Wanna go for a ride?"

"In the boat? Yes, please!" Jamie starts bouncing up and down.

"Watch your ice cream, bucko!" I warn, but it's too late. The top two scoops scud off and Buster is on them in a nanosecond.

"Oh, Jamie," I soothe, but he waves me off.

"Whatever. Too much for me anyway. C'mon, let's go!"

We pile into the wooden boat, laughing, Buster making four. Petey jumps out, grabs his sandals, pushes off, hops back in. The water of Pleasure Bay is utterly still, but the sky and earth are swirling. Only a vermilion throb to the west behind the skyline remains; to the east, where we're headed, the water is silvering with the rising moon, almost at the full.

The ripples from Petey's foot movements pick up this light, then wobble out as we leave the shore behind.

"Where we going anyway?" Jamie wonders, looking at Petey.

"I dunno. Jolly Olly Orange Land, I suppose."

Jamie giggles. Petey looks over his head to me.

"Set a course for starboard!" I cry, pulling at the oars and jerking my head outward.

The End

ABOUT THE AUTHOR

J. G. Hayes is the author of the critically acclaimed and bestselling short story collections, *This Thing Called Courage* and *Now Batting for Boston: More Stories by J.G. Hayes*. Booklist calls *This Thing Called Courage*, "An auspicious debut . . . we impatiently await Hayes' next effort. Characters' streams of consciousness and pop-cultural memories collide and overlap in Hayes' impressive stories about South Boston." *Bay Windows & Philadelphia Gay News* say of *Now Batting for Boston*, "J.G. Hayes has hit a home run with *Now Batting for Boston*, once again proving his talent as a compelling storyteller with a keen ear for authentic dialogue and a talent for crafting memorably flawed characters." He is also an artist and teacher living in the Boston area. A former reporter, he is currently working on his next novel.

Order a copy of this book with this form or online at:
http://www.haworthpress.com/store/product.asp?sku=5677

A MAP OF THE HARBOR ISLANDS

_____in softbound at $19.95 (ISBN-13: 978-1-56023-596-5; ISBN-10: 1-56023-596-9)

412 pages

Or order online and use special offer code HEC25 in the shopping cart.

COST OF BOOKS_____

POSTAGE & HANDLING_____
(US: $4.00 for first book & $1.50
for each additional book)
(Outside US: $5.00 for first book
& $2.00 for each additional book)

SUBTOTAL_____

IN CANADA: ADD 6% GST_____

STATE TAX_____
(NJ, NY, OH, MN, CA, IL, IN, PA, & SD
residents, add appropriate local sales tax)

FINAL TOTAL_____
(If paying in Canadian funds,
convert using the current
exchange rate, UNESCO
coupons welcome)

☐ **BILL ME LATER:** (Bill-me option is good on
US/Canada/Mexico orders only; not good to
jobbers, wholesalers, or subscription agencies.)

☐ Check here if billing address is different from
shipping address and attach purchase order and
billing address information.

Signature_____

☐ **PAYMENT ENCLOSED: $**_____

☐ **PLEASE CHARGE TO MY CREDIT CARD.**

☐ Visa ☐ MasterCard ☐ AmEx ☐ Discover
☐ Diner's Club ☐ Eurocard ☐ JCB

Account # _____

Exp. Date_____

Signature_____

Prices in US dollars and subject to change without notice.

NAME_____

INSTITUTION_____

ADDRESS_____

CITY_____

STATE/ZIP_____

COUNTRY_____ COUNTY (NY residents only)_____

TEL_____ FAX_____

E-MAIL_____

May we use your e-mail address for confirmations and other types of information? ☐ Yes ☐ No
We appreciate receiving your e-mail address and fax number. Haworth would like to e-mail or fax special
discount offers to you, as a preferred customer. **We will never share, rent, or exchange your e-mail address
or fax number.** We regard such actions as an invasion of your privacy.

Order From Your Local Bookstore or Directly From
The Haworth Press, Inc.
10 Alice Street, Binghamton, New York 13904-1580 • USA
TELEPHONE: 1-800-HAWORTH (1-800-429-6784) / Outside US/Canada: (607) 722-5857
FAX: 1-800-895-0582 / Outside US/Canada: (607) 771-0012
E-mail to: orders@haworthpress.com

For orders outside US and Canada, you may wish to order through your local
sales representative, distributor, or bookseller.
For information, see http://haworthpress.com/distributors

(Discounts are available for individual orders in US and Canada only, not booksellers/distributors.)

PLEASE PHOTOCOPY THIS FORM FOR YOUR PERSONAL USE.
http://www.HaworthPress.com   BOF06